The Gospel of Matthias Kent

The Gospel of Matthias Kent

Mike Silvestri

Draumr Publishing, LLC
Maryland

The Gospel of Matthias Kent

Cover art and design by Mike Silvestri.
Author photograph credit to Brad Peterson.

ISBN: 978-1-933157-32-0
PUBLISHED BY DRAUMR PUBLISHING, LLC
www.draumrpublishing.com
Columbia, Maryland

Printed in the United States of America

Dedication

For Carol

Acknowledgements

Like my protagonist, Matthias Kent, *Gospel* would not have seen print if it weren't for a host of people who shared their precious gifts with me.

That includes the honest advice of my loving wife, Carol, the patient edits of my daughter, Tessa, and the encouragement of my other daughter, Kate.

Add to them the mentoring of Ann Stewart, the sage critiquing of Cathy Ennis, the sharp eyes of Fred Schooley, the opinions of Beth Ludlum and Beth Major, the faith of Debbie Beamer, and the vision of publisher Robert Allen, who recognized what *The Gospel of Matthias Kent* needed most—paper and ink.

Genesis

Chapter 1: Verses 1-40

It was First Friday, November 1st in the Year of Our Lord 2159. A steady rain sprayed against the limousine's windows, and Matthias Kent hated every drop. There was no hope in it. Nothing would grow until spring, not a bud, or a leaf, or the grass on his mother's week-old grave.

He leaned on the armrest, dwelling on each bleak field he passed. The rich soil of his childhood had long since surrendered to decades of over-cultivation. He remembered his mother's voice calling out each crop and the way her eyes sparkled when she said, "Sweet corn." Now, the soil lay exhausted, heaped in piles the color of lead. Gone were the lush rows of corn and wheat. Gone was his mother's voice.

His eyes grew wet like the drizzle pattering on the window. The droplets merged only to be driven from the glass by the air rushing by outside. A brush of his hand drove the tears from his cheek. It was a moment of weakness, of sentimentality, and it wouldn't do—not on First Friday. He let out a huff and swatted the vinyl upholstery.

The startled driver glanced at him in the rearview mirror. "Is everything all right, Brother Kent?"

Matthias rocked back, pressing against the headrest. "I'm fine, Brother Alexander. Bless you for concern." He scolded himself for letting his weakness fester into irritation. Both were sins. He made a mental note to pay penance. Penance demonstrated his piety, and piety was good for business. Besides, today his soul needed to be as spotless as the gray polyester business vestments he wore.

The limousine bounced slightly, announcing the departure from country asphalt to urban concrete. Matthias turned away from the window, ignoring both his grief and the relentless gray slums arrayed around Philadelphia's white concrete walls. His eyes fixed upon the vid-panel before him, where the corporate logo of The First Bank of Job displayed. It was a simple design, two crosses intertwined by a bold green dollar sign. He touched the screen. The logo faded. One by one, images of the bank's officers, the Corporate Elders, slid by. One position sat vacant. Today, the vacancy would be filled.

The ride smoothed out, signaling the approach to the city's west gate. Matthias leaned against the glass, looking out at the rabble gathered at the entrance and the twin guard towers assuring peace and order.

The crowd clogging the gate parted as his vehicle approached. Matthias stiffened and stared straight ahead. The limousine halted for the requisite security screening. The images on the vid-panel disappeared, replaced by the stern officer clad in the formal black of the citadel's security force.

The officer sat straight up and barked, "Blessings, Brother. Entry approved."

The guard had never before been quite so formal. It amused Matthias. He nodded toward the computer.

Beggars neared the windows.

Matthias focused on Brother Alexander's back, avoiding the paupers' stares. He already knew how they looked, shivering in tattered clothes, their unclean hands cupped and pleading just beyond the minimum legal distance from the car. Brother Alexander canted his head toward Matthias. He watched his vid-panel and saw the security guard manipulate the remote-controlled tower guns into position. The guard nodded.

"You may begin, Brother Alexander," said Matthias.

Grabbing a stack of white plastic cards embossed with the cross and dollar sign, the driver rolled down the window and let each one drip into their grasping fingers. The crowd snatched up every card and then departed without a sound. No matter how hard Matthias tried, he could never be a cheerful giver.

Two figures, a boy and woman, lingered near the window. Matthias tensed. He looked up through the sunroof and watched the tower guns pivot toward the pair.

The sentry's voice crackled over the intercom, reassuring yet tinged in apprehension. "Please remain where you are, Brother. I am affecting countermeasures."

Matthias slid toward the middle of the car. The boy stood right outside the car, just on the other side of the glass. The child couldn't have been more than ten or eleven, his face drawn, with sodden curls hanging beneath the scrap of plastic that covered him. A pair of spectral hands rested on the boy's shoulders, mottled gray with what Matthias recognized as *Pythium cronos*, the fungus, the Rot. He swallowed hard to force back the nausea.

Despite his revulsion, Matthias traced the arms to a woman's withered face, her eyes milky and soulless. He shuddered. She was probably in her thirties—his age. *There, but for the grace of God.*

The child tapped on the glass.

Matthias waited for the microsonic cannon's blast to turn the child into a pink mist. The boy displayed neither a death wish or a panhandler's plead, only a quiet pain. Matthias understood grief when he saw it.

Clicking on the intercom, Matthias said, "Hold your fire."

The sentry's head snapped toward the vid-panel. "But, Brother."

"The result of trespassing is condemnation. Yes, yes, I am acquainted with the law. I motioned to the boy," lied Matthias, another sin demanding reparation. "He is not to blame."

The sentry's eyes widened. "Oh, I ask the Brother's pardon." The guard relaxed his grip on the control panel.

"No offense taken." Reaching into his vestment pocket, Matthias pulled out a thin wallet and removed a blue plastic card.

Brother Alexander's eyebrows flexed upward in the rearview

mirror.

Lowering the window an inch, Matthias said, "Is this your mother?"

The boy nodded.

He slid the card outside until it fell into the child's hands. "Tend to her needs." The window whirred shut.

The boy's eyes flickered with a mournful joy, and he held his gaze on Matthias for just a moment before leading his mother away.

A man in a black poncho streaked by, knocking the boy to the ground. The child's mother halted. She remained as still as a plaster Madonna, her hands outstretched.

The man snarled at the child and reached for the card lying on the pavement.

A low bass note thrummed. The man's body quivered and burst. The limousine's window turned pink.

"Are you unharmed, Brother Kent?" asked the sentry.

Rain sluiced through a film of blood and tissue. Matthias collected himself. "Yes." He saw the boy's mother unscathed, still poised in the same stance and covered in a rose patina.

The boy pawed through the debris until he found the card. The child stood, pressed his mother's hands to his shoulders, and led her into the slum.

Brother Alexander looked over his shoulder. "I've called for a decontamination team, Brother Kent. Do we require any other assistance?"

Matthias watched the pair recede into the thicket of tarp-roofed huts. "Blessed are those that mourn."

"Sir?"

"For they shall be comforted. The Beatitudes were some of the first scriptures my mother taught me." Matthias leaned back against the headrest. He was being sentimental again. It wouldn't do. There could be no demonstration of weakness in front of the Elders or the Body Corporate. He fought his grief until it subsided under a layer of indifference. "Move on, Brother Alexander. I cannot be late."

Chapter 2: Verses 1-108

Inside the wall, a smiling billboard Jesus with blue eyes and an outstretched hand welcomed Matthias to an earthly kingdom of steel and neon. Well-dressed businessmen huddled under the Almighty's chin, their hands in their pockets and their skin clean.

As the gate slammed shut behind him, Matthias smiled back at the Almighty and mouthed the caption on the billboard, "Blessed are those that dwell in My house."

The First Bank of Job came into view, the neoclassical edifice of the former art museum resplendent and imposing.

Supplicants spread their red umbrellas over the walkway. One of them opened the car door.

"Thank you, Brothers," said Matthias, rising into the dampness. A few drops of rain fell from one of the umbrellas. They missed the collar of his vestments and landed on the back of his neck, biting into him with icy teeth. He winced.

The entourage froze, their hands quaking and eyes wide. Such clumsiness could get them cast them out into the slums.

Matthias felt a rush of anger. Now was the time to demonstrate the wrath of an Elder, but a line of psalm came to mind—*surely goodness and mercy shall follow me all the days of my life, and I will dwell in the Synod of the Lord.* Reasoning that mercy, from a position of strength, would offset his earlier sins, he said, "It's all right, brothers. Nothing has touched my vestments."

A collective sigh fogged the air.

Matthias motioned, and the entourage continued toward the bank.

When they reached the protection of the Bank's portico, the supplicants departed. At the same time, attendants split open the doors of the main entrance. A white cloud of tobacco incense coiled upward.

Matthias halted, letting the breeze chase the smoke back into the lobby. The wind continued on, ruffling the vestments of those members of the Body Corporate nearest the door. Silence filled the vast lobby as Matthias entered.

Faces pointed in his direction. Some demonstrated congratulation. The remainder were as unmoving as the Rodin sculptures scattered about the hall.

Matthias basked in the moment, a rush of pride eroding his emotionless façade. He tilted his head down to disguise his feelings and stepped into what he thought was a deserted alcove. A voice greeted him from the shadows.

"Brother, do not let your ego lead you astray—astray."

The accusation stole Matthias's breath. Only one attendant spoke with that peculiar echo. "How is it, Brother John, that you peer into men's souls so easily?"

An ebony face emerged from a beige cowl. "And so formal— formal. You haven't called me 'Brother John' since your first year—year. Will you forget about me if God smiles on you today—today?"

The attendant's words teased Matthias, who was keen to know what rumors the old man heard. "And will God, and the Body Corporate, smile on me, Blind Johnny?" As soon as the question left his mouth, he realized his folly.

Johnny snapped up the reply. "Proverbs 16, Matthias— Matthias. Pride goes before destruction—destruction."

The rebuke stung him. He finished the verse. "And an arrogant spirit before a fall." Matthias bowed. "I thank you for your lesson, Brother. I will pay penance for my arrogance."

The edges of Blind Johnny's lips curled upward. "Always the eager penitent—penitent. That is a good sign—sign."

Scars on the old man's cheeks and the depthless black where his eyes used to be left Matthias unsettled, as it always did.

Blind Johnny's grin evaporated. His bony fingers tugged the sides of his cowl close. "My face still frightens you so—so?"

"Yes."

"And well it should—should. My face, my eyes, my voice, all demonstrates the wages of sin, young Matthias—Matthias. Blessed be the Inquisition and the Reformation of my soul—soul." Blind Johnny's chin tilted up, his nose sampling the air. "Yet, there are other faces to be distressed by—by. Vice Elder Rourke seems most interested in our fellowship—fellowship."

Matthias swiveled his head enough to bring Rourke into view. The Vice Elder stood outside of the assembly, gathered with the other Elders and perched at the right hand of the Chief. Rourke's glower focused on him. Matthias returned a soft look and tipped his head in far less of a bow than he gave the old attendant. A sneer creased the chiseled terrain of the Vice Elder's face, a pale reflection of the bust of Rodin's *Father Pierre-Julien Eymard* set atop on the pedestal behind him.

Blind Johnny turned to his left, letting his cowl shade the movement of his lips. "You would do well not to taunt Elder Rourke, Matthias—Matthias."

"I can imagine my uncle's vote."

"Then know what I do, young Brother—Brother. The Minutes have already been written—written."

Matthias spun around. "And the name?"

Blind Johnny turned back to him, a wide grin exposing yellow teeth. "I am a blind man—man. How could I see it—it?"

"Now, who is doing the taunting?"

"Be at peace, Brother—Brother. To everything, there is a season—season. Perhaps it is your season, or another's— another's." The attendant's hands stretched out from the wide sleeves of his robe, palms skyward and motioning as if weighing something. "Be it known, I judge each page heavier by four syllables—syllables."

Matthias found his breath stolen a second time. He mouthed

the names of his rivals. Besides his own, only one other name carried four syllables.

The Chime of Assembly sounded. The soundless wraith of Blind Johnny disappeared behind the plain oak of the Attendant's door, taking Matthias's confidence with him.

Three booming thuds resounded from the meeting room and echoed off the wood-paneled walls of the corridor where the Body Corporate gathered.

The sergeant-at-arms slammed the Staff of Order against the marble. "Blessings be to the Body Corporate of the Bank of Job."

The Body Corporate fell into two lines and chanted, "And to the Synod for which we stand, one corporation under God."

A man shuffled next to Matthias. "Am I permitted to stand by the side of an Elder?"

"You have more confidence than I do, Brother Kyalo," replied Matthias.

A grin formed on Benjamin Kyalo's lips, followed by a quiet laugh. "They'd be fools if they did." He shook Matthias's hand and pulled him close enough to whisper. "Everything is still in place for our sojourn. What should I tell our contacts?"

Matthias dug his fingers into his subordinate's shoulder, struggling to maintain a cordial smile. "Tell them that you are fool for mentioning that here. Be silent. There are far too many ears. Come to my office later. Now, laugh as though I've told you something funny."

Benjamin hesitated and complied.

Matthias forced a chuckle, his gaze scanning the faces of those closest to them. To his relief, none reacted to the exchange.

The sergeant-at-arms slammed the Staff of Order again. "Let the Processional begin."

The hallway's confines opened into the yawning breadth of the amphitheater. Each man of the Body Corporate sidled up to a metal desk, chair, and vid-panel.

Matthias stood in the first row with Benjamin at his right. Blind Johnny stood against the rear wall of the Elders' dais in his customary spot, clad in his official robes as Master of Pages. A young blond attendant walked around the Elder's conference table, passing out the Minutes from the last gathering of the Body Corporate. A raven-haired boy followed the blond, placing a Pen of Witness near each seat.

Matthias watched the boys complete the Sacrament of Pen and Paper by genuflecting at the Chief Elder's chair and standing next to Blind Johnny. He stared at the children's eyes, both as empty as the Master of Pages. Their blindness assured that they would never look upon the Minutes before the Elders witnessed them. He pitied them for a moment until the memory of the child outside the gate filled his mind. At least these boys would never have to starve, thirst, or watch their mother die the slow death the Rot inflicted.

The carved oak doors of the executive suite slid aside, revealing ten of the Elders who moved to their places at the table. Matthias followed Vice-Elder Rourke, his gaze tracking the taut lines of the man's brow. Rourke swiveled his eyes. It was as if he knew Matthias was looking. He stared back—icy, cold.

Chief Elder Vanderhaggen came into view, breaking the line of sight between the two. Arriving at the center chair, the Chief Elder paused, arms lifted and his round face fixed in his trademark benevolent smile. "Blessed are they whose transgressions are forgiven, whose sins are covered."

Matthias barked out the bank's mission statement. "Blessed is the man whose sin will never count against him."

Vanderhaggen lowered his arms. "Under the auspices of the Synod, the Most High, and His advocates here on earth, I hereby convene this business meeting of the Bank of Job."

The Body replied, "Blessed be His servants, the Synod, and all who serve the Lord. Blessed be the Bank of Job and the sinners we save."

The boys appeared behind the Chief Elder, pulling out the old man's chair. "Amen, brothers. Be seated."

Chairs scratched along the marble floor. Rourke stood and read from the sacred Minutes.

The Vice Elder's droning reminded Matthias of the times they shared at his parent's dinner table long ago, his uncle going on and on about some corporate event or another. It was all manners and congeniality—a pleasant time. A distant time.

Rourke finished and applied his stare to the assembly. "Does anyone here, in the sight of the Almighty, wish to amend the Minutes as stated?"

Matthias fought a cynical urge to laugh. No one challenged the Minutes. To do so risked excommunication into the slums.

Rourke turned to the Elders. "Having no amendments to consider, I move that the Minutes of the Bank of Job for October of the Year of our Lord 2159 be accepted as written."

"I second," murmured one of the other Elders.

Vanderhaggen raised his right hand. "Those in favor?"

The Body Corporate replied, "Amen."

The Chief Elder lowered his hand. "Brothers, you all know the special reason for our gathering. While we mourn the sudden passing of Elder Stewart, we know we must carry on. To that end, I have deliberated with the Elders to find a new executive to fill the vacancy."

Sudden passing, huffed Matthias. Everyone knew that Elder Stewart died in a moment of rapture in a bed far from the one he shared with Mrs. Stewart.

"After much prayer, we found two worthy candidates—two men of God, stalwart and fine examples to all." Vanderhaggen reached into his vestment pocket and pulled out a slender remote control. He clicked a button. A hidden projector displayed ten-foot high photographs on the wall. "I'm sure you recognize our Financial Planning wizard up there on the left, Simon Kloepfer. Director Kloepfer personally ran a sweeping audit of our budgeting methodology resulting in hard dollar savings in the millions. And, to the right, Director of Advertising, Matthias Kent. Director Kent oversaw the implementation of the penance discounting to the lower classes. These innovations put us head-and-shoulders above the competition and were responsible for winning the Synod's trust to administrate their revenue collection systems. Since then, we've gone nationwide serving the penitential needs of every man, woman and child in the United Christian States."

The Chief Elder directed his speech at Matthias and Kloepfer. "Both men, in their own right, deserve a seat at this table. But, only one may serve."

Matthias spied a subtle cant to Blind Johnny's head. The Master of Pages seemed to be looking toward Kloepfer in the second row.

The blind man's words replayed in his mind down to the echo. *"I judge each page heavier by four syllables—syllables."*

"Simon Kloepfer," whispered Matthias, his fingers counting to four. His breath came in tentative puffs while his heart slammed against his chest.

Vanderhaggen spoke to the Elders. "Brothers, I tender the name of—"

The beating in Matthias's chest halted.

"—Matthias Kent for installation as Elder of Theistic Marketing and make a motion for his acceptance."

An unnatural stillness filled the room. No one at the table offered a second. He watched the Chief Elder's smile fall for the first time in Matthias's tenure at the bank. The old man shifted and glared at Rourke.

Rourke's gaze sunk to the table. His throat cleared, the words almost refusing to leave his lips. "Seconded."

Vanderhaggen raised his right hand, his eyes riveted on Rourke. "Those in favor?"

"Amen."

Matthias mouthed the response, unable to speak.

The Chief Elder's smile returned. He rose and looked at Matthias. "Brother, do you accept the will of the Elders, the Synod, and the Most High?"

Springing out of his chair, Matthias collected himself and stood at attention. "I do."

Polite applause filled the room, though one figure made no effort to join in the accord—Rourke. Behind them, Blind Johnny stood, a serene smile across his lips.

Vanderhaggen continued, "Then, it is time to shed your former self and don the Elder's mantle. Join us, Elder Kent."

As the boys attended to him in front of the Body Corporate, reality became as blurred as the view from his rain-soaked limousine window earlier in the day.

Matthias saw the Elder's stole upon his shoulders with its intricate pattern of dollar signs and crosses, yet the garment seemed weightless. Even the tenor grate of what was now *his* wooden chair echoed in the distance.

Finally, God heard his earnest prayers. Retribution was at hand. He stood one step closer to his dear Uncle Cornelius Rourke—one step closer to having his revenge. But a veil of numbness dulled his satisfaction and Matthias puzzled over his reaction.

Blind Johnny walked over to Matthias and said, "Elder Kent, please be seated—seated."

The dark-haired boy brought a Pen of Witness to Matthias and laid it at his right hand. The blond boy arrived, his gloved hand depositing an ivory sheet of paper containing the Minutes on the table.

Matthias studied the Minutes, dwelling on the rarity of paper and its utter fragility in the presence of the Rot. Only the cleanest of mind and body were allowed to legally handle the substance. Only the most worthy were allowed to convey the Word in the tradition of the written Scriptures. Only an Elder.

Matthias drew his fingers across the page. Touching paper was a silly obsession, a rank covetousness worthy of the addicted dregs that lived outside the city's walls.

A wave of guilt tightened his stomach while fear clenched his throat. Would he be an Elder now, if the Synod found out that he already knew the texture of paper? How the page held ink? Would he be an Elder if they found out just how much of this prohibited substance he hid?

Anticipation called him away from his fears with a voice as silky as the page's surface. His eyes traced down the page, reading each stroke of black ink etched into the surface and denoting the will of the Most High as manifest by His servants at the Bank of Job.

Chief Elder Vanderhaggen cleared his throat. "Elder Kent, would you recite the Elder's pledge?"

Vanderhaggen's command sliced through Matthias's thoughts. Despite committing the pledge to memory, he had to grope for the words.

"Oh Lord, I, your humble servant, pledge to the Synod

to uphold the Word of God, as manifest in the Holy Bible, and witnessed by Your servants here on Earth. May You impart Your wisdom upon my judgments as Elder of the Bank of Job. May I be a blessing to those I lead and to whom I serve. In Your name, I pray."

"Amen," said the Chief Elder. "We welcome Elder Kent to the table and ask him to partake in the closing of the Sacrament of Pen and Paper."

Matthias drew his fingers across the paper, feeling the slightest changes and surveying the tiny unbleached bits imbedded in its surface. The pen, a sleek marriage of chrome and brass, lay in his hand, gleaming in the light. He uncapped the pen, letting the metallic scent of ink waft into the air.

The aroma conjured up his mother's face from his childhood, studying her son's hand as it swung along the paper, practicing his signature. *You would have been so proud of me, mother. You will be proud of me now.*

Matthias let his hand flow like an orchestra conductor along the contoured script of his name. He slashed the crossbar of each "T" and saved a crisp dotting of the "I" for last. It was satisfying. It was perfect.

Grimaces set on most of the Elder's faces. Even the Chief Elder's expression was less benevolent, less solicitous. Then there was Rourke, his lips neither smiling nor frowning. He remained stoic except for his eyes, as gleeful as a cat taking a mouse.

Vanderhaggen recovered. "Thank you, Elder Kent." He raised both arms. "By the witness of the Elders of the Bank of Job, I so move that this special meeting of the Body Corporate be adjourned."

"Seconded," said Rourke, his face unchanged.

With a solemn "Amen," the Body Corporate rose and marched back down the hallway.

Before the Elders walked out, Vanderhaggen's face drew into hardened lines. "We will continue in my office."

The command caught Matthias off guard. By the whitened eyes and glances cast about by the other Elders, he realized that everyone felt ill at ease. There was one positive aspect to the Chief Elder's command. The smile in Rourke's eyes had disappeared.

Chapter 3: Verses 1-73

Matthias found himself seated at the end of the glass conference table to Vanderhaggen's left. Rourke occupied the same position on the right. The seating arrangement was no random affair, and he found the unexpected honor unsettling.

The Chief Elder cleared his throat in a low growl. He glared out of the tinted windows overlooking the bank's entrance, his ruddy face reflecting a grotesque mask at the assembly. "So help me God, I will have harmony from my Elders when we address the Body. That includes you, Cornelius."

Rourke pressed his fingers to his lips, rocked back in his chair, and said, "You knew my objections, Philip."

The Chief Elder spun around and flung his chair across the office. "You gave me your word."

"I prayed over it and reconsidered."

"Oh, I suppose the angel Gabriel opened a scroll and told you to challenge me?"

Matthias recoiled from Vanderhaggen's spittle. The intensity of Chief Elder's temper was nothing new, but proximity was another matter.

Rourke stayed calm, the eye of a hurricane. "I discerned what is right."

The Chief Elder slammed the table. "Don't go quoting Job to me. You had time to object well beforehand."

"Kent lacks experience and his track record is questionable. He has a maverick spirit."

Trying to remain detached, Matthias analyzed the calm delivery of Rourke's words. Each syllable fanned Vanderhaggen's temper hotter and hotter. The lack of the title "Elder" before his own name seemed meant to nettle, to provoke. Matthias chose to ignore it. There would be another time for anger. Giving in to the taunts would make him appear exactly as his uncle said.

Instead, he allowed himself a brief look around the table to judge the effect of the exchange on the other officers. All eyes narrowed at the Chief Elder. In that moment, Matthias understood Rourke's maneuver—he sought to render Vanderhaggen impotent within his rage.

Rather than allowing things to go according to Rourke's intent, Matthias diffused the moment with a laugh. "Yes, I do have a maverick spirit, Uncle Cornelius." The intentional use of their family tie made Rourke's eyebrow rise.

The Elders focused their attention on their newest member, their steep wrinkles easing into gentle slopes.

Matthias spoke directly to his uncle. "But I carry experience far beyond the walls of the bank. Experience you don't have."

Rourke stiffened. "Wandering in the wilderness of the slums is not experience. Dabbling with a case of the Rot is reckless, and circumventing the Synod's authority is highly illegal."

"In your eyes. My mission trip to the poor and afflicted opened up new revenue streams out of the line of sight of your traditional practices."

Matthias placed his hands on the table, palms touching in a show of piety while he addressed the group. "Have we not brought God's salvation through the paying of penance to new markets? Hasn't my experience shared whatever good things the Lord gives all of us?"

Each of the Elders nodded.

Matthias caught a glimpse of Vanderhaggen's face, its redness fading to a flushed pink. Rourke stared his way, arms crossed.

Time to push dear Uncle Cornelius even further.

"So far as circumventing the Synod's authority, those are your words, Uncle. Perhaps you didn't see my picture with the Interior Minister during our mission trip to West Chester? Yet, neither he nor I had a turn with the Inquisitor afterward. It would seem that the only authority I circumvented was yours."

Vanderhaggen smiled. So did some of the Elders.

Their reactions told Matthias why he had been placed at the Chief Elder's left. The rumors of his uncle's growing stature among the corporate officers were true. Vanderhaggen needed an ally. *So be it. Let the Chief Elder be my instrument for a better purpose. Together, we will cast my dear uncle out into the slums and give him the punishment he deserves.*

Vanderhaggen said, "Your innovations have been very well received, Elder Kent. Even Elder Rourke cannot dispute the harvest we have reaped."

Rourke's face seemed to be taking on the shades of red departing Vanderhaggen's cheeks.

Blind Johnny rolled the Chief Elder's chair back into place.

Vanderhaggen sat down. "Enough bickering. Let us pray. Oh Lord, bless our assembly, guide us and make us fruitful. Amen."

"Amen," said the group.

Tapping on the keyboard in front of him, Vanderhaggen sent a display of graphs and text scrolling across the assembly's computers mounted in the table. "The Synod's General Services Administration reports a fourteen percent decrease in sweet potato production from the previous year. Soy went down eight percent, as did peanut production. That's the third year in a row and the biggest loss since the end of the Islamic Wars a hundred years ago."

The Elders gasped. Only Rourke and Matthias remained unmoved, two poker players riding out their respective hands. Matthias tried to fathom why the anger fell away from his uncle's face, replaced by straight-lipped satisfaction.

Rourke joined his hands, mimicking Matthias's piety. "My brothers, this is exactly what I have been warning you about. Our chairman put too much faith into Elder Kent's freewheeling ideas. We can all see the impact these programs have had on discretionary spending by those outside the walls. We need to focus on our core competencies."

Matthias rocked back in his chair, and he played his cards before a rapt audience. "Supply and demand, fellow Elders—supply and demand. God is simply testing the unworthy and the Bank of Job is more than worthy. Did you know that people in the slums were dealing with shortages on a daily basis long before anyone inside the city felt a hunger pang? And those poor fools spent their last credit hoping to buy salvation with the help of these." He reached into his pocket and pulled out penance cards in denominations of red, white, and blue. "From the experience gained mingling with the destitute, our marketing teams learned from the basest human yearnings how to appeal to their sinful natures and, in turn, provide them with a means of redemption. They learned just how much sin they could afford and clamored for more. By partnering with the manufacturers of alcoholic beverages, pharmaceuticals, and the vice unions, we gave these dregs the opportunity to sin they could never imagine. And these cards, these blessed cards, let them forget about their stomachs and reach beyond their means."

Vanderhaggen tipped his chin down. "What are you proposing, Elder Kent?"

Business vestments rustled. Bodies leaned forward in their chairs.

"I propose to expand our penance credit program to include the middle class. In fact, I propose we begin with this Sunday's service."

Rourke slapped his hands on the table. "There will be none of this. The city's residents are the core of our tithing base, and they pay the requisite fees for coveting and perjury."

Matthias shook his head. "They pay the requisite fees to live inside the city's walls, safe and secure from the terrors outside. We offer them basic necessities in exchange for their labors. They give onto Caesar what is Caesar's. Just what, my dear uncle, will we offer them when food becomes scarce? When there is no more old silage to burn for heat and electricity? How will we produce clean water? What then?"

Rourke folded, apparently having no other play.

Matthias stood, held up the penance cards, and dealt them

down the table. "My brothers, we need to offer them sins to drown their misery and redemption to give them hope. We need to expand the penance credit system into every town and city. Those of strong character in our Lord and Savior will continue as they always have. Those that are not will partake in industries that we already have a partnership with. Those same industries will raise their prices in response to the crop shortfall. We will dole out even more of these cards as we have done in the slums to cover the gap between earthly pleasure and salvation. They will have the illusion that their standard of living will be maintained, and we will maintain our profitability by charging handling fees all along the way."

The Elders fell silent, their eyes flitting about while they considered Matthias's words.

"What happens when their sins outweigh their ability to pay for redemption?" said Rourke.

Matthias could feel his smile broaden. "That, my dear uncle, is when we offer them a Hajj."

Rourke spit on the floor. "How dare you speak Muslim words among our holy assembly."

"Very dramatic, uncle. I do not mean the Hajj in the Islamic sense. I mean it in sense of a holy pilgrimage as did the European Christians of old when they journeyed to ancient Jerusalem. I mean it in the patriotic sense."

"Patriotic?" asked Vanderhaggen.

"Yes, sir." Matthias bowed to the Chief Elder with theatric grace. His deference to Vanderhaggen gave the Chief the appearance of being in charge and, at the same time, demoted Rourke.

Vanderhaggen's chest filled. "What do you have in mind, Matthias? Jerusalem no longer exists."

"Why go to Jerusalem when you can take a bus to Zion?"

"I beg your pardon?"

"Sir, the pilgrimage I speak of is to Saint Ronald's Zion, his bright city on the hill—Washington D.C."

Rourke rose, bellowing to everyone at the table. "The Synod will not approve such a visit. Washington is quarantined for another 400 years until the radiation fades."

Expecting such a response, Matthias said, "My marketing researchers feel that the Synod's measurements are wrong. The radiation from the dirty bomb should have dissipated enough by now to allow shielded visitors a short visit. A corporation in the Arab League has been doing precisely this for two decades for devout Muslims making the Hajj, their sacred journey to Mecca. We all know just how devastated that city was during the war. Their believers will pay any price to touch the Kaaba, even if it's with lead-lined gloves. And gentlemen, that corporation is making an absolute killing."

Rourke's thin-lipped smile returned. He punched some keys on his keyboard and the vid-panels filled with a new set of graphs. "You assume too much, nephew. The Synod's scientists have already reviewed your so-called research and dismissed the results as a house built on sand."

The statement caught Matthias off guard. His staff assured him of the quality of their findings. No one had access to the research team's data, yet the figures Rourke had on the screen countered every key point on his list.

"A more *experienced* Elder would have done more preparation before presenting something as outlandish as day trips to a poisoned city," said Rourke. "You would have us martyr our most pious citizens? How very Islamic of you."

Chuckles rose from the assembly.

Matthias fumed. His uncle managed to pierce the walls of secrecy around his project, probably through the weakest link—one of staff. Matthias realized that his single-mindedness to launch the pilgrimage made him as blind as Blind Johnny. He made a mental note to pray for humility. He made another note to pray for discernment. Once his prayers were answered, he would personally cast out the person responsible.

With the advantage lost, Matthias conceded as best he could. "Too bad Uncle, I booked you on the first pilgrimage."

"You may go in my place, nephew."

More laughter.

Vanderhaggen intervened, a bit crestfallen, but still better than his former rage. "Perhaps I will send you both to Washington so that this debate may be settled with firsthand knowledge. Elder

Kent, your plan has great merit. Until the city is declared safe, we will file your project with our other contingency plans." He raised his voice to the entire assembly. "Fellow Elders, our newest officer has made a proposal to implement the penance credit system nationwide." The Chief Elder shifted toward Rourke. "Do I have a second?"

Rourke smiled a gratuitous reptilian smile, the one that always made Matthias uneasy. "Seconded."

"Those in favor?"

The assembly replied, "Amen."

Vanderhaggen called out, "Opposed?"

Silence.

"Good. Now to our second order of business. Our dear friends at the Synod will be releasing the latest version of the online Bible, SKJ 8.2 sometime late next week. According to the press release, affected chapters are mostly limited to the Old Testament with emphasis on Proverbs and Judges. The archeological and scholarly notes show very minor changes. As usual, Elder Rourke will head up Synod compliance. Make every one of your employees aware of the changes so that we may gauge the impact and glean any advantage. People, I want to be on top of this from the get-go. Amen?"

"Amen," chanted the Elders.

"That's all I have. See you all next week." Vanderhaggen bowed his head. "By the power of the Synod who act under the Most High and the shareholders of the Bank of Job, I adjourn this meeting of the Corporate Elders. May God bless us all with unending profitability. Amen."

Matthias pushed his chair away, anxious to leave. Before he could, he felt a hand on his shoulder.

The Chief Elder stood next to him. "One more moment of you time, Elder Kent."

Chapter 4: Verses 1-90

Matthias followed Vanderhaggen past the phalanx of the Chief Elder's administrative assistants, all of them handsome young men dressed in fine business vestments. A slight man with short blond hair scurried to the door and held it open. Both Elders entered.

"Please Matthias, be seated," said Vanderhaggen. He looked up at the blond-haired man and barked, "Refreshments."

The door swung shut. Footsteps dashed along the granite floor.

The layout of the Chief Elder's office no longer intimidated Matthias as it had during prior visits. He understood the wealth the chestnut wainscoting was supposed to convey and the authority the massive oak pedestal desk was supposed to dictate. Even the position of the spindly steel chair placed squarely in front of the desk had been set there to isolate and intimidate. He angled the chair to one side, sat down, and leaned on the armrest.

"I thought you had him," said the Chief, lowering himself onto the leather wingback chair.

"As did I, Elder Vanderhaggen."

"Philip. I prefer that my Elders call me Philip when we're not performing formal tasks."

"Yes, sir. Philip." Calling the Chief Elder by his first name made him feel as comfortable as the metal chair he sat on. "I found the seating arrangement in the meeting room interesting."

"I hated being so obvious, but your uncle has been provoking me for quite some time."

"He has a talent for that."

Vanderhaggen brought his fingertips together on top of the desk and flexed. "Like uncle, like nephew."

"Or, Chief Elder and his staff."

Philip laughed. "It is my duty to provoke and challenge."

And, it is not in your nature to be provoked. "I hope I did not embarrass you before my uncle. I had assurances that the pilgrimage data was sound."

"Evidently not as sound as your uncle's data. No matter. The expansion of the penance card system was well received. I'd say that you got the better of him overall. Oh my, how angry he became."

"He is easily provoked."

"Why does he despise you so?"

Matthias felt the congeniality of the conversation leave him. An old and familiar anger smoldered inside his chest.

A knock on the door broke the gaping silence.

"Come," said Vanderhaggen, settling into his chair.

The blond servant returned, wheeling a beverage cart. He sidled up to the Chief Elder's desk and stood at attention.

Vanderhaggen passed his hand over the cart. "We must celebrate your appointment. Whiskey? Wine? Perhaps Gilead Spring Water?" His eyes never left Matthias.

The servant poured spring water into a crystal tumbler and handed it to the Chief Elder. He guzzled it without a breath.

Matthias was dumbstruck. A liter of water from the last unadulterated spring in North America cost a week's pay and Vanderhaggen drank it like common distilled.

The Elder's face brightened. "My, don't you look like a landed carp. You're an Elder now, not one of those Reformation drones reading people's correspondence. You must take time to enjoy the privileges of rank." Vanderhaggen spoke to the servant. "Another, and one for our newest Elder."

The assistant poured two full glasses and handed one to Matthias.

Before he drank, Philip said, "And no sipping. We keep it at the same temperature that it comes out of the ground. It's God's gift. One—two—three."

Matthias obliged, drinking the contents in time with Vanderhaggen. The cold liquid cooled his anger.

"Freezes the very brain, eh?" said Vanderhaggen, held the glass up to the window apprising its contents like fine wine. "We keep a stock of it here for all of the Elders. Feel free to indulge at any time."

The servant shuffled nervously toward Philip. "Sir, there is a call from Senator Levitz."

"I need to take this. It will be but a moment."

Matthias rose. Vanderhaggen waved his hand, bidding him to remain.

The conversation proved easy to ignore, the Chief Elder's solicitous tone trading small talk with the senator over the Ecunet. Matthias gazed out the window at the sagging corporate flags set against the gray sky, as limp as Vanderhaggen's authority. Only the United Christian States flag stirred in the faint breeze. Its blue field of forty-two white crosses atop red and white stripes billowed for a moment and drooped.

Vanderhaggen swung his arm while he spoke on the phone. The water in his glass swirled over the lip of the tumbler and splashed onto the desk. A drop landed on the decanter and glinted in the light. Matthias saw himself as a rotund caricature on the curved base of the vessel. While he studied the reflection, his thirty-five year old self disappeared, replaced by himself as a boy.

Matthias carried the glass decanter to his uncle's guestroom, proud that he had carried out Uncle Cornelius's command to get him some drinking water. It was fortunate that Naomi, their housekeeper, had distilled enough water the night before, or it would have taken forever to prepare.

He raised his hand to knock on the door. Before he did, a woman's sob pierced the air. The voice sounded pitiful, anguished, and unmistakable. He pushed door open to the contorted face of his mother. She lay on her stomach, her dress sloughed around her waist. Behind her rocked Uncle Cornelius, his drawn mouth grunting in time with his motions. His mother screamed. Uncle Cornelius cursed. Matthias dropped the decanter and ran.

Later that day, his mother came to him in the family chapel. She clenched a handkerchief and dabbed the corners of her eyes. He knelt, his guts boiling from a fire within.

She knelt next to him. "You can never tell your father what you saw," she said. "What Uncle Cornelius did to me was an abomination, but you must keep silent. When your uncle left, he told me what he would do to us should anyone find out." Tears streaked from eyes wild with fright.

His rage burned white hot. "I've been praying for God to strike him down."

She nodded.

"Why did he hurt you?"

"Because he was overcome by the Evil One."

"You should tell father."

"No one, Mattie. Not a soul or Cornelius will take what little we have left. We must pray for his redemption."

"I'll pray that he goes to Hell."

"Have another," said Vanderhaggen over the gurgle of the decanter.

Matthias felt the tumbler turn cold.

"You seem lost in your thoughts. Did the Senator's intrusion bore you that much?"

A chill passed from his hand to the rest of his body. Matthias shivered. "The water does freeze the brain, Philip."

Vanderhaggen returned to his chair, dismissing the blond assistant. Once the door closed, Philip's hospitable grin faded. "You didn't answer my question."

"Sir?"

"What is it between you and your uncle?"

Matthias sipped the water. "A personal dispute."

The grin reappeared. "I see."

Knowing that the Vanderhaggen wasn't satisfied, he said, "My uncle is a proud man. Suffice it to say that he does not like to be reminded of his faults."

Matthias studied Vanderhaggen's expression and found what he needed in the subtle crinkling around the Elder's blue eyes. He realized just how much Philip wanted to trust him, and, at the same time, understood just how weak the old man had become. No wonder Uncle Cornelius opposed him at every turn. The situation was worse than he realized. *Lord, let me consider these threats and enable Your servant to speak Your word with great fervor.*

Leaning forward in his chair, Matthias whispered, "When I find a way to unseat my uncle, can I count on the highest corporate authority to back me up?"

The crinkles smoothed. Philip drummed his fingers against his glass. "Your price for this bargain?"

"Why, my appointment to Vice Elder, Synod Relations."

Vanderhaggen laughed, deep and loud. The water in the glass spilled out onto the desk a second time, beading on the varnish. "That's what I call ambition."

Ambition to you, vengeance to me. "You have my word before God Himself that I will not pursue a similar course where you are concerned. Retire when you will, and I will recommend you for the Board of Directors."

The Chief Elder pursed his lips, and slowly nodded. After a moment, he slammed his glass down like a judge's gavel. "Agreed. What is your next step?"

"With the pilgrimage routes shot down, I will have to come up with another strategy."

"Understood."

"Which, I will attend to after our release of revised biblical passages."

"You have not taken any time off to mourn your mother's passing."

"There is always much to be done."

The Chief Elder said, "Policy dictates that you take three days as prescribed by the corporate guidelines, and Heaven knows that your dear uncle will remind us if we are not compliant. Get your staff started today on the updates and take the requisite time off. Return on Thursday, ready to assume your duties."

Matthias wanted to protest, but decided to accede. Better to give the Chief Elder the illusion of obedience. "Yes, sir."

Vanderhaggen produced a folder from a desk drawer and handed it to Matthias. "This is your upgraded security badge and your new corporate penance card. It will be validated by the end of the day. You know how slow the Synod's processors are."

Matthias grasped the folder, but Vanderhaggen didn't let go.

The Chief Elder leaned across the desk. "My next command to you is to celebrate your promotion. Like the spring water, use the card according to your own discretion." A smile curved Vanderhaggen's blushing cheeks. "You've earned that card, enjoy it." He released the folder.

Office gossip told of the Chief Elder's free-spending bacchanals. Matthias grinned. "As you command."

Vanderhaggen summoned the servant, "A pen for Elder Kent."

The man obliged, bringing a slender wooden box to Matthias and opening it with a gloved hand.

Philip swirled a finger at the exposed documents. "Sign the card and press your forefinger on the imprint of the bank. That will certify it. Then sign the form acknowledging your responsibility."

Complying, Matthias took the pen, signed, and handed it to the assistant.

He snapped the folder shut and left the room.

"Your handwriting is so elegant, so practiced," commented Vanderhaggen, his eyes transfixed on Matthias's hand.

The word "practiced" hung in air, the prolonged last syllable carrying an insinuation that couldn't be ignored. Philip's face bore the same critical stare during the meeting of the Body Corporate. Matthias realized his sin and its weight pressed against him. *How could my handwriting be so perfect if there are no ink and paper to practice on?*

He knew he needed to allay all of the Chief Elder's suspicions or the trust he gained would be lost. "Is it that noticeable, Philip? I had no idea that my penmanship would cause such a stir." Matthias studied Vanderhaggen's sober expression, finding the subtle crinkling around the Elder's eyes a second time. "You know how parents are, expectations."

"Ah, yes."

"Mother insisted that any man of the Word under her roof should be able to write his own name, despite the law. That, and, well, things were more lenient then. So, from my earliest years, she would make me practice on scraps of aluminum and plastic. Father used to fill these antique pens with old tractor oil." Matthias made a point of wrinkling his nose. "Horrid stuff. Then you just wiped it away." His hand acted out the motion, as if he were wiping the issue away.

Half of Vanderhaggen's face lifted into a grin, which suited Matthias's half-truth. "I see. Your mother, bless her soul, did an excellent job." The Chief Elder tapped his fingers together for a moment and moved to his keyboard. "If I may make a recommendation—"

Matthias tensed, worrying that his handwriting would draw some kind of chastisement.

Over the tip-tap of the keys, Philip said, "—Pharaoh's. I'm obtaining a reservation for you tonight."

A wave of relief swept over Matthias. "Why, thank you, Philip. Is it permissible to bring Brother Kyalo?"

Vanderhaggen chuckled. "The more the merrier. And don't let the women exhaust you. We will need you rested and focused for our formidable task."

Chapter 5: Verses 1-92

Matthias made his way from Elder's Hall to the administrative wing, receiving courteous bows.

One voice, and its familiar echo, rose above the rest. "Blessings, Elder Kent—Kent."

"After all these years, you have forgotten my name, Blind Johnny?" said Matthias.

"No, Elder, but the rules on this matter are quite clear—clear."

"I am forgotten as if I passed away."

"Psalm 31—31. Such drama—drama. You are not forgotten, Elder, only known by a new name—name. Your uncle knows your old name well enough—enough."

"How did he take our first official meeting?"

Blind Johnny laughed in a hushed baritone, his cowl falling away and revealing his wrinkled face. "Elder Rourke paid much penance today, uttering curses that would bankrupt less wealthy men—men." The laughter stopped as quickly as it started. He pulled the cowl back over his head. "Elder Kent, be it known that he seeks the stone that will make you stumble—stumble."

"Or, perhaps the rock to make me trip?"

"Do not make light of it, Elder Kent—Kent." The old attendant hunched over, his voice fading away as if he were falling into a chasm. "He has not been so vexed for many years—years."

The change in Blind Johnny's demeanor made Matthias pause. An enraged Uncle Cornelius was something to be wary of. "Then I shall be careful, old friend. Oh, and Blind Johnny, what is the penalty for disobeying an Elder?"

"Exile—exile."

"By my command, you are to call me 'Matthias' when we are not in formal proceedings."

Blind Johnny smiled, bowed, and said, "By your command, Matthias—Matthias. May goodness and mercy follow you all the days of your life—life."

Sunlight poured through fissures in the parting storm clouds, casting the shadow of a window frame across the breadth of Matthias's office. He watched it appear and disappear from his desk. The golden glow returned and beckoned. He lifted his hand into the beam. A section of the window frame drew a cross-shaped silhouette onto his palm.

A twisting of the doorknob signaled Benjamin Kyalo's entry. No one else dared enter the office without permission. He approached Matthias's desk, carrying two parcels under his left arm. "When do you move upstairs?"

"Tomorrow."

"How did it go with the Elders?"

Matthias looked out the window.

"That good, eh?"

He tried to suppress the feeling of betrayal boiling in his stomach. "We have a spy in our ranks. Rourke made our data look worthless. I looked like a damned fool in there."

Benjamin was incredulous. "I hand picked everyone. We checked everybody everyday for any kind of espionage. Our computers weren't connected to any kind of network. It isn't possible."

Matthias slid the vid-panel toward Benjamin. "Here's the access log for the project. Other than you and I, two people had full security to the room, the system, and the data—Levi Fuentes and Seth Jackson. One of them is our traitor. Any ideas?"

The research director pulled the vid-panel close, reading the computer logs.

"What's wrong, Benjamin?"

"Jackson volunteered to go to Washington with me."

"The sojourn we planned isn't going to happen. The Synod and the Elders have denied us permission. Eight months of work gone."

"Shit."

"Such an elegant word. Now we both have to pay penance."

Ben tossed the parcels on the desk. "Does that mean that I have to pay for these, too?"

Matthias held one of them up. It felt lumpy, soft. "You brought me pillows?"

"Look inside."

Tearing open the plastic cover, Matthias slid out the inner package. A folded white coverall embroidered with a red crescent moon and star lay in front of him. He lifted it up and let it unfurl. A hood with a clear-plastic visor and two rounded appendages thumped to the floor.

"Careful with that, Matthias. That's the air filtration mask."

"This is the cloak the Muslim pilgrims wear?"

"My contact called it a 'hajji suit.' It keeps the tourists alive long enough to go to Mecca, circle the Kaaba four times and get back out. Their scientists are working on a suit that will shield them during the entire Hajj."

Matthias scooped the mask up and placed it over his head. His voice sounded muffled. "Too bad you can't use them."

"I can't believe one of our staff is working for Rourke. It just doesn't add up. Even if one of them is a spy, they saw the data. They would have reported that the radiation is gone."

Pulling the mask off, Matthias said, "Then why would my uncle dispute the facts? Pilgrimages would be very lucrative and would make his position that much better."

Chuckling, Benjamin said, "It wasn't his idea. Maybe Rourke wants to present it to the Synod."

Benjamin's insinuation made Matthias reevaluate the meeting. He mulled it over, from his uncle's attitude at the table to the way he presented his material. "I really am a fool. Rourke didn't present anything new. He just rearranged it to counter us. He doesn't want us to rock the boat by asking the Synod for permission to visit the city."

Benjamin nodded.

Matthias looked off out the window, the flags moving in the wind. The image of ranks of similar flags flying along the road to Washington, buses loaded with paying pilgrims weeping at the inspirational sight filled his mind. "Are you sure of your figures? I mean, really sure?"

"We've been over it seven-times-seventy times. Washington's dirty bomb had a fraction of the radiation that Mecca got in their nuke. The Strontium 90 is long gone. The Synod's own downwind sensors validate that."

"That leaves the Americium 241 my uncle enjoys reminding us about. Just think, another two-hundred-and-fifty years and we can visit the old capitol. If my uncle wants to steal my idea and go to a poisoned city, let him. Once his teeth fall out, he will be easier to deal with."

Benjamin reached onto the desk, grabbed the other parcel, and tore it open. The object resembled a child's toy—a small flying saucer. He set it on the desk next to the hajji suit.

"Great, I've got a space suit and now I've got a space ship. We're going to offer pilgrimages to the moon next?" Matthias picked up the object.

"No, I just got this from an antique vendor down in Delaware. You're playing with Americium 241."

Matthias let the object clatter across the desk. He tried to wring his hands free of the invisible stain of radiation.

The object spun like a top until Ben placed a single finger on it. "Don't worry, it's safe." He picked it up. "This is what we were missing. It's like I told you, Matthias. Back when the Muslim terrorists set off the dirty bomb, there was a lot of controversy about the material they used. The scientists of the time could only account for about an eighth of what they were detecting. When the war heated up, they pretty much gave up on measurements. They were too busy making better bombs. Well, the word I got was that the old measurements were right all along. What's perking up the detectors is this." He pointed to the flying saucer. "In 2009, most of the homes around D.C. had at least one of these. It's called a smoke detector. Since most of the residences of that time were built of wood, fire was a constant danger. These things were everywhere."

All of Matthias's trepidation fell away, pushed aside by the rush of ideas filling his mind. "You're telling me that the Synod's sensors are picking up these devices around the rest of the city. They're getting false readings."

"Exactly."

"Then, this means that Washington can become a tourist attraction just like Mecca. Profits are going to go straight to heaven."

"Finding one of those detectors was the key."

"Have either Jackson or Fuentes seen this thing?"

"No, I just picked it up this morning."

"Then my uncle won't know about it either." Matthias picked up a brass crucifix lying next to his parent's picture. He ran his fingers over it, rubbing the lines cast into its surface to resemble wood grain.

Benjamin laid the smoke detector on the desk. "If we showed this to the Elders, do you think they'd change their mind?"

"That's unlikely." Spinning the cross between his thumb and forefinger, Matthias thought back to when he got the crucifix during a family trip to a shrine in the Maryland mountains called Mount Saint Mary's. He remembered the stunted trees at the foot of a towering statue of Jesus and his father purchasing the cross for him from a souvenir vendor.

Electricity spread from the souvenir, up his arm, and between his shoulder blades. "Benjamin, what happens if you take a religious tourist and give him a relic?"

Benjamin replied, "You have a happy tourist?"

"No. You have a pilgrim. Think about it. If we can get proof, immutable proof, that Washington is safe then no one can tell us 'no'."

"What are you saying, Matthias?"

"I'm saying that radiation estimates and Muslim garments carry little interest to anyone. We can't market that. It has zero appeal. We need something profound, something jaw-dropping that we recover from the city."

"What do you have in mind?"

Putting the crucifix down, Matthias said, "We're going to go to Washington—you and I."

Benjamin shook his head in wide swaths. "You're an Elder. You're not trained. What about the Synod's ban?"

"Aren't you the Doubting Thomas. Look, I'm more fit than Jackson and you've already answered the Synod question."

"Oh?"

Matthias jumped to his feet. "I'm an Elder. I'm untouchable. It's perfect. A ranking company official that opens the eyes of government and company alike to a brand new revenue stream. All I need is proof."

"What do you have in mind?"

"I'll know it when I see it."

Benjamin locked his fingers together, his head still shaking. "How are you going to get away from your duties? Your absence will be noticed."

"Vanderhaggen. I've been ordered to take Mourner's Leave, and I'm not due back until Thursday." Matthias could sense his associate's continuing doubt. "Benjamin, trust me, it really is perfect, but it will need a little misdirection. Tell your researchers that the Synod has shut us down. That way, the spy will tell Rourke. On Monday, we go to Washington, find a nice relic, and present it to my uncle next Thursday."

"I still don't like this, Matthias."

"Tell the team to stand down. We'll work out the details tonight."

"Tonight?"

"You are so full of questions. Tonight, you and I are going to celebrate my promotion." Matthias slipped the Elder's card from his vestment pocket. "Behold."

"Pharaoh's?"

"Yes. And here's the best part—Vanderhaggen set up the whole thing. Are you ready for a Bacchanal?"

"Absolutely," cheered Benjamin.

"Perfect. We'll talk more about our sojourn later. My limousine will pick you up at 7:00." Matthias punched some keys on his keyboard. "Until then, there's work to do. We received approval to expand the penance card system to everybody in the city."

"They actually went for that?"

"You forget, I was top advertising salesman three years in a row. Rourke had a fit. We're starting it with this Sunday's service."

"Who's preaching?"

Reading the name off the vid-panel, Matthias clenched both fists and cheered. "Yes. Reverend Isaac."

"It isn't a ratings week."

"No, but he's perfect for us. Make sure your crews are recording the crowd reactions. We can—"

Benjamin stood and rested his palms on the desk. "You can let me do my job, Matthias. You're an Elder now."

"Which you keep reminding me of. Listen. I hate to say this, but outside of this room, you're going to have to call me 'Elder.'"

Benjamin walked to the door, huffed, and pulled on the handle. "Yes, Elder Kent."

As the door closed, Matthias hung his head.

The cross-shaped shadow came into view on his desk. He reached out to grasp it a second time, but the clouds regrouped, his empty hand hovering in the gathering darkness.

Chapter 6: Verses 1-137

The ride to Pharaoh's House of Rapture began with a strained silence. The strain ebbed when the sprawling brothel loomed into view.

"Oh my God," said Benjamin.

The pulsing neon and black glass pyramid was nothing new to Matthias, but he managed a smile. "Did you know that Pharaoh's was built from the same plans as the ancient pyramid of Luxor in Las Vegas?"

Benjamin gave a schoolboy's nod as if some great lesson had been taught.

"Ah, poor Las Vegas. Scoured from the earth by the wrath of God. A perfect example of what happens when you don't pay penance." Matthias tried to imagine the splendor of the Las Vegas Strip. He couldn't. All he saw was a radiating façade, a triangular void amidst the staid granite edifices of Rittenhouse Square. The pyramid's blackness created an impromptu mirror in the car window. His face reflected no joy.

He blinked away his melancholy, and looked off at the beacons atop the Synod's congressional offices only a few blocks north. "Benjamin, to your right is the Synod's downtown offices.

Pharaoh's is just far enough away to be indiscernible by the more prudish members of government. It's also conveniently close for its less prudish members. They stop by anytime they wish. Keep that in mind when we're inside. You never know who you might be sitting next to."

"How many times have you been here?"

"I've lost count."

"Are the women as beautiful as the rumors say they are?"

"Every Magdalene I've been with has been exquisite and well worth the penance."

Benjamin fogged the glass. "For the love of God, look at what's coming."

"For the love of your wife, control your lust. It's going to be a long night."

"My wife knows her place. It's not like this is my first time with concubines. If anyone should be staying away from the brothels, it should be you. You're getting old. You need a good woman."

Matthias heard that comment one too many times and his mood switched to irritation. He knew plenty of good women— social climbers, covetous, domineering, meek and everything in-between. Each one had been hell-bent on marrying for prestige, respectability, or the fulfillment of the Bible's decree to go forth and multiply—some with more zeal than others. They were all *good* women. Good in the eyes of the Lord and the Synod, but not in his eyes. They lusted after status. They loved wealth and they had no more love in their hearts for him than the women inside Pharaoh's.

"Maybe you can marry this one," said Benjamin, prodding Matthias's ribs.

A young woman in a gold lamé robe approached the car. Statuesque, dark-haired, and long ebony arms clean of the Rot, she was the veritable picture of Solomon's Sheba. She reached for the car door's handle.

Gesturing with a graceful sweep of her hand, she said, "Greetings, Elder Kent."

He stepped into the dank air, his mood brooding and dark like the gray clouds above. Benjamin followed. City dwellers milled around the periphery, heads maneuvering to see the most current arrivals. Cameras swung in their direction and flashes bleached the night.

The grand awning overhead glowed with a moving projection of alluring women in various states of undress. Each face turned toward the viewer, their full lips red and rounded with the promise of implied seduction. In unison, they whispered, "Our love is more delightful than wine."

"Do keep your mouth closed, Ben. The press is here," chided Matthias.

The Queen of Sheba ushered the pair to the entrance. It slid aside, a puff of scented air enveloping them. The perfume chased Matthias's brooding away and replaced it with renewed twinges of anticipation.

The blonde maitre d' spoke, her voice as smooth as her tight-fitting gown. "Welcome to Pharaoh's, Elder Kent—Brother Benjamin. Your suite is ready. This way, please."

She led them along a walnut-paneled corridor, their shoes squeaking on the marble tile. The aroma of braised meat overpowered the perfume. Matthias's stomach gurgled.

The maitre d' opened a set of double doors. "Gentleman, the King David Lounge."

"This is one room I haven't been in, Benjamin. The Chief Elder has outdone himself," Matthias studied the half-dozen scarf-clad women gyrating to the skirl of a Turkish flute. They danced their way over to a replica of a desert tent trimmed in maroon brocade and golden tassels. A flock of scarves flew into the air and descended. Each woman displayed her bare left leg, toes pointed and calves accentuated.

"Enjoy yourselves," said the blonde as she closed the doors.

The troupe surrounded Benjamin and Matthias, tugging at the men's clothes, and rendering them naked within moments. A woman with caramel skin and brown almond-shaped eyes draped a gauzy robe over each man. She led Matthias to a couch, motioning for him to lie on his stomach. He complied.

An electric guitar strummed softly when the flute quieted. Smooth hands slid under the robe, kneading Matthias's legs.

The caramel-skinned woman said, "I am Lydia. Jada, Candice,

and I are here to attend to your every desire, lord. Tonight, you are our king and we are your slaves."

A long, pronounced and deep "Oh," filled the room. Benjamin turned toward Matthias. "Do you think Heaven will be like this?"

"Hopefully," he sighed, feeling six hands loosen his spine with deliberate pressure.

Between long blinks, he noticed a servant girl placing a bottle of wine and two glasses on the table next to him. She handed him a card. It read, "Congratulations—Philip."

Lydia poured two glasses with such care that not even the slightest drop was wasted. She gave him a glass.

Perching on an elbow, he drew in the wine's bouquet—sweet, rare, and luxuriant. His contemplation shattered when he spied Benjamin taking a long swig from his glass. "Slow down, this is a sweet Riesling. The Rot gets most of the grapes. At best, a few cases come out of New York every year and most of that ends up with Synod members. It's probably a hundred credits a glass and this is a quart."

Benjamin slowed to a sip. The women's hands stopped their kneading, their gaze focused on the bottle.

Matthias tipped the glass at Lydia. "Would you like some?"

"No, lord. We are not permitted to partake in the fare of our clients." Her eyes never left the glass.

He took a sip, pulled her close, and kissed her. "Is my kiss sweeter than wine?"

Her tongue swept across both lips, slow and teasing. "Yes lord, but you move too swiftly. We have many hours together. Would you spend your manhood now, or let us attend you in good order?"

Blood rushed to his pelvis. He fought back the hot surge and tried to concentrate on the sweet wine. It calmed him. "I'll try to savor you a bit at a time."

Giggling erupted at Benjamin's table. He had spun on his back, hands enveloping his torso. There would be no waiting for him.

Lydia and the other women resumed their massage. Matthias fought back the primal urges boiling within, trying not to listen to his friend's moans. Benjamin arched his back, shuddered, and fell into quiet bliss.

"No patience. It's all about the total experience. Anticipation heightens the climax," explained Matthias.

Benjamin didn't bother to lift his eyelids. "Are you sure you're not a homosexual?"

Despite Ben's teasing tone, Matthias bristled. Caresses slid between his legs. The anger dissipated. "Yes."

The wine steward returned, hammering a three-bell chime. The women ceased their massage and scurried out of sight behind another volley of pastel scarves.

Matthias lifted his head and listened for the departing servants. Satisfied that both he and Benjamin were alone, he whispered, "Have you notified our contacts?"

"Is it always business with you?"

"Business first, pleasure second."

Benjamin rested his head on his arms. "They're very nervous about the last minute change. I had to give them another five hundred credits to just to calm them down."

"Do I cause that much fear?"

"No, I had to pay them to call you 'Elder Kent'." Benjamin frowned. "They will meet us at Chillum and take us to a place where we can get past the Synod's sentries without notice. We have to be back in Chillum before four."

"Or, we turn into mice?"

"What's that supposed to mean?"

Matthias realized how stupid the comment sounded. How could his friend know the story behind it? "An old tale from my childhood. Go on."

"We pay them half the fee when we go in and the other half when we go out, a total of five-thousand credits."

Matthias said, "What? That's outrageous. I don't have that much in gold or penance cards simply lying around the house. We can't draw from an expense account. Rourke will have our banking activity monitored."

Benjamin frowned all the more. "Then we don't have a prayer."

"Damn it." Matthias punched the couch. Everything had come undone. His uncle's success chafed his ego. He cast about, analyzing a way, any way, to make the sojourn happen. Benjamin was right, they're wasn't a prayer—or was there? "Oh Lord, you have given me understanding according to Your word."

"What are you mumbling about?"

"What if we could get our hands on some untraceable funds?"

"The Black Market?"

"No. Church."

Benjamin choked on his wine. "Are you proposing the collection of a special offering?"

"Very funny. They give out thousands of penance cards every week during the service. Why couldn't we use them? I can book the expense against my Elder Card after the trip. Just like this party, no one will know."

Leaping to his feet, Benjamin took Matthias by the shoulders. "Are you insane? The cards are guarded by the troops from the Order of St. George. My family and I will be cast out."

"The guards always move into crowd control positions once the dispensers are loaded. You'll have the room to yourself for at least five minutes, maybe more. Besides, they're going to have their hands full this week."

"You've really lost it."

Brushing Benjamin's hands away, Matthias stood and stared into his associate's eyes. There could be no deviation now, not when he stood so close to defeating his uncle. "Do you want to rise to the board? Do you want to be an Elder? You must seize the moment. If my uncle becomes Chief, you'll be lucky if you get a severance package. Think it over. Are you with me, or against me? Just say no, and I'll do it myself."

Benjamin looked into the distance, his breath shallow and lips clenched. "Damn it. And I'm supposed to trust you that this is all going to work out?"

"Absolutely. You have the protection of an Elder, after all." Matthias brought his hands together in a mock prayer. "Just put your trust in the Old Testament."

"Moses will appear and part the security doors to the card vault?"

Trays rattled in the hallway.

Matthias glanced at the door, rushing to finish. "Listen for the number of the chapter and verses of the Old Testament reading. That's the code to the lock."

"How did you do you know that?"

Matthias smirked. "Remember Phoebe, the vault manager's plain daughter?"

"The one blessed with the ample bosom?"

"And, a lot of insecurities. She talks in her sleep. Do you think you can do it?"

The women returned, bearing trays of steaming delicacies.

Benjamin said, "I don't know."

"We'll be legends, my brother. Our trek will be heralded in the Minutes and I will be

most happy to sign them myself." He sat down, his hands raised and shaking with every syllable. "Matthias Kent and Benjamin Kyalo—the men who opened Saint Ronald's Zion."

Benjamin took a deep swallow of wine and slapped the couch. "Yes. Yes. All right. The men who opened Zion."

"This calls for a toast." Matthias drained the last of the Riesling. "Lydia, a bottle of Shiraz."

The women came in parading a rack of lamb and bowls overflowing with spiced vegetables.

"Lord, may I attend you?" asked Jada who proffered a heavily laden dish.

Lydia returned and poured generous glasses of red wine.

Matthias sat back on the cushions, taking each bite Jada served and washing it down with ample pulls of the full-bodied vintage. Lydia refilled the glass each time he set it down. Before long, the edges of his cheeks numbed. The emptiness he felt when he arrived disappeared with the contents of the bottle. Soon, he'd have his relic and his uncle would look like a fool before the board. "Another bottle."

Benjamin pitched a bone onto the table. "You're the one who needs to slow down, Matthias."

"I am an Elder of the Bank of Job." He tapped his glass until Lydia filled it to the brim. The numbness in his jaw made his voice sound like someone else spoke. "I will eat what I want, drink what I want, and take what I want." Matthias wrapped his arm around Lydia and yanked her close. The plate tumbled to the floor. He kissed her hard and ran his hands over her body. At first, she squirmed in his grasp and then turned as pliable as clay. He could feel no passion in her, no ready desire. Pushing her aside, he said, "Clean this up."

Jada and Candice joined Lydia, snatching food off the floor and shoveling it into their mouths. Matthias's lust retreated. "Is it that bad for you all?"

The women froze, hands quaking in front of their mouths.

Matthias regarded the large amount of food still left on the serving tray. He spoke as best as he could despite his wine-clouded thoughts. "Lydia, do you know the penalty for failing to obey the direct order of an Elder?"

She crawled to his feet; her head bowed and ends of her hair trembling like her hands. "Yes, Elder Kent."

"Get up and pour me more wine. Take this food away." When she rose, he seized her arm. "And Lydia, none of it is to be returned to the kitchen. Divide it equally among the dancers and yourself. You are to tell your masters we were pigs and ate every crumb. Do you understand my order?"

Relief washed across her face. "Yes, my lord."

As they carried the meal away, Benjamin said, "The beneficent Elder Kent."

Matthias hoisted his glass. "To me."

While draining another glassful, the lights dimmed. Curtains parted at the far end of the room revealing a backdrop painted to look like the rooftops of biblical Jerusalem at sunset. Dancers appeared from the wings in another cascade of scarves. They spun and jumped in time with the flute's allegro pace. The dancers stopped center stage when the music halted in a dramatic pause then curled off into the wings.

A new dancer appeared on one of the rooftops, a touch of backlight silhouetting her profile against the sheer muslin drape she wore and making her long, auburn hair glow. She knelt, unfastened a cord, and let her dress fall to the ground.

Transfixed, Matthias drank in every supple curve.

"Dear Lord," said Benjamin.

The dancers twirled onto the platform, carrying a washbasin.

Matthias slurred out a discovery, "I get it now. The King David Lounge. She's Bathsheeba."

Bathsheeba rose from her knees, like a flower opening for the sun. The dancers loosed a knot on their shoulders, parting the last scarf surrounding their bodies. One by one, they pirouetted and passed the scarf through the washbasin, curling it around Bathsheeba. She writhed with scarf's embrace.

Looking at Matthias, Bathsheeba covered herself with her hands. She dipped her chin, eyes never leaving his. Her hands slid down to her abdomen, revealing her breasts.

He followed the woman's contours from part of her long hair to the curve of her hips. The urge to touch her, to see her head rocked back in ecstasy engulfed him. But the barest hint of doubt flickered in his brain. Dismissing the feeling as a part of the wine's fog, Matthias decided it was time to be King David. "Bring her to me."

The dancers reappeared and took Bathsheeba to their king-for-a-night. They presented her before him.

She spoke in a low soprano, velvety and lush. "What is thy bidding, my king?"

Matthias's uncertainty increased. He suppressed it again and said, "Come here." She did as he commanded, his hand caressing her body. She was perfect, too perfect. He caught sight of a beauty mark on her right cheek. "How long ago did you have surgery, Bathsheeba?"

She didn't reply.

"Answer me."

"A few months ago, lord."

His hands traversed her hips while he studied her face. "And the rest of you?"

"The same, lord," she said, her legs shifting.

Benjamin said, "What's going on?"

Matthias snapped his head toward his friend, the hot rush of lust transforming into a flame of anger. "Vanderhaggen sent me a changeling."

Benjamin grimaced. "A homosexual? How can you tell? She's… he's perfect."

He hurtled the wineglass at the floor. "Nobody's that perfect.

Look at her beauty mark. It's the trademark of the Synod surgeons."

"I'll be damned. At least she's a government-approved homo, Matthias. Nobody's probably had her yet."

"That's how it's going to stay." Matthias pointed to Bathsheeba. "Get him… her… it, out of my sight. Damned changelings. You are an abomination." He got dressed. "I am going to the bar. See to Mister Kyalo's needs and make sure that he has transportation home."

A dancer yanked Bathsheeba's arm and pulled her out of the room.

The third chalice of soy vodka tasted as bad as the first, which, Matthias considered, was the drink's only virtue—consistency. The pleasant buzz from the fine wine had been squandered the moment his rage took over. "Damn it, Vanderhaggen," he snarled, slamming the cup onto the table.

The bartender, a full-figured woman overstuffed into a leather corset jumped, her chest nearly leaping from the bustier.

"Another," he yelled.

The bartender filled the chalice and retreated to the far end of the bar. Matthias grabbed the woman's corset and groped her breasts. "These are real enough." The look she returned puzzled him—equal parts fear and fury. He shoved her away, saying, "Thank God there are still some real women around. Perhaps I should marry you."

Matthias spotted the ersatz Bathsheeba being escorted to the door by some of the dancers. "Yes, a real woman. A real whore. Not like that changeling, that homosexual. He's an abomination to his gender and an abomination before God. Get thee behind me Satan." He turned around.

The door slammed and a muffled pounding began. Hard shoes clattered on the tile, getting closer with every step. The bartender screamed. Matthias looked over his shoulder and saw an enraged Bathsheeba charging at him. She swung her foot around and kicked the barstool out from under him. His world turned sideways, weightless. Then he hit the floor.

Bathsheeba screamed, "God damn you. You think I want to

be this way?"

Matthias curled his body against her kicks, each one burning more than the last.

"I was born this way. God made me a man but you can't handle it. You have to screw with nature—you're the God damned abomination!"

Matthias felt the point of a high heel dig into his thigh.

"I'm a man, damn it. God damn you. God damn you all."

Between anguished blinks, the lobby doors burst open. A pair of glossy black boots strode across the floor and aligned themselves behind the kicking high heels as though a tango were taking place.

A single hollow thump filled the room. Bathsheeba's rants silenced. The changeling's knees buckled, and she collapsed next to Matthias.

The jabs of pain blended into one dissonant chorus of torment. He stared back at her still open eyes until his vision dimmed, darkening until the world around him turned as black as Bathsheeba's Synod trademark.

Chapter 7: Verses 1-66

Matthias drew in the scents of home, a hint of bleach in the polyester bedding coiled around him and his housekeeper's all-too-sweet perfume. Naomi wore that scent ever since he could remember. Its aroma, and the rising tide of a hangover, set his stomach to heaving.

Matthias flopped out of bed, and crumpled on the floor. He caught another whiff of the perfume. He felt the bile rise up in his throat. The heaving resumed. Crawling to the toilet, Matthias threw up. Every convulsion rippled through him in an agonizing circle—nausea, breathlessness, dry heaves, repeat. He finally collapsed onto the tile, a trail of spittle connecting him to the toilet bowl.

Naomi stepped into the bathroom. She flushed the toilet, and opened up the curtains to a burst of rare fall sunshine, all the while whistling the *Battle Hymn of the Republic* with shrill intensity.

When she reached the third verse, Matthias had enough. "Please stop." A bath towel fell over his lap.

Naomi's short, stocky figure loomed over him, her tightly curled hair gathered in stormy gray clouds around a knit cap. Her voice thundered in the small room. "Even Adam was ashamed of his nakedness."

"It's Eve's fault that men were kicked out of paradise and forced to wear clothes," he croaked.

She produced a mop and slapped it to the floor. Its tassels reeked of bleach. "Adam had a choice. So do you. If your mother could see you now."

"Then she would see an Elder throwing up like Jonah's whale." Matthias got to his knees and looked into the toilet. "Jonah? Jonah? No, no Jonah's in there." The combination of Naomi's perfume and bleach cut through him again. He vomited in dry, rasping gasps.

She pulled open the medicine cabinet. "Red or white wine this time?"

"Red," he wheezed between spasms. "And vodka."

"A new low. Drink this." She handed him a tonic. "Back in my time, we had hangovers that lasted all day. Count your blessings."

Matthias grimaced at the tonic's flavor. There was simply no understanding how the medicine could be any viler than the taste festering in his mouth, but it did. Relief seeped into his gut. He brushed his mouth with a forearm. "You're not going to give me a good-old-days lecture, are you, Naomi?"

She slapped the mop into a bucket and yanked on the wringer. "Not any more than your mother is going to tell you bedtime stories."

Matthias read the anger in the lines of her face, the sorrow in her eyes. The sorrow spread to him. "No. No, she isn't. But, she never lectured me after any of my bacchanals."

Naomi yanked his towel away. "That was always left to me. Your parents couldn't abide you in the morning after one of your binges. I have a stronger stomach. Now, go get cleaned up or your penis is going to catch the Rot. Then you will be an Elder eunuch."

Matthias knew the tales of men made insane by the Rot's wasting long before it killed them. Motivated, he sprinted to the shower.

The water tasted of metallic filtration as Matthias scrubbed himself over and over. The bathroom door creaked.

Naomi shuffled in. "I put a robe on the chair for you. Breakfast is ready."

After drying off, Matthias used the towel to wipe the vanity mirror. Amidst the stubble of his unshaven face were welts and cuts all over his right cheek. Lightning flashed in his mind, each burst carrying the impact of a woman's shoe. "Damn it." Matthias stood back from the mirror, looking over his body and finding it smudged with yellow and purple bruises. He closed his eyes and saw Bathsheeba's stunned visage looking back. "Oh, damn it—damn it—damn it."

"You're mouth is still filthy. Brush your teeth and get down here. Breakfast is getting cold," commanded Naomi.

Matthias hurried through grace and then yanked the spoon out of his oatmeal as if he were King Arthur freeing the sword in the stone. He bit into the gruel and wished he hadn't.

"I told you it was getting cold." Naomi poured tea from a flowered teapot, steam curling up and around her weathered hands. "Benjamin's called nine times. He sounded worried."

"Tell him I'm fine."

"He said that you were on the Ecunet this morning."

"Oh my God." Matthias pulled a vid-panel toward him and tapped the screen. An image of him being carried by Benjamin and a policeman appeared on the screen. "Wonderful, just wonderful." He shoved the screen toward Naomi.

"I saw it already." She plopped another glob of oatmeal into his dish and pushed the screen back. "Eat, or you're going to feel worse."

"I don't know if that's possible," said Matthias, studying the picture and its caption: *Elder Attacked at Downtown Entertainment Complex.* He forced another mouthful down, all the while staring at the fresh cuts on his face in the photograph. His gaze shifted to the background where two more officers carried Bathsheeba's body. Behind them, at the edge of the picture, stood a pair of glossy boots worn by a black-suited man with a solemn face and close-cropped dark hair. Matthias clicked on the picture and zoomed in on the man's coat. An emblem came into focus, a black cross set on top of a lick of red flame. Matthias choked on his breakfast.

"Do you need the bucket again?" said Naomi as she jumped to her feet.

"Only if it's to drown myself."

Naomi sat back down.

He tapped on the vid-panel. "That, my dear Naomi, is the mark of the Order of Saint George."

She swallowed hard, her hands twisting a napkin. "I remember their uniforms."

"You read the article?"

"Yes."

"He was the man who saved me last night. You see, the party was going along very well until I took exception to being paired with a changeling. Words were exchanged and the changeling assaulted me. This Soldier of the Order came to my aid."

"Did he kill her?"

Matthias zoomed the picture back to normal size. "With his bare hands."

Naomi unraveled the napkin, and sat down. "From the way you look, I'd say you were lucky that he was there. We should thank God."

Matthias took her hand and bowed his head. His mind drifted far from giving thanks. Instead, he calculated the odds that God would provide divine intervention by way of a brother of the Order of St. George. Then he factored in that their members never patronized Pharaoh's or any establishment like it. That left a margin of infinitesimal proportion. There was more to last night's photo opportunity, and he needed to reason it out.

He squeezed Naomi's hand. "Amen. I also thanked God for you speeding my recovery."

"Again."

"It will ensure your place in heaven. I will make a plea for your swift canonization."

She slapped him with a dishtowel. "I will make a plea for you to settle down."

Matthias felt a grin lift his sore cheeks. "Someday."

"Don't forget to call Benjamin."

"I'll call him later. Right now, I need to pray."

Matthias made his way to the family chapel. Its floor glowed with blues and golds, the dazzling result of sunbeams pouring through a reproduction of medieval stained glass mounted above the nave doors. The brightness stirred a recollection of morning prayers back when all fifty-seven members of the household staff and farm hands were in attendance. It was only twenty years ago. *Or was it a hundred?*

Even now, he heard their fervent whispers, saw their cracked lips intone petitions to God. They prayed like it was the first Passover. The Angel of Death stalked them all and there was no lamb's blood to paint on the lintel.

Every animal was consumed long ago.

And the mob outside the chapel wanted something to eat.

A cloud obscured the sun. The whispers of the past quieted. Shadows overtook the ghosts, and Matthias surveyed the empty sanctuary. He missed their faces, their smiles, their jokes, kneeling with them at the communion rail and breaking bread. He missed praying with them even if their prayers, and his, went unheard during that awful time.

Sunlight returned to the faces of God and Adam in a mosaic replica of Michelangelo's *Creation of Adam* on the back wall. "I wonder if You hear them now."

There was no reply.

"I hear them." He plopped onto the kneeler, wincing at the pain jutting into his knee. Rocking backward, he wedged his rump against the metal pew. More pain. He remembered all the bruises administered by the changeling. "Damn it."

There was no sense in what happened last night. Vanderhaggen might have chosen just such an entertainment had he been there, but he wouldn't have selected a changeling for Matthias. It lacked the Chief Elder's sense of style. Then there was the coincidence of having a Soldier of the Order in the neighborhood.

A realization brightened in his mind like the sun through the window. The events at Pharaoh's carried the taint of hurried contrivance, clumsy and blatant. The characteristics had a familiar pattern.

Only one man had access to Vanderhaggen's communications

as well as the right connections within the Synod to bring a scheme like this together. Matthias swatted the pew, a loud clank reverberating across the transept. "Rourke."

He lifted himself off of the pew. "Damn it," echoed off the walls each time he thought about his stupidity, and he chided himself for not heeding Blind Johnny's words.

"He seeks the stone to make you trip—trip."

Damage control would be needed. So would saying just the right phrases to soothe a frazzled Chief Elder. *And what better way to dismiss this trivial scandal than to present Vanderhaggen with a holy relic?*

The roar of his limousine roused Matthias from his plotting and announced the departure of Naomi and his driver, Brother Alexander. It was market day. Solitude.

Matthias regarded the mosaic from Adam's reclined body, across his outstretched hand and onto the face of God. He lifted his hand up like Adam's, and spoke to God. "Perhaps You can see to it that I am not shamed or that You let my enemies defeat me?"

Matthias walked past the altar. He ran his hand along the mosaic, fingers bumping over the irregular surface of smooth tiles and rough mortar. When his palm met God's, the texture of each of the Lord's fingertips felt slightly rougher. Matthias matched his fingers to God's and pressed. A hollow click echoed in the room followed by a low rumble deep in the bowels of the earth.

He took one more look around, grabbed the edge of the wall, and pulled its mass back a few feet. The huge door parted with a whoosh of air. The pallor of fluorescent lights greeted him. He stepped into a tunnel containing a long, descending staircase and closed the vault behind him.

Chapter 8: Verses 1-49

Standing at the bottom of the access tunnel, Matthias could almost hear his father's voice reverberating in the narrow space.

"Mattie, this is an oath before God, not just before your mother and me. No one can know about our secret place except us, okay?"

"Not even Naomi?

"No."

"Why, father?"

"Because there is only enough room for us." His father pointed to the bottom of the steps where his mother stood. *"If anyone else finds out, they'll kill us."*

Matthias reached for the latch to the family bunker. His hand twitched with the same clammy dread he felt all those years ago. Shrugging, he tried to sooth his apprehension by telling himself that there hadn't been food riots for three decades. There were no cadaverous mobs hammering on the chapel's doors. All was well.

It worked until he turned the latch. The old mechanism screeched in protest and he could instantly hear the shrieks of the damned when the Order of Saint George arrived on that fateful day.

Matthias's heart thumped in time with the soldier's march on the ground above the bunker, each step carried them through the fields and purged their farm of the human plague.

When his parents and he emerged, the fortunate looters lay dead. The unfortunate writhed on the ground. Near misses from the Order's microsonic cannon left the survivors' faces wrenched in agony with blood hemorrhaging from their ears.

Matthias watched the soldiers hunt them down. Each rioter died the same way, hands pleading for mercy, a bayonet, and a shriek.

A soldier strolled past Matthias, his bayonet a wet crimson. He displayed a proud smile, saluted, and said, "You're safe, young brother. All is well."

Considering the irony, Matthias huffed. Twenty years ago the elite corps rescued his family. At Pharaoh's, he was saved yet again.

When he slid the door to the bunker aside, another rush of air blew Matthias's hair back. He stepped into a plain white room studded with steel nozzles and inhaled a stale aroma reminiscent of Naomi's mop.

Matthias removed his tunic and shoes, tossed them outside, and closed the door. The nozzles rotated toward him. He closed his eyes and said, "Purify me from everything that contaminates body and spirit, O Lord." The nozzles hissed. Within moments, he felt antibacterial gel ooze over his body. A blower came on, evaporating the gel and leaving him with gooseflesh. Another door slid open. He opened his eyes to a thousand stars.

The ceiling of the central chamber lifted his spirits with its tapestry of light emitting diodes mimicking a twilight sky. The room brightened to full daylight. Ventilators hummed, freshening the stale air. He lifted a coverall from a peg and slipped into it.

Everything was in its place, from an array of scenic photographs to a large family picture hung above a plastic table and three dusty chairs. There was a time when the chairs never had dust, a time when the bunker held more wonder than fear.

His mother pointed to a mountain peak in a photograph. "That's snow, Mattie. The Himalayas are the only place that gets any. Grandma said she saw some once when she was little."

Matthias felt awestruck. Frozen water covering a mountaintop was as miraculous as Jesus with the loaves and fishes.

They walked around the room talking about each outdoor scene, him with a hundred questions and his mother with a hundred answers.

He marveled at it. "It's so white."

His mother's face fell. "Yes, it was."

Matthias remembered the look of loss on his mother's face as if she were in the room with him now. He wrapped his arms around himself, his mouth open in a roar of silent grief.

It felt good to cry, good to mourn without being observed. In the bunker, there was no need for posturing or posing for a corporate audience. Down here, it was just he and his memories. He rubbed the tears away with the coverall sleeve and faced a door labeled "Library."

"Civilizations come and go, but duct tape lasts forever," his father joked the day they hung a comic book on the library door with a piece of duct tape.

"You were right, father," said Matthias smoothing the cracked and peeling edges of the tape against the library door. The cover, a picture of super hero turning a gigantic key to open his secret fortress, was as bright as the day they sealed it in plastic and stuck it there. He opened the door.

Neat rows of reference books lined oak shelves according to his mother's meticulous attention to order, but the shelves were bordered in chaos. Piles of children's books engulfed the floor. Each stack looked like it would topple if it weren't for the pile next to it pushing back.

Matthias picked up a copy of Cinderella, dusted it off, and threw it back on the pile. The pile toppled over onto a stack of coloring books next to a desk and chair.

"Mattie, pick those up," demanded his mother.

Matthias dropped his pen, and scrambled to straighten out the coloring books he accidentally kicked over. Some of the books fell open.

She crossed her arms. "You've been practicing."

Pushing the pages closed, he hid the coloring books at the bottom of the pile. "Uh-huh."

"Let me see."

Matthias reluctantly handed one over to her and sat back down.

Her finger traced along the letters he had written. "It's wonderful, but there's a problem."

Slumping in his chair, he said, "Now what did I do wrong?"

His mother brushed a lock of his hair back. "The problem is that I can't call you 'Mattie' anymore." She turned the pages over, her eyes scanning dozens and dozens of cursive signatures. "I need to call you 'Matthias.'"

Matthias stacked his old, yellowing coloring books. He fanned the pages, bright crayon colors on one side, and his signature *ad infinitum* on the reverse. It didn't look any different than the signature he used when he signed the Minutes during his installation.

His stomach tingled when he remembered the Elder's reaction to his ability with the Pen of Witness. It upset them that he was so good at it. If they were so bothered by a practiced signature, he wondered what they'd think if the blessed Synod found out about this room.

Matthias ran his hand along the stacks. He knew he should turn the contents of the library over to the Synod. Every good citizen was bound by the Preservation Law to do just that, but the Rot would consume it in a month. This wasn't the durable stuff that made up the pages of the Minutes. The fortune within these walls would be lost almost as fast as his career. And Uncle Cornelius would be especially grateful to God for Matthias's downfall.

Lifting a hardback off the shelf, he caressed the rough edges of the pages. The book was unsoiled, free of advertising and instructional Bible verses—just words to a story. He opened it, his finger racing along the text of Cooper's *Last of the Mohicans* like Hawkeye bounding through the forest. His finger halted at the period. He sighed, closed the book, and rested it on a rickety stack. *It stays here with me.*

Chapter 9: Verses 1-74

Saturday's sunshine fled, chased away by Sunday's impending rain. Matthias's thoughts of the bunker, its treasures, and its memories disappeared with the sunshine, chased by the infinite details of the upcoming church service.

He sat in the back of the limousine, studying the vid-panel. There were ad timings and placements to coordinate, sermon scripts to review and endless research to make sure the target audience got saved every week at precisely 10:00 AM.

While he knew Benjamin and the other subordinates would have everything covered, it did little to curb the up-tick in his heartbeat. His project, his secret sojourn to Washington, was mere hours away from launch.

Allowing himself a break from the anticipation, Matthias glimpsed out the front window. The great gray dome of Nation's Church with its four brightly-lit spires marking the compass points came into view. Today, he would enter through the south gate, the gate of government officials, high-ranking ministry and, of course, corporate Elders. *Time to harvest the fruits.* A tinge of pride hung in his thoughts. He promised to pay penance.

The limousine slowed and stopped.

"What's wrong, Brother Alexander?"

The driver looked to his left. "There's a checkpoint."

Alexander spoke to black-uniformed officer from church security. The security man stood board-straight. His fingers tapped his thigh. The display of obvious nervousness for delaying an Elder amused Matthias.

Alexander closed the window and turned around. "The lieutenant said that there is already a crowd near the church. They are moving the people off the road so that we may pass. He extends his apologies."

Checking his watch, Matthias was surprised at the delay. The city's poor rarely assembled hours before a service, and he couldn't remember the last time he stopped for a group of any size.

As the car climbed a slight grade, Brother Alexander said, "Elder Kent."

"I see them, Alexander. I see them." On his right, Matthias followed the long gray thread of people shuffling toward the church. Just as many were on the left, all dressed in tarps and tatters. They barely raised their heads.

"Praise be Jesus. Think of how many souls we'll save today."

"Yes indeed, Brother." Matthias returned to his work, not wanting to disillusion his naïve driver. Better to let him believe that the faithful were flocking to this week's altar call instead of clamoring over free penance cards.

Matthias paused.

How could these dregs know they were handing more out this week? He touched the picture of Benjamin on the vid-panel. The research director appeared on the screen.

"Nice of you to return my calls, Matt... Elder Kent," said Benjamin, his eyes flitting about a bustling control room. "Can I call you back later?"

"No," said Matthias. "Have you seen the line outside?"

Benjamin pressed some keys, his brow lifting. "Oh my God."

"Did anyone in our department leak anything about the penance cards this week? Rumors? Spin?"

"No, that's company classified. I didn't even tell my wife."

"Did you babble anything at Pharaoh's?"

Benjamin's face hardened. "Did you?"

"This is too much of a coincidence." Matthias's thoughts raced. There was something more he noticed in the crowd, but what?

"Coincidence? They always get free cards. Why are you so upset? Maybe they're here for Reverend Isaac."

"Even Isaac doesn't attract a crowd like this." He punched the upholstery. "Damn it, something's not right."

Brother Alexander's head jerked up with the curse.

"Keep your eyes on the road," said Matthias. The word 'eyes' stayed in his mind. A picture formed of the crowd at the checkpoint, their eyes downcast and edged in white. They weren't coming to church for the usual handout. They were far more sullen.

The car stopped for another checkpoint.

Matthias stomach tightened. He knew the look—hunger.

"All is well. Move on," said the guard.

The phrase shook Matthias from his thoughts.

His driver glanced into the rearview mirror, watching Matthias. The car resumed its ride toward the church. "Elder Kent, is everything all right? Please pardon me for saying this but you don't look well."

"I'm fine."

Benjamin joined in, "Are you sure? You just kind of faded on me. Should I order more cards for the service?"

"I'm fine." Matthias read the intent in Benjamin's face. "Yes, get more cards. We'll need them. Oh, and do you have the order of worship?"

"Yes. Reverend Isaac gave us his favorite hymns. The place is going to be a-marching today. No scripture yet. The Synod is running true to form."

"I'm sure it will be, Benjamin. I'll be inside in just a few minutes. I'd like to see the stage placements once I get to the control room."

Benjamin crossed his arms. "We've got it, Elder Kent. Go and enjoy the service from the Elders' box. I'll talk to you later."

He understood the obvious body language. Benjamin knew what to do and expected Matthias not to micromanage. The sudden idea of not being personally involved behind the scenes of the church service left him numb. How long had it been since he sat through a service as a participant—not as an employee? Ten years? Twelve?

Brother Alexander pushed the shifter into park. "Elder Kent?"

"Yes?"

"We're here."

All told, Matthias figured it took less than five minutes to reach the Bank's luxury box on the Concierge level. He thanked the cart driver and strode over to a young woman in an unkempt custodial vestment who leaned against the door to the suite.

She sprang to her feet, tugging on her robes. "My deepest apologies, Elder." The custodian glanced inside the box and kept checking the wall clock. "We are still preparing the room. Last night's game went into overtime."

Matthias noted the wringing of her hands, the bags under her eyes. Like most of the women on the church's janitorial staff, she probably had been up all night cleaning up the debris from last night's football game. He usually ignored their presence on Sunday mornings when there were souls to be saved and quotas to be met.

Rather than evoke any further discomfort on the custodian's part, he said, "Who won?"

"The Saints."

"Of course." He forced a smile to dilute the tension. "Perhaps you can direct me to the concierge."

A tall, blond woman in a tailored blue suit stepped alongside Matthias. "I am she, Elder Kent. We apologize for your inconvenience. Should we expect you at this time every week?"

Studying her face, he realized that his early arrival breached some kind of minor sanctuary etiquette. It was unfamiliar territory. "No," he said. "Where might I find some breakfast?"

"Please, follow me."

For the better part of an hour, Matthias sat in the opulent dining room, the only other diner being his reflection on the mirrored ceiling.

While he savored a plate of real eggs and toast, he peered through the dining room's windows. Preparations for the service were in full swing. The groundskeepers unrolled a tan mat to protect the artificial turf. The lighting crew ran through their sequencing, stage lights flickering on and off around the altar at the far end of the church. Florists arranged groupings of plastic palms. A thirty-foot-high sports fan downed gulp after gulp of soy vodka on the big screen monitors positioned on either side of the altar—the first of the morning's advertisements. The image brought bile to his throat. It was business as usual except that he was now an observer. He felt detached, like a person adrift in the ocean and seeing his ship move away.

"Is this seat taken?"

More bile churned in Matthias's mouth. "Why, yes Uncle Cornelius, it is."

"I don't see anyone."

"It's reserved for Bathsheeba."

Rourke's lips slithered into a smile. "You didn't approve of my gift?"

Matthias struggled to maintain a civil tone. "I worried that you had assaulted her beforehand and that she would be mentally scarred. It makes for poor entertainment."

Rourke pulled out the chair and sat down before a servant could assist. "Ever the victim, I see." A waitress sprinted over to him. His voice trailed off, and he waved her away.

Despite his uncle's calm manner, Matthias detected a subtle tilt to Cornelius's head. It was as if the man was trying to gauge who heard the conversation—probably the closest thing to fear his uncle would demonstrate in public. Matthias leaned toward Rourke. "I'm not the victim. I buried the victim last week. I'm the witness."

Rourke's nostrils flared, his chin jutting upward and eyes looking down. "Then you shall be a witness yet again when I become Chief Elder. Be mindful of that."

"I shall be mindful that Elder Vanderhaggen is still in charge," said Matthias.

"To everything is a season."

"Ahem," said the concierge. "Elders, the hour of the service nears." She produced a small black touchpad and a stylus. "Your wine selection?"

Rourke leveled his head, transforming into the pontifical executive. "Do you still have that Carolina Merlot we had last week?"

She nodded.

"Two chalices, one for me and for my dear nephew. Oh, and the sourdough bread for communion. My thanks."

The concierge tapped the order into the touchpad and departed.

Matthias rose from his seat. He wadded his napkin and hurled it on top of the remaining breakfast. "Don't ever order Communion for me again."

Rourke wove his fingers together. "Why not? You need to get used to me giving orders."

Chapter 10: Verses 1-159

The concierge led Matthias and Rourke to the Bank's skybox and held the door open for him.

"Matthias, so glad to have you join us. Please, have a seat," said Chief Elder Vanderhaggen, his face lit up a jovial red. "I'm sure you remember Claudia."

"Blessings and prosperity, Mrs. Vanderhaggen." He stepped behind the Chief Elder's chair and grasped her slowly moving hand with both of his. Claudia's hand felt clammy and limp, features that matched the appearance of her mannequin-like face.

Her expressionless eyes swiveled toward him. "Blessings."

Matthias forced a grin despite the pharmaceutical staleness of her breath. He lowered her hand to her lap and turned back to the Chief Elder. "Blessings and prosperity."

"I take it you've seen the crowds?" Vanderhaggen retained his jovial exterior, but his words didn't match his apparent mood. "A rumor has run around the slums that the harvest came up short and that famine is beckoning."

Matthias surveyed the church, every chair filled and the center black with an overabundance of the impoverished. He had never seen the stadium floor so full. "I've already ordered the release of more cards."

"There are concerns that we should postpone the expanded release."

The Chief Elder's lack of confidence irritated Matthias. This was no time to waver. "There should be concerns that someone leaked classified information. We should demand an investigation. Besides, if the beggars know about the harvest, so will the citizens, and the citizens will not be happy if we lavish penance cards on the undeserving." He laid his hand on Vanderhaggen's shoulder, trying to bestow his confidence upon him. "This is precisely the right time. I feel God has ordained it."

The church's electronic organ began the service's prelude as if it were background music to his appeal. Matthias almost laughed at the coincidence.

"Please, sit." The Chief Elder pointed to an empty seat at his left.

"My thanks," said Matthias. He looked around the room, each Elder filling in the remaining ranks of plush chairs behind the Chief Elder leaving only the seats to Vanderhaggen's left and right conveniently vacant. Each Elder's wife regarded him with equal portions of disdain, questioning, and, in a few pairs of eyes, lust. It made him miss the chores of the control room even more.

Vanderhaggen said, "I see that the Synod has brought out the big guns to break the news to the faithful."

"Yes, having Reverend Isaac is a coup. Our ratings will be very strong this week."

"Blessings and prosperity," greeted Rourke, entering the suite and sitting down at Vanderhaggen's right.

Vanderhaggen said, "How is Pricilla?"

Rourke sat down, lifted the armrest, and pulled up a computer workstation. "She is having one of her bad days."

Matthias remembered Aunt Pricilla, a prim and righteous woman whose strongest belief was the denial of her husband's depravities. Now, she lay bedridden and wasting away from the Rot's all-too-frequent cohort—tuberculosis. Bowing his head, Matthias thanked God that He took his mother by way of a heart attack. "I am sorry for her illness."

"Thank you," said Rourke, whose face didn't shift away from

the vid-panel.

Matthias watched him after his nonchalant response. No change in focus on the computer screen. No swallowing back any emotional burden, just a dismissive *thank you*. Rourke simply didn't care, and it rankled Matthias. He said, "May God free her from *all* of the demons around her."

Rourke's head lifted from the vid-panel, his eyes cold and pale lips drawn into a straight line.

The prelude faded, replaced by the boisterous introductory measures of *A Mighty Fortress is Our God* being hammered out on the organ. The big screens filled with a panorama of Philadelphia in the background and the words to the hymn in the foreground. Prompters around the stadium lifted their arms. Everyone stood and joined with the choir.

Matthias noted the significance of this hymn and the others on the Order of Worship. There wasn't a contemporary piece on the list contrary to the Reverend's style. Each tune meant to remind the faithful of their duty and patriotism. It smacked of outright Synod intervention. It smacked of his uncle.

Matthias glanced at Vanderhaggen who seemed to have no problem singing but every problem of being in tune. Claudia remained seated, her head bobbing one beat out of time with the rhythm.

Rourke neither sang, nor paid attention to the song. His eyes were locked onto the vid-panel.

Matthias recognized the document being displayed—the Order of Worship. A line on the Order blinked yellow. He squinted. Someone at the Synod finally sent the scripture for today's service. Matthias felt a chill slice down his back like the cold drops of rain on First Friday. *Did Benjamin see it?*

Reverend Isaac dashed across the stage, his royal blue robe flowing along behind him. He slid to a stop in front of the microphone, plucked it off its stand, and shouted, "Can I get an Amen?"

"Amen," shouted the applauding crowd.

He stared down the audience with his accusing blue eyes. "Weak! I need strong voices. I need strong voices calling up to Heaven."

"Amen!"

"Now that's what I'm talking about. Come on now, give it up for our choir director Nabal Shultz, and Obadiah Norris, our three-time National Organist winner."

The big screen monitors switched to a live view of the audience, the camera tightening its focus on those who were the most ardent in their applause.

"Now brothers and sisters, I'm not going to let you fall. Are you going to let me fall?" Isaac bent backwards in a mock faint.

The crowd roared, "No!"

"We must be ever watchful. We can't let our family fall, or our neighbors, our servants. True?"

"True."

He clapped his hands over his head and the whole church followed along. "Now, you know who's going to win the battle between good and evil."

Heads shook in agreement.

"And who's going to lead us?"

"Jesus!"

"Who?"

"Jesus!" cheered the crowd, enough to make the windows rattle in the suite.

"Jesus is going to lead us, just like a shepherd leads his flock. Just like a coach leads his team. Just like the Saints winning again last night. I want to be on Jesus' team. How about you?"

"Amen."

Vanderhaggen leaned toward Matthias. "I love this man. You can give him any audience, and he'll have them dancing in the aisles and kicking in their tithes."

Matthias made sure to shake his head in agreement despite wondering how many of those dancing in the aisles would be there next year. Many of them were already little more than blue-tarped scarecrows.

The prompters motioned for the worshipers to sit when the first commercial break began.

As they did, Rourke addressed everyone in the room. "I've just received the scriptural advisory from the Synod's Parochial Affairs office. Our verses for today are from Genesis 41: 17-32 and Matthew 6:19-27. Alert your departments."

Matthias recognized the passage of Genesis. It was the story of Joseph interpreting famine from the dreams of Pharaoh. The Synod was preparing the flock for the shortages that lie ahead. He tapped the panel, trying to notify Benjamin. All the screen showed was an empty chair.

Soldiers of the Order of St. George appeared at the top of each staircase and made their way to their assigned post over the lower classes. He worried and imagined Benjamin keying the combination to the lock one too many times. An alert would be triggered. The guards would run to the vault. Benjamin wouldn't stand a chance.

Stay calm, he urged himself. *The guards are where they should be. They haven't moved. Take your time. Make it a part of official business.* He contacted the site producer who looked more than annoyed by the interruption.

"Um, Elder Kent." The man pointed to a variety of monitors on his right. "Go six, now. I'm sorry, sir. How may I help you?"

"I'm looking for Mr. Kyalo. Is he there?"

The producer looked around the room. "He must have stepped out." The annoyance in the man's face grew. "Would you like to leave him a message? I can put you into his mail queue."

Matthias eased up on his tone, both to soothe the producer and himself. "No mail, I'm afraid. Official business. Have you received the biblical verses for today?"

"We've been alerted as is the protocol," said the producer, his face souring and head swiveling back to the bank of monitors. "No. No. The man on camera four. Yes. Go there now and get the next commercial ready to run." He faced Matthias for a moment. "I'll see that he gets it."

The screen went black.

"Amen," yelled Claudia, with more volume than Matthias ever thought possible.

"There, there, dear," said Vanderhaggen.

The door to the skybox opened. Two stewards entered, pushing a silver cart bearing everyone's communion wine and bread. They placed the Communion elements on tables between the Elder's chairs and departed.

"It's about time," said Rourke, taking a pull from the silver cup. Others in the room did the same.

Matthias picked up his cup, watching his trembling hand jostle the wine around the rim. He placed it back down before he could spill its contents.

The organ music rose once again, announcing the end of a commercial showing two fat children with candy smears all over their faces. Matthias saw the stage director counting down with his fingers—three—two—one. He imagined Benjamin pressing the combination in time with the countdown. Alarms would sound. His plan would fail before it began.

Reverend Isaac appeared on the big screen, holding a bottle of wine. "Friends, remember to celebrate communion the old fashioned way with Grace Vineyards' blend of fine red wine. Grace Vineyards, at your local supermarket in the Celebration section."

The screen switched to a brightly flickering word, "Alleluia," and the crowd roared "Alleluia," in response.

Matthias tried Benjamin a second time. The screen came up empty. He clenched his fist. *Damn it.*

"Problems, nephew?" said Rourke, leaning out from his chair.

Matthias didn't realize his uncle's scrutiny. "I'm making sure Benjamin got the scripture."

"You would do well to let your underlings fend for themselves. Perhaps they need more discipline."

Forcing himself to relax, Matthias said, "Benjamin knows what he's doing, but I can't resist keeping my hands in things. Old habits die hard, Uncle, as you well know."

Claudia yelled, "Alleluia!" before Rourke could reply,

Spotlights traversed the assembly and swung toward Reverend Isaac. The minister approached the microphone. "Now brothers and sisters, we're going to do things a little differently today. We're going to read from the good book and then have our collection after we share Communion."

A chime sounded on Matthias's workstation.

"Yes, Elder Kent?" said Benjamin, his eyes following the activities in the control room much the same way as the producer.

Thank God. "You've seen the verses?"

Benjamin's glancing about halted, his brow raised. He checked a monitor on his desk and swallowed hard. His face remained stoic. "Not a problem. The staff has it well in hand."

Matthias listened to Benjamin's words and studied his expression. There was a modest lift on the left side of his lips. He understood the message. "Then I shall quit interfering with my employees. Blessings and prosperity, Brother Kyalo."

"Enjoy the sermon, Elder Kent."

The church darkened except for the cones of light converging on Reverend Isaac. The spotlights bleached his platinum hair white. He was Moses. He was Abraham.

The words to Genesis 41: 17-32 filled the screens to his left and right, white letters across a black background. One hundred thousand parishioners drew in a collective breath.

Isaac raised his hand and brought the microphone to his mouth. "Brothers and sisters, we all know our sins. How we drink too much. How we indulge our pleasures. I bet that some of you even bet against the Saints last night."

Laughter rippled through the congregation.

"But betting against our Saints is just plain dumb, and the last I heard, the good Lord hasn't made a sin out of stupidity. Now, I know you're not stupid. I know you can read the Word behind me on these screens. You know that the good Lord put Joseph in charge of interpreting Pharaoh's dream about the seven years of famine."

Matthias could feel the weight of Isaac's words weigh upon the audience. Even from the skybox, he saw every face transfixed upon the Reverend.

"Our blessed leaders at the Synod want to be honest with you. They want you to know the score. That's why they picked this week's scripture. They've tried their best, but the sins of the past are still with us. We have the rain. We have that tool of the Devil, the Rot. The Devil and his servants are still trying to send our souls to Hell. But, brothers and sisters, we're going to beat Satan like Saint George beat the Arabs, like Saint Ronald beat the commies."

Amens burst from the crowd.

Matthias watched Isaac pick up a glass of water and drink it, making sure the logo of Gilead Spring Water stayed oriented toward the camera.

Vanderhaggen leaned toward Matthias, "He has the most amazing skill for product placement, don't you think?"

The Reverend wiped his lips and brow. "And the road to Hell is paved with these heathen Arabs, these Chinese Jews, these liberals from the Hindu Lands that covet our lives here in God's Kingdom. The Devil can starve us, he can parch our throats, but you know who is looking out for us. Who is that?"

"Jesus!"

"Who?"

"Jesus!"

"You know that God is looking out for us."

The screens faded out and reappeared with the words to Matthew 6: 25-33 appearing against a photograph of blue sky and puffy white clouds. The house lights brightened.

"Christ Jesus told us not to worry. He told us He'd keep an eye on the birds and the grass. He told us not to worry about what you need to wear or when you're going to eat."

On the stadium floor, heads drooped.

"Oh, you of little faith. Your salvation is right before you and you fall short. Now, when I came in here, I asked if you were going to let me fall. Are you going to let me fall now?"

"No," yelled the congregation.

"No," yelled Claudia.

Vanderhaggen tapped on Matthias's forearm. "This is why he's worth every penny."

"You're not going to let me fall?" continued Pastor Isaac.

"No!" said the parishioners.

"Are you going to walk in righteousness with me and Jesus?"

"Yes."

"I hear you brother and sisters. But how can we do that in our sin?"

"How?"

"I'll tell you how." Reverend Isaac reached into his vestment sleeve and pulled out Penance cards in denominations of red, white, and blue. "We can't let our guard down when we sin. We can't be caught short of the Heavenly goal with the stain of sin on souls. We're going to sin brothers, sisters. We're going to be weak. We're going to bet against the Saints because the Devil tells us to. It's only human. But, my children, the Bank of Job is going to be right there for you, leading you back to righteousness, leading you back to Jesus, all at less than twenty-five percent average percentage rate. Your sins will be forgiven each time you make a minimum monthly payment. So when the hard times hit, know that the Bank of Job will be with you on the road to salvation. Don't give in to sin. Spend. Keep us strong."

Isaac lifted his hands skyward, the spotlight following his hands and continuing on to the roof of the church. The organ trumpeted *Ode to Joy*, and penance cards fell like parade confetti.

Matthias turned toward Vanderhaggen. "The dispensers have been modified to cast the cards into the middle and lower class ranks as well as those on the floor. Hopefully, the congregation in the upper decks will pick them up and keep them."

"Can I get an alleluia?" cheered Isaac.

"Alleluia!"

The spotlights followed the cards as they fell. The destitute standing on the church floor looked up, their arms lifted and hands groping the air.

The church members in the seats stood with their arms down, cards falling upon them.

"They're not buying the message, nephew. This is a waste of capital," growled Rourke.

Matthias almost missed it. It was the vaguest of movements, a drop of rain in a downpour. A little boy in the middle class section reached down, picked up a blue card and handed it to his father. The man took it and tucked it in his suit pocket.

The same scene played out again and again.

Matthias smiled. "Perhaps you spoke too soon, Uncle." He felt slaps on his back from the rest of the Elders.

People in the upper decks pocketed still more of the cards, and Matthias couldn't have been happier. He tapped away at the keyboard of his computer, sending out e-mails to the Bank's commercial partners. There would yet be a bountiful harvest in the face of famine.

He folded the computer away and joined a few Elders near the skybox window.

"Very good," said Vanderhaggen.

Before Matthias could reply, his gaze was drawn to an immense guard wading through the lower class and heading toward a small mob of beggars. Through the glass, he saw their mouths open in pantomimed rage, their hands pointing at the feet of someone in the lowest row.

The guard stood above them, shouldering his rifle. Most of the mob backed away. One woman surged forward, snatching the penance card from under the person's foot. A flash burst from the muzzle. The woman fell backward.

The mob held still for a moment, like the pause between a wave's ebb and flow, then crashed upon the guard. They pushed the rifle into the air, fire spitting from its muzzle. A single round pierced the skybox window, shattering it.

Everyone in the room dove for the floor. Screams flooded into the suite, drowning out the shrieks of the Elders and their wives. Shards of glass peppered Matthias as he crawled away from the window. More gunfire resounded in every part of the church, then silence.

A hush filled the vast sanctuary except for the moans of the injured and the crunch of broken glass. Matthias picked himself off of the floor and brushed the debris off of his vestments. He stood, surveying the sanctuary. Dozens lay dead or wounded on the stadium floor, some still gripping their penance cards.

Vanderhaggen and Rourke rose and peered out of the broken window with him.

"Alleluia!" yelled Claudia.

"Is everyone all right?" asked a fully armored trooper who appeared in the doorway of the skybox.

Vanderhaggen shoved the soldier aside. "Out of my way," he said, leading a procession of the rest of the Elders and their wives.

"Blessings and prosperity, young man," whispered Claudia to the soldier.

Matthias looked at the worry carved into the trooper's brow.

It told him all he needed to know. "We are fine, no thanks to your comrades. What happened?"

The guard chanted out a reply. "God's wrath comes on those who do not obey."

"I ask for a reason and you quote Paul. Were you not told of the card dispersal? Were you not told to be tolerant?"

Another voice intercepted the questions. It was Rourke. "Tolerance does not include a lack of discipline, my nephew. Private, you are dismissed. Rejoin your unit."

The solider tromped out of the room, leaving only Matthias and his Uncle amidst the debris of the skybox.

Matthias growled. "Tolerance implies mercy. These people have nothing."

"Tolerance means nothing of the sort. Only the strong may give mercy. You give them handouts, and they riot to show their gratitude. They need to find work and earn their way to heaven."

"There aren't any jobs."

Rourke turned, walked to the broken picture window, and looked down at the church floor. "They will find work when their stomachs are empty enough."

The insinuation in his uncle's words cut through Matthias's anger. In an instant he realized the awful logic. "You're the one who leaked the news about the famine. That's why church was so packed today."

Rourke turned around, a broad smile painted across his face. "I wish I could take credit for the idea, but it was really yours. My associates at the Synod simply added a lesson."

Matthias felt as though the blood were leaving his body. The sight of the people on the floor cowering as the bullets tore into them filled his mind. "The guards were instructed to suppress the first sign of trouble."

His uncle's smile fell away. "We will not have a repetition of the last time."

"The last time? No, there will be no repetition of last time. She's dead, after all."

Rourke's head dipped, eyes smoldering. "Your mother did her duty."

Matthias strode across the room, thrusting his palms against his uncle's chest and sending him sprawling. "Rape is a duty?" He bent down, picked up a chunk of glass and wrapped it in a fabric napkin until only its point protruded. "Too bad there aren't any stones in here."

"Rape?" Rourke stood up, dusting himself off as if the blow never took place. "You're still the stupid child. Your mother traded herself for you, your father, and your decrepit farm. Why do you think the Order came to your properties first when there were so many other farms being pillaged?"

Rourke's eyes were black and cold. It was business and only business—a debit to sexual assault and a credit for services rendered. Matthias sized up the channel below his uncle's ear and an area just below the back of his jaw. The glass shard would fit there well enough. Then his business would be concluded.

Benjamin appeared at the door. "Is everyone okay? We heard that the Bank's skybox had been hit."

Rourke headed for the door. "Tend to your boss, Brother Kyalo. He seems to be having some kind of difficulty."

Matthias let the glass fragment fall from his grasp. It shattered and glanced off of his vestments.

Rourke left the room.

Benjamin said, "Matthias?"

Down on the stadium floor, crews heaved bodies into a series of wheeled dumpsters. No one prayed over them, not Reverend Isaac, or a single member of the choir. They fled at the first sign of trouble. Above the carnage, the big screens replayed the commercial of the fat children.

Matthias wanted to feel pity. He wanted to feel rage. He could feel neither, only numbness.

"Matthias?"

"Did you get the cards?"

"Yes."

"Then all is well, Benjamin. Go home and get some rest. We leave tomorrow before dawn."

Chapter 11: Verses 1-75

It felt wonderful to rock in his mother's arms, hear the softness of her voice singing old lullabies. She smelled of the lavender and basil she picked from the greenhouse earlier in the day. But her face swelled with tears. Just behind her, Uncle Cornelius loomed.

Matthias stirred, a shudder rippling through him.

Benjamin tugged his cloak. "Are you okay?"

It took a moment for him to wake up and get his bearings. The air stank of perspiration and urine. No one sang. He peered out from his hood and took in the drawn faces of the other passengers. They were mottled with Rot. "I'm fine," he said, happy to be anywhere but in his dream. "Where are we?"

Benjamin leaned close. "We're almost in Hyattsville."

The pair boarded the ramshackle flatbed truck near Newark, Delaware. Various contacts handed them off along the way and they now were in the care of a driver who hauled cement for the Synod and riders for the price of a bottle of vodka.

Matthias slumped down against the hard bags of cement, tugging his cloak around him to fight the cold. He allowed himself another fleeting look at his fellow passengers. Satisfied that they were asleep, or otherwise occupied, Matthias lifted his coarse vestment sleeve up, and checked his watch. Disgust churned in his belly. They had been on the road almost five hours. It took far longer than he thought to get to Washington.

The driver slid the cab's back window aside. "Everybody off." The truck slowed, but didn't stop.

All of the men scurried off, disappearing into the rubble on either side of the road. Matthias and Benjamin jumped. They stood in the truck's dusty wake listening to chugging biodiesel pick up speed and looking out on a wasteland of chipped bricks and broken asphalt.

Within minutes, a three-wheeled cart appeared, its engine the soprano whine to the diesel's bass.

A bald and goggled man with a greasy face brought the vehicle to a halt. His smile displayed one yellow tooth. "You the guys from the bank?"

Benjamin said, "Hi, Tommy. Been waiting long?"

"No, not really. The cement guy runs a better schedule than any of the government's buses." He slapped the broad metal plate behind him. "Hold on."

By the time the cart stopped, Matthias understood why the man had only one tooth. The ride had been so jarring that he ran his finger along his gums to make sure every one of his own teeth were still in place.

The trio walked across a sprawling yard full of discarded subway cars. Tommy picked up a steel rod and whacked one of the carriage wheels. A door on one of the subway cars opened. Two gun barrels retracted.

Tommy spit, and said, "Home sweet home, sojourners. Let's to business."

The cabin was warm enough for Matthias to open his outer cloak. Tea appeared in porcelain mugs, brought by a pair of little girls with untamed hair and guns slung over their backs.

Benjamin gave his boss a nod. It was safe to drink.

The girls disappeared down the aisle.

While Matthias sipped the bitter contents, he took in the surroundings. It was a haphazard version of an antique shop coated with what was probably the same veneer of grease on Tommy's face. The wind whistled through the cabin. When it died down,

Matthias could swear he heard cooing.

"Been damned cold the last two days and getting worse. Coldest it's been as long as I can remember," said Tommy. He grabbed a cracker, crushed it in his hand, and yanked a tarp off of a series of birdcages. "Here you go, sweeties." He cast the crumbs toward a dozen or so pigeons in the cages. "Do you have my money?"

Benjamin reached into his messenger bag. He pulled out three stacks of blue cards. "Half now as we agreed."

Tommy's tooth jutted out. "Very nice." He walked over to a counter where an odd machine stood, a series of buttons marked in the old currency—a dollar sign without a cross.

Matthias remembered the machine from a history lesson where Americans used to trade paper money for goods. Millions of people touching paper every day, he marveled, millions. Now, that past sat on a forgotten shelf in a forgettable shop. No one touched paper for three generations—no one except an Elder.

Tommy's hand flurried over its surface and he pulled a lever. The machine let out a ka-ching. "Transaction approved."

Looking at his watch, Matthias said, "Now, to the city."

"Aren't you God damned impatient. We charge extra for that." Tommy spun toward Benjamin. "Keep this stupid city boy quiet Ben, or he'll be the death of both of you. Washington has a goddamned battalion of them Saint Georgies standing guard over the sacred burial grounds over there, and they'd sooner gut you than look at you. They been shooting people left and right these days. We hardly go in any more."

Benjamin swallowed, his feet shuffling. "We heard they guarded the perimeter of the city. Are they inside, too?"

Tommy's eyebrow rose. "They're all over the damn place. You can't get near the city center no more."

Matthias felt a rush of anger. "Then what are we paying you for?"

Tommy poked him with a single unclean finger. "Benjamin, one more word out of this boy, and you can keep your stinking cards."

Matthias recoiled and bumped against the birdcages.

The pigeons fluttered madly.

Tommy picked one up and calmed it by stroking its back and cooing. "You're upsetting my birds, damn you."

"Look Tommy, we're sorry," said Benjamin. "But you told us that we could find some nice artifacts inside the city. If you can't make that happen, then the deal is off."

Setting the pigeon on a small perch, Tommy scuttled to a lopsided filing cabinet. He shuffled through a stack of plastic sheets, pulled one out, and brought it to a table. "A deal's a deal. Here you go. Your treasure map."

Matthias came close and read the map's title, *Metro DC Area.*

Tommy moved his finger in circle near the middle of the map. "The Saint Georgies own the city and everything west to Arlington." His finger slid across to a dot on the northeast side. "We're near Hyattsville. Even if you started walking now, you'd never get to any of the monuments before nighttime."

This just keeps getting better and better, thought Matthias, biting back a rising tide of anger.

"Besides, that whole area is picked cleaner than a carcass on an anthill. The Synod's had people in there for a year and a half."

"What?" yelled Matthias.

"Damn it. They beat us to it," said Benjamin.

The yellow tooth jutted out of a smiling lower lip. "This is why you paid me what you did, Benny." Tommy tapped an area close to the Hyattsville marker. "This was pretty much all residential."

"So?" replied Benjamin. "We're not collecting old kitchen appliances. This is useless."

Tommy picked up the pigeon and balanced it on his index finger. "Tsk, tsk, Benny. You're missing the point. That's where your little smoke detector came from. The Georgies don't give a rat's ass about those old neighborhoods. It's all about dead presidents and finding Saint Ronald's sacred underwear so they can venerate it."

Matthias studied neighborhoods on the map, each rectangle neatly arrayed next to another and another. His eyes stopped on a tiny black cross. "I get it. Where there were people, there were churches."

Tommy licked his thumb and pressed it against Matthias's

forehead. "You get the gold star, city boy." He tapped his finger on the map again. "There were churches here, here, and here. But that's not the big deal. The big deal is here."

Revolted, Matthias scoured his forehead with his sleeve. His eyes returned to the map and some small print—*Commissariat of the Holy Land.* "What's this?"

"A Franciscan monastery. Downright pretty one too. You should see all the stuff in the basement and in the grounds. Pretty damned amazing if you ask me. All made of stone, steel and tile so there's no Rot. Can't say the same for pretty much everything else around there. If you're going to find something, that's the place."

It seemed too easy to Matthias. These junk dealers seemed far too shrewd to let a prize go unmolested. "How do I know it will be worth the trip?" He expected another tirade, but saw Tommy's tooth flicker in his mouth.

"Most of the stuff to see weighs a damned ton and it ain't gonna move without a truck and a hoist. That ain't gonna get past the guards. Besides, the Synod has the monopoly on all things churchy. Something goes on the market from a church and the Georgies show up. You disappear. It's not very businesslike, but they're the defenders of the faith and all that bullshit. I would imagine that you city boys, boys that run around with stacks and stacks of penance cards, should have enough pull to get away with a little parochial larceny. If you can't, go on home. Just remember, I'm keeping the money."

"What do you want to do, Matthias?" said Benjamin.

At first, he wanted to scream. To have ridden on common trucks, subjected to the sights and smells of human vermin while freezing his ass off, and then finding out that the city was effectively sealed, was simply too much. But defeat was worse. They were here *now* and ready to go. Returning without proof was unthinkable. He studied the map. His anger eased. An unadulterated Franciscan monastery awaited him. Franciscans were among the most devout of God's believers on earth before their franchise went bankrupt. Surely there had to be something there.

Matthias tapped his finger on the map. "We're still going. I take it the map is included in our price?"

Tommy stroked the pigeon. "I guess. Can't have you city boys wandering around town. Now come on, time's a wasting."

Tommy led them across the yard to a low hill. A row of subway cars leaned against the rise like a giant snake. Tommy yanked open the door. "Gentlemen, your train awaits."

Matthias pulled himself along the handrail, struggling to plant his feet along the shattered plastic seats.

Tommy stood midway through the car, tugging on the car's sliding doors. The pigeon roosted on the handrail next to him. "This will take you right under the feet of those damn Georgies. It's a maintenance tunnel. Don't worry, no rats, no bugs. Follow it to a cave-in. There'll be a hatch on your right when you get there. Don't bother trying any of the doors along the way. Thems been welded shut a long time ago. Once you get out, stay on the God damned rocks. Don't leave no footprints."

"Where will we be?" said Matthias.

"On the green line, city boy. Just hail a cab when you get there."

Benjamin slipped between the pair. "The old subway, I get it, Tommy." He reached into his bag and pulled out one of the Hajj suits.

Tommy's eyes widened. "What in the rotting hell is that?"

"It's a radiation suit."

Tommy spit against a plastic chair. "For the love of God, you stupid city boys just don't get it. Didn't them two other assholes you sent down here tell you?"

"Tell us what?" said Benjamin.

"I ain't never seen those troopers wearing no radiation suits, and they got every toy in the book. You put that bright white thing on and I may as well have my kids just shoot you for being so damned dumb. Hell, I've been in there lots of times. Do I look all irradiated?"

Matthias studied the man's hairless head, his split fingernails and single tooth. He looked over at Benjamin.

Benjamin folded up his Hajj suit. "What do you suggest?"

Tommy narrowed one eye. "You want these tarps. Rusty brown and gray—camouflage. Georgies come around and you can just melt into the ruins." He winked. "Use 'em myself, I do when

I roam around in there. I ain't got my ass shot off yet."

Matthias realized Tommy's entrepreneurial bent. He would be the right person to deal with once the pilgrimages began. There would be money everywhere. Tommy might even be able to afford some more teeth.

Grabbing the suits from Benjamin, he said, "Trade you even up for our suits." Matthias tossed both packets on the train floor.

"Transaction approved, city boy." Tommy pulled out another tarp and flung it to Benjamin. "Now, on your merry way. Take your little sojourn and then get the hell out of there. Hell, take some pictures for the folks back home. Whatever, I don't care." He cupped the pigeon in his right hand and stroked its back. His face turned to stone. "And city boys..."

Matthias and Benjamin looked back through the doorway.

The pigeon cooed.

"Don't come back here if you get your asses in trouble, understand?" Tommy grabbed the bird by the neck and snapped it against the cabin wall. "Have fun. I'm going to lunch."

Chapter 12: Verses 1-116

They walked in near darkness for almost an hour, the way lit by the narrow cone of Matthias's flashlight. "How much penance do you think Tommy pays a year for that mouth of his?" He swung the light around the corridor and hoped to find its end. A pile of dirt came into view.

Benjamin replied, "What? Sorry. I was thinking about the troopers. Do you think Tommy was serious about them shooting us? We didn't know anything about that when we planned this."

"Don't worry about them. You're with an Elder."

"Well, that's the point. Look at how we're dressed."

Matthias halted and shined the flashlight on himself. "Damn it."

"Exactly."

"Then you'd better make up your mind."

"About what?"

"Going or heading back."

"Why is that?"

"Because we're here." Matthias pushed open a hatch. He squinted at the overcast sky and felt the slightest icy brush of wind. "Well?"

Benjamin pushed past him and stood in a clump of boulders huddled around the small door. "How did I let you talk me into this?"

"We are going to bring the faithful to Zion and Christ."

"I thought it was for fame and profit."

"Same thing." Matthias studied the small rocky cleft. The hatch became invisible after only moving a few feet away. No wonder it remained undiscovered.

He noted the surroundings, the limestone outcropping they stood on, the Rot-stunted thickets, and an overpass strangled by vines. There weren't any structures. "Where are we?"

Benjamin produced Tommy's map from his messenger bag. "Fort Totten." He pointed to the right. "We need to head this way."

Matthias looked at the featureless horizon. Something didn't feel right. "Are you sure?"

"God, you're such a micro-manager. This is just like yesterday when you kept calling me every five minutes. I have it under control. I can read a map."

"But you didn't have the Old Testament verse."

"I didn't need the scripture because I didn't pull the cards from the dispensers. Once I had your official order, I made the guards help me carry them from the vault. They were in such a hurry to get to their posts that they never saw me take a bunch." Benjamin patted his messenger bag.

"I should have believed and not doubted. Lead on, brother." He fell into step behind him, hopping from rock to rock as Tommy instructed. "Let's not forget where we came out."

Benjamin halted. "I do have the map."

Matthias guessed he was in a residential area, each lot delineated by the jagged remains of brick walls. A peeling sign announced the corner of Galloway and South Dakota Avenue. "It's not what you see. It's what you don't see. The Rot's eaten all the wood. I'm surprised the walls are still standing. But that's God's will."

Benjamin kicked a small chunk of concrete across the street. "God's will?"

"Go pick up that rock. Look, the debris ends at the curb. These streets have been cleaned." Something rumbled in the distance and approached. "We need to get off the road."

They darted for a low wall, curled up in a ball on the ground, and spread their tarps out over themselves. The rumbling grew louder.

Matthias pressed himself to the ground, the vibration shaking the bricks near his face.

The vehicle passed and the noise of its engine faded.

He lifted up a corner of his tarp. A dump truck trundled up the street, chuffing out black exhaust. He allowed himself a breath. It wasn't the Order of St. George. In its hopper were girders, pipes and wire, not troopers. He called to Benjamin. "All is well."

A voice called out from underneath the tarp. "I'm going back."

"We just got here. Come on." Matthias pulled the tarp away revealing a set of accusing eyes looking back from a man tucked into a fetal position.

"This is insane. We're going to get killed."

He looked down at Benjamin's motionless figure. His friend looked like an infant from the slums, clad in rags, and laying in dirt. He was someone who should be pitied. But Matthias could only feel contempt, the same contempt that he ascribed to Vanderhaggen at church—spineless.

His mind shifted to the one person who was neither spineless nor fretting—Rourke. Rourke the Terrible. Rourke the Unflinching. Rourke the Rapist. Perhaps his uncle would flinch when he shoved a holy relic in his face.

He huffed and shook his head. "There are worse things than getting killed. Going back empty handed, for instance."

Pulling Benjamin to his feet, Matthias said, "There is something, somewhere in this dung heap that will be my proof of concept, and I'm not leaving until I find it. Are you with me or against me?"

"You sound like a trooper," said Benjamin.

"Go back."

Benjamin stared off at the rocks they came from. After a moment, he reached into his bag and pulled out the map. "This way. I'll keep us off the main streets."

Another half-hour slipped by according to Matthias's watch. He hated every passing second, each passing step through the withered suburban landscape.

There was nothing remarkable about any of the residences that couldn't be found in a proper antique shop, nothing that would impress the faithful into financing a pilgrimage. Frustration added to the weight of every step.

He walked faster, trying to pass the journey by peering into the scrubby remnants of suburban yards. Matthias wondered what life was like back then when children were fat and their books were made of paper. All he could envision were the well-fed children inside the walls of Philadelphia studying on the Ecunet while the ones outside grew skinnier and skinnier.

They came to a wide lot. A familiar shape held a rough outline among the weeds—a baseball diamond. Not too far away he could make out the lines on a few basketball courts. They were standing near a playground, but there were no backboards, no bleachers.

Benjamin glanced down at the map. "10th and Shepherd. Only a few more blocks."

Matthias looked at the sidewalk, neat holes a foot across evenly spaced along the way. Wooden telephone poles used to stand in those holes, he remembered. They used to stand like Orthodox crosses carrying power and communication lines to each and every house. The Rot ate the poles, but where were the wires? His head spun around; there were no low-rise buildings, no glass, no steel—only piles of chipped bricks and broken concrete. "They're stripping the city."

"What? Who?"

"The Synod. That's why they don't want anybody here. There should be wires all over the place, buildings. This is why the roads are clear. They've already come through here and taken everything of value. No wonder Rourke vetoed the trip." Matthias threw his hood back, dug his fingers into his hair, and growled. "This is useless. This trip was useless. My uncle has me by the balls."

"What you Elders do during board meetings is entirely up to you."

"How can you be so flippant?"

"Because." Benjamin smiled, his eyes gleaming. "Look."

Matthias followed his friend's finger pointing the way. It was hard to see the top of the hill just above the rubble, but it was there nonetheless—an intact tan wall with a tiled roof. Beyond the wall stood a domed building with a cupola perched atop its roof. "My God."

The pair dashed across the field and up the hill. They arrived breathless at the double-arched gate.

Matthias bent over, arms on his knees, and eyes lifted to the five-fold crusader cross near the building's peak. An inscription on the main gate proclaimed, *Hosanna to the Son of David. Blessed is He who comes in the name of the Lord.* He recognized the church's architecture, a Byzantine dome in the center of a nave and transept. His eyes caressed the slope of the dome and the arches of the windows. Not a pane was broken, not a tile out of place. It was a physical and spiritual oasis in a foul, foul, desert. It would make billions.

"It's a miracle," whispered Benjamin.

"Blessed be the name of God," said Matthias.

Slack-jawed, they stepped inside the gate.

Matthias spotted the only flaw. The doors were gone, probably wood and certainly rotted. Reproductions could be made. The faithful would never notice.

He looked around the grounds. Statues in varying shades of gray gazed down at the weeds climbing the pedestals. Leaves blew around the courtyard. More roofs loomed just outside the walls.

There had to be something here, something to take back to the next meeting at the bank, thought Matthias. Faces would be dumbstruck. Mouths would hang open, just like Benjamin's. He patted his friend on the back. "Don't just stand there. Let's go in."

The sights inside dwarfed whatever delight Matthias experienced outside. Stained glass saints gazed down at him in saturated hues of blue and gold and scarlet. This was a church of the old America, grand and reverent at the same time. Pews instead of stadium seats. Paintings instead of big screens. "Look at the ceiling."

Benjamin fell to his knees.

Matthias kept walking to the altar. It stood atop three steps, a majestic pink marble table that had seen untold Communions. To his right, Doubting Thomas inspected the wounds of Christ on a sweeping stucco mural. To his left, Christ spoke to his disciples. In the middle was a dove flying in golden radiance. It was stunning, magnificent. He turned again and looked down at his friend.

Tears poured from Benjamin's eyes. "God has blessed us beyond riches, Matthias. This place is untouched by the ravages of war and of time itself. It is truly a miracle."

With his friend's words, Matthias's elation fell away. There should be dust, flecks of paint left over from wood consumed by the Rot. God might have left it standing but housekeeping was a human task. This place was bright, immaculate—impossible.

A tremendous chime sounded, deafening, and radiating from above them. A moment later, the chime repeated.

Benjamin's tears stopped.

Matthias sought out the source and spotted a long black cable running from the ceiling downward.

The chime sounded again.

Sprinting, Matthias grabbed Benjamin by the cowl and pulled him along. "Run, you fool."

More chimes played out as they ran across the courtyard and near one of the gates. The statues remained unfazed by the great peal, and were seemingly content to watch Matthias and Benjamin dash among them. The pair reached a gazebo with arched windows and came to a halt.

The chime sounded one more time, and quieted.

Panting, Matthias checked his watch. "It's noon. The clarion rang twelve times, just like Nation's Church."

Benjamin still hadn't caught his breath or the faintest clue of what just happened. He sat on the floor and said, "The old clarion still works?"

"I wish that were so." He squinted at the cupola. "Somebody put speakers up there and recently. This isn't just *like* a church. It *is* a church. Somebody's restored it."

Rumbling sounded in the distance again, this time deeper, stronger and resonating inside the gazebo. A second engine joined the chorus and a third. Matthias pulled his friend to his feet. "We need to get out of here."

Matthias peered out from the gate. Three olive drab trucks approached, helmets bobbing with the bumps. The far side of the street looked so far away. He knew he'd never make it. Instead, he pushed Benjamin back inside the courtyard and against the wall. He brought his finger to his lips. "It's the Order. On your life, be silent."

The rumbling transformed to a roar. Matthias listened for it to pass. Brakes squealed. The trucks halted. Boots thumped onto the pavement.

He looked at Benjamin whose lips trembled. Their sojourn failed. It was time to announce his Elder status and face the Order. Explanations would be given. Penance would be paid. Uncle Cornelius would be pleased.

Matthias stepped away from the wall. A hand clamped over his mouth. The arm pulled him backwards and out of the gateway.

"Are you out of your mind? Look." Benjamin released his grip. He shoved Matthias to a slender break in the wall and showed him the back of a soldier manning a heavy machine gun. "Remember what Tommy said." He produced the map. "If we cut to the right there are some shrines and outbuildings. We stand a better chance to hide out there."

Before Matthias could protest, Benjamin ran across the courtyard and through an archway in the wall. He took one more glance at the troops and followed his subordinate.

Matthias's gaze slew around the statues, gazebos, and small buildings scattered around a winding pathway. Somewhere in the jumbled landscape, he lost sight of his companion. "Benjamin? Benjamin?" whispered Matthias.

A guttural "Attention!" sounded. Heels clicked and stomped as one. "Right face, march." The troops marched into the church, their boots echoing in the sanctuary.

Matthias called to Benjamin again to no avail. He cast about, judging each hiding place and ruling it out. They were far too obvious. He moved further away from the church along a stone pathway overrun with weeds. A column lay on its side among some debris. In the mess he spotted a collapsed dome like the gazebo they had been in earlier. The marching stopped. It was as good as it was going to get. Matthias hunkered down in between the stone blocks and next to a pile of twigs. He pulled his tarp around him and prayed.

From inside the church voices shouted with military cadence, "Our Father, who art in heaven. Hallowed be thy name-."

Matthias let out a nervous chuckle. They were praying the same prayer, just with different intensity. His humor stopped at prayer's end and a "Ten shun!"

The troops marched back out of the church. Matthias opened his eyes. "Thank you, oh Lord."

His relief lasted three seconds. Another vehicle approached, this one sounding higher-pitched than the trucks, moving quickly and screeching to a halt. The marching stopped. Voices murmured. Boots hustled back into the courtyard.

One voice bellowed above the rest. "Brothers of the Order. Our scouts report signs of two looters. Fan out. Find them and rid God's earth of the vermin who dare violate this holy city. A three-day pass goes to the man who brings me their bodies. Amen?"

"Amen!" answered the troops. Boots hustled out of the courtyard.

Matthias pushed further into the debris, pulling twigs over himself and rearranging his tarp. Boots approached. Someone prodded the weeds. He heard the slap of running footsteps, the action of a gun snapping shut. Gunfire. A thump.

A soldier called out, "Three days for me."

More prodding snapped branches near him. Stones fell on the tarp.

"Got one," said another soldier.

Matthias got ready to stand. *I'm an Elder. You can't shoot me.* He heard his father's voice. "No one can know about our hiding place." It quieted him, and he lay still.

A girl screamed. Gunfire sounded.

"Two down."

The shriek cut through him, punctuated by the smell of cordite. Footsteps moved away, stopped, and began again, this time with the scratch of cloth being dragged.

The troops marched out of the area. Cheers rose from the courtyard. Trucks started and departed. Matthias lay in deathly stillness imagining Benjamin's bullet riddled body slumped across the hood of the truck—a trophy to effective security.

When the sound of the engines faded, Matthias pulled the tarp down to see if it was safe. The twigs on top of him shifted and he came face to face with a pair of wireframe glasses wrapped around a skull. "Oh my God," he shouted, leaping out of his hiding place. The skeleton tumbled after him, snagged on the tarp.

He brushed himself off, trying to shed the decay from his clothes. A gold wristwatch lay in the jumbled remains. He reached down and picked it up. The dead man's entire forearm came with it. Matthias dropped the watch in disgust.

As the bones landed, they scraped dirt away from a large white object. Matthias bent down and brushed more of the dirt away. It was an envelope. It shouldn't be there. Nothing survived the Rot, yet there it was in his hands.

Picking it up, he understood why. It was plastic. Bright red lettering spelled out, "Priority Mail." It was addressed to Sally Ludlum from Senator John Weaver—Kansas.

A rectangular object slid out of the bottom and landed on the debris. Matthias chased after it and picked it up. The yellowed cellophane crackled in his hand but held firm. He knew the shape, knew the feel all too well. His eyes welled up. It was a book. The cellophane preserved it—not a sign of Rot anywhere. It should be gray dust. It was a bigger miracle than finding the church. The book's title made his hair stand on end. "My God."

"You're alive!" screamed Benjamin.

Matthias dropped the book.

Both men embraced.

"But who?" said Matthias, standing up and noticing flies circling a dark pool of blood.

"I don't care, but I am getting the hell out of here. No more treasure hunting."

"No, no more treasure hunting, Benjamin. I have what we need. We're going to open up Washington wide for the pilgrims. The Synod isn't going to get away with secret contracts and special deals. We have him."

"You're giving up? Wait? What?"

"I have my relic." Matthias bent down and picked up his

treasure.

"A book?"

"No, it's not just any book." Matthias brushed the dirt away softly, lovingly. "It's a Bible."

Chapter 13: Verses 1-35

Her brown hair hung in confused tangles, but no confusion clouded her eyes. One was held tightly closed. The other squinted in deliberate alignment with the small bead at the end of the shotgun she pointed at Matthias's head.

"Your father told us he would give us a ride back to the truck," said Matthias, his hands up. He stared at the barrel, and the way it followed his nose. The gun seemed bigger than the child brandishing it. He wished Tommy had waited for them. "Will he be back soon?"

"Soon enough. You got the other half of the money?"

He lowered a hand in slow motion, unclipping the flap of the messenger bag enough so that she saw the blue cards inside, but not its other contents. "Three thousand as we agreed."

The girl cradled the gun in her arms like the way other children held teddy bears. She took the cards and skipped over to the register. Ka-ching. "Transaction approved. Come on city boys, or you're gonna miss your bus."

However bone-jarring Matthias felt the ride in was, it didn't compare to the sheer abandon with which the child drove the trike on the return trip. By the time they made it to the rendezvous, he figured he'd have bruises for life.

"Thank you, come again," she said over the engine's putter. With a happy shriek, she gunned the engine and flew off into the distance.

Matthias felt a cold wind cut through his vestment, both from the freezing weather, and from the timbre of her voice. Her shriek carried a hint of familiarity, like the scream of the girl gunned down at the monastery. The absence of Tommy and his other daughter took on a darker significance.

A verse of David's psalm drifted into his thoughts—*Even though I walk through the valley of the shadow of death.* The rest of the verses disappeared in a fog of fatigue. He slumped to the ground next to a guardrail. His bruises protested, but he didn't care. "You know Benjamin, this isn't exactly green pastures."

Benjamin sat on the steel barrier. "God, I'm hungry."

Matthias agreed. They hadn't eaten, hadn't drunk a thing since the tea they had earlier. Hot tea would be wonderful, he thought. Something to fight this damned cold.

Tugging his vestment closed, he could make out flecks of Rot dotting his skin. A rush of adrenaline jumped through his body.

"What's the matter?" said Benjamin.

"I need to get home and get cleaned up."

A pair of weak headlights appeared on the horizon and headed toward them. Matthias recognized the strain of the truck's engine that delivered them there.

The truck came to a halt. A voice called out, "All aboard!" It lurched forward before they were in the back. They crawled behind the cab and hunkered close together for warmth. It didn't help.

"We're here," said Benjamin.

Matthias awoke from an exhausted, dreamless sleep. He spoke through his shivers. "Thank God."

The pair walked from the roadside to a parking lot near a brightly-lit motel. Benjamin unlocked the trunk, and they heaved their soiled outer vestments into a plastic bag.

Matthias opened the car door and sat with the messenger bag

on his lap. Benjamin started the car.

"8:06," said Matthias, his hands reaching for the heating vents.

"I know, I know. If anybody asks, we were looking at retirement villas until a little after eight." Benjamin leaned over Matthias and opened the glove box. A dozen or so placards with mansions depicted on them fell into his hand. "Pick the one you liked best."

"Very good. You remember the decontamination routine? I already have spots."

"Diluted bleach and soap scrubbing then rinse and repeat. I know the drill."

"The best part is the cure."

"The cure?"

"Gargle three shots of vodka, and then snort one."

"You can't be serious."

"It's a trick the Interior Minister taught me. The alcohol kills the Rot in your mucus membranes if you get it early enough."

"What a way to end this sojourn."

"Indeed." Matthias looked out the car window, past the lights of Newark toward Washington. He dreamt of spotlights traversing the sky and the dome of the monastery bathed in brilliant illumination for all to see. It really would be St. Ronald's bright city on a hill. The Order of St. George would have to relinquish control. There would be transports full of pilgrims clogging the roads, all thanks to him. "I'm glad you decided to keep going. When I move up, you're coming right along with me, brother." Matthias held out his hand.

Benjamin shook hands. "No more God damned mission trips for me, boss, and I'm not paying penance for saying that. Get the interns to do this from now on. This was crazy. We could have been killed."

"But we weren't. Our adventure will be exalted in the Minutes. We're hands-on self-starters, the kind of mettle the Bank was built on. Your family will be able to get an estate. I'll see to it that you have your own account at Pharaoh's." He watched Benjamin crack the first smile he'd seen in hours. "I need you to head up the advertising campaigns we're going to have when the pilgrimages begin."

Matthias leaned back against the headrest, his chest swelling and his hand patting the messenger bag. "I can hardly wait to see my uncle's face."

Chapter 14: Verses 1-81

The view of his bedroom looked unchanged, as if he never moved during the course of the night. A lingering trace of vodka burned in his nostrils. Matthias stretched, feeling the soreness in his legs and arms. An unfamiliar shape blocked the extension of his hand under the pillow.

The book.

Matthias flung the bedspread aside and jammed the pillow against the headboard. *My holy relic.*

Footsteps padded toward his room. The door swung open.

Matthias lay on his stomach with his head on the pillow, blocking any view of the book, and faced Naomi. "Good morning."

She walked past him and opened the curtains. Her head canted to one side, nose sniffing the air. She let out a breath and said, "Don't think soap can mask that awful vodka you drink. Good Lord, did the real estate broker beat you up? Will you be on the news again?"

He tugged the sheets up over his torso to cover his bruises old and new. "No, it's a long story."

"I'm sure it is." She picked up clothes splayed about the

furniture. "Breakfast is on the table. Will you be needing Alexander today?"

He noted unease in her tone. Had she seen what was under his pillow? Was she going to the authorities? "I may need Brother Alexander to take me to the bank after all."

"Oh," she said. "I visit my sister on Tuesdays. Brother Alexander usually takes me while you're at work."

Matthias's tension eased. His hand brushed against the book, a tingling spreading through his body. The rush to present the Bible to Rourke and the Elders fell away, replaced by burgeoning anticipation. "No. No. Go ahead. Blessings and prosperity to your sister."

Naomi turned toward him, her unease fading quickly. "Why thank you, Matthias. Oh, and be sure to look outside, there was a frost last night."

After waving goodbye, Matthias walked to the chapel. He stood on the pathway, regarding the glaze coating everything white. His hand clenched the book. *A rare day for the rarest of substances—paper. It is ordained.*

The stained glass shepherds of the chapel stood over him as he entered. Inside, Matthias heard no prayerful ghosts or anguished poor, only the rustling of the aged plastic enveloping the Bible. The sound fueled his curiosity and sped his steps.

He made his way to the mosaic of the *Creation of Adam*, faced the image of God, and lifted the Bible over his head. "On Mount Zion will be deliverance. It will be—" He paused, mouth open and groping for the words. Annoyed, he lowered the book.

"It's Micah or Obadiah," Matthias said to the mosaic God. He remembered what he could of the verse from school. It was one of those trivial passages his Biblical History professor used to spring on the students just to knock their grades down. They'd mumble and guess—not Matthias with the outstretched hand. Matthias with the nimble mind. But the words to the verse failed him now. His teacher would have been pleased to click a red mark next to his name on the grading computer.

Matthias lifted his eyes toward the visage of God bestowing life to Adam and pictured himself receiving God's knowledge instead. His fingers tightened around the Bible. Glee replaced his annoyance. "I'll just look it up." He brought his hand up to touch God's. The vault door opened.

Matthias lathered decontamination gel into every crack and wrinkle of the wrapping then repeated the procedure. The plastic turned cloudy. It blocked his view of the wording on the cover. *Might there be Rot inside?* He peered down at his naked body, goosebumps covering his skin. There was only one way to find out.

Matthias flipped up an edge with his fingernail and managed to pinch a hole in the first layer. The old plastic proved resilient, the product of abundant and naïve days when they thought petroleum would last forever. It parted reluctantly, stretching, cracking, and giving way. Another layer presented itself. He tore at it.

Each successive layer took him back in time, less cloudy and more transparent. One layer remained. He read the title aloud. "Holy Bible—Contemporary International Version."

On closer inspection, Matthias studied the golden edges of the unopened volume. There was no visible sign of Rot. It would be safe to bring inside the shelter. He cast his eyes toward the ceiling. "My thanks."

The last layer surrendered. His hands trembled. The cover felt like vinyl, but more supple. He followed the irregular lines texturing its surface with his eyes. *Leather. My God, it's worth a fortune.*

Fanning the pages, he sniffed for the slightest sign of decay. The Bible seemed pristine, amazing considering the mold's relentless appetite. He looked at his arms, the goosebumps seeming to double, then triple.

The book would be hailed as a miracle, a God-given sign to usher in the pilgrimages. The Synod would be forced to allow the Bank access to Washington. Uncle Cornelius would be exposed for complicity in whatever schemes were underway to loot the city. *Perfection.*

He reached for the shelter door and hesitated. All it took was one spore *of Pythium cronos* to devastate his collection. A dot smaller than a grain of salt would consume his library.

Matthias looked down at the book, his stomach knotting. "You are the pearl of great price. I hope you're worth it." He turned the handle. Air hissed from around the door.

After donning his coveralls, he quickly walked to the table where he had laid the Bible down, reddish-brown against the white surface. Matthias grasped it, drinking in every detail, the maroon leather, the gold lettering. He envisioned it under glass in the Synod's National Museum next to the Second Constitution. *Yes, the Kent Bible.* The line would stretch out the museum's door.

Matthias ran his fingers down its surface, lifted a corner and opened it. The sheets were impossibly thin, graceful, delicate, not like the Bank's thick Minutes. Very few of the books in his collection came close to this level of sophisticated construction. Like them, it had to have been machine made and commonplace like the oil that made the plastic. It was all gone now. No wood for the paper—no oil for the plastic—no food for people.

He turned the page. The knots in his stomach tightened.

Handwriting.

The cursive script was masculine, narrow like his writing, not his mother's flowing hand. A cursive heading on the page said, "Presented To," and he read the message.

"August 31, 2017. Dear Sally, Congratulations on your ordination and good luck in Guatemala. May God bless you, Senator Weaver."

"Ordination? Guatemala? Sally? A nun perhaps," said Matthias. His eyes were drawn back to the date and then to the memories of the skeleton in the rubble at the monastery. It didn't take much to picture the spectacled skull having skin and bone—perhaps a woolen suit and one of those odd neck scarves.

Matthias imagined the scene in the monastery garden one day after the date written in the Bible when the immense dirty bomb killed thousands. They died weeping blood and drowning in their own sputum. He regarded the Bible. "And you have laid there ever since September 1, 2017."

The date marked on the book made its value grow ten-fold, a hundred-fold. It was pre-Ecunet, from before the Synod was given control of the government. Oh, how the faithful would clamor to see this holy treasure resurrected from Washington's ashes.

Matthias placed his hand on the upper corner and leafed gently through the pages. Space was set aside for weddings, baptisms, and deaths, but no more writing followed.

An index appeared denoting the books of the Bible, subject index, maps, and best of all, a concordance.

"What was that verse from Micah? Yes, deliverance." He scanned the concordance. "I was wrong," said Matthias, hearing his professor scold him in the back of his mind. He turned to where Obadiah began, all two pages of it.

But on Mount Zion will be deliverance. It will be holy...

Matthias looked away, realizing that now he could finish the rest. "And the Synod will possess its inheritance." He shook his head, chiding himself for not remembering the context of the law that gave the government clear religious title to all non-Christian land and property since the time of the First Islamic War.

His eyes parsed the chapter and came to the seventeenth verse. *And the house of Jacob will own its inheritance.* He blinked and read it again.

It was a subtle difference, something that might have been wrong in the past and corrected by Synod scholars. He tried to dismiss the discrepancy. The knots in his stomach drew taut. *Was the book legitimate?*

He could imagine himself before the Order of Saint George, not only for his forbidden sojourn, but for presenting a heretical fake to the Synod. *Heresy.* It would not end well.

Flipping the pages forward, Matthias found the Lord's Prayer tucked right where it should have been in Chapter 6, verse 9. He pulled in a breath and mouthed the words. Each sentence rang true. He sat back in the chair and breathed. His stomach loosened up.

Matthias scolded himself for the foolish expectation that this old text would match the modern, well-researched Bible that Reverend Isaac preached from every Sunday. "I should have listened to your sermon and not let my spirit be troubled, Pastor Isaac," he said, turning another page and looking for the scripture used the previous Sunday. Verse 19 came into view.

"Do not store up for yourselves treasure on earth where moth and rust destroy."

He read on through to the 24th verse, the words foreign, but sounding like they were an extension of the previous verses.

"No one can serve two masters. Either he will hate the one and love the other or he will be devoted to the one and despise the other. You cannot serve both God and money."

Matthias's stomach coiled like a snake. The Bible fell out of his grasp. *This is heresy. There are no such verses.* His treasure was tainted. "Damn it, it may as well have the Rot!"

His words echoed in the room.

The verse echoed in his mind.

He stared at the book until a frightful curiosity bloomed. Matthias picked up the Bible and ran his hand along the pages.

The Synod.

Yes, he thought, the government would be most impressed when he would show them their name confirmed in this old tome. Its value would be immense.

Plying through the concordance, Matthias searched for "Synod." It didn't appear. The snake in his belly tightened again. *But every version had "the Synod" in it.*

He tried "government" and only found Isaiah's familiar Christmas scripture about the government on Jesus' shoulders. Electricity ran down his neck, his page turning becoming more and more frantic. Each sheet rustled to the point of tearing.

Authority.

Matthias couldn't breathe. There was no mention of the Synod, not like the Bible he had been brought up on.

His hands tugged at the pages, his eyes scanning for any mention. The old book refused. There was no Elder's Oath given by Paul to the Ephesians, no Soldier's Prayer in Hebrews. Even the Rule of Law, taught to every first grader, was missing. Only the book of Samuel bore up to his scrutiny on rulers and masters—the foundation of Synod citizenship.

The room seemed to spin, his breaths short. Questions came in spasms. *Why are these verses missing? Where is the Synod? Why is this Bible so wrong?*

His hand trembled against the page, a single thought dropping onto his consciousness with the same icy intensity of the drop of rain that fell upon his neck at the bank the day he became an Elder.

It's not the book that's wrong.

Matthias set the Bible down and cradled his head in his hands. His mind raced. *This Bible erodes the Synod's authority like a foundation built on sand. Those in power won't want to be challenged by this old book.*

The weight of it all pressed against him. His book, his holy relic, and the tool of his uncle's undoing could never leave the shelter. *No one can know. No one can ever know.*

Benjamin.

Matthias sprang up. He needed to talk Benjamin. They must keep the Bible a secret. They would work out a plan.

Yes. All would be well.

Matthias picked up the book, held it away from himself, and walked to the library. He placed the Bible on top of a stack of coloring pages. It looked silly there, this staid maroon volume squatting atop a jagged pile of paper adorned with primary colors on one side, and his ever-repeated signature on the back.

As he left the room, he took one more look at it, dwelling on the implications boiling up in his mind. It was too much to fathom.

"My pearl indeed." Matthias closed the door.

Naomi looked stricken, her curly hair even more askew. "Where have you been? The Chief Elder's office has been calling every five minutes. They are demanding your presence at the bank."

"Be calm, woman. I was strolling the grounds. Weren't you at your sister's?" said Matthias.

"The Bank contacted Brother Alexander, and he brought me home to find you."

Matthias sat at the table and pulled the vid-panel close. He clicked on Vanderhaggen's address. Rourke appeared.

"How kind of you to contact us during your time of bereavement. You are commanded to return to the bank immediately. There has been an incident."

"What's going on, Uncle?"

"Inquisitor Gideon Stanmore of the Order of Saint George is conducting an investigation. He needs to have an audience with you."

"What's going on? Let me speak to Elder Vanderhaggen."

"You are in no position to give orders." A savage smile filled Rourke's face. "I am."

Chapter 15: Verses 1-114

The Order's motorcycle escort buzzed around Matthias's limousine like black beetles stirred up in a freshly reaped field. Rarely did anyone get such special and unwanted attention.

Matthias paid little notice to the riders in their black helmets and body armor. He hadn't spoken a word to Alexander since they departed for Philadelphia, nor did he want to. His thoughts churned with questions.

Where was Vanderhaggen? Why was Rourke in the Chief Elder's office? Why hadn't Benjamin returned his calls? Did the Synod find out about the sojourn? If they did, so what? What could they do to an Elder?

Nothing.

Rourke's visage appeared in his mind and spoke. "You are in no position to give orders. I am."

Matthias growled, trying to blink away his uncle's face. He gave up and concentrated on the corners of Cornelius's lips where his damned smile ended. "I shall wipe that smile away."

Brother Alexander's brown eyes glanced in the rearview mirror, his face as pale as someone with Rot Fever. Matthias glared back until the chauffeur looked away. As far as he was concerned, there had been far too much fear on the faces of Benjamin, Thomas, and every stinking peasant slinking into church last Sunday. That's why they died—fear. *Enough!*

In that moment, Matthias found clarity. He couldn't analyze, couldn't control his anxieties, and he whispered, "Increase my honor, oh Lord, and comfort me." The anxiousness stilled. His mind sharpened.

Yes, the Synod knew of the journey, and they would have sent their Inquisitor straight to Rourke. *So be it.* As an Elder of the Bank of Job, Matthias would don the whole armor of God and confront this civil servant with the truth about Washington.

As he mustered his strength, Philadelphia's white walls loomed in the windshield. The tower guns didn't track his approach. The limousine didn't slow at the city gate. Beggars scurried to get out of the way. Inside the walls, sullen businessmen glanced toward the entourage and turned away. Only the billboard Jesus smiled.

"You look too small for that chair, Uncle," said Matthias, flanked by the four black riders who marched with him the entire way to the Chief Elder's office.

Rourke sat back in Vanderhaggen's chair and ignored him. "Soldiers, you are dismissed. Glory and honor."

The soldiers clicked their heels together and shouted, "Glory and honor." Their marching jarred the floor all the way out of the office suite.

Matthias planted his fists on the desk. "Don't think that those troopers intimidated me, Uncle. Where is the Chief Elder?"

Unruffled, Rourke folded his hands on his lap. "I'm surprised that you didn't ask about Brother Kyalo first."

"Why? What have you done?"

"More precisely, what have you done?" The question came from someone else.

Matthias followed the voice from a serving cart where Blind Johnny dispensed coffee to a man dressed in black vestments.

The man brushed his thin, dark hair into alignment and strode across the floor to where Matthias stood. The soles of his boots made a familiar sound. "Gideon Stanmore, Elder Kent. *Commander* Gideon Stanmore of the Order of Saint George, former Commandant of the Capital Host and Inquisitor General to the Master of Laws."

Fear cut through him. *The man from Pharaoh's.* Just as quickly, he drew in a breath and smothered the growing apprehension. Matthias moved toward him, offering a handshake and studying Stanmore's poise, his gestures. They gave away nothing. Only his clothes told any kind of story. The cut and style spoke of standard government-issue, a lack of tailoring, yet edified somehow. Matthias got the message. Gideon was uniform, and the uniform was Gideon.

"You don't look any better than the last time we met, Elder Kent."

"I see your boots are still shiny. You must spend a lot of time polishing them."

Gideon flashed teeth as white as the starched white blouse he wore under his vestments. "That is a duty for our recruits. Perhaps you are interested in joining the Order? Your dossier mentioned that you're certainly physically fit enough to do so and your mental abilities are far above the norm."

"They offered me a commission. I turned them down. Let's just say I'm not into polishing shoes," said Matthias, fighting an urge to laugh. The reference to the dossier meant that Gideon sought to assert his authority. It was a cheap marketing trick, making the customer think that the salesman held all the cards.

"No, I would imagine that you aren't. But then again, I knew that from your file as well. Your psychological profile indicated a high desire to challenge authority coupled with an equally high index of creative thinking."

"Two qualities undesirable in the Order and commonplace in Elders. Speaking of which, I'd like to speak to the Chief Elder."

Rourke pushed the chair away from the desk and swaggered to the front. "You are speaking to him." His arrogance hung in the air with the same odor as fertilizer spread on a humid day. No smile filled his face, but his eyes smoldered with glee. "The Synod has temporarily invoked control of the bank. Elder Vanderhaggen has been relieved and placed on indefinite sabbatical. I am in charge."

The answer chafed at Matthias, but he dared not show any

objection. An Inquisitor's presence, an Inquisitor General no less, meant strict enforcement of the Synod's interests. He regarded the pair, smug righteousness practically oozing out of their pores. They knew all about the trip. He imagined Benjamin, perspiration running down his face as he answered each and every one of the Inquisitor's question. That would not be him. There would be no weakness. There would be truth, and the truth would set him free. "All this over a trip to Washington?"

The glee in Rourke's eyes departed, replaced by fire. "I forbade you to enter the city."

Matthias faced the Inquisitor, whose head tipped downward, favoring his left ear. It was a common trait among the Order—a certain amount of deafness caused by the frequent discharge of firearms. "What is forbidden is the looting of this holy place without the approval of a Corporate Convention. All recovery profits must be shared as stated in our covenant. Am I not correct, Inquisitor Stanmore?"

"Yes, Brother Kent," said Gideon. "However, the Synod chose to award contracts in secret. Elder Rourke knew of this, as did all other members of the Corporate Convention. You, Brother Kyalo, and Elder Vanderhaggen are in contempt of a direct order."

Matthias pulled his Elder Card from his wallet. "Elder Rourke has a penchant for saying no to almost everything. Tell me the penance I must pay and release Brother Kyalo. Really, all this fuss."

Stanmore held a single hand aloft. "It is not that simple. I understand you carried out an artifact, a religious artifact?"

Gideon knows, thought Matthias. *There can be no denial.* "You mean, a Bible?"

Gideon took a gulp of coffee, the picture of nonchalance. "You haven't, per chance, opened it?"

Rourke leaned forward with the question.

Matthias needed a moment to consider his answer. "Brother John, you have been remiss in your duties."

Blind Johnny rounded the beverage cart. "I have, Elder Kent—Kent?"

"At least someone here knows the proper way to address an Elder. You have not offered me hospitality. A glass of Gilead

Spring Water, please."

"I offer my contrition, Elder—Elder." Blind Johnny, touched the bottle caps and produced a bottle of water.

As the servant grabbed a glass, Matthias gave another look to Rourke who now stood, arms crossed and face reddening.

"Your cup, Elder Kent—Kent."

Matthias reached out for the tumbler. Blind Johnny placed it in his palm, wrapped Matthias's fingers around the glass, and squeezed. The unexpected gesture surprised Matthias, but not as much as the expression on the servant's face.

Blind Johnny mouthed the words, "Be careful—careful."

Matthias yanked his glass back while Johnny poured. Water splashed on the floor.

"Idiot," yelled Rourke.

"My apologies, Elders—Elders. I will clean this up—up," said Blind Johnny.

Rourke's face turned even redder. "Just get out you old fool. You have no better aim now than when you had eyes. Out!"

Blind Johnny fled through the servant's door.

The Inquisitor spoke as the ruckus subsided. "So, Brother Kent, did you open this Bible?"

Matthias guessed that Benjamin told the Order about the trip and the Bible. They couldn't know anything more. "No, I didn't. The Rot would have compromised the find in an instant. The best I could do was read the title through all the plastic." Matthias caught Gideon reclining a bit more, his legs crossed—a transparent shift from feigned nonchalance to forced disinterest.

The Inquisitor produced a datapad. "And that title?"

"For the record?"

"Yes."

"If I must. The Contemporary International Version."

Rourke fell back against the desk, his Adam's apple making a tidal rise and fall.

Gideon's manner remained unfazed. "When will you be surrendering the book to us, Elder Kent?"

Ah, another shift. I am an Elder again. "I won't be doing that, at least not yet."

Rourke said, "How dare you defy an Inquisitor. Stanmore,

take him away and teach him some manners."

For the first time, Gideon broke his character with a smirk. "You miss the point, Elder Rourke. Elder Kent is bargaining with us. Am I correct?"

"You read people so well, Inquisitor Stanmore. If you ever decide to leave the Order, please see me for a consulting job in our sales division."

Gideon nodded.

"What I want is quite simple. I want exclusive pilgrimage rights to the city all the way down to transportation, food, and vice concessions. In return, the Synod gets equal partnership in the profits and never a word is said about all the pillaging."

"Is that all?" said Gideon.

Matthias sipped what little water landed in his tumbler, his fingers recalling the grasp of Blind Johnny. "I want Brother Kyalo released and Elder Vanderhaggen reinstated."

Rourke bellowed, "This is absurd. There will be no bargaining."

Gideon motioned for Rourke to settle down. "Elder Vanderhaggen's sabbatical is non-negotiable, I'm afraid. According to my latest update, Brother Kyalo has already been released."

Matthias nodded. Someone needed to be the fall guy, and the Chief Elder had been slipping. Better him than Benjamin. "I see."

"I can't believe this. You have no authority," howled Rourke.

The Inquisitor sprang up, his expressionless countenance now punctuated by a protruding jaw. "I have every authority, Brother Rourke. Don't you dare forget that. Elder Kent bargains in good faith and has shown spiritual due diligence with this pilgrimage." Gideon performed another chameleon change to a casual smile directed at Matthias. "And when may we expect delivery of the book?"

He is most anxious. Then he can have it, but not yet. All will be well. "Not for a while, I'm afraid. I need to see considerable good faith on your part considering how much has gone on in Washington without corporate oversight. The Bible will remain in its hiding place until the pilgrimages rights are formalized, agreed?"

"Agreed." The Inquisitor extended his hand.

Matthias took it and shook. "I knew we could do business, Gideon. Won't it be wonderful to see the pilgrim's faces in Saint Reagan's Zion? Oh, and of course we will commission a museum honoring Saint George and the Order."

Gideon flashed a smile worthy of a recruitment poster. "Wonderful, I can hardly wait."

Matthias flung aside the pall of menace cast over him by both Blind Johnny and the Inquisitor. Satisfaction filled him with more warmth than a good bottle of wine. New ground had been broken with Stanmore, his new and immeasurably valuable contact within the God-blessed Order of St. George. It was business the good old-fashioned way.

Best of all, the Inquisitor General erased Rourke's sanctimonious smile. The rebuke was exquisite. Matthias basked in the glow of success until a hand cupped his elbow.

"My deepest contrition for the spillage, Matthias—Matthias," said Blind Johnny.

"It was nothing."

"Matthias, how long have you known me—me?"

The hand cradling Matthias's elbow tightened and shoved him into an empty office. "What are you doing?"

Blind Johnny shut the door. "Brother Kyalo is dead—dead. He went to the Lord during inquisition—inquisition."

The blind man's words hammered into him. "Dead? Stanmore said he has been released. Has the Rot eaten to your brain? Inquisition? We don't torture managers."

He studied the contours of the old man's face, the forehead smooth with concern, the lines to the jaw taut, and his damnable lack of eyes confounding Matthias's ability to read honesty or guile.

"I have heard them speak—speak. Stanmore is most distressed by your Bible—Bible."

"How do you know about that? Benjamin is dead?" Matthias felt the giddy breath of self-congratulations wane, yielding to a vacuum of numbness. Thoughts suffocated faster than he could form them.

"The Order is searching your home as we speak—speak. Is it true you have found a Bible, a *paper* Bible—Bible?"

Matthias leaned against the desk, his mind reeling. "They can't do this to me. I'm an Elder. I've bargained in good faith."

Blind Johnny pawed the air until his hands fell on Matthias's shoulders. "My brother, the Synod has ordered your arrest the moment you return home—home. Inquisitor Stanmore has been commanded to locate the book using all means at his disposal—disposal."

"Well, the Synod's not going to be happy with what they find."

Every line on Blind Johnny's face turned as smooth as a plaster saint. He sank to his knees and clasped his hands. "You have seen the Word of Yahweh? You have seen the Word as it was before the wars—wars?"

Yahweh? The confusion snuffing out Matthias's sense of reason ebbed. It was the first time in his life that Blind Johnny didn't repeat himself. "Say 'Yahweh' again, Brother John."

"Yahweh. The great I am—am."

Suspicion filled Matthias. "The mention of God's name suppresses your echo?"

Blind Johnny sat on the floor. "I did not lose all of myself during my inquisition and reformation by the Synod—Synod." He ran his hands over his eyes. "Their techniques were clumsy then, not like now—now."

"Interrogation and torture are better now? Brother Kyalo might not agree."

"Brother Kyalo was a dead man as soon as the government learned of the Bible—Bible."

Matthias shook his head. "Benjamin is my direct report and protected by me. I am an Elder."

"Your rank is irrelevant to the Synod and the Order, Matthias—Matthias." Johnny's face brightened. "You have seen the Word of God—God?"

"Yes, and the Synod will be most unhappy when they see it."

Blind Johnny's fingers trembled. "To have seen the true Word—Word. You must be blessed—blessed."

"I am cursed."

"God does not curse those He has revealed Himself to—to. For many years, I cursed Him for my fate—fate. I learned of the Synod's treachery many years ago when I worked for your uncle—uncle."

The revelation jolted Matthias. "You worked for Rourke?"

"He cast me into the arms of the Order—Order. They reformed my soul back when the inquisition was new—new. Afterward, Cornelius would not let me out of his sight—sight. Not a day went by that I didn't ask the Lord to call me home—home. Today, I understand His will—will."

Matthias let a hushed laugh fill the room. "I am hiding in some clerk's office in my own corporation with a sightless fool who tells me God has spoken to him. Well, alleluia! I am filled with faith beyond measure. It will serve me well when I join Brother Kyalo."

"I hear the defeat in your voice, Matthias—Matthias. I sounded the same way when they took my eyes, but you have been given the vision to see through the Synod's lies—lies. You are one of us now—now. You must retrieve the Word, and let its truth be known, my brother—brother."

"One of us? What on earth are you talking about?"

"You must spread the true Word—Word."

"Why don't I just go on tour with Pastor Isaac? A paper Bible will get huge ratings." The flag waved outside the conference room window. Near the flagpole stood the four escorts that brought him to the bank. Defeat engulfed him. "I may as well turn myself in now."

The servant stood, arms raised to Heaven, and his cowl falling down his back. "You forget the power of He who gives sight to the blind and was raised from the dead—dead. He is the way—way. He is the truth—truth."

"Thank you for the theatrics. They're much better in church. I am no Christ."

Blind Johnny reached into his vestment, produced a vinyl business card and slapped it into Matthias's hand. "No, you are not—not. You must become Lazarus, and then you must flee—flee."

Chapter 16: Verses 1-42

Flee.

Blind Johnny made it sound so simple. Matthias could count the servant's teeth pressed tight against his lower lip forming the "F." The word hung there, as much prayer as demand.

Brother Alexander closed the door to the limousine. Outside his car, the parking garage hadn't changed much. Concrete. Institutional purple paint blistered by rust. *Not all that different from a burial vault.* Only the limousine's biodiesel exhaust let him know he still lived.

"The usual way home Elder Kent, or Pharaoh's?" said Brother Alexander.

"Home."

The billboard Jesus smiled as they passed by.

Matthias grunted. *You have forsaken me. Delivered me into the grip of the evildoers. Have I not prayed well and often to You? Have I not paid penance according to the law? Have I not tithed?* He drew in a breath, studying the Lord's blue eyes. *At least you could flee to Egypt.* "Ha."

"Sir?" said Brother Alexander.

"Nothing, Brother." Matthias ran his hands through his hair, trying to brush the chaos tangling his mind into some semblance of order. Flight was impossible. Flight to where? To what end? All over a book?

Flee.

His temples throbbed with the command, the gesture, the card. Matthias pawed through his pocket.

The card was a simple affair, a bland advertisement for discount liquor at a vendor along Broad Street. Perhaps he could drink himself into unconsciousness before the torture began.

How magnificently stupid he felt, the perfect pawn. Stanmore played him so well, even to the point of chiding his Uncle. And his Uncle, dear Uncle Cornelius. *So close to casting the vile old goat out. Now who was cast out?* The sound of his own laugh filled the ersatz crypt of his limousine. *I have failed you, Mother. Uncle Cornelius had his way with me as much as he had with you.*

Anger mixed with bile in the back of his throat. *I will see you soon.* He crushed the card in his hand. A corner stuck out, defiantly standing straight and exposing some handwriting. Matthias squinted, his hand relaxing. The card unfurled into a lurching scrawl.

SalVal. Genesis 5:29 Main Line.

The Salvation Army. Matthias remembered the sound of their musical instruments filling the alleyways of the slums. It was a joyous sound among the joyless. They catered to a market share unable to afford redemption, whose bodies were consumed by Rot, liquor, disease. They catered to the hopeless. Would they cater to him?

"I guess you set the Order straight," said Brother Alexander, his bright grin framed in the mirror.

Matthias looked at him, debating what to say. A volley of curses might suit the moment. The Synod would never be able to collect penance after all. But it was better to let Alexander believe that all was well, right up to the moment the bullet left the barrel on the way to his skull. "The Order are of stout heart and mind. We both work to the good of all of God's corporate citizens."

The limo slowed and stopped.

The gate's sentry appeared on Matthias's vid-panel, standing at attention. "Blessings Elder Kent. We beg your patience."

Yes, thought Matthias. *Good theater, indeed.* The tower guard played the earnest soldier. It was back to the normal routine. Even the escorts were nowhere to be seen. "Proceed."

The gates opened. A sea of beggars parted for the vehicle like Moses parting the Red Sea. Their faces turned toward him, hopeful of a handout.

"Brother Alexander, did you refill our penance cards?"

"Yes, sir."

"Let us show our beneficence." *One last time. Perhaps I can still get a decent mansion in Heaven.*

The chauffeur pulled into the crowd, their hands outstretched. He stopped the car and rolled down the window.

"Alexander."

"Yes, Elder Kent?"

"I will give out the cards."

"Sir?"

"Please."

Brother Alexander passed a small stack back to him.

Matthias looked out at milky eyes, swollen bellies and withered hands—dead men and women all. "Is this all of the cards?"

"No sir."

"Give me all of them."

Three more stacks of white cards came back followed by a stack of blue. It was the monthly allotment of an Elder and a small fortune. Matthias lowered his window. He held out a card. A beggar's hand grasped for it, but Matthias snatched it back. He unlocked the door and stepped into the throng.

Raising his hands, Matthias spoke to the crowd. "Brothers and sisters, the Angel of Death is an equal opportunity employer, is he not?"

People murmured, nodded, and chuckled.

"I stand among you for a chance at redemption." He looked into their anxious eyes, every able iris focused on the cards. Looking skyward, Matthias studied the tower guns. They hadn't locked onto him and were pointed away.

Flee.

The word screamed in his mind as if Blind Johnny were standing right next to him. Matthias tossed the stacks of white cards into the air to his left and right where they descended like falling leaves. The mob surged.

He pushed through the crowd and ran into the slums, praying, *Into your hands, oh Lord.*

Chapter 17: Verses 1-52

Matthias dashed past a jumble of shanties and stopped to catch his breath. Rain fell on his hair, sinking down, and chilling his scalp. His skin tingled with an awful excitement.

He was out in the rain, the Rot, and surrounded by two-legged vermin. His mind raced. *What am I doing? I must go back. They will surely listen to an Elder of the Bank of Job. I will give them their old book, and all will be well.*

More beggars jostled him on their way to the cards. Panic numbed his body and his emotions. It was as though he stared through a rain-pattered window into Hell and watched its residents tear each other apart.

One woman bit down on the ear of a toothless man. Blood gushed across her face. Two Goliaths swung metal bars at each other. A terrified child disappeared underneath the incoming tide of the crowd. White penance cards crowned the wave of people, undulating on a sea of hands.

A siren sounded above the screams and curses. The gates to the city clattered shut. The mob quieted. Faces lifted. Matthias followed their line of sight up to the tower's microsonic cannons. Their muzzles rotated into firing position and pointed at the crowd.

A guard at his post atop the wall lifted his hand and dropped it.

Matthias could feel an intensifying vibration in his feet. Every part of him shook with it. The rain that seeped onto his head warmed. He wanted to run, wanted to scream, but the panic robbed him of any rational act.

Hands in the mob dropped their white treasures and pawed their way against the current of incoming people. Just as quickly as the tide rushed in, it sped away.

They flowed around Matthias. He wanted to go with them. Rainwater on his hands steamed in concert with a low thrum. His scalp burned.

The cannon's sonic pulse slammed into nearby clump of people with an alto shriek. Those at the beam's focus burst apart.

The shockwave tore at Matthias's eardrums, and knocked him to the ground with dozens of the rioters. He couldn't breathe. The wind had been knocked out of him. Everyone pawed at him, desperate to get away. Some hobbled. Others crawled. Matthias gasped and looked on, unable to close his eyes.

One old man cried while he pulled penance cards from a dead woman's hand. Ears bled. Arms dangled the wrong way.

Matthias rose, unbalanced and disoriented. He saw dirt all over his vestments, and brushed his hands over the stains. They would never come clean. His ears would never stop ringing.

Another volley of the microsonic cannon dimmed the streetlights. About a block away, he watched more bodies hurl into the air when they were hit by the invisible blast.

Even with the ringing in his ears, Matthias heard the hiss of boiling flesh as the ultrasonic waves rent its victims apart. It was just like his view from the limousine only a few days ago. There were no screams then, no sizzling flesh, no stench of fear. The car window kept it at bay. But he was outside now, without a prayer. The thought froze him in place even more firmly.

One by one, victims fell away in a steady line to where he stood. A collective moan rose from those around him anticipating who would be the weapon's next target. To his surprise, the thrumming ceased.

A man next to Matthias fell backward, two holes appearing in the beggar's head. It was a different sound—gunfire. Security troops poured out of the gate. Licks of flame spat out of their rifles. People fell like wheat cut with a sickle.

The security forces sliced deeper into the mob. Four men appeared behind them at the gate. They wore the black armor and helmets of the Order. Their heads swiveled about.

The sight of them jarred Matthias out of his stupor. They hadn't yet seen him, and he considered it no small bit of luck. A single word screamed in his brain louder than the ringing in his ears, louder than the shrieks of the crowd.

Flee.

Matthias shoved beggars aside and bolted around a corner. The crackle of gunfire sounded again, and the crowd spilled into the street behind him. Children ran past. Adults scrambled into the doorways. Shacks crumbled from the weight of the crowds pouring into them.

Matthias felt the mob shove him forward amidst the huff of panicked breaths. Every time the throng slowed, a gunshot would resound. Everyone ran until their feet could carry them no more.

An hour later, the automatic rifle fire waned from boom, to a sputter, and then to a distant pop. The mob staggered away in twos and threes until Matthias halted in a waste-strewn alley.

Around him lay the detritus of the slums—bits of concrete, shreds of plastic, petrified feces, and dozens of eyes peered at him from inside their hovels. When he looked at them, they turned away, disappearing into darkness. The fear in him ebbed.

"What do we have here?"

Matthias faced a young man who brandished a pair of metal rods connected by a chain, a crude nunchuck. The youth spun it with slow intensity. A greasy hank of black hair sloughed across one eye. The other eye held a glint of adolescent defiance bordering on malice.

Others youths joined the first teenager. They all wore the same type of the black vinyl jacket dotted with an array of steel studs and carried the same look in their eyes.

"I'm talking to you," said the young man, halting the spinning weapon and jabbing it at Matthias.

He realized he had the vulnerability of the victim in the Good Samaritan. No one out here would care if he were beaten or killed.

Fighting the urge to run, Matthias forced himself to think. He watched the adolescent's stance and the way his gaze kept shifting back to his friends. *What does this child want? Authority? Power? Only fear will stop him.* Matthias grabbed the nunchuck and shoved a blue penance card into the adolescent's other hand. "I am Elder Kent of the Bank of Job. The unrighteous are paying for their sins. Those that treat me well will be rewarded. Those that don't will feel the Synod's wrath."

The gang murmured, most of them staring at the blue card. The expression on faces swung like the weapon, oscillating from anger to fear and back again.

All except the kid with the black greasy hair.

The kid snapped his weapon back out of Matthias's hand and set it spinning. "This is what I think of the Synod." He raised the weapon and brought it toward its target.

Before the weapon stuck, Matthias heard the crack of a rifle. The adolescent arched his back and fell. The gang turned toward the sound of the shot.

Four men in black armor crouched in firing position. Anger returned to the gang's faces. They yelled and charged at the soldiers. Matthias ran the other way.

Over his labored breathing, Matthias heard gunshots and screams. Then everything became silent except for the squish of his shoes.

Darkness and rain fell. Fatigue set in. He slowed to a walk among the brick and cinder block shanties dotted with Rot and graffiti. Matthias continued on, deeper into the slum. There was no telling where he was. Every alley and path looked the same, smelled the same and sounded the same down to anonymous wet coughs emanating from the hovels.

The steady drizzle permeated his vestments. Matthias came to a break in the corrugated roofs stacked haphazardly next to each other. Philadelphia's white walls were invisible in the distance. He shivered. There was no place for him now.

He came to a puddle, its surface pierced by drizzle. The man he saw in the reflection stood in soiled vestments. His face carried the sheen of sweat, the look of a criminal. Only hours ago, he made a bargain with Stanmore and the Order. All was well. All was so well. His body drooped with his sodden clothes, heavy, hopeless.

Matthias heard rustling in the huts nearby. Around him faces appeared like rats peering out of a hole. Their eyes seemed to bulge, but he realized it was the hollowness of their cheeks that made them look that way. They walked toward him, hands extended. Voices cried out.

"Do you have any food?"

"Please take my children. Save them."

"I need your help."

"Some money, brother. Please. A penance card or two for my family."

One voice rose above the rest, loud and deep. "Let him be."

The others stepped back.

Matthias followed the voice back to a large red-haired man whose cheeks were much fuller than the others. The man wore a plaid skirt.

The man slapped Matthias on the back and spoke to the crowd. "Brothers and sisters, you're not going to get anything out of this missionary. Look at him."

The excitement in their faces returned to emptiness and they scuttled back into their homes.

"Welcome to Glenolden, brother."

Chapter 18: Verses 1-75

Matthias straightened his stance. Perhaps there was hope to be found after all. At least one of these filthy rabble knew rank when they saw it, and being mistaken for a missionary couldn't be more fortuitous. It was an illusion worth pursuing. "I am Brother... Royer. And you are?"

"Abner MacEwen, Chief Executive Officer of Glenolden."

They shook hands. By the size of Abner's arms, Matthias wasn't surprised at the tight grip he offered up, but the bare legs were another matter. It took a few moments for him to remember the significance of the skirt's pattern. His earlier mission trips still paid dividends. "Scottish Mafia?"

There was nothing friendly in Abner's eyes. "What's it to you, missionary?"

"Then let's have a bargain, or I'll say 'Latha math' and be on my way." Matthias hoped he pronounced the phrase correctly because those were the only two Gaelic words he remembered.

Abner's expression changed. "I wasn't aware of any corporate missions in our humble part of town."

"I was further east in Colwyn when all hell broke loose," lied Matthias.

"There's been a riot at the Vine Street Gate, and it's spread out all along the Schuylkill. City Security has been gunning down everybody near the wall. Word has it that the Synod has called in the Order."

"God must have had a hand in your saving me during this time of tribulation, Brother Abner. Are you saved?"

Abner's brow lowered. "Oh yes, at least twice a day. You spoke of a bargain?" His eyes swept over Matthias. "What do you have to trade?"

"A blue."

Abner's brow rose. "What do you want for it?"

"Dry clothes, something to eat, and perhaps a ride?"

"The first two are easy. The ride is another matter. No can do."

"Why not?"

"Marshal Law has been declared. Curfew is about to start. It'll be shoot-on-sight if they see us move toward the city."

Matthias had no intention of heading back to Philadelphia. "Then I would ask for sanctuary. Do so, and you will receive a righteous man's reward."

The straight line of Abner's lips curled into a vague smile. "Why don't I just ransom you instead, missionary?"

"Then it will be the last time any corporation hands out food and penance cards in Glenolden. From the look of things, Brother MacEwen, you could use a friend inside the walls."

His grin slipped back into a straight line. "Follow me."

An occasional gunshot echoed through the slum, its report hollow and distant. Matthias walked a step behind Abner. Neither spoke until they arrived at a broad lot of rumpled asphalt bordered by a low wall of cinder block chunks and rimmed with barbed wire. Two more men in skirts guarded the only pathway to a brick building beyond the wall.

Abner gestured to the sentries who bowed and moved aside.

To Matthias, the building looked more like a medieval castle than the suburban low-rise it once was. Cinderblocks formed crude battlements around the periphery of the roof. Steel sheeting, complete with arrow slits, hung where windows used to be. Bullet holes pock-marked the brick walls. Some of them were fresh enough to show the original red with no veneer of Rot.

Abner leaned in front of Matthias, close enough for him to see patches of the mold on his face. "We're outside the walls now, city boy. There's no God-blessed Order of Saint George out here to save your ass. Just the Irish mob to the east in Darby, Ghurkas north of us in Melbourne, and ravenous squatters to the west. Occasionally, the neighbors get a little cranky, but good old Caesteal Glenolden holds up just fine. Best keep low if they pay us a visit and don't shit your pants. Laundry service isn't included in that blue. Now, give it up."

Matthias reached for the penance card. There were still a few of them in his pocket and he wondered if he had enough to buy safe passage. His hand brushed against the rough plastic of the business card Blind Johnny gave him. He thought about it for a moment and decided that it would be better left hidden until he could think things over.

Pulling a card out, Matthias held it out of Abner's reach. "Our agreement included food, water, and dry clothes."

Abner yanked open the thick steel doors of the castle. A pale blond woman stood in the entrance, saw the red-haired man, and winked. "Suzie here will attend to you in whatever way you see fit." He gave her a wink back, whispered in her ear.

Suzie pushed him away.

Abner turned and snapped the card from Matthias's grip. "Don't let her exhaust you."

A strong arm propelled him through the doorway and the door slammed behind him.

A bare bulb hung over Suzie, its filament oscillating between dark red and amber. She wore a plaid skirt with the same pattern as everyone else. It crowned a pair of skinny legs, tiny compared to Abner's. Still, she wasn't as waifish as the street people. Her green eyes flickered at Matthias and then down at the foot-long stiletto blade in her right hand. "Touch me, and I'll circumcise you."

Matthias worried about the knife. "I am unarmed."

"It's not your arms I give shit about. Abner makes his jokes, but I'm not one of his whores. He knows better."

Matthias couldn't read any fear in her, not in her body language or in the lines of her face. Any time he moved, there was an alteration in her stance. It was like watching a soldier of the Order, one that knew hand-to-hand combat all too well. He opened his hands and stood still. "I will mind my manners and expect no favors. I expect only what my bargain was for. Agreed?"

Suzie slid the knife into a hilt concealed inside the sleeve of her blouse. "Agreed. Your bed is over yonder."

She led him down a hallway and into a large room. "This used to be a police station." Suzie pointed to a cell with rusting bars. "Don't worry, the lock doesn't work. Abner said we weren't holding you for ransom. Now, off with your clothes. I'll bring you fresh ones along with bread and soup. It won't be that hoity-toity shit you rich bastards eat behind the white walls. Piss and moan about it and I'll eat it myself. Now, on your way."

Matthias obliged.

The cell had three concrete walls and a window sealed with crumbling mortar and pieces of asphalt. The graffiti seemed as old as the cell. A crude mattress lay across a thick slab of metal hung by two chains.

He pulled everything out of his pockets and shoved it under the bedding. Matthias tugged his vestments over his head and dropped them to the floor. He never heard Suzie come in.

"Now that's a fine ass if ever I've seen one. My, that's pretty. Back in the old days, the men in these cages used to fight for pretty asses like yours." She dropped a bundle on the bed. "Clothes and sheets. Best pull the sheets tight around the mattress or you'll be feeding bed bugs all night. Damned things eat better than most of Glenolden. And tie your shoes to the bed. No telling who'll try to pinch them when you're not looking." She slipped away as quietly as she arrived.

The trousers were short and the shirt a rough polyester fleece. Both were uncomfortable, but dry. He did as Suzie commanded and tied his shoes to the chain near his head. They were still wet and stunk of every foul thing he stepped in to get himself this far.

This time he heard Suzie's footsteps.

"Here's the last of the potato bread and some starling stew. You're lucky."

Matthias caught the aroma. It was worse than his shoes. "How am I lucky, Suzie?"

"Last night was rat and the night before was nothing."

"My thanks. Blessings be to the cook." He looked straight into her eyes and tried to be his charming old self, the Matthias the ladies fawned over.

Suzie let a smile grace her pale complexion for just a second and frowned it away. "Rattle your spoon against the bars and I'll come for the dishes. Chamber pot is in the corner."

Matthias glanced at a rusting metal can in the corner. "Oh."

"What did you want, indoor plumbing? Stay inside your room, missionary. It's best. You don't want one of our warriors slitting you open in the middle of the night." Suzie paused at the door and watched him.

He took a bite. Naomi's mop tasted better, but he swallowed it down. "It's good." How he wished for the food he gave away at Pharaoh's.

"It tastes like shit." She laughed and walked down the hall.

After forcing down another mouthful, Matthias tore at the bread. It was rock hard. He banged it against the chain, knocked off a piece, and soaked it in the broth. Combined, they weren't all that bad, and the meager meal soon disappeared.

A rattle of his spoon brought Suzie. She picked up his dishes and stood at the bars once again, her face hardened in bulb's glare. "Sleep well."

Matthias lay on the cot fighting exhaustion. He wanted to get a look at Blind Johnny's card, but made himself wait until everyone in the castle turned in. Once it felt safe, he groped under his bedding and found the card. The handwriting was hard to read in the bulb's glow.

SalVal. Doing the Most Good. Genesis 5:29 Main Line.

The Main Line, thought Matthias. That was the name of the old communities near the Lancaster Road where the elite used to live in grand wooden houses and tended yards full of shrubbery. Once the Rot consumed their homes, they ate their house pets while the destitute carted off their foundation stones to build their shacks.

He knew the area, a desolate back road from his estate in Valley Forge to the city, and a trip that made Brother Alexander especially pale unless they had a security escort. "Like craters on the moon," his driver used to say. "Too bad I hardly ever looked out the window," said Matthias.

With SalVal franchises all along the Main Line out as far as the Turnpike Wall, finding the one person that would understand the mention of Genesis 5:29 would take forever. He laughed. *But what else do I have to do, tend to my estate?* His laugh trailed off into silence. *What are they doing to my house? Have they found their precious book? Naomi. Good God.*

Matthias looked over the scripture on the business card. "God won't help you now, Naomi. Not the God of Adam and Enos and Cainan and Enoch and everybody else in that chapter."

He could remember the pain of the teacher's rod when he had to memorize every ounce of lineage and the number of years each ancestor lived. Back then, it hurt like the devil. It seemed so insignificant now.

His eyes grew heavier. The specifics of the verse eluded him. There would be time to think things over tomorrow. He let his body fall onto the plastic sheets.

In the midst of his fatigue, Matthias dreamt in bursts of anguished faces, of trampled children, of himself being hurled like a doll in the cannon's concussion. He'd awaken, unsure where the nightmare left off and reality began.

Sweat pooled along the sheet. It made his arm itch. The idea of feasting bed bugs jolted him off the mattress. He peeled away the fleece shirt and found nothing.

"Can't sleep, missionary?" said Suzie.

"I thought bugs were biting me."

She opened the cell door, walked over to him and ran her hand along his chest. "My, you are a pretty one."

"I never thought of myself as-." Matthias closed his mouth when he felt the stiletto's point against the base of his chin.

"Shhhh. Can't wake the clan, can we now?" She pushed against his chest and forced him to lie on the bed.

He squirmed and grunted.

"What did I say?" Her eyes were gleeful, animal-like.

A deep voice bellowed from down the hall. "Susie? Suzanne MacEwen? Where in the hell are you, girl?"

Her glee disappeared in an instant. She let go of him while putting more pressure on the blade. "My husband Abner is looking for me. All I have to do is scream, and he'll feed you to the rats. Do we understand each other?"

Matthias blinked in agreement.

Suzie smiled and crept back down the hall.

Chapter 19: Verses 1-59

Sunlight beamed through the ragged holes in the sheet metal windows. Matthias's breath fogged the air, coiling around the light as if clinging to the warmth. But there was no warmth on the spare bed, no blankets to retreat under.

"Good morning, Elder Kent," said Suzie, curtsying and sliding a metal bowl of orange paste through a slot in the bars. "Breakfast is served."

Her salutation jolted him like the concussion from the cannon. "How do you know my name?"

She laughed. "You stupid gowk. You never even realized I picked up a few souvenirs when I stopped by last night." Suzie held up his wallet.

Matthias jumped up, flung the mattress aside and found nothing there. "Damn you." He kicked the bowl and yanked at the cell door. It held fast.

She stepped closer. "Peckerhead—Peckerhead. You even believed us about the door. God, how dumb you are."

Abner entered the cell block. "You look cold, brother. Should have kept your hand on your belongings like she told you."

Matthias rattled the bars. "Why are you holding me?"

A third set of footsteps walked into the room. "For me, Elder Kent. Get your shoes on. We're leaving."

Matthias could make out a man's silhouette and followed it down to the floor where the sunbeam fell on glossy boots. Whatever anger he had ebbed in a wash of defeat. "Damn it."

Gideon moved into the light, its glow highlighting the obvious satisfaction on his face. "I see that your vocabulary has improved since yesterday."

Abner slid into the space between the two. "So, he's the genuine article?"

"You have captured the heretic, Matthias Kent, Brother MacEwen." Stanmore brushed him aside and stepped up to the cell door. "I trust that he hasn't spread his gospel of hate to your people?"

Matthias tied his shoes, watching Gideon and the way he smoothly delivered the question that worried him most. "Don't worry, Inquisitor. Their souls are untarnished."

"I'm sure they are." Stanmore turned and nodded to Abner. "Let your sentries know we have a bargain and please tell my troops that we have our man." He wrung his hands together. "Mission accomplished."

"All right then," said Abner. "Suzie, unlock the door and send this bastard on his way. The sooner he's out of here, the sooner we get our money."

Suzie did as Abner said. She stood next to Matthias and gave his face a long lick. "I'll miss that pretty ass."

The point of her knife dug into his back.

"Now, let's be on our way."

Matthias stepped out into the courtyard. Clouds gathered and smothered the sun. A crowd murmured just beyond the castle gate, their bodies pressing against the sentries. Wild eyes locked on him.

Gideon stopped. "Brother MacEwen, what's going on?"

"Five million credits is what's going on. The word must have got out. Everybody wants a look-see."

"Please tell your sentries to make way for us, or I shall order my troops to do so. I will wait here with the heretic."

Abner's eyes narrowed and his face flushed red. His hand slid into his sleeve.

Suzie shook her head. "Let's give him what he wants, and we'll have what we want, dearest."

With a nod, Abner and Suzie waded into the crowd.

As they yelled at the people of Glenolden, Matthias said, "That much for me? You haven't found the Bible yet, have you?"

The Inquisitor turned toward him. "No, we haven't, but you'll tell us in due time. Why not tell me now and save yourself from considerable pain? I mean, for the life of me, it makes no sense why you're withholding the book from us."

Gideon's statement made Matthias pause and think. "No, it doesn't make any sense, does it? I mean, here I am, the lamb being led to the slaughter."

"Don't blaspheme our Lord."

"You already have—you, the Synod, and my uncle."

Gideon lifted an eyebrow. "That's what this is all about, your uncle?"

"Would you put a bullet in Rourke's head in exchange for the book?"

"What caliber?"

The rapidity and willingness of the Inquisitor shook Matthias. "You really are afraid of that old Bible, aren't you?"

Gideon brought himself to within an inch of Matthias. "I am afraid of nothing, for I serve the Synod and the Most High."

"You serve power. I've read the pages. I know the difference."

"As do I. I know of old Bibles and old religions. They were a bane upon this land. America was a land where milk and honey flowed. Now look at it." The Inquisitor yanked Matthias by the hair and spun him toward the crowd. "I said, 'Look at it.'" Gideon pulled Matthias back. "Religious freedom, they called it. Jews and Hindus and Muslims, all running around preaching their poison in God's Own Land, the land of Washington, of Lincoln, and Bush. Even the Christians couldn't agree on just who God was. Then God smote us all. Wars and Rot and heretics just like you until there was nothing left but the Synod and the Word. And there you stand, you stupid salesman, peddling vice to the masses, all indignant because you think you found the truth? The Synod is the truth, Kent. We hear God's Word and dispense it to the people."

"Then you are as much a salesman as I." Matthias collapsed as a white-hot burst of agony erupted from his pelvis.

Stanmore drew his knee back and spit on him. "I will enjoy conducting your inquisition personally, brother. Now, get in the car."

The Inquisitor's voice sounded distant, like speaking through a hollow tube. Over Gideon's shoulder, Matthias could make out men on the roof of Caesteal Glenolden, their hands waving and mouths open. He could barely make out what they were shouting.

"Irish! The Irish are attacking!"

The first explosion burst in the dirt near the castle, sending bits of rock in all directions. A man on the parapet fell to the ground.

The crowd broke through the gate like water bursting through a dam. Sentries tried in vain to keep them out. Warriors rushed to the perimeter wall.

Above him, Gideon stood, calm and collected. He spoke into a microphone on his lapel. Machine gun fire started off in the distance. Another explosion sounded, this time hitting the castle. Mud flew up around Matthias. Something hot sizzled in a puddle near by. People in the courtyard were knocked off their feet.

Gideon held his ground. The gunfire moved closer. "Get up. We're leaving."

Matthias felt a grip close around his arm and jerk him to his feet. A black armored car appeared at the gate.

"Move!"

Soldiers of the Order leapt from the vehicle and fired in all directions. People fell. A path cleared and Gideon hurled him at the vehicle. He tripped and fell next to a pile of cinderblocks.

"Get up," commanded Gideon, waving a pistol in Matthias's face.

The flash of a hundred suns lit up the courtyard as another explosion hit the sentry post. Matthias squinted in the brightness, watching Gideon flail in mid-air and disappear. Debris pattered down on him like rain. He rolled away from the blocks. The soldiers of the Order lay motionless around their burning armored car.

Around him, warriors manned the wall and began firing.

Matthias ran for the gate.

The outside of the compound was more hellish than the inside. Bodies lay like the litter he walked through the day before. Bullets slapped off the wall every time he stuck his head outside the wall.

Another explosion burst down the street, this one bigger than the rest. A black cloud rose. The rat-a-tat of weapon fire followed, all from the castle wall. No one in the street fired back.

He peered out. A truck burned in the distance. It was his chance, and he crawled out onto the road over bodies and blood.

Suzie lie dead, her cloak shredded and legs twisted about. Matthias scrambled over to her body and ran his hands through her pockets. He found his wallet, a few blue penance cards, and a metal flask. Lifting her arm, he unsheathed the stiletto, wrapped it in a rag and slipped it into his belt.

When the gunfire subsided, Matthias crawled the entire length of the block, hoping to God that no one would see him flee.

Chapter 20: Verses 1-47

Matthias moved through the alleys, an anonymous face among anonymous faces. No one bothered to give him anything more than a passing glance, and he was glad for it. He was just another stranger clad in soiled clothes—with a price on his head.

The sun peeked out from behind the clouds, much the same as his skin appeared through holes in his garments. The rough texture of the clothes made him miss the comfortable weight of his vestments, the way they fit around him. Naomi always kept them clean and pressed. The thought of her stabbed at his heart. Was she, like him, cast out? Was she even alive?

Matthias looked northwest, toward home, toward the accursed book, wondering what the Order had done to his house. Would he ever see it again? *Perhaps, when the time was right.*

His foot landed in a puddle. The cold water gushed into his shoe. Somewhere in the shanties, children giggled. Matthias looked down at his foot and then skyward. Deuteronomy came to mind. *You will find no ease, nor shall your foot find rest.* He laughed like the children. *Was that verse even in the Bible?*

He shifted his gaze to the hovels, the lean-to's, and tarps that bordered the heaved pavement that passed for a street. A family clustered together inside a single blanket, every eye dark and listless. Next to them, an old man slept rolled up in sheets of milky plastic like a caterpillar in a cocoon. A young couple said Grace over a stack of hardtack bread and water. Matthias's stomach gurgled.

He reached for a blue card to trade for a meal and withdrew his hand. The use of a penance card only a few miles away from Glenolden would spark suspicion.

Just take it. Matthias shook off the urge, incredulous that he coveted the hard-as-stone crackers. *But what else do I have?* His hand bumped against a metal container. *The flask.*

He sniffed the contents and found it a surprisingly agreeable blend of imitation scotch. The idea of trading it for hardtack sat worse with him than not being able to use a blue card. His stomach beckoned. "Brother and sister, I am a stranger and seek to bargain with you."

Their hands surrounded the bread.

"Fear not." Matthias held up the flask. "I will trade you a swig of this fine whiskey in return for few crackers and enough water to make it pliable."

The man pushed his wife back further into the hovel. "We are devout before the Lord and do not drink."

Great. A million souls outside the wall, and I run into the only two that don't drink liquor.

"Be on your way," the man said, his hand tightening on a metal rod.

Matthias raised his hands. "I mean no harm to you and yours, brother."

"Go."

Lowering his hands, Matthias spied a brass crucifix and a Synod-approved print of the Last Supper set off to the side in the neatest part of their home. Compared to the rest of their possessions, those items were well kept, hallowed. He shifted tactics. "So much for doing unto the least of your brothers. I'm sorry for interrupting your dinner, friend." Matthias bowed and shuffled away.

"Wait," said the woman.

Matthias turned back to the pair. They whispered to each other, brows wrinkling, easing and wrinkling again. The discussion ended with a nod of both heads.

"Here." She proffered a single cracker to him along with a pint of water.

He took it. "You shall know kindness in our Father's house."

The couple smiled.

Matthias picked up an empty plastic bottle and poured some of the contents of the flask into it. "This is decent whiskey."

The man cut in, "Brother, we do not drink."

Pressing the container into the man's hand, Matthias said, "You don't, but others do." He couldn't suppress a smile. "Trade this to someone with a taste for it and your supply of bread will grow tenfold."

"All right," said the man.

"My thanks." Matthias held the hardtack in his hand. It was embossed with a shield and the words, *Salvation Army*. "Where did you get this?"

The man sniffed the whiskey and coughed. "The SalVal in Overbrook."

"Where am I?"

"Springfield."

Matthias recalled a map of Philadelphia, where the city wall began, the principle slums, and outlying ghettos. Overbrook stood just outside the old city limits, where the Main Line began—where the first Salvation Army center was. Springfield lay to the south and west of it. That was where he would start looking for a SalVal. "My thanks." He started walking.

The woman spoke up. "God bless your travels."

Matthias said, "Blessings to you both."

The man receded into the shanty

Matthias could feel the man's eyes studying him, halting at his feet. There was no time to waste. Five million credits made every stranger suspect, especially one with fine shoes.

Matthias hiked a few blocks and found an empty lean-to. The corrugated metal seemed ready to collapse into a pile of rust with the slightest touch. The clouds above him regrouped, ready to unload another volley of rain. Whatever time it was couldn't be reckoned. Afternoon? Evening?

He hunkered down, rubbing his arms over his sleeves. The street quieted, and the lean-to was a safe place to prepare his meal.

The hardtack proved more resistant to water than it was to the Rot, which dotted its surface with grains smaller than ground pepper. Matthias mixed the scotch and water together—another mission trip lesson. Booze killed the Rot. Even the cheap stuff did the trick. He remembered on those outings how the servants would cleanse the food with it, mix it in the water. An hour after dinner, nobody could walk straight. Everyone sang hymns off-key, and it sounded better than any church choir. By dark, everyone slept soundly. *The good old days.*

Matthias shook the water bottle. Only half of the contents remained. There would be no singing tonight, not if he wanted to prepare any food or drink he might happen to find.

Flecks of Rot drifted to the top of the portion of water he had in his container. He poured the top layer off. Dinner was ready. Footsteps neared. Matthias tensed, expecting a famished soul like him peering in with an outstretched palm.

No face appeared.

A figure passed the lean-to. Matthias looked through one of the holes in the corrugated metal. It was the man who gave him the bread.

Matthias pulled the hardtack from the water and gnawed it into submission. Only the scotch gave it any taste. He ate it all. His stomach gurgled again. It didn't matter. There wouldn't be time to soak another piece even if he had it. He slurped down the water, pocketed the flask and set off to follow the man.

Peeking around the corner, Matthias watched him hurry along a broad avenue and head northeast. Not once did he look back or check to see if anyone else followed. He was a man of purpose, and it didn't take a lot of imagination form Matthias to guess that the man was headed to the nearest security station—Overbrook. The same place he was heading.

With his destination compromised, Matthias leaned against the building, shaking his head. "Damn it." He took a pull from the flask. Troops would be coming right down the avenue looking for him. *Where else on the Main Line can I go?*

An old middle school mnemonic about the Main Line came to mind. "Old maids never wed and have babies." The phrase sounded odd in his voice, not that of the venerable geography teacher, Mr. Giordano. The old man always wore rumpled business vestments when he taught and never missed when he swung his steel yardstick. Matthias flexed his hand in remembered pain.

The town names to the Main Line materialized, each one in concert with the old mnemonic; Overbrook, Merion, Narbeth, Wynnewood, Ardmore, Haverford and Bryn Mawr. The Order would be in Overbrook by nightfall, he considered. They would spread south and west to find him. The further away he was from the man he got the hardtack from, the better. "Bryn Mawr it is."

Rain fell, a patter at first followed by a steady drizzle. Matthias yanked a brown tarp from underneath some debris. He pulled it up over his head like Blind Johnny's robe. He blanched at the smell. A rod slid off the pile and landed at his feet. Matthias picked it up to use as a walking stick. As he stood, he saw himself in a shard of glass. He laughed. *I am Paul of Tarsus.*

Chapter 21: Verses 1-109

Matthias made his way from suburb to suburb until his legs felt like pillars of salt. He sat down on a chunk of shattered stone near the husks of blackened foundations. Familiarity swept over him. He knew the place from a pilgrimage during middle school—Haverford College.

Every school child memorized the story of the Battle of Haverford, the high water mark of the Second Civil War. Only by the grace of God did General Barnabas Connor defeat the Amish Secessionists a mere ten miles from the capitol. The win here, along with the victory in Salt Lake City a week later, assured the dominance of the United Christian States. A year after that, the Chinese and the Arabs signed the Armistice of Rome. Peace reigned. Alleluia. *Now we're all fat and happy.*

I should have been a tour guide. It was better to think of old victories than the screams of the doomed.

A meager brightness fled the western sky. Mercifully, there had been no rain for hours. Even the clouds seemed starved. Matthias pulled himself to his feet with his walking stick. It had already begun to color his palm orange with rust.

At dark, he reached the Lincoln Highway, old Route 30, the

road that Brother Alexander disliked so much. Matthias squinted, trying to make out the vile souls that usually lined the road. His footsteps were the only sound except for the drone of a vehicle some blocks away. Moving back into the cover of a side street, he listened to their movements.

A searchlight sliced through the darkness, illuminating the rutted asphalt and piles of God-knew-what. The light hovered, traversed a semi-circle, and then winked out. Red taillights blinked on. The drone increased. The vehicle moved on—away. It was safe to cross.

Another searchlight winked on. The world around him transformed from night to day.

A man's voice shouted, "Halt."

Matthias turned away from the searchlight beam, dropping the walking stick and raising his hands. He felt his garments move as if someone blew a puff of air on them. The sound of a shot followed. He dove behind a pile of rags. More shots rang out, spattering off the sidewalk. One hit the rags in front of him with a wet thud. He raised his head. A woman looked back, her expression fixed in the open-mouthed rigor of somebody three days dead.

The shooting stopped. Matthias peered over the body. The vehicle approached, its searchlight lurching around. When it swept away, he ran down an alley. Gunfire and footsteps pursued him.

The alley opened into another street and then another. Behind him, the pale circles of flashlights danced along the walls. They moved down a different street. Matthias let out a breath.

Night turned to day again. Matthias didn't wait for a command to halt this time and ran into the next block. An engine roared. Soldiers ran. The rat-a-tat of machine guns chipped stone off the walls. Fragments stung his face and propelled him onward.

The light blinded him, but he ran in breathless desperation. His feet caught on something. He tripped. The building walls around him disappeared. The ground beneath him withdrew. He plunged into the black void of a shallow ravine.

Something sharp tore through his tarp and into his skin. The searchlight pierced the void. The beam lit the branches of a great tangle of brush. Despite the agony of every movement, Matthias pulled himself further into the thicket and plunged into the mud.

The searchlight hunted after him. Bullets peppered the brush pile. None came close.

Matthias heard the voice in the vehicle talking to someone else. "Go and get him."

The other voice replied, "I'm not going down there. You go."

"I'm in charge. Get down there."

"No."

The sound of a gun's action being snapped open and closed got Matthias's attention.

"Fine, have it your way. Just put that thing down."

In the dim cast of the taillights, Matthias made out a small silhouette crouched nearby. He tensed, fearing that that his pursuers caught up to him, but the shadowy figure held still.

Seconds passed. The searchlight powered off. The engine revved and the vehicle drove away.

The person, a boy, approached, but kept a few strides away.

It took a few moments for Matthias to get his breath and night vision back. The boy's features were impossible to make out in the darkness, just the unruly curls of his hair and that his chest high height—ten, maybe twelve years old.

To Matthias's surprise, he felt the child take him by the hand and lead him down a path through the thicket. At first, he wanted to pull away, to run, but he gave in to the gentle guidance. Maybe he was too tired to go any further, too tired to fight, but he could sense no malevolence in the child.

The clouds thinned just enough for the moon to brighten the path. They walked for a while. Matthias had no concept of time, just the jabs of thorns still embedded in his skin.

The child stopped, looked around, and pulled away a pile of debris that stood in front of a culvert. He pushed Matthias inside, pulled the debris back, and urged him to go further into the blackness.

The urging stopped. A flame appeared, neared the wick of a candle and lit it.

Matthias looked at his host. His first impressions weren't too far off the mark. The child's age seemed right. His hair jutted in all directions, matted and dirty.

Sweat dripped in Matthias's eyes, and it blurred his view of the child. A chill swept over him. He knew the face, the hair, the age. "You're the child at the gate."

The crescent of a wide smile glowed in the candlelight, but no words left his mouth.

"Your name?" said Matthias.

The boy shrugged.

"Can't you speak, boy?"

The boy swung his head.

"Do you know who I am?"

A nod.

Matthias's sweat ran cold. "You could have turned me in, made a fortune for you and your mother."

The boy looked down, his chin pulling in and wavering.

"She's with God?"

Another nod.

"I'm sorry."

Despite the tight confines, the child slid past Matthias, taking the candle further down the culvert. He came back with hardtack and water.

"For me?" He took the bread and water. The kindness touched him but also made him wary. "Why?"

The child opened a metal box, pulled out a vinyl placard, yellowed and cracked with age.

Matthias looked at an illustration of two children. One held out food to the other. The caption read, *Do onto others as you would have them do onto you.* "Ah, Matthew 18, the Golden Rule. I don't suppose you've got Genesis 5:29 in that box?"

The boy stared at him.

A red shield stood out on the bottom right hand corner of the placard. "The Salvation Army," said Matthias. He held up the hardtack and ran his thumb over the emblem. "Is there a SalVal nearby?"

The boy nodded.

"Would you take me there?"

The child's lips pursed and he took away the placard.

"Not sure you want to, eh?" Matthias shifted his weight and another wave of pricking made him twitch.

The boy fumbled around in a bag. A pair of needle-nosed

pliers appeared, their jaws opening and snapping shut as the child made a yanking motion.

Matthias took off his tarp and tugged his shirt up over his head. He could feel the warmth of the candle, followed by a tug and a bright jab of pain.

The boy repeated the process until all of the thorns were removed. He tossed Matthias his shirt.

"My thanks, little brother."

The child moved down the tunnel, lighting up drawings on the concrete. They were simple things, stick figures, a cross.

"Did you make those?" asked Matthias

A nod.

"They're very good." Matthias turned his attention to the hard tack and chewed down anything that had softened. It did little to ease his hunger. Exhaustion overwhelmed him.

When his eyelids fell, the boy noticed and ushered him to a bed of rags. Matthias lay down and settled in. He looked up at the child and gave him a smile. "My thanks."

The boy sat near the candle, smiling back.

Matthias let his eyes close. The rustle of plastic brought them open again.

The boy shook a bag full of toy animals onto the floor of the tunnel and arranged them two by two.

"Are they headed off to the Ark?"

Another nod.

The sight jarred his thoughts. He chuckled. "Now I remember. Genesis 5:5-25. 'And he was called Noah, saying this name will comfort us.'"

The boy stopped playing, his hand knocking the animals over and the smile gone from his face.

"Did I say something wrong about Noah?"

The child's eyes opened wide.

Matthias tried to gauge the conflicting sides of the child's reaction. Fright? Recognition? Anger?

The boy picked up the candle and moved closer to the opening.

In the darkness, Matthias dwelled on the child's face, but could find no answers in his weary mind. The need to sleep trumped the desire to understand what just occurred. He closed his eyes. Whatever the answer, it would wait.

Matthias couldn't tell if it was morning, such was the darkness blanketing him in the culvert. A blatant mustiness hung in the air from the mix of biodegradable bedding and the stink of his unwashed self. Only the flexing of his eyelids gave him any indication that he was awake.

The wall felt slimy, damp. There was nothing to pull himself up with. He turned and got up on his hands and knees. Every muscle, every joint, cried out in painful rebellion.

How nice it would be if Naomi brought him an aspirin and a cold glass of common distilled. *Heaven.* Even better would be the aroma of oatmeal on the kitchen table. *If she were still alive. If she weren't in a hole in the ground like some rodent—like me.*

His thoughts weighed him down, made him unable to rise. The events of the last week swirled through his brain. *Funeral. Promotion. Washington. How can a man go from Elder to cast-off in less time than it took God to create the Earth?*

Blind Johnny's words came to mind. "Pride goes before the fall—fall."

"How right you were." Matthias lay down. The opening of the culvert came into view, a ghostly crevice of light creeping into the first few inches of the tunnel. There was no silhouette of the boy, no trace of his belongings, or of the candle. Matthias was abandoned during the night.

Something on his scalp moved. He scratched at it. The image of lice crawling through his hair made him jump out of bed and head for the opening.

Matthias kicked the brush concealing the door aside. Light poured in. So did the rain, falling in sheets on the thicket. The path that brought him there the night before lay inundated under a pond. He moved back inside the tunnel and sat, listening to the drops hitting the water.

Both the sound of the rain and the ache in his bladder forced him out of the shelter.

He stood in the frigid ankle-deep pond, relieving himself. The water turned warmer near his feet, and he blanched in disgust. *This is my Nineveh, my future, standing in my own filth, and worrying where my next meal will come from. All who see me will run.*

Matthias returned to the tunnel. He tugged on the rope belt, cinching his garments tight. His hands lingered on the cord. It was stout stuff, rough and strong. His hands ran along his clothing. They were soiled, holed, and coarse. Even Paul of Tarsus wouldn't wear such tatters. He brought his hands to his face. Each cut, each gash, lay under a crust of dried blood, the skin around it an angry red. Weariness penetrated every fiber of his body. The worst of it came from his empty stomach.

I wonder what Uncle Cornelius is having for breakfast?

The thought stuck in his gut, gnawing at him. Matthias imagined his uncle downing coffee and scones, reading the updates of his nephew's flight on the Ecunet. All the while, he'd be grinning that smug bastard smile and knowing that he'd won.

"I have made a fool of myself."

His laughter echoed in the culvert and rebounded to mock him where he sat. He looked around the embankments to crumbling buildings and upward at the clouds, where the ever-grayness blocked the sky. *All this over a relic. A relic they've probably found by now. I have nothing to bargain with. I have nothing at all. My loss is complete. I'm sorry, father. I'm sorry, mother.*

His hands fell to his lap, his thumbs nudging the rope belt. Matthias ran his fingers along the cordage until they reached the knot that kept his garments closed.

The knot loosed with little fuss and he coiled the rope in his hand. Matthias's eyes searched out a thick branch or just the right piece of metal that might be high enough. A steel girder protruded from the bank over his head.

He tied a slip knot into one end and crawled up on top of the culvert's concrete apron. It took a few tries until he lassoed it.

The dark thicket sprawled out before him in a pool of muddy lather. The end of the line swung in the breeze. Matthias snagged it and tied another knot to form a small noose. He set it in motion and it swept back and forth like a pendulum. *Is this what Judas saw?*

"You'll need to put a few more knots in that thing before you step off."

The words jarred Matthias back from the edge. His chin dipped. The boy stood in the water next to a man in a dress military uniform. The man's clothes were old fashioned, even down to the dark tie, collared shirt and red epaulets. Two patches embroidered with a white "S" stood out on his coat along with a bright green shamrock pin. The pond concealed his shoes, and Matthias wondered if the man's boots were as glossy as Gideon's.

"Let me get Samuel out of here before you do it. He's seen enough."

The boy glanced up at him and then looked down at the mud.

"Fine," said Matthias.

The man grabbed Samuel's shoulders, turned him around, and gave him a push.

The boy looked back over his shoulder at Matthias and mouthed the word, "No."

The man walked up to the foot of the culvert. "Before you go to God, I just want to know if you're Matthias Kent, Elder of the Bank of Job."

"Yes, now you know what five million credits looks like."

"That doesn't matter to me. I'd rather meet the man who has seen the Word of God."

Shock rippled through Matthias. "How can you know that?" He pulled the noose close. No one would take him in for torture and reformation.

The man smiled up at Matthias. "Blind Johnny told me of you. I'm Noah, Captain Noah Finney, of the Salvation Army. You told the boy you sought comfort with us."

A rush of emotion washed over Matthias. His knees trembled and he fell. "Genesis 5:29?"

"That would be me."

Matthias looked up at the noose swinging in the breeze. Nausea overwhelmed him and he heaved into the mud.

Noah climbed up next to him and patted his back. "I'm not here to collect the reward. My reward will come from God Himself on the day I am judged. Now, let's get out of here before someone sees you. Please, I have food and drink. Come."

Chapter 22: Verses 1-102

"Welcome to the Main Line," said Noah, his feet creating muddy swirls in the water.

Matthias watched the eddies and tried to stomp some feeling into his toes.

"You might want to keep the noise down." Noah brushed aside a thorny limb. "Not everyone is friendly to us."

"Understood."

"This used to be a railroad line up until maybe a hundred years ago. Ran the whole way to Pittsburgh."

He looked past Noah to a never ending thicket arched above them. "We're not walking to Pittsburgh, are we?"

"Oh, heavens no. My church is about a mile from here. We just got our coal allotment. The sexton might've even fired up one of the old boilers by now. Fresh distilled on the way. Maybe even some soup."

He looked at the back of the captain's head, his thinning, gray hair combed in neat ranks below his cap, his face wet, but shaven. The promise of warmth, of cleanliness, and of food lent an extra step to Matthias's plodding. It was all so wonderful, too good to be true. He halted. "How did you know it was me?"

"Blind Johnny told us you might be coming our way. We didn't know what you looked like, but figured you'd have all the trademarks of the recently cast out—a full face, no tinge of Rot."

"Samuel spotted me easily enough, even in the dark."

Noah laughed. "You do stand out. The boy told me the security forces were chasing you."

"They weren't chasing me. They were trying to kill me."

"City Security is very jittery. They're quite frightened to be outside the wall. Been shooting everybody they see."

"All this because of me?"

"You've got them scared out of their wits. Is it true you killed an entire squad of the Order of Saint George?"

"Me? An advertising Elder taking on the Synod's finest? I've come a long way in just two days. The truth is that a rival gang attacked the place I was being held. The Order's troops were caught in the middle. I did nothing except flee."

"That's not what the Secretary of Mass Communication said in his address last night. 'The heretic Matthias Kent exhorted his followers to murder defenseless ministers of God.' Somewhere in his speech, I think he also called you a 'terrorist.' They haven't called anyone a terrorist since the Second Civil War. It's big news on the Ecunet."

"So, I'm a heretic, murderer, and a terrorist, eh? Shouldn't you be worried?"

"Not in the least. You're no more a terrorist than Samuel is. If anyone is afraid, it's the Synod."

"What makes you so sure?"

"The reward." Noah turned around and headed down the path. "It's been expressly stated that you must be delivered alive to atone for your sins and to recant your terrorist ways."

"Alive?" To Matthias, it didn't make sense. Killing him would insure that his secret would remain a secret. The answer sprang into his mind. "They haven't found it."

"No, it would seem they haven't. If they get you, they'll render your mind for answers, and you'll tell them everything you know. No one ever goes before the inquisition and returns with their soul."

"Not even Blind Johnny?" said Matthias.

"John clings to his soul by a thread, and that thread is hope. You have given him much to hope for, Elder Kent. Much hope for all of us. Just the thought of seeing an unmolested copy of the Word brings tears to my eyes. Truly, a miracle of the Most High. I can't wait to hear about it. Come on, let's get going before someone sees you and makes good on your bounty. John tells me it'll be ten million by nightfall."

The Rot drew charcoal lines along the mortar of the humble, granite church. Sheets of corrugated aluminum painted to resemble stained glass stood in its window frames. Smoke rose out of a chimney. Warmth. Food.

Samuel appeared from nowhere, tugged on Noah's sleeve and pointed.

Noah looked at the church. "Thank you, Samuel. Brother Kent?"

"Yes?"

"Please follow Samuel. I must go in the front way. We have several new faces looking for hospitality today. Not all of them seek God."

Matthias understood. "You mean they're looking for me."

"Most likely. The local folks know we're out of rations. They wouldn't expect a handout. Still, some come to our door in the hope of God's unfailing love."

"I'm sure they do." Matthias found Noah's words funny. He saw plenty of God's children along the way, diseased, dead. In the eight years since his trip into these areas things had gotten a lot worse. "Unfailing love" weren't the words he would use if he were making up a marketing slogan to sum up this trip.

Samuel waved for him to follow and crouched along the rubble.

Matthias had a tougher time moving like the child, clumsy, loping.

More than once, the boy looked backward at him.

"I'm doing the best I can."

With one more street to cross, Samuel took in the surroundings, eyes following unknown contours. When he had seen enough, he pulled a hunk of metal sheeting out of a pile of trash. A stairway appeared. It led down into darkness.

"You do love your tunnels, don't you?"

There was little to see inside and too much to smell—sweat, Rot, sewage.

Samuel took Matthias's hand and placed it on a handrail. He let his fingers slide along, his feet slipping on the greasy surface beneath his shoes. More than once, his foot slid into unseen depths. The stink made him gag. He wanted air. The blackness overwhelmed him, closed in around him like a coffin. He backpedaled and headed back out to the opening.

Samuel gripped his hand, the boy puffing in normal, even breaths.

Matthias found a measure of calm in the child's actions and moved further into the tunnel. A black rectangle appeared a few yards away, a door rimmed in fluorescent light.

Samuel rapped on the door. It opened.

Noah stood in the doorway. "Thank you, Samuel. How did Elder Kent do?"

A shrug.

"I'm afraid the boy doesn't think much of your stealth."

Matthias could feel heat pouring through the entrance and stepped inside a bleak concrete room with pipes running to and fro along the ceiling. He warmed his hands on a heating pipe. "Where are we?"

Noah removed his hat, sliding his palm along his hair to smooth it down. "SalVal Franchise 207 - Merion. 238,135 souls saved since our incorporation here fifty years ago. This was a former Baptist church before they abandoned it. At least they refurbished it with girders and plate steel before they moved out. It used to be all wood. I wish you could worship with us in the sanctuary, but I'm going to ask you to remain here."

"As you wish. Do you have anything to eat?" said Matthias, leaning his tired body against the wall.

"Yes, but we're down to one meal a day right now, and we eat at the dinner hour. Preparing a single meal might draw unwanted attention. Samuel will see that you get dry clothes and a washbasin to get cleaned up. I'll be back later with dinner. And then we'll talk about the Bible."

Noah left, leaving Samuel and Matthias in the pallid glow of the lamp.

Samuel yanked on Matthias's tarp.

"Clothes, got it." He pulled the tarp off and tossed it in a corner. A cockroach scuttled across the floor. Matthias stepped on it and looked at Samuel. "See, I am a killer."

A nap followed Matthias's bath and change into clean clothes. His bed, a concrete slab, was even less comfortable than his stay in Glenolden, but he was dry and warm. From time to time footsteps would thump above him, an organ would let loose a peal of low notes and he would hear the vaguest sound of hymn singing, all set to the random clanking of pipes running through his room. The door to the other parts of the church remained locked. He had opened the passageway to the tunnel once. The smell beat him back.

During his waking time, he mulled over ways to get to the Bible and give it away. Let Finney and Blind Johnny do whatever they had in mind with it. Let it be gone.

His knew his home would be closely watched. Not even the boy could sneak in and get it without discovery. Or, more likely, eventual capture and torture. The Order would find him. He would be the next withered man on the Ecunet confessing his sins and begging forgiveness of the Synod. There would be mandatory viewing of his execution by the faithful during prime time Sunday—the Heretic Matthias Kent. It might even preempt football, and that was saying something. His chances were no better than the cockroach he killed earlier in the day. *All because of a relic.*

Someone tapped on the door. The bolt released. Noah stepped inside. Behind him stood some old men, regarding him suspiciously.

Noah lowered a tray onto the slab. "As I promised, soup. I think the cook got hold of some starlings, but don't hold me to that. Please, eat."

The aroma was questionable, but Matthias scooped the broth into his mouth as fast as he could. Four hearty slices of mission bread lay next to the bowl. He forced himself to slow down, dipping the bread and letting it soak up the broth. Matthias spoke to the entourage. "My thanks, gentlemen. What will this meal cost me?"

The murmurs stopped.

Matthias watched Noah's graciousness slide away. "What have you told them, Captain Finney?"

Noah motioned to close the door.

Once it latched, the room became much smaller with six people inside. Matthias nibbled on the bread, watching everyone's eyes. Some were fearful, others wary. Noah's were beaming.

"These are the trustees of our church, Elder Kent. They know your secret. We're wondering if you would answer some questions for us?"

"Is this an inquisition?"

"Hardly. You may leave at any time."

"What do you want to know?"

"Have you seen the Word of God?"

"Yes, I had it, held it, read some of it, and hid it. To my knowledge, it is still hidden. A Contemporary International Version published right before the radiation poisoning of Washington. "

Every gaze locked onto him, their faces transfixed.

"Gentlemen, you look like Christ Himself is coming for a visit. Trust me, the Synod will find it soon and that will be that."

A gray bearded man fell to his knees. "Praise be to God."

Another knelt down next to him. "The miracle is true. Praise God indeed."

Every man in the room cried, all but Matthias. In that moment, he realized the full power of the book in his possession. To believers, it was the Word of God, a miracle manifested on the rarest of substances—paper. The Synod would be unable to deny a certifiable miracle and be doubly unable to contain the controversy its pages would create. No wonder they pursued him with such intensity.

Noah tugged the other men to their feet. "As you can see, we're quite amazed. Having only the Synod Edition and our oral traditions, we're quite interested in obtaining it."

The inflection Noah used when he said "oral traditions" piqued Matthias's suspicions. "You mean that the lessons handed down to you don't match the official version. You need my Bible to back you up."

"We need your Bible to renew faith. It was written for everyone, rich and poor alike, not just the wealthy inside the walled cities across America."

Matthias heard this philosophy before. "We both know that God blesses those that are successful. Besides, the Synod isn't going to be happy with what I found."

"Do you know how silly that sounds? You are cast out here with us, yet you speak like a tool of the government. Are you sinful? Unclean? Worthless? Do you deserve your fate?"

"I was doing my job."

"Your job is why I minister out here. People just like you created the poor and afflicted. Because of you, these beggars feed their addictions rather than their children. What will happen to them when there are no more of your penance credits to buy the things that make them forget what they wake up to every day?"

"Perhaps you can feed them the Bible."

Noah pushed the trustees out of his way. He stared down at Matthias. "Enough of your blasphemy. Tell me, Elder Kent, which one are you?"

"What do you mean?"

"I mean that I don't see an Elder here. I see a terrorist. Is this God's doing? Is He righteous in His holy judgment upon you?"

Matthias became as speechless as Samuel.

Noah frowned and shook his head. "I'm sorry for my outburst, brother. It's just that I've seen the results of the Synod's hold on the Bible. I believe, as do many others out here, that our salvation comes from God, not from those that say they speak for God. And you have proof. The Bible given to you by the Lord will save the souls of millions upon millions in this world and the next." He laid his hands on Matthias's shoulders, his face softening. "God blessed you for some reason with its discovery. He has blessed us with finding you, and that is a miracle all on its own. Don't hide this under a basket."

Matthias gnawed on the bread, trying to dismiss the Captain's words.

Noah looked around at the trustees. Each one nodded their

head. He sat down next to Matthias. "We offer you a bargain. Sanctuary, in exchange for the Bible."

Hair stood up on the back of Matthias's neck. "What are you saying?"

"I'm saying that we will arrange safe passage for you out of the country. When you reach your destination, you will disclose the Bible's location to those that convey you to safety. We will take it from there."

"As simple as that?"

"Yes."

Escape. Five minutes beforehand, there was no hope. Now, however, was another matter. But there was no mention of where he would be going. Canada still extradited criminals back to America. Mexico was a violent wasteland. "Where is this sanctuary?"

"The Hindu Lands."

"The Federation of Free States? Wonderful, I'll be with liberals and secessionists. The Synod will add 'traitor' to my list of titles."

"You'll be alive."

Noah's comment trumped Matthias's protests. He would be gone, away from the fray, and away from the Synod. "Agreed. When do I leave?"

Noah stood and headed for the door. "Tomorrow night."

Chapter 23: Verses 1-42

Alone, Matthias sat against the wall of his room under the SalVal church. Its coldness numbed the reminiscence and the grief that hollowed him. He shook his head, loving the irony.

Every school-age child knew the Federation of so-called Free States by the epithet, *The Hindu Lands*. Matthias remembered outlining the region in second grade, and God forbid if a student couldn't perform the task.

In his mind's eye, he saw the pointer on the computer screen highlighting everything east of the Hudson River, from the no-man's land of New Jersey to where Maine abutted New France in the north. It was a land of pagans, criminals, Devil worshippers, cannibals and unchurched Democrats.

The more he thought about it, the more the deal soured in his mouth. There was no guarantee of what would become of him once he got there. No guarantee that he would even get to where they said they were taking him. The people upstairs might even be conspiring to turn him over to the Synod.

Doubts festered in his mind until he recalled the passion Noah displayed. *He believes*. Matthias saw enough posturing, enough bluster over the years, not to be fooled by liars in official garb. He was one of them after all. He traded in it, used it, built a career on it.

Noah displayed none of those traits. Matthias laughed and looked at the ceiling. "I do believe that You put one honest creature on this Earth after all."

The door flung open and Samuel charged in, his face frowning. He carried another bundle of clothes.

"What's the matter?"

Before Matthias got an answer, the boy pulled him up off his seat.

Noah stepped into the room. "Someone saw us. I've received word that the Order is on its way. We need to move you tonight."

Matthias could feel his heart pound. There were no more choices, no more doubts. "What do I need to do?"

"Change into these vestments. They belong to one of our trustees. Once you're ready, come upstairs and meet me down the road. Samuel will lead you."

Matthias did as commanded, changed, and made his way through the sanctuary. Churchgoers scrambled around the narthex like they were abandoning ship. No one paid him any mind. He walked outside into the evening darkness.

Samuel waited for him near the entrance. The boy waved and Matthias followed. They walked for a time past crumbling walls and desperate people moving away from the church. The walls gave way to muddy tracts and finally, a road. A stink hung in the dampness, the unmistakable odor of decay, death. Matthias halted.

Samuel tugged on his sleeve.

"They're going to kill me."

The boy gave a quick nod and wide grin as if happily acknowledging the statement.

Matthias could feel his body quake. The hour of his death was upon him. The Order probably stood a few yards away waiting for their chance to capture the man that killed no less than four of their number.

Samuel brought his hand to his nose, pinched it, and resumed walking.

Before the boy left his sight, Matthias jogged ahead, not

knowing why his feet carried him with such urgency. He grasped for control of his fears. The smell got worse. He pinched his nose shut like Samuel. No soldiers sprang from the shadows.

A truck idled in the distance, growing louder with each nearing step. Matthias imagined a full squad sitting inside a military truck, each man waiting to avenge their comrades.

Noah appeared. "Your limousine, Elder Kent." The captain led the Matthias and Samuel through the darkness to the vehicle, a tractor-trailer chortling on biodiesel.

The truck's headlights lit a bald man who leaned against a tire. A gas mask rested on top of his head, making him look like some kind of insect. "Let's go. Time's a-wasting."

Matthias looked past the driver to the trailer. He turned toward Noah. "I'm riding with a reaper?"

"Technically, yes."

"Do I at least get to wear a filter mask?"

The driver shouted, "I'm leaving."

Noah glanced at the driver and back to Matthias. He produced a long black plastic bag, its zipper glistening in the headlights.

"Oh, for the love of God, no. I am not riding with these bodies." Everything spun. He rested a hand on Samuel to steady himself.

"It's the only way out. We've used this method many times. The bag is marked with the proper codes for your size and weight. Keep quiet and no one will know. Think of yourself as Lazarus."

The name "Lazarus" cut through Matthias's fears, borne on the memory of Blind Johnny's voice. "You must become Lazarus."

The driver revved the engine.

Noah climbed up the ladder of the trailer. He waved to Matthias.

Samuel pushed his rump.

Noah was nervous. "Perhaps you'd like to be here to greet the Order personally?"

Matthias climbed up the ladder and straddled the trailer wall. He looked down at the stacks of bodies, each layer oriented to show off its identification code for tracking, delivery and burial.

Noah stepped on top of the bodies and spread out the bag. "We've alerted our contact. He'll retrieve you once you've safe.

Now, get in."

The bag lay unzipped, a black maw waiting to consume him. He slid inside. Noah pulled the zipper closed, Matthias caught sight of Samuel standing nearby. The boy nodded with a placid grin, unaffected by the stench. The zipper closed. Darkness.

The truck lurched. Matthias felt bodies shift around him. He sank down. Wrestling against them made him sink deeper. The bodies pinned him in place. He was trapped inside. His breaths went from rasping, to wheezing, and to emptiness before he passed out. As he did, he could have sworn he heard another zipper being pulled.

Exodus

Chapter 24: Verses 1-40

Matthias awoke, his mind adrift. The truck idled, its rhythm out of synch with a random electronic chirp. The bag covering his face prevented him from seeing the noise's source. He tried to push it away but found his limbs pinned under unseen weight. The mental fog cleared in a black, blinding instant.

Bodies.

The beeps grew louder. He froze and took in a breath. Any movement risked exposure. A mélange of putrid odors assaulted his nostrils, and he found himself yearning for the smell of Naomi's bleach-soaked mop. Matthias prayed.

I walk through the valley of the shadow of death. You are with me. I walk through the valley of the shadow of death. You are with me. I walk through the valley of the shadow of death. You are with me.

Two men came near. He concentrated on the ease of their exchange, the occasional laugh.

The beeps grew in intensity and moved in a 1-2-3 beat as if stepping through some monotonous waltz. The sound had the familiarity of machinery, of someone performing a tedious task. The realization sunk in. They were checking identification codes on the bags.

The volume of the beeps peaked, and he imagined the scanner inches from his head. His lungs cried out for air. He fought to remain motionless knowing that a rise and fall of his chest would give him away.

The scanner moved on, never hesitating in its dance with the dead. 1-2-3. 1-2-3. 1-2-3. Matthias allowed himself a shallow breath and another. His lungs filled. Relief.

Murmuring followed the beeps until all that was left was the motor's chugging. A door slammed. The engine roared. The truck pulled away, and Matthias sensed it picking up speed.

The faster it went, the more the stench got carried away on the wind. He considered it no small blessing. Each time the vehicle hit a pothole, he moved his arms until they freed. Bringing a sleeve to his face, Matthias inhaled the stale polyester fibers of the trustee's garments, the smell of soup and coal smoke. The aroma was as much liberating as it was reassuring. He could feel his hands on his face. He was alive.

The dead jostled him at every bump, and Matthias wondered who he bumped against. How many of these poor souls begged cards from him on his trips through the gate? How many died at the hands of troopers? How many died at church? He hoped for one consolation—that Gideon Stanmore's body lay next to his, still wearing those damned boots.

It felt odd to be counted among the dead, weighed and measured like a talent of coal. Along with it came a modest sense of security. No gunfire. No pleading. No screams. They had all gone to meet God. All except him.

Matthias slid his arms under his head and listened to the truck tires howl against the asphalt. It was good to be in an anonymous cocoon, away from the city where most citizens hunted him. He swayed with the trailer, cradled in the arms of the dead, and nodded off.

His eyes snapped open to the same darkness, but it was the absence of sound that made him nervous. The engine was silent. From his body bag he heard the scuff of shoes on pavement and little else. Bags rustled around him, creaking springs, clumsy footsteps, cracking bones.

Something prodded his bag, a hand, or a stick, or the toe of a boot. Matthias kept quiet and rigid. The prodding stopped. The object withdrew. He allowed himself half a breath.

The zipper pealed away. A rough paw of a hand yanked Matthias from his shroud and into the dank night air. As soon as he caught his breath, he got a look at the immense man who exhumed him.

Black armor.

Shiny boots.

The Order of St. George.

Disorientation fled behind a gush of horror. He had been given up for the reward. They would take him, rend his mind apart, and kill whatever still functioned after their tortures. He swung. His fist slammed into the soldier's face.

The hand released.

Matthias scrambled across the macabre landscape, the dead buckling under his weight.

The trooper took hold of him again. "You're safe, Lazarus. Captain Finney sent me."

Matthias spun around, looking at the only bit of humanity jutting out of the helmet, clean-shaven, chiseled, scarred. His heart pounded all the more, and he fought to free himself.

The trooper dropped him onto the body bags. "Have it your way. Walk to the Hindu Lands."

Finney? The name broke through the panic. "Sal Val?"

"No, Elder Kent. I am Jeremiah Sanford, Sergeant Major of the Order of Saint George, retired, and here to raise you from the dead."

"You're of the Order?"

"Was. You have nothing to fear."

The driver shouted, "You going to give me a hand?"

Matthias glimpsed over the side of the trailer. The driver looked back at him, a limp and naked body draped over his shoulder. "My God."

Jeremiah pushed him aside. "Excuse me, Elder Kent," and leaned over. He hefted the body and slid it into the body bag that Matthias occupied.

The driver called out again. "Here's the other one."

The sergeant tugged the second body over the rim and plopped it next to the first. It was small, a child.

Matthias looked on, amazed and unsettled at the same time. "Two?"

Jeremiah zipped Matthias's body bag closed and unzipped another. Samuel appeared, his fingers pinching his nose.

"What's the boy doing here?"

Jeremiah rolled the second body into the bag as soon as the boy crawled out. "Captain Finney said that he will be your messenger when we get to the Hindu Lands. He said you'd understand."

Matthias considered Finney's choice for a moment and understood. A mute child would be a perfect vessel for secrets.

"Pick up the other end." The sergeant zipped the bag closed and lifted.

Matthias grabbed it without thinking. Together they tossed the body further into the load. He stared at it as it landed, just another sack of flesh and bone.

Jeremiah brushed off his hands. "The Synod's bookkeepers are sticklers about this kind of thing. They weigh every body when it leaves Philadelphia and when it arrives in Palmerton. Any big discrepancy is noted, and the driver down there will get a bad review." Jeremiah leaned back over the trailer. "Isn't that right?"

Matthias bent over. He caught sight of the driver sliding his finger across his neck, tilting his head to the side and sticking his tongue out.

The sergeant lowered Samuel to the driver and motioned to Matthias. "Come on, now. Let's get out of here before a patrol sees us and starts asking questions."

Chapter 25: Verses 1-133

The trio left the road and walked a short distance to a weedy tract. Jeremiah stopped, gave a look around, and started pulling on some shrubbery. A squat military vehicle appeared in the vegetation. "It's no limousine, Elder Kent, but it's got an honest fuel."

Matthias didn't understand.

"Hydrogen, not biodiesel."

Samuel nodded and smiled.

The sergeant pointed to seats in the front and back. "Don't be too impressed, boy. Damned thing uses solar to make the gas. The rocket scientist that invented this thing didn't take all the cloud cover from the global warming into account. Takes weeks to fill." His gaze fell on Matthias. "I just hope you're worth it."

Matthias rode in the front seat, a cold breeze slapping him in the face and his mind awash in questions—the greatest of which was whether to trust the trooper beside him. "How do you know Captain Finney?"

Jeremiah chuckled. "Suspicious, eh? No wonder you're still alive. How I know him is my own business." He spun the wheel to avoid unseen obstacles in the darkness. "You needn't worry, Elder

Kent. Noah told me about the Bible. Is it true?"

"Yes."

"Noah made me swear to get you to the Hindu Lands. Made me swear on my life." The sergeant blinked away the emotion welling up inside him.

The unexpected crack in the sergeant's façade made Matthias look away. *There can be no demonstration of weakness.* A crescent moon winked at him from a break in the clouds.

The sergeant hacked and blew his nose.

It reminded Matthias of another time. He looked at the moon, just as he did when he was a child. He could hear his father's wet coughs, see the worry lines on his mother's face grow as distinct as a newly plowed field.

A sudden lunge of the transport brought Matthias back to the present.

The sergeant's eyes never left the road. Samuel lay against the rear seat, his sleep unfazed by the vehicle's jostling. Locks of the boy's hair moved in the breeze. Dry, clean hair, not like the sodden child he gave a penance card to just a few days ago.

He dwelled on Samuel's mother, her eyes as gray as the moon. Not like his mother's eyes. They were clear right up until the day she died.

A wave of grief engulfed Matthias. He fought it back down inside. *There can be no demonstration of weakness.* The grief abated. He looked back at Samuel again, thinking of the coincidence that brought them together at the gate. For a moment, it all seemed too convenient, almost providential, a minor miracle. A phrase from Matthew's gospel sprang forward in a sing-song chorus. *Let the children come to me.*

Matthias laughed. *If those words were even in the Bible.*

"We're here," said the sergeant.

"Where is 'here'?" said Matthias.

"My graveyard." The sergeant reached for a switch. Headlights bathed the night in a blue glow. A great iron gate hung between brick columns parted for the rover. "I am the caretaker of this place, Elder. While we pass I expect respect, not for me, but for the dead."

An infinity of neat white crosses stretched out into the

darkness. Matthias understood. "A military cemetery."

"Fort Indiantown Gap National Cemetery, to answer your question. Around us lie my brothers." The sergeant slowed the vehicle near a particular set of crosses that bore the Order's insignia.

The dates embossed on them marked a time from twenty years ago. Matthias sensed the change in the soldier, his loss, his reverence. There was more than one grieving person in the vehicle. "May they rest in honorable service to our Lord as I'm sure they did on Earth."

Jeremiah jammed on the brakes, his eyes smoldering. "Honorable service on Earth? There is no such thing." The sergeant snapped his head back, growled, and punched the accelerator.

Gravel sprang off the tires.

Jeremiah lifted his chin and shook his head as if trying to shake off an offending insect.

Silence resumed until a Quonset hut appeared at the bottom of a shallow hill just past the cemetery.

"Stay in the vehicle until we're inside," said Jeremiah. He stopped the transport, keeping the headlights trained on a garage door, and got out.

Samuel woke up.

The sergeant walked to the door, a pair of giant shadows from the headlights walking with him. "Keep in mind that we have no titles here, no last names. First names only. It's safest that way."

"We?"

"There are others who seek escape from the Synod. They are brought here until transport to the Hindu Lands can be arranged. From now on, you will travel as a part of a group. And, for the love of God, don't tell anyone that you're an Elder."

"Was."

"Most of these folks have been out of touch with the news for weeks. They won't know about you. But if they do find out, some of them may want to buy their way back into the city if they get the chance."

Matthias thought about the Synod's penchant for surveillance. Yet, the sergeant seemed quite confident of their ignorance. "Can you be so sure?"

"We're entirely off line from the Ecunet and are in full accord with the Greenbriar Protocol. Our isolation makes us safe."

Greenbriar. It was funny to hear that anyone still followed the old wartime protocols. Only an old soldier would do such a thing. Matthias mused over the paradox—the Treaty of Rome forbade wars, yet the Synod still maintained wartime shelters throughout the country for government and business leaders. The even bigger paradox was the dutiful sergeant standing before him who smuggled human beings for a living. Grief. Smuggling. Duty. Honor. It just didn't add up.

Jeremiah pulled a brass key from his pocket. "Most everything here is pretty ancient—the vehicle, the solar arrays, and even the locks." He slipped the key into the lock. It moved easily. "Two hundred years old, and it still works. They knew how to build things back then." He put the key away.

"Aren't there ever any patrols?"

"Not even the Order comes here anymore."

Matthias felt the intensity of the soldier's contempt from ten feet away. "Really?"

"I am the commander of a deserted outpost that no one comes to inspect, and the caretaker of a cemetery where no one mourns. Only that fat-assed District Superintendent ever comes around."

The sneer painted across the soldier's lips told Matthias how much scorn Jeremiah bore. "Will he be stopping by any time soon?"

"No, he was here last week. I won't see him for a month, may he rot in Hell." With one hand, the sergeant lifted the door. "You'll be long gone by then."

A group of people stood just outside the headlights as if the light would dissolve them. Matthias counted six.

The sergeant hopped back into the transport and pulled it into the garage bay. Everyone blanched from the headlights.

Jeremiah switched off the transport, walked over to garage door and gave it a yank. It clattered down. Fluorescent lights came on.

Matthias hopped out with Samuel following close behind.

Questions peppered the sergeant as soon as the door latched.

"Did you bring food?"

"What's going on in the city?"

"Was there any formula this time?"

Matthias focused on the last question. It belonged to young dark-haired woman. The robe she wore consumed her scrawny frame. A baby rested in the comfort of an olive drab blanket cradled in her arms.

Jeremiah cut in between Matthias and the woman. He handed her an unmarked container while nudging Matthias. "Yes, Johanna. I couldn't get very much. You have to make it last."

Johanna peeled the blanket away from the infant's face. "We have your formula, Joshie."

Matthias recoiled. The face of a doll peered back, its cheeks rosy and blue glass eyes fixed at the ceiling. "It's a—"

Jeremiah's grip made a tourniquet around Matthias's upper arm. He spoke his words like he was hammering nails. "Josh is the best baby in the world, don't you think so, Matthias?"

The pressure jolted Matthias enough to halt his sentence. The grip relaxed. The sergeant stared at him. The woman held a pleasant smile and an expectation of praise for the child.

Her quivering iris's told Matthias how closely she danced with madness. "A fine name for a fine boy. May he grow strong and tall."

"Yes, indeed." Jeremiah moved behind the transport and opened the tailgate. "Give me a hand, you all."

Matthias watched the group hurry to the back of the vehicle. Their faces glanced his way like frightened mice—the way his face must look to them.

Another dark-haired woman approached him. She was older and fuller-figured but carried a resemblance to the woman with the baby. "Thank you for playing along. My sister fights the demons of her past. I'm Elizabeth, but everybody calls me Beth."

"Matthias."

The sergeant marched by with two sacks draped over his shoulders. He gestured toward the boy. "This is Matthias's son, Samuel. Can't speak a lick, but he can hear well enough. Girls?"

Two girls, with straight blond hair and bright eyes, bounded up to the soldier and saluted. "Yes, Sergeant Major?"

Matthias watched Jeremiah's harsh face round into softness.

"Ten hut!"

The girls stiffened and giggled.

"You will convey Private Samuel to the barracks. Draw stores for his bedding and personal hygiene. You are to have him turned out and ready for inspection before morning mess."

The girls nodded.

"Dismissed."

The pair bounded over to Samuel, took him by the hand and led him off. The boy turned toward Matthias, his face a portrait of desperation. It was the first time since they traveled together that the child looked unnerved. All it took were two girls.

"My son thanks you." He had a son. The evening was full of surprises—surprises like the vestments the girls wore. They were made of fine polyester, finished to look like silk. Expert hands crafted the tailoring. It spoke of upper middle class, perhaps a minor executive. Would they know him?

"Hi, I'm Tim, Timothy Kosloski," said a brown-haired man who held out a quaking hand.

Matthias noted the man's receding hair and chin and smelled the man's fear when he blurted out his last name. His eyes dodged any kind of direct contact. The clothes he wore reflected the quality of the children's vestments. He must be the father. "Matthias. Your daughters?"

Tim's face brightened, but his demeanor remained unsettled. "Um, yes, my two little jewels—Susanna and Ruth. This is my wife, Mary."

Matthias shook the woman's hand. It was cold. He noted the way her eyes never left the floor. Concealing some shame, he figured. This couple had demons as well. They all had them, just like him. No stones to cast among this lot.

Cradling her hand in both of his, Matthias gave her a quick assessment. She carried none of the usual surgical alterations the well-monied wives of the Elders underwent to make themselves more appealing. Mary was the picture of a middle-class housewife. What made them flee their comfortable life?

Her frown never lifted. "Blessings, Matthias."

Matthias dipped his head and met her gaze. "And to you."

Her eyes narrowed, and the briefest of smiles appeared.

The sergeant returned empty handed. "Come on, Matthias. Everybody pitches in."

The sack held fifty pounds of rice. Matthias shouldered the bag, its bulk uncomfortable but manageable.

Jeremiah bore a pair of sacks branded *sweet potato flakes* on each shoulder. "Follow me."

They passed through a room lined with metal bunks, mattresses neatly dressed with sheets and blankets. The floor glistened under a coat of wax. Matthias wiped a bead of sweat away. "Ready for inspection, I see."

Jeremiah said, "The barracks maintain a state of one-hundred percent readiness to accept the Order. Ha. Until they return, my guests make use of it. Some of the group have become quite proficient in maintaining their rack. Have you ever made a bed?"

"Yes."

The sergeant looked back at him. "Without your servant's help?"

Matthias hesitated.

"I'll send the girls over to show you the proper procedure."

"My thanks."

Jeremiah headed for a door on the other side of the room. "You'd best get used to it. There are no servants here, or in the Hindu Lands. Everyone is expected to carry their own weight."

The door burst open to the smell of bleach and detergent. His mind flashed to Naomi, and her visage stung at his heart.

"Our laundry," said Jeremiah. "Matthias, meet Theresa and Thaddeus."

"Blessings," called out the couple who stirred clothes in a large vat.

"Blessings to you," replied Matthias. The name 'Theresa' hung with him. It wasn't on the approved list of biblically authorized names.

The sergeant spun around, his brow pulled tight and his tone low. "Closet Catholics. She insists on the name Theresa now that they've outed themselves. Thaddeus is a good guy, but she's headstrong. I worry about her the most."

"Why is that?"

"Won't hold her tongue. Totally outside the Book of Ruth, you know what I mean? Whatever you do, don't bring up the Virgin Mary, or they'll be doing that rosary thing all night long."

Matthias nodded. *I'm hiding with fugitives.* He heard his uncle's laugh the whole way from Philadelphia.

Jeremiah led the way through yet another pair of doors. The odors of the laundry yielded to the aroma of food cooking. He leaned his sacks against a wall. "Put that one over here."

It felt good to rid himself of the burden. Matthias noticed the way Jeremiah gauged his actions. "Did I pass muster?"

"You're stronger than I thought you were. You Elders are usually inadequate."

"You mean 'useless.' In my younger days, I passed all the physical exams to join the Order. Was something of a marksman, too."

"So, why didn't you join?"

A picture of Stanmore loomed in his mind. "I have problems with authority, or so I've been told."

"Me, too," said the sergeant. He pointed toward two men laboring over the cookstove. "Gentlemen, meet Matthias. He'll be joining us."

A trim older man stepped out from around a huge kettle, his bald head sweating from the heat of the pot. "Another sojourner, eh? I'm Nathan." He nodded but didn't offer a hand. "Sorry, the sergeant says that cleanliness is next to Godliness."

A much younger man never left the kettle. He glanced up revealing a sullen face with a fresh red scar on his right cheek, and chopped some kind of plant stalk.

Nathan said, "This is Luke. Doesn't say much, but is a whiz in the mess hall. He found rhubarb growing out along the tree line. Rhubarb! That would have cost a fortune back in the city. It's going to liven up this porridge a good bit, how 'bout Luke?"

Jeremiah said, "Luke told us he was something of an amateur chef back in Philadelphia. Circumstances brought him here to us, and we are blessed by his talent. Which brings me to your duties. Can you cook?"

"Not particularly."

"Iron clothes? Mend?"

"No."

"Do you know any mechanical trades?"

Matthias looked up at the sergeant. "I guess I am useless."

Jeremiah crossed his arms. "I see. Only one real skill."

The insinuation made Matthias wonder what the soldier meant.

The sergeant continued, "You will help Timothy wash the dishes after each mess call and clean the latrines at oh-nine-hundred every day."

Protest boiled up in Matthias but cooled quickly. Anything would be better than lying with the dead. "As you command, Sergeant."

Jeremiah looked at his watch. "Good then. Go wash up. Breakfast is in twenty-three minutes."

Chapter 26: Verses 1-60

Matthias basked in the hot shower. The water tasted of chlorine. It rinsed away the muck of his escape, the stench of the dead. But the Rot was stubborn. Flecks of black dotted his skin. Matthias stared at it with equal parts revulsion and fascination. It never wasted any time adhering to flesh, assaulting it, consuming it one organic molecule at a time.

He scrubbed, looked, and scrubbed again. The flecks disappeared in the steaming water. The moisture amplified the smell of disinfectant. Under such surroundings, the Rot would be kept at bay—for now. It was good to be clean. Good to be safe.

As the mold left his skin, he hoped his trail to this haven had been washed as clean. Matthias imagined the parishioners at the SalVal being questioned. All it took was one person to say the wrong thing. His stomach tightened.

After the shower, he found his stained and reeking vestments replaced with clothes wrapped in thick cellophane. The outfit consisted of a dark green shirt and trousers, cadet fatigues about two sizes too big and a pair of dry socks. *Praise the Lord*. It all reeked of mothballs. At least the boots he tried on were a decent fit.

When he saw himself in the mirror, he laughed. Everything about him was disheveled, from his ill-fitting clothes to his helter-skelter hair. A fine cadet he made. Gideon Stanmore would have shot him on the spot for making the uniform look so bad. He cinched up the belt as best he could and combed his hair.

Bugles blared over the loudspeaker. A hint of sweet potato porridge found its way to his nostrils. Time for morning mess. He gave his reflection a salute.

A line formed at the end of the mess hall's serving area. Matthias stepped to the end. Samuel reappeared, hand in hand with the girls, his face showing none of the earlier reluctance. It didn't take long for the beggar to become a child at play.

He patted the boy on the shoulders. His hair was wet, like the first day they met. "Having fun?"

The child turned and gave him a broad smile.

Matthias watched the others to learn the routine. They formed a straight line, each picking up a stamped metal tray, napkin, and utensils. Each took their turn presenting their tray to Luke who dumped a slurry of sweet potato porridge into its deepest indentation. Nathan plunked a piece of mission bread next to it. Very military, very precise.

A line of cups beyond Nathan awaited pickup. Matthias counted them—fourteen. He counted the people around him. Twelve. The sergeant made it thirteen. One cup too many. *Who else was here?*

Luke said, "May I have your tray?"

"Oh, sorry," replied Matthias.

Matthias followed Samuel to a pair of seats. He glanced around. No one touched their food. All eyes focused on a door at the other end of the hall.

When the second hand on an old institutional clock reached precisely 6:05 AM, the sergeant entered, got his food and brought it to the table. "Almighty Father."

Everyone bowed. Matthias and Samuel followed suit.

Jeremiah continued, his arms raised and eyes closed. "Instead of their humiliation, my people will receive twice the share, and instead of disgrace they will have joy in their freedom. And so they will inherit double the land, and eternal joy will be theirs. For

You, the Lord, hates evil and loves justice."

Matthias couldn't resist the urge to watch people's faces when they prayed. He did it every Sunday for a decade. Most wore a mantle of piety—all except for Timothy who buried his face in his hands. *Humiliation*, thought Matthias, lowering his head.

The sergeant's words grew louder. "In my faithfulness I will reward them and make an unbreakable contract with them."

"Amen," replied the group.

The rustle of clothes and the clanking of utensils signaled the all-clear. Matthias grabbed his spoon and saw Thaddeus making the sign of the cross. To think that he, Matthias Kent, Elder of the Bank of Job, was labeled a heretic.

But the man's actions calmed Matthias's nervous stomach. It had to be completely safe here. Back in the city, just the rumor of doing such a thing would get a person reformed. Afterward, they were little more than automatons barely able to hold umbrellas over the Elders.

Samuel held onto his spoon with his fist and stoked his mouth full.

Matthias ate the porridge. It tasted good, very good, as a matter of fact. He took another bite and felt the weight of someone watching him—Luke. Matthias nodded. For a moment, the cook's face broke into a thin smile then returned to quiet disdain.

Murmurs rose and fell at the table, none of them leaving the family or friend that started them. It was odd not to make small talk. To Matthias it was almost painful to be silent. He looked down the table at the sergeant. "Was that Psalm 80 you prayed from, brother?"

The sergeant's head swiveled like a gun turret locking onto its target. "85. You didn't like my choice?"

"My mistake. It was fine. Good word. Good word indeed. I'm just surprised you didn't pick Numbers for today."

"Numbers? Why? Which chapter would you recommend?"

"Why, fourteen."

"That's not what I had in mind for today." Jeremiah's eyes narrowed, glanced at the remaining cup, and then fell back on Matthias. "You're spoiling my surprise, brother."

"Oh?"

The soldier stood. "Brothers and sisters, today we have a guest among us. I know some of you have been waiting weeks for deliverance. Your prayers are answered. A representative just arrived with news. Let us prepare a place for him among us."

Cheers went up from the group.

Jeremiah took his cup and raised it to the group. "To God be the glory."

"To God be the glory."

A man appeared at the entrance, thick plastic military-issue glasses perched atop a narrow nose and a neck bordered by a black ministerial collar. A patch on his lapel bore the maroon "S" of the Salvation Army.

He made his way across the floor to the table. "Blessings, brother and sisters. I'm Lieutenant Schooley, and I bring news from Captain Finney."

Matthias regarded the man and the way he addressed each and every one in the room. It wasn't simply good public speaking. He searched for someone. When the lieutenant's eyes fell upon him, Matthias saw them flicker and heard the man's voice change timbre for a fraction of a second.

"The Order is greatly distracted by riots in the capital. We've chosen to begin your journey to the Federation tomorrow."

A collective gasp rose.

Matthias wondered if he had to clean the latrines now. He could feel a smile filling his cheeks until he looked down the table at Jeremiah. The sergeant wore a broad smile, but his eyes portrayed stony coldness. Matthias felt queasiness return to his gut and a quickening in his heart.

Schooley served himself and sat down. "I see we have twelve this time, like the apostles. A fortuitous number to be sure."

"Indeed," said Jeremiah. "Lieutenant, we should give thanks."

Schooley bowed his head and cleared his throat. "Heavenly Father, we thank You for Your unending grace as we take our next step toward freedom. In Your name we pray."

"Amen," replied the group.

"Amen," said the sergeant, a little louder than the rest. He crossed behind Schooley and patted him on the shoulder. In a fluid movement, the sergeant grabbed the lieutenant by the chin and twisted his head.

Schooley made no sound, his body falling toward the table and hand still clenching a napkin.

Porridge dripped from one of the girls' spoons. Johanna whimpered. Matthias could feel air filling his gaping mouth. The silence burst into chaos worthy of Genesis.

"My God," said Mary, scrambling to cover her children's eyes.

"What in the name of God are you doing?" said Nathan.

Theresa kissed her rosary.

"Shut up," commanded the sergeant in a voice that set the girls to cowering. "This man wasn't from our friends in the Salvation Army. He is probably with the Order of Saint George. We don't have much time. Whoever sent him will be expecting him back."

"How can you tell?" demanded Luke.

"He gave the wrong countersign," said Jeremiah.

"My God. We're going to be executed," said Timothy.

A glance at Jeremiah's eyes told Matthias that the soldier had no doubt in his actions.

The sergeant beckoned to him. "Give me a hand. We need to take this worthless piece of shit off of holy ground."

"Yes, sir." Matthias hurried over amidst the still gasping onlookers. He tried not to look at the man's body, his still open eyes. Bodies in a bag were easier to ignore. Instead, he looked down at his own hand wrapping around the corpse's leg. Matthias spotted a black dot under his fingernail. It proved more disconcerting than the warmth of the body in his grasp. A fleck of Rot lurked under his thumbnail, clinging, fighting to stay on its host.

It was then he realized how just how much like the Rot the Order was. They would never give up. It wasn't in their nature.

Chapter 27: Verses 1-77

They made their way across a field. Matthias wobbled along behind the sergeant, carrying Lieutenant Schooley by the legs. "How did you know?"

Jeremiah walked backward, hands underneath Schooley's shoulders, and no effort displayed on his face. "He used last names and said the wrong prayer."

"This is why I didn't join the Order. Your punishments are way too severe."

The sergeant halted. "This is no time for jokes, Matthias. We've been compromised. The contact was to recite Psalm 58 as his prayer with us."

He caught the significance. "85 and 58. Sign and countersign, eh? Clever. Do you think we have a traitor among us?"

"No. Look at his uniform."

Matthias studied the coat. It looked like a standard issue SalVal frock. "I don't see anything special."

"On the lapels. See the 'S'?"

"So?"

"It's a captain's insignia, not a lieutenant's. See the shamrock next to the 'S'?"

Jeremiah's words stabbed at Matthias. "Do you think it belonged to Captain Finney?"

"Yes." Jeremiah dropped his end of the body and kicked it.

Matthias let go and thought of Noah's kindness, the way people respected him, followed him. He remembered the man's look of absolute wonder when he told him about the Bible. He should have told the captain where it was so he could die a happy man under the Order's interrogation.

"Let's go," said Jeremiah, his face red with rage.

Matthias grabbed the dead man by the legs, grunting at the burden. "What's the plan now?"

"I'm surprised you're not throwing up. You Elders usually have neither strong backs nor strong stomachs."

"Compared to what I smelled yesterday, this is nothing." Matthias stopped. "Should I take that as a compliment?"

"Yes." The sergeant gave him a grudging smile. "Whatever plan we had went up in smoke the minute this imposter came in the door. You were supposed to have transportation north."

"Now what?"

Jeremiah started walking and didn't answer.

They came to an embankment. All manner of rusting equipment occupied a shallow ravine. Garbage filled the spaces around the hulks. Rats scurried away at the sight of human beings. Jeremiah swung Schooley and counted to three. Matthias tossed the man in time with the sergeant. The body rolled against the husk of some long defunct armored vehicle.

Jeremiah lowered his head and clasped his hands in prayer. "May he rot in Hell."

"Best prayer I've heard in a while. You didn't answer my question."

"I don't have an answer, only an idea."

"Considering my options, I'm willing to try pretty much anything that doesn't involve me ending up like him."

"I'll send the rest of the group in different directions to confuse anyone trying to track you. Take the boy and head north." Jeremiah pointed to a barely visible path slithering up the side of a mountain. "There."

"I'm walking to the Hindu Lands?'

"You only have to walk as far as the town of Palmerton. You and the boy can cover the terrain in seven or eight days. It's easy. I've used it myself many times."

Matthias looked at the mountain studded with leafless trees. "Where in Hell's hot fire is Palmerton? Are you insane? What about food? Water? The Rot?"

The sergeant squinted into the gray sky. A large black bird appeared and then another. "There are worse things to worry about."

"What are those?" More birds appeared. Matthias marveled at their size. The starlings in the capitol were miniscule in comparison.

"Buzzards. Hurry, or we'll wish we were as dead as your friend down there."

They moved away quickly but didn't go back to the barracks. Instead, the sergeant led him to a large metal door set in a hillside. Matthias glanced back at the embankment where Schooley lie, a black-winged cloud blotting out the horizon.

Jeremiah slid a cover aside on the door, revealing a keypad and a narrow slot. He punched in some digits and turned to Matthias. "Do you have an Elder card?"

"What do you need it for?"

"Greenbriar."

The word keyed a memory, an insignificant bit of text on an insignificant document he read on the Ecunet the day Vanderhaggen gave him his card. Matthias concentrated on the memory. A full screen dealt with the Greenbriar Protocol, but it was so incomprehensibly boring that he scrolled right on by.

Matthias blinked away the recollection and palmed at his right pocket, then at his left. A hot rush ran up his spine. "My wallet."

"What's wrong?"

"I left it in my old clothes. Somebody took them away."

"Wonderful," said the sergeant.

Samuel came at a gallop, his face stricken by the sight of the birds.

"What are you doing here?" said Matthias. "Get back inside."

"We should all go back to the mess hall," said the sergeant.

Samuel reached into his back pocket and pulled out Matthias's wallet.

"Did you take it?" said Matthias.

The boy's shook his head no, making a motion as if picking something up off the ground.

"You found it."

Samuel nodded.

"My thanks to you again." Matthias pulled out the card.

Jeremiah took it from him and inserted it into the slot. "To answer your question, we're requisitioning supplies."

"Won't this give my identity away?"

The door whirred, thunked, and hissed. The soldier pulled on a handle. "Does that matter now?"

They stepped inside a pristine white room. To Matthias, it carried the look and feel of his family's bunker.

Jeremiah pulled the door shut, and the lights winked on. He opened an interior door.

Racks of automatic weapons created a kind of hallway. Bunks stood behind them, rank upon rank well into the darkness.

"There's enough space in here for a company of troops," said Jeremiah.

"Somebody had to keep the citizens out while we leaders waited out Armageddon," said Matthias. "God, how naïve we were."

"Indeed," said Jeremiah. "You're looking for the galley and lockers marked with the letters 'I-R-D-R'. Inside the lockers are irradiated food packs. Sing out when you find them."

Samuel and Matthias walked deeper into the vast bunker. The room smelled of stale air and lubricating oil. Fluorescent lights winked and buzzed all around them.

Samuel tugged on his arm. A sign on a door proclaimed "Galley" and they went in.

The room was a tribute to stainless steel. Sinks, gigantic mixers, and appliances of all kinds filled the space like the skeletons of dinosaurs in a museum. Matthias wondered how much the salvage value for just this room alone would be worth.

He got another tug on the sleeve. Samuel pointed at the lockers.

"Found 'em," yelled Matthias.

Jeremiah appeared at the galley entrance carrying two camouflaged backpacks and some clothes. "These are yours. The packs have a sleeping bag, shelter and water purification tablets. Throw as much food as you can carry in there. The coats will keep you warm but I don't know how they'll do in the rain. Now, don't screw around. The Order could be out front by now."

Matthias regarded the sergeant's new uniform. He didn't wear a backpack, only a large, bulky vest. On top of the vest was a harness with rectangular pouches attached to it. Holsters sat on his right and left hip. He knew what they carried. "Planning a little target practice, Sergeant?"

"I will treat my brethren to a worthy adversary. You'll have as much time to get away as I can give you." He patted one of the pistols.

The look on the soldier's face told Matthias that there would be no bargaining at this point. "Have it your way."

They made their way to the door, weighed down by the packs. Samuel looked as if a soldier of the Order had been shrunk to half his size.

Jeremiah grabbed two rifles, slung one over a shoulder and carried another one in his hands. "Wait here while I check things out."

"You don't have to do this."

Jeremiah said, "You saw the shamrock. Noah wanted me to do this. Now remember, head north. Stay on the trail and don't come down the mountain until you reach the biodiesel plant at Palmerton. You can't miss it. Just follow your nose. Stinks every bit as bad as that truck you rode up on. Ask around for a man named Felix. He'll help you." Jeremiah flicked the safety off on the rifle. "When you meet him, recite the first verse of Psalm 86. You know it?"

Matthias groped for the words. "Something about being needy. Yeah. Hear oh Lord for I am poor and needy."

"Good," replied the sergeant while he grabbed the door handle and gave it a twist. "Now, shhh."

A crease of light sliced into the room. Jeremiah stepped outside.

Matthias and Samuel huddled by the door, waiting for the sergeant's all-clear. The boy kept his hands on the door handle. Matthias understood. The child would shove it closed at the first sign of trouble. They could end their days eating rations and sleeping in all the bunks, safe until madness overtook them. Matthias figured he would last about a week.

Footsteps neared the door. Matthias listened for Jeremiah to beckon or for the sound of gunfire. Instead he heard a single word.

"Shit."

Chapter 28: Verses 1-37

"It's clear," yelled the sergeant. "More or less."

Matthias shielded Samuel and peered out from the door. Ten people stood in a semi-circle around the soldier. It was the rest of the cadre.

Nathan stepped forward. "Just where are you three going?"

Luke moved alongside Nathan. "I told you. He's going to double-cross us. Kill us for our money and feed us to the buzzards like that Sal Val man."

"I will do no such thing," said the sergeant. "There are supplies inside the bunker. Gather what you can and run."

"Run?" said Luke. "Run where?"

"Anywhere you can. Stay off the roads," replied the sergeant.

The fact that Jeremiah didn't tell anyone else about the trail told Matthias to keep his mouth shut.

Nathan said, "Which way are you going, sergeant?"

"To my grave. I will buy you time. For the love of God, grab what you can and get going."

Matthias saw Nathan studying him. He already knew the man's next question.

"Which way are they headed?" asked Nathan.

The sergeant said. "They are headed north. It's better if you all split up."

Nathan pointed at Matthias and Samuel. "It's better for them, you mean."

"Sergeant," said Matthias. "There is another way."

"No. No, there isn't."

"If I can be Lazarus, you surely can be Moses."

"What?"

"Lead us through the wilderness to the Promised Land."

The sergeant's head swung between Matthias and the group. "I told you not to make jokes. Fleeing together will just hasten the hour of your death. The Order will gut us all by nightfall. Better to stay and fight it out."

Matthias sensed that the sergeant wanted one last confrontation, but now was not the time. Everyone's chances were better with Jeremiah than without. But how to convince him? Matthias looked around and saw the little girls hugging their mother. "Will these children make it to the Hindu Lands without you?" He gestured toward the graveyard. "Would your fallen comrades welcome a brother who fell to an empty cause?"

The last comment brought a sneer to Jeremiah's lips. "It would be something we all had in common. Go."

Playing one more card, Matthias said, "Would Noah have abandoned these people in their most dire hour?"

Jeremiah mulled the words, pursed his lips, and let out a great heaving breath. "It is a fool's mission."

"No. We would be fools not to try," said Matthias. "We are at your command, sergeant. What are your orders?"

Ruth and Susanna came to attention and saluted.

Jeremiah looked down at the little girls, and his face softened. "Gather equipment and food. Samuel, show them where everything is. Bring as much food as you can carry."

As the group moved inside, the sergeant spoke to Matthias. "Even Noah would know this is suicidal."

"No more than facing the Order alone like you intend. Did you see their faces? You have given them hope."

"False hope."

Matthias glanced back at the door and the rocky outcropping

that surrounded it. A spine of granite ran all the way to a creek, and the creek led to the trail the sergeant showed him. He turned back around, spying footprints in the mud and trampled grass. "Perhaps not. It's perfect."

"What is?"

"Does the Order have access to the bunker?

"No, only Synod representatives and Elders."

"God is infinitely merciful. When the group comes out, get everybody up on the rocks. Have them follow the boulders down to the stream."

Jeremiah surveyed the terrain. "The Order won't see our tracks and think we're inside." He laughed. "You should have been a solider."

"No, my dear Moses, I am who I am. Only an advertising man could sell them on the wrong idea. I can only hope this will confound them long enough for us to get away."

Chapter 29: Verses 1-71

Their journey began in silence, as if the Order could hear their steps, a splash of water, or the sniffles of the girls.

Before long, the pack on Matthias's back chafed, weighed down by equal parts food and desperation. *I am an Israelite fleeing from Pharaoh's army.*

Weeds gave way to shrubs and shrubs to thickets of stinking ailanthus trees. Matthias hesitated before plunging through the spindly branches. He looked down at the valley. Gray rectangles of fallow ground reminded him of his estate. A damp breeze blew along the mountainside, and a wave of regret came with it. Matthias tried to push it aside, pretend it wasn't there. More than ever, there could be no weakness demonstrated out here. It would be fatal. He tugged at the pack straps and plunged ahead.

When the ailanthus thinned out, he found his breath stolen by the sound of leaves underfoot. Rank on rank of stunted timber stood before him, each trunk wearing a mantle of Rot where the rain didn't wash it off.

The rustling halted when Jeremiah stopped the column and dropped to one knee. "Let us pray." His hand never left his rifle. "Keep us, oh Lord, from the hands of the evildoers. Protect us from evil men. They have set traps for us along our way. Hear, oh Lord, our cry for mercy. Amen."

A group "Amen" dissolved quietly into the air.

Everyone stood and shouldered their packs. Everyone except the sergeant.

Jeremiah stayed on his knee, his eyes narrowing and head swiveling. "Shhh. Listen."

Timothy spoke first. "What do you hear?"

"I hear you talking. Now, shhh," commanded the sergeant.

Matthias felt the way Timothy sounded. *What does he hear?* At first, the only sounds he heard were his beating heart and a chorus of breaths.

Theresa turned ashen, her mouth fixed in an "O."

It began as a kind of howl, not that of an animal but of the constant pitch of something mechanical. The noise grew louder, more rumbling. Matthias recognized the sound and the dread that accompanied it. Tires on a highway. Trucks.

Jeremiah stood up. "They're here. Let's move out."

At lunch, only Jeremiah and Samuel ate. Matthias tried one of his rations. The bitter herbs of the fleeing Israelites would have tasted better. He pushed it away and found the others as disinterested in the food as he. The look in their faces told him what he already knew. Everyone's stomach was sour on a diet of fear, and that fear took hold of him.

Matthias's thoughts closed around him like the shroud Noah Finney zipped him into to escape the city. Behind him was the Order. Around him, the very air was laden with Rot. Ahead of him lay uncertainty. He couldn't move, couldn't breathe.

"Matthias? Matthias," said Jeremiah.

Matthias heard the sergeant's voice like it was far off. It forced him to think, to inhale. "Yes, sergeant?"

"Get up. We're moving out."

Matthias looked up, watching clouds scud by swollen with rain and began to walk. He shucked off his fears and laughed. *I bet the Israelites didn't have to deal with rain.*

"This is where we stop tonight. Take your packs off." The

sergeant shouldered his rifle and pulled a broad knife from a scabbard on his leg. He picked up a Rot-speckled branch about the size of a broomstick and sliced it with the blade. A crude point appeared at the end of the twig.

Matthias felt a jolt run through him. He had just seen wood, *wood,* reduced to the crudest of spears.

Jeremiah held up the branch. "Girls, Samuel, find me as many sticks like this that you can. The winner gets a special treat."

Whatever exhaustion the children bore when they arrived departed. They ran off the path in a frenzied quest.

"No more than thirty paces, and don't break any saplings. Deadfall only," ordered the sergeant.

Matthias approached him. "Spears? Are you expecting us to fight the Order with spears?"

Jeremiah constantly moved his head, watching, waiting for something. "It'll be dark within the hour. The Order is not our concern right now."

Picking up the stick, Matthias felt suppleness and resiliency. He inspected it closely, noting the lack of Rot on its surface. "Why isn't this twig dust?"

"We're up above the frost line. The Rot can't stand the cold. Trees down below last maybe a decade at most. Up here, they can grow for twice that."

Amazed, Matthias handed the stick to Nathan. "Why the sharp end?"

"Other things live twice as long up here. Coyotes, for instance. Buzzards." Jeremiah kept looking in the distance.

Nathan laughed. "Clever sergeant. A fairy tale to scare the children and keep them close. In the old days, it was tales of the big bad wolf."

There was no humor on Jeremiah's face. "Well, history teacher, you tell them there aren't any. Then go sleep outside the pickets." He addressed the group. "You will all help. This will be our lives while we are out here. When we camp, the women will set up the shelters. Children will gather sticks. Men will gather rocks, logs, and water. At night, we'll sleep four to a tent."

Beth marched forward, hands balled up into fists. "Do you want us to sweep the floor and wash your clothes, too? Are you saying that women cannot do what men do?"

Great. First it was Catholics and now it's a feminist. Matthias waited for the sergeant to reach for his sidearm to quell the insubordination.

Jeremiah made no such move. A smirk grew on his lips. "No, it's quite the opposite. There is something women do that men cannot."

Beth crossed her arms. "What's that?"

The sergeant blushed. "Menstu... The curse of Eve. I assume you and your sister are still able to bear children."

"Yes."

"Blood of any kind will attract predators out here. They are keen to it. If you aren't menstruating, feel free to gather as the men do." Jeremiah grasped her arm. "But first, set up the shelters. Three of them. Close together. And don't sweep a thing. We want to erase our presence as best we can in the morning."

The woman's face showed more hurt than anger.

"Beth," said the sergeant. "Your sister does little except coddle on her baby. Theresa and Thaddeus are in their own world, and Mary wants to be anywhere but here. You seem like a strong woman. I need somebody like the prophet Deborah. I need somebody I can trust to get things done out here. Will you do this?" Jeremiah shifted out of his military demeanor. "Please?"

Matthias watched Beth regard the sergeant, the way their eyes softened for just a moment.

Beth said "Yes," and went to work on the campsite.

Jeremiah nodded and watched her walk away.

Matthias couldn't resist. "Which shelter will you be staying in tonight, sergeant?"

Jeremiah regained his official self. "None. I will guard the perimeter. The family will share one tent. Beth, Johanna, Theresa and Thaddeus will share another. The rest of you will occupy the third." He looked down at Matthias. "What's the matter?"

"Back in the storeroom, you said the shelters sleep two."

"It will be cold tonight, colder than anything you've ever felt in the city. Cluster together and you'll be warm."

"As you wish."

Dropping his pack, Jeremiah reached inside and pulled out

what looked like a large, reinforced plastic bag with a nozzle at one end. He picked up a makeshift spear and tossed it to Thaddeus. "There's a stream about a hundred yards down the slope. Fill this up and come right back. Don't tarry. All of you get to work. It's getting dark."

The children returned. Samuel carried quite a bundle of sticks, but Ruth carried even more. The boy's lips pursed when he sensed defeat. But no one paid either of those children any mind. They circled Susanna who came back a few seconds after the others, a great, green fern branch in her hand.

Matthias marveled at the way it glowed in the midst of grayness around them. His voice joined the others in a collective gasp. Only the Synod's greenhouses grew plants so exotic.

Mary stepped closer to her daughter. "It's beautiful, honey. Where did you get it?"

"There's a bunch of them mommy. You should see."

Jeremiah knelt down next to the child. "You didn't follow orders."

"But it was so pretty. Don't you want to see them? There's lots of them."

The idea of seeing a place full of green made the group halt their chores.

"Get back to work, everyone," said the sergeant. "Now." He turned back to the child. "It's pretty. But please, Susanna, you need to stay close to camp and do your duty. Okay? Don't ever go out of sight again."

By the time Thaddeus returned with water, the fortification was nearly complete.

The mish-mosh of branches and stones hardly fit Matthias's idea of a fortress. Three tents stood in its center. They were olive, squat, things that had far too much of a resemblance to a body bag. At least his prison cell in Caesteal Glenolden was open and had a light bulb.

"It will do," said Jeremiah. He threw a few pills into the water bag. "Everyone is to eat one of your meals. Eat it all, no exceptions. One cup of water each, and one in the morning." The sergeant reached into his pocket. "Before I forget, your reward,

Ruth." He tossed a small packet at the girl.

She caught it and tore open the packet. Her face burst into glee. "Chocolate."

Faces stared at the two squares in the girl's hand and showed more amazement than when Susanna brought the fern.

Matthias felt his mouth water. Chocolate was rarer than good wine. He pulled his eyes away from the delicacy and looked up at the sergeant. The man wore a satisfied smile, that of a happy uncle bestowing gifts. The way uncles were supposed to be.

Darkness fell more rapidly than Matthias anticipated. He heard more than saw. Zippers unzipped. People groaned with fatigue. Fabric brushed against fabric.

He peered into the tent, another black maw waiting to consume him. Matthias backed away. A hand reached out and grabbed him. It was small. It tugged gently. Samuel.

Squirming into the tent, he could smell the sweat of the others. He fought a rising panic until Samuel let out a peaceful sigh. It calmed him.

But, there was no such ease for Matthias. Melancholy and worry washed over him. *Where is the Order? How is my house? How is Naomi? How will they treat me in the Hindu Lands? Will I make it there? Have they found the Bible?*

The last thought burdened Matthias the most. The book and its location were both his freedom and his shackles. The Order would never halt their chase. He could be running out here forever, trapped on the mountaintop like the trees around him.

Fatigue overpowered Matthias's worries, and his eyes closed. Just before he fell off to sleep, he could have sworn he heard something yipping off in the distance.

Chapter 30: Verses 1-53

Matthias awoke in blackness. Bodies pressed around him. All he could feel was the cold. He tried to free his arms, but the weight of unseen others pressed against him. Electronic beeping rang in his ears. Matthias wanted to scream, but any noise, any movement meant death. The weight pressed against him harder, suffocating him. All around, the bag imprisoning him shook and shook.

"Wake up, Matthias. You're going to knock the tent down," said Luke.

Hearing the agitated voice, Matthias awakened from his nightmare. The odors from his comrades assaulted his nostrils. It was a million times better than what he smelled yesterday. "Sorry."

His clothes were cold with sweat, and he cracked the tent door open to get some air.

Somebody in one of the other tents coughed. It was a wet cough, something between a croak and a clearing of the throat. To Matthias, it was a sound of illness, a sound from his past.

The image of his father appeared in the darkness, coughing in the night at a campsite. They were in the Maryland mountains, not far from the town where his father grew up. His father retched until Matthias slapped him on the back hard and fast. Each time a fit occurred, it took more and more effort to free his father's lungs from the demons smothering him.

"Thanks, son," said his father, fiercely embracing him the way those in need of rescue cling to their rescuers.

Matthias felt his father tremble as he patted his back.

"Everyone up," commanded Jeremiah.

Matthias opened his eyes and found morning darkness indistinguishable from evening darkness.

The sergeant's voice was no dream. "Let's go. We're moving out in one hour. Fifteen minutes for breakfast."

As they ate, meager daylight crept into the forest. Jeremiah yelled again when his watch counted off the time. "Take down the fort. Scatter the rocks into the forest."

Samuel ran up to the sergeant, the boy's face knotted with concern. The child tugged at him and pulled Jeremiah's bulk about twenty yards into the woods. Matthias and the others followed.

The girls stood, eyes fixed on a muddy spot. Samuel pointed at the ground.

"Paw prints. Coyotes," said Jeremiah, his voice as matter of fact as could be.

Matthias felt a chill run up his back. "They were this close?"

Jeremiah crossed his arms. "They were this far away. Good. They are wary of us."

Mary gathered the girls to her side. "Good? Wild animals next to our camp and my daughters are out running your damned errands? How can you say 'good'?"

The sergeant said, "They sense that we are strong and prepared, or else they would have probed our defenses."

Matthias studied the marks in the mud. "At least we know our enemies are near." He reached down and picked up one of the spears. "I hope the apostle Matthew will forgive me, but I have no intention of going out like a sheep."

Nathan picked up another spear and spoke to the sergeant. "I take it that pointed sticks are permitted?"

"So long as you don't hurt yourself," said the sergeant.

Nathan returned a flat smile and a limp salute. "Yes, sir."

Everyone else picked up a makeshift spear.

Jeremiah laughed. "My, aren't we the Royal Guard of David himself." He pulled his knife out and shaved a far more menacing point on Samuel's spear. "There, boy. Now that thing means business."

After morning prayer, Matthias positioned himself at the end of the line. He stayed a step behind Thaddeus and Theresa, who somehow managed to walk side by side along the narrow path. They teased each other and talked of things they saw along the way. Occasionally, she produced her rosary and they would follow its beads in whatever strange ritual it called for. The way they looked at each other made Matthias wistful. It was how his parents looked at each other, right up to the last time they were together.

Matthias shifted his attention to Johanna and her ersatz child, Joshua. She carried an air of tragedy. In another time and place, he might want to hear her story. It might have made a poignant addition to a Sunday service.

Samuel and the girls whirled into view. His *son* never stopped moving, sliding back and forth within the column in a flurry of crunching leaves and snapping sticks. Matthias envied their playfulness and innocence.

Jeremiah halted the march. He pressed a finger to his lips and beckoned everyone to come near. "There is a road ahead of us. Make no noise. If there are patrols, this is where they will be. Stay put until I return."

Luke nudged Nathan with an elbow. The two spoke in low, angry tones.

Matthias recognized the behavior, skeptical, questioning, *dissenters in need of quieting.* He moved toward them and whispered, "What's the matter?"

Luke drew circles in the leaves with his spear. "I don't like the way he gives orders to us all the time. It's like he's an Elder, and we are his servants."

The remark stung Matthias.

"You may think he won't turn us in, but I'm not so sure."

Matthias chuckled. "He can't like camping that much. What kind of idiot would venture into a land rife with Rot and hungry beasts?"

"The kind of idiot marks a trail as he goes." Luke pointed to a broken tree branch near the trail.

"An accident. Any one of us could have done that." He kicked the leaves around the circle that Luke just made.

"Ye of little faith. How about there or there?" Luke pointed further down the path.

Matthias followed the accusations. Broken branches traced the path behind them. "I see."

"We need to get away from him."

The words galled Matthias. "Luke, Nathan, have you ever gone into the woods like this before?"

They shook their heads.

"I have, and I'm not sure I would have made it this far let alone where ever it is we're going. Now, unless you've got a transport hidden in your pocket somewhere, I suggest you listen to orders, or the sergeant's going to break more than twigs. Understand?"

Jeremiah approached. "Understand what?"

Matthias felt a hot rush. "Understand the need to keep silent."

"I see." Jeremiah's eyes swept over the trio. "The road, such as it is, appears safe. Let's get moving."

They marched along the trail, much deeper into the forest with trees almost twice as high as the day before. The sight of so much priceless lumber should have left Matthias awestruck. Instead, his thoughts were focused on another broken branch about waist high. One or two would have been a coincidence, but this was the tenth since they left the road. The problem was he never saw how the sergeant was doing it.

Chapter 31: Verses 1-40

The sky grew darker with the threat of rain. Matthias studied the clouds trying to gauge when it might begin. When he lowered his gaze, he found Theresa and Thaddeus glancing at him over their shoulders. Words fell instead of rain.

"Your son has your eyes," said Theresa.

Yes, we've both seen our mothers die, thought Matthias. "Thank you for noticing," he replied.

"How old is he?"

"Ten."

Near the front of the column, Samuel turned and shot him a grimace.

"I mean, eleven."

Samuel nodded.

"They grow so fast," said Matthias.

Thaddeus chimed in. "Once we get married, we'd like to have children, lots of them."

"Will they be Catholic, too?"

Thaddeus halted. "Do you have a problem with that?"

"I'm just always puzzled by God-fearing Christians who buy into a religious franchise that went out of business long ago. No wonder you're going to the Hindu Lands."

"I'm not buying anything," protested Thaddeus.

Theresa chimed in. "We heard the Federation has religious freedom. They'll be plenty of Catholics. There's even synagogues and mosques."

"Buddhists, too," added Thaddeus.

Matthias dwelled on his comment, the slippery slope of old prejudices. He never considered the idea of church in this unknown land, let alone having to deal with dozens of competing corporations and their congregations. Then there was the whole idea of just what religion the old Bible supported. He wished he had more time to see just what else the Synod hid from the people. The more he thought about it, the more foolish he felt. "Look, I'm sorry. Old beliefs die hard."

Nathan slipped back a step to join in. "Don't apologize, Matthias. Those that cannot learn from history are doomed to repeat it. To think that America, in its Golden Age, took the Constitution at face value and allowed such things. It tore us apart until they corrected the First Amendment."

Matthias studied the man's ease of delivery, the confidence in his eyes as he lectured instead of conversed. He thought back to the sergeant's remark calling the man a *history teacher*. It carried more weight than he first considered. "What grade did you teach, Nathan?"

The man hesitated for half a step. "Sophomores, high school sophomores. I taught American History in Pittsburgh."

Teachers were extremely well-screened instruments of the Synod. This man's presence was more of an enigma than Johanna's baby. Matthias pressed on. "I take it that you're not a Catholic."

"Good heavens, no," said Nathan. "I was dismissed."

The admission shocked Matthias. A dismissed teacher was the moral equivalent of being a cast-out Elder. "The Synod rarely dismisses teachers."

"No, they don't. The police took my wife away, may she rot in Hell. A neighbor called me while I was at school. When I realized why they took her, I knew they'd be coming for me. It came down to running away or getting my mind sucked out by an inquisition."

The framing of the reply piqued Matthias's interest. This man was a kindred spirit. They had both fallen from a great height.

Thaddeus said, "What did she do?"

Nathan darkened from the top of his head to where his neck met his coat. "Keep your wife in line, young man. Trust the word of God and keep reminding her of Paul's letters to the Colossians. That was my mistake." The teacher shook his head. "Tabitha, my wife of eighteen years, had a great mind—for a woman. But for all that knowledge, she didn't know her place."

Matthias noticed how much Theresa bristled at the teacher's remarks. If Thaddeus wanted to live through the night, he probably shouldn't quote Paul to his beloved.

Nathan let out a sigh. "I used to let her help me with history articles I posted on the Ecunet and took her with me on outings to historical sites. One day, she showed me this study she did of the Second Civil War. It was brilliant, especially for a woman, but fundamentally flawed. Her thesis was that the Amish were non-violent and that she could prove it with evidence she gathered at the Haverford battlefield."

"Was she addled?" said Matthias. "The Amish fought to the last man."

"No, not addled in the least. She was incensed. Said I was ignoring the facts. I told her to knock off her revisionist ways and deleted her research from our computer. The next day, the Order arrested her and came after me. The rest, as they say, is history." Nathan turned and prodded Thaddeus in the chest. "Keep her in her place, young man."

Thaddeus smiled a nervous smile at Theresa who lips were drawn into a straight line. The young man edged away from Nathan and said, "How about you, Matthias?"

The question caught him off guard. He'd been concentrating on the teacher's tale so much that he didn't see it coming. "Well—" He groped for enough facts to knit a veil of lies together. "I'm an inconvenient husband, so to speak. I spent my life in service to the largest financial institution of its kind, The Bank of Job. I never suspected my wife was involved with the Chief Elder. He dismissed me from my job and had our marriage annulled. My boy and I were to be cast out, but I fixed her. Our accounts were fat with the Chief Elder's favors. I transferred all of it into penance cards before they evicted us. That paid our way north. So, here I am trodding the wastelands with disgraced teachers, Catholics, and feminists. All we need is a homosexual and we can host a diversity seminar."

Luke spun around, his middle finger extended.

Matthias spotted him. "Don't tell me."

Theresa choked back a giggle. "Didn't you know?"

The volley of conversation triggered more exchanges among the company though Matthias intentionally kept out of most of them. Instead, his mind spun on his own fall from grace—the Bible. Too bad he didn't bring the relic with him. It would have made him an instant celebrity in the Hindu Lands, and that social capital would help him rise again to importance. Just the idea of presenting it to the Federation would gall his uncle beyond measure.

Uncle Cornelius. The old rage burnt in Matthias's chest and his uncle's victory over him made it burn all the brighter. He closed his eyes and prayed. *Pursue my enemies, oh Lord. Have them die upon your sword. Avenge me, oh Lord. Avenge my family. Do you hear me? Pursue them Lord. Smite them.*

When he opened his eyes, another broken branch hung before him.

Chapter 32: Verses 1-105

At day's end, the sergeant pronounced their sojourn concluded for the day. Orders were given, meals consumed, and another fortress of Megiddo erected out of the detritus of the forest.

Matthias happily slid into the tent, exhausted.

Rain, and the sergeant's bellow, peppered the tent before first light. Everyone ate inside, unwilling to venture out.

The tent flap flew open. Jeremiah stuck his head in. "Let's go, ladies." His face proved more unpleasant than the weather.

Matthias stepped out into rain. Drizzle ran off of his coat. The precipitation would be kept at bay. A dollop of rain landed on his neck. He rubbed the drop between his fingers. Much to his horror, he saw what looked like fine, black hairs in the water—filaments of Rot. He pawed at his neck all the more.

"Hold still," said Luke.

Matthias felt a coarse cloth rub his neck. Being touched by a homosexual, *an abomination*, riled him. They were never to touch a member of the same sex. "Stay away from me."

"I'm cleaning it off, you ass. Hold still."

Unable to reconcile his fear with his prejudice, Matthias

froze. The coarseness disappeared followed by a tugging around his collar. A moment later, a hood unfurled from his collar and slipped over his head. Relief pushed the horror aside. He regained his composure. "My thanks."

Luke walked away saying, "You know, I'm a human being, just like you."

Matthias stood in the rain, feeling foolish all over again. Old beliefs died hard.

They disassembled the fort and prayed.

Jeremiah donned his hat. "Today, we will cross a road near the town of Port Clinton. They distill water there. As you can imagine, it's a busy place, and one where we don't fit in."

Matthias regarded the motley state of the cadre. *That is an understatement.*

"If it is anywhere along the way that we must be cautious, this is it. Our luck has held so far. Even the weather helps us. Let us pray that God continues to shield us from the eyes of our enemies, and we will be in Palmerton in no time."

The mist hung over the mountains, a white pall held aloft by a procession of trees. Matthias trudged along under the canopy. Dampness seeped into his coat, and he fought the growing chill.

Timothy moved alongside Matthias and pushed his hood back. "You worked for the Bank of Job?"

"May they rot in Hell," said Matthias. He couldn't help but notice how much older Timothy looked in just two day's time. Even the roots of the hair on the man's temples were grayer, but the shafts still dark. The camouflage of wealth was washing away. "Where did you work?"

"Zion Logistics."

The name rang familiar to Matthias, even if it seemed like an eternity that he thought of anything as mundane as a bank client. They were a middling account. There was talk of an audit of the company's books a few months back. "Zion. Hmm. Yes. I remember them. Something about financial irregularities. Its Elders were blamed at first, but the investigation turned up widespread corruption at lower levels."

"That's what the press was told. You are well informed," said Timothy, his head lowering.

"I take it that you were one of the 'lower levels?'"

"Yes."

Matthias let out a brief chuckle. "That's the way it always happens. Ethics, it seems, are for underlings. Now, your children are far from safety, crushed in court without a lawyer."

Timothy looked at him. "I beg your pardon?"

"Job, Chapter 5. Sorry, it's a talent of mine. I can remember a lot of what I've read. It seemed appropriate considering your situation. Mine, too. Perhaps we can find more ethical employers in the Hindu Lands."

Timothy brightened and nodded.

Ruth sidled up to her father, "Daddy, my tummy hurts."

The man switched from repentant sinner to doting father. He scooped the girl up and patted her belly. "Too much of that irradiated food. Come on, let's catch up to mom."

As Timothy carried his daughter, Ruth snagged a low branch and folded it.

Relief came over Matthias and he laughed. The mystery of the sinister trail marker was solved.

The day blurred on. Step followed step. Raindrop fell after raindrop. The only perception of time was a certain dimming in the East. What conversations there were dwindled with the daylight.

Jeremiah thrust up his hand and the group stopped.

The persistent whine of tires on pavement and the chug of a diesel engine announced an approaching vehicle. The noise held none of the Order's familiar drone.

Jeremiah seemed unperturbed by the sound. He waved everyone close. "You hear the traffic? The main road to Port Clinton lies just down this hill." He pointed to Luke and Nathan. "Lead the group to a clump of rocks just shy of the road and wait for my signal."

"Where are you going?" said Nathan.

The sergeant cradled his rifle across his arms. "Across the street where I can get a look-see at traffic. It's a busy road. We'll be out in the open for more than fifty yards. Timing is everything here. God forbid there's a patrol. Pray that our luck holds." He sped off down the trail.

Nathan came up to Matthias. "Do you think he plans a trap for us up ahead? Maybe we should move deeper into the woods."

The idea amused Matthias. They could wander up there for forty years and never find their way out. He put his hand on Nathan's shoulder. "You've been listening to Luke too much. When we get to safety, I'm going to buy both of you the biggest glass of vodka I can find. You need to be more at ease, brother."

Nathan cast the hand aside. "I'll be happy when I'm in the Hindu Lands."

"Then we'll both be happy. Until that time, we must abide." Matthias understood the teacher's distrust, but the sergeant hadn't shown any signs of betrayal—quite the opposite. The whine of the tires grew much louder. Matthias looked across the road at Jeremiah beckoning to them. "The sergeant is ready."

"Not now," said Beth in a roaring whisper that made everyone jump.

Johanna countered, "But Joshie needs more formula."

"Honey, we'll do that another time. Joshua has more than enough to get him to town. Okay?" said Beth.

"But there's cars out there. Maybe someone can take us to a store," replied Johanna.

Luke crawled over to her. "Johanna, there's a better place up ahead that has formula. We can't stop here for your boy." He stroked the blanket and grinned.

Johanna didn't buy it at first but eventually smiled.

Nathan hustled to the side of a large boulder. "The sergeant wants three of us. Luke, you, Beth, Jo and the baby. Go!"

Luke and Beth rose. Johanna stayed put.

Beth said, "What's the matter now?"

"Can't you smell that?" Johanna held up the baby. "You little stinker." She fussed with pins on the doll's diaper.

Jeremiah waved all the harder.

Nathan's eyes were as big as saucers. "For the love of God. Luke, take Susanna and Mary."

Luke grabbed Mary's hand, who took Susanna in tow. Their feet clomped across and into silence.

Beth said, "Please hurry, Jo."

A vehicle approached. The sergeant held up his hand. When it passed, Matthias saw him motion for more to cross.

"Thaddeus, Theresa, go," said Nathan, slapping their backs.

The rest of the group sat quietly until Jeremiah signaled again. Timothy carried Ruth over the road in a dead run and plunged into the brush.

"All done?" said Beth who hovered over Johanna.

"Don't rush me, sister. You know how he fusses if I don't keep him clean," said Johanna.

The doll lay on the ground, a blaze of pinkish plastic against a mottled gray carpet. Johanna sang and cooed.

Another vehicle came and went. Jeremiah waved.

Nathan tugged Matthias and Samuel. "Let's go."

It seemed as though Matthias's boots got heavier in the last few minutes. He couldn't run fast enough to keep up with the child who disappeared into the thicket along the shoulder.

Jeremiah said, "Is she done yet?"

Matthias let out a puff. "Just about." He followed the sergeant's gaze down a shallow hill. A pair of lights hugged the road. Jeremiah waved frantically.

Beth and Johanna ran. The sound of tires on pavement approached. Their feet slapped the pavement in a mad sprint and they leapt off the road. The vehicle passed. Matthias allowed himself to breath.

Jeremiah sighed. "Is Joshie dry?"

Beth looked as pale as the doll. "Yes."

"Good, let's get out of here."

Matthias rose and started down the trail.

Beth shouted, "Johanna!"

Johanna stood in the middle of the road, bending down to pick something up. "It's okay. I dropped a pin."

Vehicle lights arced upward in the mist.

Jeremiah bolted toward Johanna.

The lights swept down, converging on the young mother and the bundle in her arms.

Beth dashed past Matthias, shoving him aside. He gaped at the truck, the young mother, and wished to God that he couldn't hear the brakes or the scream.

The truck came to rest on its roof, its horn blaring. Its door swung slowly and a man lay on the ground nearby. Johanna was nowhere to be seen. Matthias ran down the hill.

Jeremiah held onto Beth, who flailed in his grasp.

She cried, "No! No!"

The sergeant called out, "Matthias, give me a hand here." He turned Beth toward him. "There's nothing you can do for her now. Let me attend to her."

She wailed even louder.

"I need you to be Deborah all the more."

"I can't."

"Yes, you can. Matthias?"

The pain in the sergeant's face was more than evident. Matthias took Beth by the shoulders and felt her violent quaking. He tried to talk calmly, as if to soothe himself as well as Beth. "I'm sorry. I'm so sorry."

"I need to see her," protested Beth.

Jeremiah looked into her eyes. "No, you don't. You don't want this memory. I'll take care of her."

Beth pushed off Matthias's hands, sobbing and falling to her knees.

Matthias looked skyward. *Why?*

The blaring horn fell silent. Matthias searched for the sergeant in the distance. He saw him picking up the doll, holding it as if it were a real baby.

Matthias and Beth walked up the mountain in the failing light, stopping whenever she felt like it. In time, they caught up with the others who were already setting up camp.

Samuel walked up to him, rubbing his stomach.

"Stomach ache?" Matthias felt the same way.

The boy shook his head.

"I think those rations are getting to everybody." He patted his stomach. It had been unsettled since Ruth complained to her father.

The boy paid him no mind and looked off down the trail. Matthias looked too. The sergeant appeared from the mist.

Beth rose from her seat and took a step down the trail.

Jeremiah stood in the distance, his face taut. She ran to him and they embraced. He spoke to her, but Matthias couldn't hear anything but murmurs and sobbing. The sergeant pulled the doll from his pack and gave it to her. She held it, brought it to her face, and collapsed.

The sergeant carried to the camp. "Help me get her inside her tent."

Chapter 33: Verses 1-85

Dawn broke clear and cold. A breeze tossed the bare branches. Ordinarily, such a rare morning would have brightened Matthias's spirits. He would have risen from his warm bed, admired the blue sky, and walked to the kitchen for a hot breakfast. That was before he found the Bible—before Johanna died.

Matthias zipped up his coat to fend off the cold. He stood in silence. No vocal reveille roused the exhausted. No curses assailed the slothful, and no orders barked at the disorderly. Sergeant Jeremiah Sanford was missing in action.

Somewhere, in one of the other tents, a man sucked in air suddenly, as if roused out of his slumber. To Matthias's surprise, Jeremiah popped out of Beth's tent. "How is she?"

"As good as can be expected, considering. She is a strong woman to be sure. She will survive this." The sergeant looked at the ground, patting his arms to keep warm. "Good heavens, I had no idea it was this cold. What would you say it is?"

Matthias noted the discomfort in Jeremiah's body language, the way he avoided whatever grief he might be feeling by changing the conversation. He let it go, and gauged the sting on his cheeks. "I'm not sure. I've never felt this cold before. Forty?"

Picking up the water container, Jeremiah shook it. It rattled. He unscrewed the cap and looked inside. "My God. Ice. Lots of it. It has to be in the twenties."

"Impossible. We're hundreds of miles from the Arctic Circle."

"Look for yourself."

Matthias peered in. A thick blanket of slush came into view. It was like looking at the picture of the snow-covered mountain on the bunker wall at home. "No wonder I feel so cold." A cramp made Matthias twist.

"You don't look well. How did you sleep?"

"Between Johanna and those rations, badly."

The sergeant gripped Matthias's face with one hand and yanked down on his cheek with the other.

He squirmed in the soldier's grasp. "I said it was my stomach."

Jeremiah studied his eyes. "How long have you felt this way?"

"Since yesterday."

"Damn it. Rot Fever. Pray that it doesn't get any worse."

Whatever chill Matthias felt vanished. Rot Fever killed. "I need to get to a hospital."

Jeremiah pointed south. "Go that way, fifty miles or so. Good luck."

"I'm serious."

"So am I. Other than prayer, there is little I can do for you. Look, the fever is like the coyotes. It preys on the weak, the old, and children who haven't built up a resistance to the Rot's devilishness. You are strong. You may recover."

Trembling spread through Matthias. The fever took far more souls than it left alive. He wanted to be home, laying in clean sheets.

Another person moved in their tent. Samuel pushed the flap aside. Matthias's anxiety spread. "What about the children?"

"They're safe. It is an affliction from the mold. You can't give it to anybody."

"Samuel and Ruth had stomachaches before I did."

"Damn it. Damn it all. Everybody up," yelled the sergeant.

"Front and center, now."

The sergeant inspected each shivering person for the same signs of Rot Fever as Matthias. Samuel had it. So did Ruth. The others were clear—for the time being.

Jeremiah came up to Matthias. "I don't know what to do. We can't wait here. But Noah gave me orders. We can carry the children. I…"

The die was cast and Matthias knew it. "I know. I'll try and keep up. How long to Palmerton?"

"Two nights and a morning."

Samuel drew close.

"Stay with the sergeant, son."

The boy shook his head.

"God, you are stubborn." Matthias thought about the journey ahead, wondering if he'd see Palmerton, let along the Hindu Lands. He faced the sergeant. "If I can't keep going, take Samuel with you. He will carry what I know and my bargain with Captain Finney will be fulfilled. Understood?"

Jeremiah said, "Understood."

They broke camp and formed a circle around Beth.

She hugged Johanna's doll in her arms. "My sister had a hard life and now she is at rest. I hoped we both would grow old in the Hindu Lands where husbands don't beat their wives and kill their unborn children. May God hold her in His loving arms."

Theresa pulled out her rosary, her hands shaking. "Eternal rest give her, oh Lord."

Thaddeus followed. "May perpetual light shine upon her."

"Amen." Matthias glanced up at the couple and listened to their earnest benediction. He wondered if God listened to them, or anybody in the group. Did the Almighty hear Johanna's scream at the moment the vehicle crushed her? Did he hear Benjamin's anguish under the Order's tortures? Did He hear the cries of the destitute of the city when God's Holy Order cut them down like weeds? Did He fill the farms with loaves and fishes to stave off the deaths of thousands? And, did He ever, ever, ever strike down Cornelius Goddamned Rourke?

The sergeant knelt. "Almighty Father, he who dwells in the shelter of the Most High will rest in the shadow of the Almighty. I will say of the Lord, You are my sanctuary and my fortress in whom I trust. Surely He will save us from traps and from disease."

"Amen," said Matthias, wondering if the word was worth the breath.

Cramps and fever hit Matthias in waves as he marched along the trail. Samuel trudged along beside him. Gone was the bouncy boy who played so freely just a couple of days ago. He touched the child's forehead and found it hot. Samuel pulled away and walked all the faster. *Stubborn, indeed.*

Ruth, on the other hand, grew more and more listless. Most everyone took a turn carrying her. Theresa sang a hymn to keep the child's spirits up. Matthias halted, watching the group move on and listening to the hauntingly beautiful song carry in the forest like vespers at Christmastime.

The sergeant halted the column, ordered a break, and sat down next to Beth.

Matthias watched her stare off into the forest as if her sister would join them at any moment. He thought of the state of mourning they each were in. Beth's raw grief. Jeremiah's, old and festering. For him, lingering. And who would mourn for him?

Samuel rested his head against Matthias's knee, his eyes almost as sad as the day he stood begging with his mother outside of the limousine. He felt the comfort of the boy's warmth and drew strength from it.

Perhaps somebody would give a damn if he died out here after all.

Matthias walked on, his mind clouded with fever. Samuel stayed with him. The fever slowed their march, and they found themselves slipping further and further behind. All he could hope for was that the camp would be over the next rise, or the next, or the next.

Matthias heard a snarl, at least that's what he thought. It was like a storybook noise his father made, or the low roar of a football player posturing for fans on the Ecunet. He shook it off. The fever obviously made him imagine things that just weren't there.

He heard it again—a growl.

Matthias bumped into Samuel. The boy stood immobile on the path. "What's the matter?"

Samuel backed up against him, trembling.

Another growl joined the first.

Looking down the path, Matthias felt his illness leave, replaced by a rush of chills. Two coyotes stood in their way, their lips raised and teeth bared. He pushed the boy behind him.

Something padded through the brush to his right and left. Matthias caught glimpses of them. A yellow eye. A pricked up ear. The flicker of a tail. There were too many to count, and they were getting closer.

Samuel crouched beside him, lowering his spear.

Matthias did the same. Something primal rose from within, his muscles tensing each time a coyote came into view.

The beasts coiled closer, just outside the length of the spears, drool falling from their jowls. One of them lunged, bloodlust in its eyes

Matthias jabbed his stick at it. It slipped back. Another and another lunged and retreated.

More growling emanated behind him, but the sound was all wrong. It had a human tone, tenor, and childish. Matthias cocked his head around to see Samuel baring his teeth back at the animals and growling in defiance.

Matthias growled, too.

The coyotes halted their skirmish for a moment, then pressed their attack.

Matthias jabbed at them. A great yelp burst out of one of the beasts, and it hobbled backward, blood pouring from its haunch.

The wounding of one of its pack enraged the others. One jumped at Matthias. He brought an arm up to shield himself from its open jaws. The animal topped over, impaled on Samuel's spear.

Two more coyotes rushed from the side. Matthias knew he'd never get his spear around in time to stop them. He spun around, shielding Samuel from claws and teeth.

A gunshot pierced the snarls. Ears pricked up. Tails tucked

under their bellies. They vanished into the woods.

Matthias turned around. The sergeant stood about thirty paces down the path, his eye still locked onto the sights of his rifle.

Relief swept over him, and he gave Samuel a hug. The boy hugged back, hard and shaking at the same time.

"Thank goodness," said Matthias.

The sergeant approached a wounded coyote thrashing in the leaves. He pulled out his knife and slit the beast's throat in a quick motion. The thrashing stopped. "I told you they can sense the sick and the weak."

"We may be sick, but we aren't weak. Isn't that true, *son*?"

Samuel grinned.

"Would you believe the boy actually growled at those things? Growled."

The sergeant looked stunned. "God's truth?"

The boy nodded.

Jeremiah saluted the child. "A miracle to be sure." The soldier's face resumed its warrior's veneer. "The real miracle will be that the Order didn't hear my weapon. Don't fall behind again. You may not be as fortunate next time."

Chapter 34: Verses 1-103

The next day passed in an endless repetition of clouds, trees, rocks, and fever until the overcast broke apart late in the day into great silver clouds.

Matthias halted with the rest of the column at a great rift in the forest. Sunbeams leapt out of breaks in the clouds, and he likened them to spotlights in a church service. A vast field of rocks and boulders stretched out before them. To either side, the mountain sloped away into valleys. The forest resumed a half-mile beyond.

"What are you all gaping at," said the sergeant. "Move out. Another hour's walk and we can stop for the night. Tomorrow, Palmerton."

Matthias glanced down at his *son*. "How are you feeling?"

Samuel nodded, his eyes droopy.

"You're doing better than me." Matthias felt hot as Hell, and the allure of a warm tent was the only thing propelling him onward

Out on the boulder field, Matthias winced from the slicing cold of the wind. He slid his face into his coat as far as he could.

The company spread out, each trying to pick their way through the jumbled landscape. Theresa carried her rosary and spoke her prayers in a soothing tone, following Ruth and the rest of her family.

About midway, the sergeant halted. Matthias sensed the tension from ten yards away. The sudden shift made his cramps all the worse.

Jeremiah turned around, his face lined with urgency. "Get down."

Everyone remained where they were.

Matthias heard a high-pitched drone. The others canted their ears to follow the noise.

"Get down," urged Jeremiah.

Matthias understood. There was no cover for hundreds of yards. Someone could easily spot them from the valley floor.

But the sound wasn't coming from below. It came from above.

It was a beautiful sight, a gleaming aircraft lit by one of the sunbeams as if an angel were descending from Heaven. Matthias ignored Jeremiah and stood transfixed. For the first time in his life he saw an aircraft, one actually flying. It was amazing.

A flash leapt from under its fuselage, and a plume of smoke drew a line from the aircraft toward Matthias. Dread supplanted wonder. He knew the object from the histories in the family bunker, knew its intent.

A missile.

Before he could act, Matthias felt the full weight of Luke tackling him. Pain jabbed into his side as he banged into the rocks.

The missile hurtled past.

Matthias turned in time to see it burst into a dazzling fireball of red and orange. In the fireball's wake stood Thaddeus and Theresa. They held on to each other, their mouths open in silent torment as the flames consumed them. Matthias recoiled from the heat. He choked on the fumes, but couldn't tear his eyes away.

There wasn't anything he could do.

No shouts of warning.

No calls for help.

No prayers for the innocent.

Luke grabbed him by his hood. "We have to get out of here."

He looked at Luke knowing that he should run, but he couldn't will his limbs to move.

A second blast jolted Matthias out of his shock. It smelled the way he imagined Hell would. His ears rang. His eyes cast about and saw Jeremiah laying top of Beth and Samuel. The boy reached out for Matthias, trying to break free of the sergeant's grip.

The aircraft arced around, its engine roaring.

He caught sight of the sergeant rolling off of the others and removing his pack. Jeremiah's motions were fluid, economical— the precision of a machine. He produced a slender pipe no longer than a forearm from his pack, rose, and held it out like a magician's wand.

Another explosion rocked the mountainside.

The sergeant disappeared in a torrent of smoke.

Panic flashed through Matthias. Somehow, amidst the cacophony in his brain, he heard the plea of Blind Johnny.

Flee.

He tried to get to his feet.

"Stay where you are," ordered Jeremiah, still standing unfazed among the falling debris.

A bright plume leapt out of the sergeant's wand and darted into the sky. The aircraft veered wildly. Both objects maneuvered in an abrupt choreography, smoke intertwining until they merged, exploded, and fell like Lucifer himself being cast out of Heaven.

"Are you all right?" said Jeremiah.

Matthias felt wobbly though he wasn't sure whether it was the impact, the fever, or the rush of adrenaline. "I'm okay, thanks to Luke." Every time he blinked, he saw two writhing silhouettes. "Thaddeus and Theresa, I… They…" The very thought of it made his heart ache.

Jeremiah looked away. "I know."

Samuel ran to him and yanked him to his feet.

Luke got up, spitting at the wreckage of the plane. "Burn in Hell, you bastards. Burn in Hell!"

Matthias spotted Nathan coming out of the forest. How he made it back there, Matthias had no idea. Before he could ask, apprehension swept over him. "Where are the girls?" A hollowness formed in the pit of his stomach, like all hope was being sucked out of him.

Jeremiah jumped from boulder to boulder, frantically searching for the family.

Matthias wanted them to pop up out of some hiding place, sobbing, but healthy. All he wanted was to hear the sergeant say "All is well."

Jeremiah halted, his hands dropping to his sides.

Matthias went after him. He scrambled up next to the sergeant and wished he hadn't. The girls and their parents lay just as lifeless as Johanna's doll. He wanted to cry. He wanted to scream, but he could do neither. Emptiness engulfed him.

The sergeant swallowed hard, his voice faltering. "We're the only ones left. Take everyone to the far side and keep them out of sight."

Matthias walked to the forest's edge, every breath heavy laden with fever and sorrow.

Luke sat on the ground, his face caught in the turbulence of grief and shock.

Matthias looked back out at where Theresa and Thaddeus died. If Luke hadn't knocked him down, he would have been burned alive. "Thank you for my life."

Luke glanced up at him, his voice drained of emotion. "It isn't often that I save heretics."

The words hit Matthias almost as hard as one of the missiles. "You know me?"

Luke huffed. "You're Matthias Kent, fugitive Elder and heretic. I saw your picture on the Ecunet the day I escaped the city."

There was no use in denying it. There were no cocks to crow. "I am he."

Nathan approached and said, "Good God, a heretic. That explains it. There's about twenty flyable aircraft in the whole country, and to arm one with missiles. It staggers the mind. Goes against the Treaty of Rome. If any of the Arab nations found out, there could be a resumption of hostilities. Oh my God. They must really want you dead." His eyes grew wide. "Just what in the name of God did you do?"

Disgust welled up in Matthias. He found a relic, a pointless sheaf of papers that had different words than the government had on their sheets of paper. "I questioned the Synod."

Luke cut in. "They said you're a murderer. You killed members of the Order of Saint George and led your followers on a rampage. Thousands died around the city. And here you sit with us in the wilderness. You cut and run on them, leaving them to die. How many more people have to die so you can escape?"

Beth stepped between the two. "Where's Jeremiah?"

Matthias took in a breath and went back to the clearing. "He was just there a minute ago."

Beth said. "Spread out. He's got to be out there somewhere."

Luke's indictment played over and over again in Matthias's brain. *How many more had to die to save him and his accursed secret? Over what? Words on a page?*

Beth called out, "Jeremiah?"

Matthias heard the concern in her voice, the way it sounded less like a call and more like a plea. He pushed his recriminations aside. They needed the sergeant, or they'd all wind up dead. Matthias called out, "Sergeant?'

He came to the spot where Jeremiah fired his anti-aircraft missile. Other than the launching tube, there was no sign of him. It was as if the rapture claimed him while they had their backs turned. "Sergeant Sanford?"

Their calls went unanswered.

A few more steps brought Matthias to a charred spot. A glint of metal caught his attention. It was a scorched metal chain with melted beads and a crucifix—Theresa's rosary. He picked it up, and slipped it into his pocket. His spirit fell even farther, and the recriminations began anew. He looked upward. "Why?"

Matthias made his way to the second missile impact, another pile of charred granite. The rocks were still warm. A dark puddle lay in a dip on one of the boulders. He reached out to touch it when the breeze wafted its essence toward him. Blood. Was it Ruth's? Susanna's? *I have brought lambs to their death.*

Crimson spots led away from the crater, and he followed them to the trees and beyond. The sergeant sat in a grove of ferns about fifteen yards inside the shelter of the forest, his back turned.

"Thank God, you're okay," said Matthias.

Jeremiah didn't turn, his head lowered. "I told you not to fire."

"What?" Matthias didn't understand. Was the sergeant accusing him of ordering an air strike?

"Women and children. We spoke with them. They were leaving of their own accord. All was well."

The words sounded distant, an ache in every syllable. Matthias wondered just whom he was talking to. "Sergeant, what's going on?"

"You killed them, sir. Every one of them and most of my men. They were leaving. All was well. No shots. They were good and repentant citizens. We gave them the peace of the Lord. Didn't you receive my message?"

Matthias kept his distance and circled to the right. He stopped. The weight of a hundred boulders filled his heart. Susanna lay in the sergeant's arms, lifeless.

Jeremiah stroked her hair. Tears streamed out of his glassy eyes. "All was well."

"I'm sorry, sergeant." Matthias approached a bit closer. Timothy, Mary, and Ruth lay in the fern grove, side by side.

Jeremiah dropped the girl's body, spun around, and grabbed Matthias by the throat. In an instant, a pistol pressed into the base of his chin.

"Sergeant!" yelled Matthias.

"I told you not to fire. I told you we granted them peace. You killed them. You killed them all."

Fingers dug into Matthias's larynx, but he forced out a desperate breath. "Matthias. I'm Matthias."

Jeremiah tightened his fist. He blinked, and blinked again, then released his clench.

Matthias heaved on the ground, spots before his eyes.

Jeremiah sputtered, "Brother. Dear God. Brother, I'm sorry." He clicked the safety back on.

Holding up a hand, Matthias said, "I'm okay. Just give me a second. What just happened?"

The sergeant sat down on a rock, pulled the cap from his head and ran his fingers through his sweaty hair. "Demons."

"Demons?"

"I am tormented by Satan himself. He tortures my memories. I must have been weak during the battle and let him in my mind."

Matthias gulped in air and glimpsed at the sergeant. Gone was the glassiness, replaced by pain. He realized the sergeant's symptoms from a psychological primer years ago—post traumatic stress. "It's okay. I saw no weakness demonstrated. You have strength beyond us all, bringing us this far."

"Until now," said Jeremiah.

"Nonsense."

Buzzards squawked overhead, circling and descending.

Jeremiah looked up and then back down at Susanna. He drew in a breath, lifted the girl's body, and laid her with her parents.

Matthias gathered rocks to cover them. "Let me help."

Jeremiah transformed back into his soldier's demeanor, dutiful, driven, and colder than the wind blowing against them. "No."

"Aren't we going to bury them?"

The sergeant walked right past Matthias and headed back to the trail. "No, we're out of time. We march to Palmerton tonight."

"Tonight?" said Matthias.

"Tomorrow will be too late."

Chapter 35: Verses 1-92

It was near dark when Nathan asked, "What's that smell?"

Matthias knew the stink of decay. He imagined the body bag, scores of the dead surrounding him. His fever returned, wracking his body. All he wanted was to get away from the smell and go to sleep.

"Lights," said Beth.

Matthias broke out of his trance and saw dozens of pinpoints glowing below them.

Jeremiah nodded. "The Lord my God brightens my darkness. Welcome to Palmerton and our transport to the Federation of Free States."

Jeremiah left them at a bend in the road, well out of the reach of headlights. The group clustered together to keep warm.

After the better part of an hour, a vehicle chugged up to their hiding place and stopped.

"Let's go," came a yell.

Matthias knew the sergeant's voice. He got to his shaky feet and hoped that their transport had heat. When he got to the vehicle, his hope fell. The transport was a tractor. Attached to it was a trailer with a large metal tank and a pair of sprayer arms.

"Get in," said the sergeant.

Matthias knew what it was right away—a fertilizer spreader. "Get in where?"

"The tank."

"We'll suffocate in there."

The driver of the tractor turned around. "No you won't. The valves are open. I just hope the old girl holds together. Say a prayer everybody."

Curses, not prayers were on Matthias's mind as he bounced around the interior of the tank. The ride abruptly ended and the hatch popped open.

The driver stuck his head inside. "We're here. Everybody out."

One by one, the group clambered out of the tank and stood in front of a fine stone farmhouse. Lights glowed in the windows, and smoke rose from the chimney. Jeremiah and the driver shook hands and smiled.

The driver said, "Welcome sojourners. Please, let's go inside."

Matthias followed the others into the house. A coal stove sat in front of a hearth. He found himself in ecstasy over the warmth. A pot gurgled on its top and the aroma of home cooking held the fetid stink at the door.

Jeremiah came in last. "We owe this blessing to my friend and comrade, Felix."

Felix followed Jeremiah inside. He was cut from the same fabric as the sergeant, broad shoulders, brown eyes and receding gray haircut high and tight. "Brothers and sisters, I welcome you and am in praise of Christ Jesus' unending grace in bringing you to us."

To Matthias, grace was a matter of perspective. There was no grace for Theresa and Thaddeus, none for the girls, none for their parents, none for Johanna.

Felix bowed his head. "Let us pray. Let God arise, let His enemies be tossed into the wind. Let them that hate Him flee before the wrath of God."

The words of the Psalm weren't all that familiar to Matthias. It certainly wasn't Psalm 86, the pass phrase that Jeremiah had him memorize back at the camp.

The sergeant approached Felix, one arm raised and the other at waist height. Matthias looked away, expecting the crunch of bones.

"A good word indeed, Brother Felix."

The two men embraced.

Then it hit Matthias. Felix offered up Psalm 68, the countersign. But there was more. They were in the hands of a friend.

Felix gestured to the food. "Please, all of you, help yourself. The Lord has been most bountiful. There is stew on the stove. Bowls are on the table over there."

"Smells good," said Jeremiah.

Matthias agreed though his cramps began anew.

"Coyote," said Felix. "Been simmering all day."

The thought of the encounter with the beasts soured Matthias's appetite.

Samuel already had a bowl in hand.

Felix continued, "Caught three of them in my south-side trap lines the last couple of days. Never had such bounty. Especially since it's been so dang cold out. The Lord provides."

"Have others done as well?" said the sergeant.

"We all have meat on the table, praise God."

The flush of welcome drained from the Jeremiah's face. "That's not good."

Felix laughed. "You were always a spoil sport. What troubles you about our four-footed manna?"

"These creatures aren't stupid. They keep well away from us unless they have the advantage." Jeremiah walked over to the stove and warmed his hands. "Something is driving them north. They only attacked us once." He looked at Matthias.

Wrapping a rag around his hand, Felix grasped the stew pot and ladled out portions to anyone with a bowl. "The coyotes are running because the Order is moving through the mountains. I heard that they went to the base and blew away half the mountain trying to get to you and yours." Felix drew in a breath, unable to continue.

"What else have you heard?" said Jeremiah.

"Captain Finney is dead."

"I know."

Pain flashed across both men's faces.

Felix recovered first. "When they didn't find you, their commander was quite vexed. They spread out the Order across every compass point to locate you. They've even pulled City Security to fill in the gaps."

"They found us this evening," said the sergeant, slurping down the stew.

"Then, that was the rumble of artillery I heard."

Matthias joined in. "It wasn't artillery. It was an aircraft, and it was armed."

Felix choked back his surprise. "They haven't used one of those since you and I were cadets." He jabbed Jeremiah in the ribs. "Is he worth it, Jeremiah?"

The sergeant wiped his lips with his sleeve. "Noah thought so."

"Well then, he's a wreck. Rot Fever, from the look of him. Got it bad, too. Anybody else got it?"

"The boy, but he seems to be doing a lot better."

"Well then, let's get some food in them and get them cleaned up. Matthias, I'm going to go make a toddy."

Matthias felt the rawness of his skin from the scrub brush and whatever pungent soap the sergeant used on him. At least his belly was full.

"I've done what I can, Matthias," said the sergeant.

Matthias knew Jeremiah couldn't get it all. Black flecks dotted his skin. It had bonded to him. At the present rate, he'd have ten or twelve more years before the Rot killed him as dead as Samuel's mother. Considering that the missile volley, or the Scottish Mafia, or Gideon's troops should have killed him already, ten years didn't sound all that bad.

The illness was another matter. He kept feeling worse. He imagined his temperature going higher and higher until his vital organs shut down. It would have been far more merciful had Jeremiah shot him at the edge of the boulder field. "What happened out there, in the forest?"

The sergeant pretended not to hear him.

"A poor acting job, Jeremiah. I study people for a living."

"A demon visited me on the boulder field when I found the girls."

"That much I know," said Matthias. "When I saw you, you were in a different place."

"Have you heard of the Wichita Six?"

Matthias knew the tale. Traitorous civilians attacked a small group of the Order outside Wichita, Kansas. The Wichita Six were the survivors of that unit. They counterattacked the mob and killed every last one. Every schoolboy wanted to be one of those brave soldiers. "The Wichita Six were the brave soldiers of the Order that broke the back of the Kansas Riots."

The sergeant's face widened into a sneer. "It is a lie."

"What are you saying, sergeant?"

"There were twenty men in my unit—and an officer. He was a greener than green lieutenant and he ordered us into an encampment of women and their children. When we saw them, we talked and offered them the peace of God if they left the farmer's fields they occupied."

The idea of a soldier of the Order negotiating anything surprised Matthias. "You offered them safe passage?"

"There were no weapons except diaper pins. The intelligence on them was completely wrong."

"That's not what the history texts say."

"That's because the Synod tells you what to read. My wonderful lieutenant needed a notch on his gun so that he could get promoted. He gave the order to fire from the safety of his command post before me and my men could get clear. We were caught in the crossfire, dying amidst the screams of women and children. I hear them still. Only six of us survived."

The recollection of Jeremiah jamming the gun against his chin stuck in Matthias's mind. "What happened to the lieutenant?"

"He became a captain. Posthumously. I shot him myself that day, may he rot in Hell. Both weapons operators killed themselves months later. The radio man ended up in an institution. Within a year, the six were down to three. One retired and joined the

Salvation Army. Another quit and ran a farm near a biodiesel plant. I remained in active service and was assigned to Indiantown Gap to be forgotten, just like the facts."

The care of the gravesites became clear to Matthias. The dead were the only ones that knew the truth. "Was Noah Finney one of the survivors?"

The sergeant blinked and turned his face away. Twice he tried to speak. Twice he failed. On the third time, he managed to croak out an answer. "He was the best among us. Told me and Felix he'd found redemption in the saving of others and invited us to do the same. It was outright treason."

"Did you find redemption?"

"I've tried. God knows I've tried, but the things I've seen, Matthias. I can't stop seeing them."

"Which is what you saw today."

"Yes."

Matthias put his hands on Jeremiah's shoulders. "You did what you could, brother. You didn't kill them, the Order did. The Synod did."

"I saw them die. I've seen many die."

"Then it is time to stay focused on the living." Matthias rose and headed to the other room. "You know, I've seen the way you look at Beth and the way she looks at you."

"What of it?"

"Jeremiah, there is redemption in her eyes if ever I saw it."

"Do you think so?"

"Yes," said Matthias, wishing for some redemption of his own.

Chapter 36: Verses 1-49

Matthias found redemption in a mug of Felix's herbal toddy. His nose and his throat burned from whatever the former soldier mixed into the heady brew.

When their host distributed blankets, a renewed Samuel returned with two. The child laid the blanket on the floor and pointed.

"Thank you, son." Matthias flopped onto it and drifted off to sleep. He soon heard his father's words in his dreams.

"Thank you, son," said Matthias's father. His voice was garbled, his breathing labored.

Matthias tried to be so much older than twelve, touching the back of his hand against his father's head the way his father used to. "Shhh, you're burning up."

His father sputtered some more. Gone were the great heaving coughs. "I'll be fine soon enough. Thank you for coming out here with me."

"We should have stayed home." Matthias wished his mother were there, but father insisted on going to the woods at the edge of the farm to camp out while he still had the strength. They used to walk for miles around their acreage when it was in bloom, and he would be none the less for the wear. It was always Matthias who was tired. Now, the farmer, the outdoorsman, handyman, teacher, and father lay. It took all of his being just to get this far.

His father wheezed. "I love being out here. It's not that I don't want to be at home, but I thought I'd come out here for a night."

Matthias stood over him, wanting to keep him warm, make him well. But there was nothing to do but pray. "Almighty Lord, heal my father. He is a good man. Take Uncle Cornelius in his stead."

"That's not a very nice prayer, son."

"You are seven-times-seventy the man Uncle Cornelius is. If there's really a God in Heaven, He will hear the words of my heart and make it so."

"We cannot question the ways of the Lord our God."

Matthias didn't believe that for a second. It was what people said when things didn't go their way. He wanted answers. He wanted to know why his father lay near death while his miserable rapist uncle sat in the city fat and happy. He wanted to know why the crops didn't grow, why people starved. He wanted to know why his prayers, and theirs, were never heard. It would have to wait. Right now, all that mattered was his father's rest. "Yes, father."

His father's voice lowered to a whisper. "Tell me son, has the sky cleared?

Looking out of the window, Matthias said, "Some."

"What do you see?"

The sound of urgent whispers woke Matthias.

"What do you see?" said the sergeant.

Matthias turned over and found Jeremiah and Felix staring out of the window. Both men were tense, as tense as when the aircraft attacked. They took turns looking through a small pair of binoculars. He got to his feet and moved alongside Felix. On the road below, headlights stretched out into the distance. "What's going on?"

"The Order is here."

Matthias wished he would have remained asleep. "Now what?"

"We wait."

"Shouldn't we be getting out of here?"

Laughing, Felix said, "How far do you think we'd get on my tractor before they caught up to us?" He passed the binoculars to Jeremiah. "What did you think?"

The sergeant pressed the binoculars to his eyes. "The trucks keep coming. They'll be up to regiment strength by morning."

"How many is that?" said Matthias.

"Fifteen hundred at least. They must really, really want you."

"Are we safe here?"

"Yes, my guess is that they've come to search the boulder field for our remains."

Felix took the binoculars. "No bivouac equipment, one assault rifle per man, two clips, and a pint of water. Standard body armor and boots. They're in a hurry."

Jeremiah nodded. "Fast and light. They expect to be done with the mission in less than a day. Wait till they try running up that mountain in those boots."

Felix chuckled.

Matthias didn't get the joke. "What's so funny?"

The sergeant said, "They're wearing a standard issue kit. It's meant for light duty around the city, not out here. It's pretty stuff, but not right for this terrain. They don't even have field jackets."

Focusing the binoculars, Felix said, "Speaking about pretty, take a look at that one."

Jeremiah gazed down into the valley. "Oh, he is a pretty one. He's got to be the commander. Would you look at his boots."

Matthias snatched the binoculars out of the sergeant's hand and focused them on the troops. A man materialized out of the haze, impeccable uniform, overly dignified bearing, and black boots reflecting in the headlights. He could almost hear them clomp on the asphalt. A pall of dread descended over him.

"Something the matter, Matthias?" said the sergeant.

He handed the binoculars over and tried to collect himself. "The officer is the Inquisitor General, Gideon Stanmore. The last time I saw him, he was dead."

The sergeant took another look. "He seems well enough to me. Was he dead more than three days?"

"Very funny."

"Did you slit his throat?"

"No."

"Well, he is no Risen Christ. You were mistaken. And I am, too. I've underestimated our enemy."

Felix leaned against the wall. "True enough. With all those troops down there, there can be no transport north."

The sergeant stroked his chin, his eyes casting about. "Once their sortie to the boulders proves fruitless, they will look elsewhere."

The implication caused a flurry of cramps in Matthias's stomach. "We're trapped."

Chapter 37: Verses 1-60

To Matthias, Gideon's presence was a huge joke perpetrated on him by the Almighty. The man appeared hale and hearty while he shuddered under the weight of infirmity. *I pray, Dear Lord, that the Rot takes me before this stooge brings me to heel before my uncle.* Matthias rolled over on his bed. *If You hear me at all.*

About an hour before sunrise, the sergeant roused everyone and recounted the details of what they saw during the night.

The group sat on the floor, numb, defeated.

Nathan was the first to speak. "Why don't we just give them what they want? They will surely reward us for our loyalty."

Standing up, Luke pointed to his scar. "You see this? This what the Synod gave me for years of loyal service in the halls of government. When they found out I was gay, they marked me for Changeling surgery with their damned black dot. I escaped and cut if off myself." He spat. "There's hundreds of places like this refinery all across the nation. This is where you're sent when you don't submit."

Felix nodded. "Oh, they'll send you there all right, but you won't last long. The Order wants their man and will probably toss anyone traveling with Matthias right into the fermenting tanks."

It was another reference to biodiesel refinery that Matthias didn't understand. "You make it sound as if the Order will cook us for dinner."

"Hardly," replied Felix. "Surely you can smell the dead."

"The crematorium? Yes, how can I not smell it? The dead are brought here for disposal."

Luke laughed. "Our distinguished Elder doesn't know about biodiesel."

"What are you saying?"

Luke's face filled with disgust. "The only worth of the worthless is death. Their carcasses are brought here for rendering and refining. Just how many bodies to the gallon does your limousine get, Elder?"

Matthias stood motionless, remembering the smell of his vehicle's exhaust. He felt a wave of nausea come over him. "I never knew."

"That's enough," said Jeremiah. "Felix and I discussed our tactical situation. We've come up with two strategies."

"Death and what else?" said Luke.

"Continue on foot."

The room transformed into a noiseless vacuum.

To Matthias, the thought of any more hiking in his current condition was beyond comprehension. God laughed at him again by granting his prayer. He could die out there in the wilderness or wait for Gideon to show up at the door. It took less than a second to mull it over. Perhaps the coyotes would crush his bones and make the Inquisitor General search for him until the end of days. "Certain death or uncertain death. My, what wonderful choices. Put me down for 'uncertain death.'"

Nathan shook his head. "How arrogant you are. We should remain here."

"Not half as arrogant as the man that chases us," countered Matthias. "Is there anywhere we can hide, sergeant?"

"Hiding just makes us easier to catch." The sergeant crossed his arms. "You are men and women of free will in the eyes of God. Your choice?"

Beth spoke to Jeremiah. "Wither thou goes, so shall I."

Jeremiah looked stunned, dumbfounded by the words of the prophet Ruth and an implied marriage proposal.

Matthias could feel the smile rise on his lips. *Redemption, indeed.*

The sergeant recovered, his face beaming. "Then walk by my side."

Matthias felt Samuel stand next to him. The child smiled broadly and nodded.

Luke looked out the window at the lights of the refinery. "May the Synod rot in Hell. I walk to freedom. I walk with you, sergeant."

Nathan simmered in his thoughts. "It would seem that I have no choice."

"Very well, then." Jeremiah turned to Matthias. "Were you not an Elder of the Bank, a minister of the corporation, and a captain to your employees?"

The sudden and formal recitation of official titles puzzled Matthias. "Yes."

Jeremiah took Beth by the hand. "Then marry us."

Beth blushed.

A great laugh leapt out of Matthias. When he settled, he found the couple less than entertained. "I'm sorry. I don't demean your intent, holy that it is. Marriage performed by Elders is an old wives' tale. I have no legal authority to do so."

Beth laughed. "What do any of us have to do with legal authority?"

"Point taken." Giddiness took the edge off of the fever. A little doubt slipped in. Wedding verses weren't something he was well schooled on. "I don't know if I know all the right words."

"Just do your best."

Matthias said, "Your full name?"

"Elizabeth Ann Meade."

Samuel darted away. The door opened and closed.

"Samuel, where are…," said Matthias, who wondered what just happened. "Nathan, you, and Luke are the official witnesses. Does this suit everyone?"

They nodded.

"Then, by the authority of the Bank of Job, I ask you, Jeremiah

Sanford, do you take Elizabeth Ann Meade as your wife, here before the eyes of God Almighty? Do you pledge your love to her, to have and to hold, from this day forward, in richness and in health until death do you part?"

"I do."

"I ask you, Elizabeth Ann Meade, do you take Jeremiah Sanford as your husband, submitting unto him before the Lord? Do you pledge your love to him, to have and to hold, from this day forward, in richness and in health until death do you part?"

"I do."

Matthias turned toward Jeremiah. "Do we have a ring?"

Felix called out, "Um, yes." Felix grabbed Beth's hand, sized up her ring finger and disappeared into another room.

The outside door opened and closed. Samuel appeared, a fern branch in his hand. He trotted over and gave it to Beth.

"My bouquet. Oh, Samuel, thank you."

Felix returned and opened his hand. An assortment of plastic washers lay in his palm. "One of them is bound to fit."

After the couple fumbled with the washers, Matthias continued. "Jeremiah, repeat after me. With this ring I wed you and pledge my love to you."

Jeremiah slipped the washer over her finger. "With this ring I wed you and pledge my love to you."

"Elizabeth, repeat after me. With this ring I wed you and pledge my love to you."

"With this ring I wed you and pledge my love to you."

"By the power of the Most High, I pronounce you man and wife. You may kiss the bride."

The couple kissed.

A shrill whistle resounded in the valley. Soldiers marched and their steps could be heard heading away from the cabin.

Jeremiah and Beth broke their embrace, the flush of romance gone from their cheeks.

The sergeant's face soured. "We leave in fifteen minutes. Gather your gear."

"So much for the honeymoon," said Matthias.

Chapter 38: Verses 1-95

Felix handed a bundle to each sojourner. "Wedding gifts," he called them.

Matthias undid the coarse blanket that served as wrapping and found mission bread inside. "Looks like more of a Going-Away present."

"The weather's getting colder. Haven't seen anything like it. You might need something extra to keep you warm," said Felix. He turned and shook the sergeant's hand. "I expect your little ones to be calling me 'Uncle Felix' when we meet again."

Jeremiah hesitated for a full second. The idea of children caught him by surprise. He let out a gentle chuckle and said, "You'll make a good babysitter."

At the forest's edge, Matthias stared down into the valley at the empty troop transports. Gideon's men were on their way up the far slope. It gave them time, but how much?

Samuel came up next to him, looking off toward the refinery and nodding.

The scene perplexed Matthias. The biodiesel plant was probably the final resting place of the child's mother, yet serenity filled the boy's face. "Do you see your mother there?"

The boy's lips formed a "no."

Matthias found himself even more perplexed.

Samuel bent down and dug a shallow hole with his hand. He picked up an oblong stone, laid it in the cavity, and covered it up with dirt.

"She's buried?"

The boy nodded.

The sergeant joined them. "Ready?"

"Just about," said Matthias. "Samuel seems quite satisfied that his mother was buried."

"Would you like one of your loved ones cooked into biodiesel?"

The very thought of it tore at Matthias's heart. "Agreed, but I don't see how a beggar could afford such a thing. Was it Captain Finney's doing?"

"Noah didn't have the means. Even if he did, he would have bought food for the living and left the bodies to the Synod. It was a funny thing, though."

"Oh?"

"When we discussed helping you escape, he mentioned the boy's good fortune. 'A blessing of the Living Christ,' he called it. Samuel came into a lot of credit right before his mother died—a blue card given out by one of those sanctimonious rich fools on their way to the city. The boy could have lived well for a while on that card, but he chose to lay his mother to rest. It was such a noble act that Noah asked the child to be our messenger."

Matthias looked down at Samuel, remembering the moment outside the gate, the look in the child's eyes. Perhaps he did something worth a damn after all. "You're a good son."

Samuel's face beamed. His arms opened, and he hugged Matthias.

The embrace caught him off guard. He choked back his emotions and said, "I buried my mother, too."

The boy hugged him more tightly.

"May they rest in peace until the last day when we will see them again."

The further Matthias got from Palmerton, the more he felt the mountain's chill against his fevered cheeks. Weariness soon returned and hope was something he left behind on his mother's deathbed.

He shifted his attention away from his own discomfort and watched Samuel move ahead of him. The boy's pace was stronger now. His bout with the Rot Fever was short, and Matthias envied the child's resiliency. He also noticed the way Samuel never looked back, not at the refinery, or at the past. It was a characteristic that Matthias envied even more. If only he could ignore the child's embrace and the rush of memories it brought to him now.

Warm rain poured on the Kent family farm from clouds the color of steel. Eucalyptus trees swayed in the wind. The breeze bore the smell of wet soil from the barren fields and up to the hilltop where he stood. A lone granite monument proclaimed the name of "Kent." It occupied the center of a plot of land defined by a wrought iron fence. Arrayed around it were the headstones of his forebears. Some were so worn that the names upon them were fainter than the memory of the person buried beneath them. One headstone was newer than the others, its memories much deeper than the inscription carved into its face. It bore the name of his father, gone more than ten years.

Matthias hadn't come to visit the dearly departed. His purpose was far more troubling to him. It was the idea, the certainty, that he'd be erecting another headstone soon -- his mother's.

He left the family graveyard and headed home. The physician's terse "congestive heart failure" played over and over in his mind.

There had been scares in the recent past. Coughs. Relentless fatigue. Heart murmurs. All ignored, until Naomi called him one awful night.

He chided himself, then tried to dismiss it. After all, there had been business to attend to, plans to execute and favors to cash in. An appointment to Elder lay within his grasp. He'd sit at the table with dear Uncle Cornelius, just inches away from his revenge. It was proof positive that God answered his prayers.

He prayed another prayer. Restore my mother oh Lord, so that she may see her enemies perish. Let their time be at hand. Make me the tool of Your Almighty will.

Matthias walked into his mother's bedroom, watching the blankets move so slightly that Matthias fretted each time she exhaled.

"Mattie?" she said without opening her eyes.

"How are you, mother?"

"Tired. I'm glad you're here."

"What'd the doctor say?"

"I should rest."

"Then you should listen to him."

"Mattie, I want you—"

"Rest."

She fought his command at first, then closed her eyes and fell off to sleep.

Matthias watched each rising of her chest and prayed.

A frigid wind brought an ache to Matthias's hands, but the memory was far more cutting than the wind. It reopened a gaping wound, a black void out of which poured nothing but grief. Until that moment, Matthias hadn't allowed himself to recall that time.

He cursed the fever, the devilish thing that weakened his spirit enough to hear her voice again—to hear *those* words again. *How could you ask that of me, Mother?*

The sergeant halted the column, pulled his blanket out of his pack, and draped it over Beth. Beth did the same for her husband. The others followed suit.

Samuel stepped off the trail, grabbed a long branch and tore off its smaller limbs until he made a crude staff.

The boy offered it to Matthias and he took it. "I guess I am Paul of Tarsus again."

Samuel flashed a grin and set off down the path.

Matthias followed, pleased that the blanket kept some of the wind and cold at bay. His comfort fled as quickly as it arrived.

A broken tree branch hung near the trail some dozen or so

yards behind them, waist high and just like before. It couldn't have been Samuel's doing, and Ruth was dead.

"Is there a problem?" barked the sergeant.

Matthias regarded Jeremiah's glare, the authoritative inflection in his tone. In no condition to engage in repartee, he replied, "No, sir."

The sergeant rolled his eyes. "Then keep up."

"Yes, sergeant," he said, thoughts simmering in his ailing mind. Was Jeremiah simply playing soldier or conveying a warning to ignore what he saw? Why would he do it? Weren't they almost within shouting distance of the Order just a few hours ago?

Whatever questions Matthias had fell away when another wave of fever hit him. The pounding in his head matched the pounding of his feet. Each step required more and more of his will. There would be time to consider the sergeant's actions later when he hunkered down for the night.

Dusk came early borne on thickening clouds.

Jeremiah halted and said, "We stop here for the night. There will be no need for a fort."

Relief spread over Matthias. He knew he didn't have the strength to go one more step let alone carry rocks around.

Nathan glanced around. "Is it safe?"

"From the coyotes, yes. They are afraid of the same thing we are."

Nathan dropped his pack. He pointed a finger at Matthias. "I'm not sleeping in the same tent with him. Look at him. He will spread his disease and kill us all."

Beth pulled her tent out of her pack. "Rot Fever isn't contagious."

"What about pneumonia? Tuberculosis? He could have anything now. I didn't come this far just to die in the middle of nowhere."

I did, thought Matthias.

The sergeant helped Beth set up her tent. "You're being foolish."

Nathan barked back, "Then he can sleep with you."

"My own company will I keep," said Matthias. He dumped

the contents of his pack on the ground, pawed through it, and found his tent.

Another set of hands took the tent from him. They belonged to Samuel. In just a few minutes, the tent took shape. Samuel collected Matthias's gear and tossed it inside. He grinned and held open the flap.

"You are a good son," said Matthias. He went inside and slid into his sleeping bag. It warmed him, but not enough to blunt the utter cold. He shivered, blinking in and out of consciousness until he finally trailed off to sleep. Dreams began anew.

Matthias sat in the family cabin, his knees drawn up against his chest. It was cold and damp, but that didn't stop the crickets outside from chirping loudly. His father wheezed and turned over on his cot.

He had seen his father fade like the great trees on their property. They were once proud, towering. Now, they lay withered and drawn.

To Matthias, it was madness to come out here, madness to sleep far from one's comfortable bed. But it was at his father's request, and there might not be many more of them.

Sleep evaded him and he prayed. Why should my father die, while my uncle lives? Why, Dear God, should it be so?

The wheezing continued, long and slow.

Matthias tried to pray even harder. While he could recite so many verses from the Bible, words failed him. Instead, he wondered how many prayers went unanswered. There were times that God just didn't bother to respond—if there was a God at all.

At that moment, he realized he couldn't wait for God. He would answer his own prayers. He would ascend the ranks. He would cast Rourke out in the name of God. All would be well.

The wheezing slowed.

The change in rhythm set Matthias on edge. He moved closer and kept a watch over his father until early morning.

The moon broke through a momentary opening in the clouds. Matthias watched the light fill the room, and then retreat. Shadows returned. A dank breeze slithered into the room. The crickets outside fell silent. He shivered.

His father shivered, too. Matthias covered him with his bedroll, but there was no sound.

He tore the covers off and felt for a pulse. There was none. His father's skin was cool to the touch.

Matthias fell to his knees. Tears streamed from his face.

A fire burned within his chest. Did You hear me? Have You ever heard me?

There was no reply.

Chapter 39: Verses 1-82

The fire of Matthias's fever told him he had lived through the night. There was a decided warmth around him, yet his breath fogged the air. He sat up and found a pair of blankets on top of his sleeping bag. Beside him slept the boy, his sleeping bag open and partially draped over Matthias.

"Samuel."

The child awoke.

Matthias noted the tinge of blue in the boy's lips. He pulled a hand from his sleeping bag and touched the child's face. It was frigid. "I owe you my life again."

Samuel grinned.

Pulling the blankets off, Matthias took them, and wrapped them around the boy. He looked at the tussled hair, the brightness in the child's eyes. No more could he burden the child with keeping him alive. "Please, don't do that again. My life is in God's hands now."

Samuel shook his head yes.

"The Bible is hidden in my family chapel back home. Match your fingers to the hand of God on the altar mosaic and a door will open." Matthias spread his fingers and mimed the action. "Do you understand?"

Samuel nodded.

"Good then, our bargain is fulfilled." He could feel the chill seep into his sleeping bag and he shivered. One end of a blanket came around him. Samuel pulled in close. Warmth returned.

It was such a simple act, but one that Matthias couldn't fathom. Their transaction was complete. The boy should abandon him on the spot. But there he sat next to him, the way Matthias used to sit with his father.

A distant and familiar drone shattered the moment. It was the mechanized sound of tires wailing in the distance.

A tent flap unzipped and a voice broke the morning stillness. It was the sergeant. "Get up now. The Order is on the move."

An hour into their flight, Jeremiah gathered them together. He took a stone and scratched some lines in the dirt.

He pointed to one line on the right. "The Order is moving along this highway, here." His hand shifted to the left. "We are here in the mountains. It doesn't take a great strategist to guess our movements at this point. They will deploy troops all along the highway and work their way north. We must stay ahead of them. With the help of the Lord Jesus, we will reach the river."

Nathan glanced down at the drawing and back up to the sergeant. "The Delaware. We're headed to the Delaware River and the demilitarized zone."

"Yes. The Order will not pursue us into the DMZ. It would be an act of war far greater than using an aircraft. Sanctuary awaits us on the other side. From there, it's less than a half-day's ride to the Hindu Lands."

Beth studied the drawing and wrinkled her brow. "If they deploy as you say, their troops will cut us off."

The sergeant winked at her. "Only if we continue in the same direction. We will turn north. Now, eat your rations. You will need your strength."

As everyone pulled food out of their packs, Matthias spoke to the sergeant. "Jeremiah, a moment?" He waved the soldier aside.

Matthias lowered his voice. "I can't keep up."

"Don't quit on me now. We're close."

"The boy knows the location of the Bible. Our agreement is fulfilled. Take the others and go."

Jeremiah grinned. "You forget who I am."

Matthias had no idea what the sergeant meant. "Eh?"

"I'm Moses. I'm taking you to the Promised Land."

"New Jersey is not the Promised Land."

"True enough, but why not let God decide your fate instead of giving me excuses now."

"This fever isn't an excuse. I can barely walk."

The sergeant laid the back of his hand on Matthias's forehead. "Yes, you do burn with hellfire to be sure."

Desperation grew in Matthias's soul. The sergeant now knew just how sick he was. The group had to leave him behind. It was just a matter of time before the fever or the Order took him. He preferred the fever. The doctors of the Order might restore his health. Then they'd squeeze his mind for the Bible's location. All would be for naught. "I don't want to be taken alive."

Jeremiah's face darkened. "The Rot has maddened you for sure. I will not take your life."

The sergeant's words struck Matthias as funny. A day ago, the sergeant seemed all too willing to do just that. "Just give me the means to end things on my own terms."

"I will not provide you with a means to go to Hell."

"Suicide isn't what I have in mind. I wish to send someone on to St. Peter before I go."

"The Inquisitor?"

"He is to me what your lieutenant was to you."

Jeremiah seemed unconvinced.

"All I'm asking for is a pistol with few rounds. His death will end the pursuit." Matthias gripped Jeremiah's shoulder. "Ease my way to Heaven, brother."

The sergeant pursed his lips, looked around, and pulled out one of his sidearms. "There are fifteen rounds. Use them well. Go with God."

"If I were going with God," said Matthias, "we would already be in the Hindu Lands." He took the gun.

"This is no time for blasphemy."

"There can only be blasphemy if God is listening."

The sergeant's face turned blood red. "In this hour of your life, you should be praying to God for deliverance."

Matthias cocked the pistol and slid it into his belt. "You've given me my deliverance."

At first Matthias kept up, but the illness slowed his progress. The others moved on, out of sight. All but one. Samuel.

"You should catch up to the sergeant."

The boy shook his head and walked along the trail. It was easy enough to follow—one broken branch at a time.

It baffled Matthias as to why the sergeant permitted the boy to fall behind. It made no sense. The Inquisitor might find them at any moment. Sickness darkened his reason more than the clouds obscured the sun. Soon, all he could do was follow Samuel like a beast of burden and walk on.

Late in the day, Matthias regarded the faltering daylight and clouds stacked together like the scales of a fish. The blanket no longer staved off the deepening cold. All he wanted to do was sleep.

Samuel tugged his hand.

"Let me be."

The boy shook his head and pointed.

"I can't walk anymore."

Tugging turned into yanking.

"I said, 'Let me be.'"

"We heard you," said Jeremiah. "Well done, Samuel."

Matthias couldn't stop shaking even though Beth, Jeremiah and Samuel gave him their blankets. His mind drifted in and out of sleep. When night fell, he couldn't tell if his eyes were opened or closed.

Faces appeared before him, nameless souls in rags, colleagues from the bank, Benjamin's energetic eyes, and Samuel's placid smile. Colors burst inside his mind until they faded into shades of gray. He saw himself in his office, his hand outstretched and grasping the silhouette of a cross. Blind Johnny appeared, the emptiness of his eyes pulling him into the void. Blackness drowned him until he fought his way to its surface.

At the far edge of the void stood his mother's deathbed. She lay on it, resting what was left of her heart. His mouth opened in a roar of grief, but no sound came forth. The blackness consumed it.

He made his way to her side and knelt down. His knuckles turned white with the zeal of prayers.

The whisper of her voice answered him. "The Lord calls me home, Mattie."

"Don't say that, mother." Matthias could feel the tears leave his eyes. "My time is at hand, God willing. I will become an Elder and unseat Uncle Cornelius. The Lord's vengeance will be ours."

She turned toward him, her hand cupping his chin as if he were a child instead of a grown man. "The Lord's vengeance or yours?"

"Not mine, mother. Yours."

Her eyes turned sorrowful. "It is not my prayer."

"Not your prayer? He defiled you. He defiled our family. God heard my prayers. He has laid a path to righteousness. You will live to see him cast out and gnash his teeth with the unworthy."

"Matthias." She pulled her hand back, her voice becoming fainter and stronger at the same time. "Have you forgotten that justice and vengeance is the Lord's? Not yours. Not mine."

"I am the Lord's instrument."

"The Lord is your instrument."

"How can you say that?"

"Pray to God to forgive your uncle."

Her words seared Matthias's heart. It was a weak and ridiculous statement. Anger burned white hot within him. "I cannot. The Lord has set this before me."

"Then I shall pray for your forgiveness."

Matthias clenched her hand. Her grip didn't tighten around his. He looked into her eyes and found a depthless black staring back. His anger fled when a cold rush of grief poured into him.

He wrapped his arms around her. "Give her life, oh Lord. Give her life."

There was no reply.

Chapter 40: Verses 1-56

Matthias awoke, trembling from his nightmare and bathed in sweat. Another gray dawn lit the walls of the tent. As the day before, his face stung from the cold air, but no illness clouded his thoughts. He felt hungry, thirsty, spent. The fever had left him.

"Samuel? Samuel. All is well. I am well."

There was no movement.

Samuel lay next to him uncovered, his sleeping bag draped over Matthias. He brushed the blankets aside. "Didn't you hear me? The fever is gone. Samuel?" He touched the child's face. It was cold and his lips were blue. "Samuel! Samuel! Dear God, no. No!"

Someone tore the tent flap open. It was Jeremiah. "What's wrong?"

"Samuel."

The sergeant pulled the boy outside and placed his fingers on child's neck.

Jeremiah's shoulders slumped. "He is with God."

"He's dead, you mean."

Jeremiah rocked the child in his arms, both of his fists balled up. "He is with God."

Matthias could feel the old rage, the old fire burn in his chest. He clambered out of the tent. "There is no God."

The sergeant's face turned from anguish to anger. "It is by your blasphemies that God punishes us all."

"My blasphemies? I am an Elder of the Bank of Job. It is by my hand that prayers are answered. By my blasphemies thousands upon thousands are saved every Sunday. Now look at me, Rot-ridden and filthy like some cockroach in a sewer. Don't I deserve to be saved? Haven't I paid penance? Haven't I prayed? Women and children are massacred before us, and you have the nerve to put the blame on me? Even King David didn't have to put up with this shit."

Jeremiah sprang from the ground and pounced on Matthias. He grabbed him by the hair and shoved his head toward Samuel's body. "You sanctimonious ass. This poor child gave his life for you. He believed in God. He is worth more to God than you. Cockroaches are worth more to God than you." With his other hand the sergeant pulled out his remaining pistol and pressed the barrel against Matthias's temple.

The others poured from their tents.

Matthias stared at Samuel, guilt twisting in heart. *Why?* He fought in the soldier's grasp. *No more.* "Do it. Ease my way, brother."

The safety clicked off.

Matthias awaited the blast. It would be good to be done with this world, he thought. *No more deaths. No more Order. No more Synod. No more Uncle Cornelius. Good riddance and Amen.*

"Jeremiah," said Beth, her voice distant yet strong.

The timbre of her voice startled Matthias. It was right out of his dream. She sat next to Samuel, her hand caressing the child's dark locks.

"Let him go. You are my husband, and my husband is no murderer. You are no longer a soldier of the Order. Justice and vengeance is the Lord's. Let us pray for him and let God decide his fate."

The sergeant released his grip.

Matthias collapsed to the ground. He pushed himself up on his elbows and glared at her. "How do you know those words?"

Beth looked back at him. "What words?"

"The words of my mother." Tears ran down his face.

She shook her head. "You're mad."

Matthias knelt down beside her and touched Samuel's cheek. The sight of the boy extinguished his anger. "I wish I were. I wish I were."

The sergeant holstered his pistol. "Get up. We need to leave. The troops may have heard you."

"Not without burying him."

"You truly are mad," said Jeremiah. "We cannot linger."

"He cared for me in life. I will care for him in death."

The sergeant nodded and spoke to Beth. "Get the others started. Head north. We'll catch up."

"You heard the man," said Beth, shooing Nathan and Luke into action.

Matthias gazed at the countenance of the boy and softened his tone. "I'm not looking for help, Jeremiah. Allow me to honor him in my own way."

"As you wish. I will wait for you."

"There is no need to wait. I want you to get Beth and the others to safety. Nobody else dies because of me. I will tell you what I told the boy. What you seek is in my family chapel behind a mosaic of God. Place your fingers against Jehovah's hand and press. The rest will become apparent."

Jeremiah shook his head. "The Order will find you."

Matthias patted the pistol. "Yes. Yes, they will."

Matthias hugged Samuel, then gently slipped the boy into a sleeping bag. One by one, he began stacking rocks atop it, one for each measure of guilt he felt. Matthias looked over the pile of stones. There would enough to cover the boy, but not enough to cover his guilt.

Jeremiah approached, rifle in hand, and face fighting back tears. He took a handful of earth and cast it onto Samuel. "Ashes to ashes…"

"Dust to dust," said Matthias. "He was a good son born in hideous times. May perpetual light shine upon him."

"May God hold him in the palm of his hand." The sergeant

extended his hand. "May God do the same for you."

Matthias shook Jeremiah's hand. As he did, the sergeant embraced him. Beth and Luke waved to him in the distance. Nathan stood, his back turned, and his hand grasping the branch of a small tree.

Two swats on the back jarred Matthias back to the sergeant's hug.

"If you run into the Order, remember to aim for the head or hit them from the side. Their body armor will fend off anything else. Arms and legs are good too, but that will only slow them down. Understand?"

"Yes."

Jeremiah took a few steps and stopped. "If you manage to elude those fools, keep heading north for a couple of days then turn toward the sunrise. It will lead you to the Delaware. Cross it and tell the first person you see, 'Bilal.'"

"Bilal?" replied Matthias. "I don't remember anything in the Psalms about 'Bilal.'"

"Good," said Jeremiah, heading off through the brush to catch up to the others.

Matthias finished burying Samuel. The aftereffects of the fever left him drained. He sat down next to the grave. *Why did you save me? You held the secret, and yet you stayed with me. We had no blood between us, no account unpaid.* His mind flashed with Samuel's smile, the curls in his hair, and the tug of his hand leading him on when he could go no further.

Matthias fought back more tears. His heart ached, and he could feel his mind falling toward the same void of grief as when his mother passed away. He could not go there now. It was weakness. It was shameful.

And he didn't care.

He cried in silent spasms. Tears flowed until all that was left was emptiness.

After a time, Matthias stood, his hand brushing against an object in his pocket. It was Theresa's rosary. He pulled it out and let it dangle from his hand. The crucifix spun until the face of

Christ stilled and gazed down on Samuel.

Matthias pulled a few rocks aside and laid the rosary on top of the sleeping bag. "Go with Theresa and Thaddeus. Have them show you where Ruth and Susanna are playing. If there's a heaven, that's where you will be, my son."

Chapter 41: Verses 1-114

As he shoved his gear into his pack, Matthias heard a single gunshot. He tracked the report into the hills ahead of him. His eyes surveyed the woods, and his ears strained to hear anything else beside the wind in the trees. When he did, he saw a broken branch on the sapling where Nathan stood a short while ago. "My God."

Matthias moved cautiously, spotting the next bent limb before leaving the last. Unfamiliar voices murmured ahead of him. It was the sound of orders being given, and of obedient replies.

The Order.

Leaving the path, he swung widely around the main source of chatter—a group of four troopers lounging on the rocks. Another set of voices loomed nearby, and Matthias moved deeper into the forest to see who it was. Yellow eyes greeted him. It was a large coyote, its pelt thick and the fur along its back raised in a ridge.

Another shot rang out, and an unearthly wail burst through the woods.

The coyote's fur and ears lowered. It scampered away.

The wail resounded again, longer, deeper and more pained. Matthias could feel a creeping dread inside his skin. The cry was that of a man—a man in supreme anguish.

Jeremiah.

Glancing down to avoid branches and rocks, he took his steps slowly. Laughter joined the moans, taunts, and a certain baritone that reminded him of glossy black boots. Matthias peered out from beside a boulder.

Luke lay on the ground, his eyes wide open and a bullet hole in his cheek. Matthias closed his eyes, hoping the scene was a part of some waking nightmare. When he opened them, Luke stared back at him with soulless intensity.

When he glanced away, he saw her lying on her side.

Beth.

A wound in her temple wept blood.

No, Dear God. No.

Thoughts of her raced through his mind—the way she cared for her sister, her strength, the tenderness in her voice when she spoke her wedding vows to Jeremiah.

A wrenching scream echoed in the woods.

Matthias ducked back behind the rock, cringing from its intensity. It took him a few seconds to muster his courage. He looked out again and choked back nausea.

Jeremiah stood bound to a tree with his shirt cut away. His abdomen lay open, dripping blood while Gideon turned a long, slender knife in his gut. The group of troopers he heard earlier looked away.

"I can do this all day, Sergeant Sanford," said the Inquisitor.

Jeremiah howled.

"Are you convinced he knows the location, Nathan?"

Nathan took a swig from a canteen. "Kent had to have told him where it was. He would have never left without it."

"Rot in Hell," gasped Jeremiah.

Gideon turned the blade again. "It is you who will rot in Hell for your traitorous acts. I will ask you one last time, sergeant. If you don't cooperate, we will get our answers from Kent."

The sergeant writhed. Recognition lit up on his face when he looked toward the boulder.

Matthias retreated behind the rock, afraid that the sergeant would give him away. Chaos gripped him.

Flee.

In that moment, rage and purpose melded in his heart. He would not abandon Jeremiah. A singular thought pierced the veil of fear.

There will be no weakness.

Matthias slid the pistol out of his belt and crept around the boulders.

The troopers' voices grew louder as he neared.

When he reached a clearing in the rocks, Matthias drew in a breath. He held it, letting the images of Beth and Luke sear his soul.

Matthias thumbed the safety.

Vengeance wasn't waiting for God this time.

He leapt into the troopers' midst, their faces frozen in shock. The surprise only lasted an instant, and they groped for their rifles.

Matthias brought the gunsight even with the nose of the closest man and pulled the trigger.

Before the trooper died, Matthias swung toward a second man who charged at him. He squeezed the trigger. The bullet punched a hole in his forehead. The soldier tumbled backward.

A third man cocked the action of his rifle and raised it to his shoulder. When he did, his side became exposed. Matthias remembered Jeremiah's advice and fired the pistol again and again until the man collapsed.

The last trooper brought his gun to bear on Matthias, and Matthias did the same. They faced each other. The young man's eyes glowed brown and bright like Samuel's.

Matthias hesitated.

The young trooper pulled the trigger. The firing pin clicked. The bullet never left the barrel. The trooper forgot to chamber a round.

Clarity returned. Matthias concentrated on a single brown eye and squeezed the trigger.

"Enough," commanded Gideon, his knife at the sergeant's throat.

Nathan stood beside them, one hand limply holding a pistol while the canteen quivered in the other.

Gideon hid behind the sergeant. "Drop your weapon, or I will finish what I started."

The sergeant groaned and opened his eyes. Matthias read the expression. His face held the pain of having what he loved most torn from his soul. But a different kind of look followed the first. Jeremiah kept glancing down and to his left.

Matthias followed the sergeant's queue. It led to a single exposed body part—a leg in a glossy black boot.

"All right, Gideon," said Matthias. He lowered his gun.

The Inquisitor pulled the knife away.

Matthias squeezed the trigger. The black boot split in a puff of pink mist. He brought the gun back up and pointed it at Nathan.

The history teacher froze, his mouth agape.

"Rot in Hell." Matthias pulled the trigger.

The bullet punctured the canteen. Nathan watched the water spill out. When it emptied, the teacher wobbled and fell.

Gideon crawled toward Nathan's gun.

Matthias dashed around Jeremiah and fired again. The bullet hit the Inquisitor square in the back, but didn't penetrate his body armor. The Inquisitor screamed. The concussion of each round slammed him into the ground. Matthias kept pulling the trigger until Gideon quit moving.

Matthias grabbed the knife and cut the ropes binding Jeremiah to the tree.

The sergeant fell in a heap, his eyelids blinking at the edge of consciousness. They opened. "I didn't tell them."

Matthias blanched at the wound and pressed his hand over it. Even the Synod's doctors would have a difficult time mending something so severe. "Be still my brother." His mind cast about, trying to think of what to do next.

Jeremiah sobbed. "They killed her, Matthias. They killed my Beth. That bastard put a gun to her head and killed her. I saw it. Oh God, he made me watch, but I didn't tell him."

The clarity fell away. Guilt rushed into Matthias's veins. "I'm sorry. I've killed you all."

Jeremiah shook his head and coughed up blood. "He killed her, not you. He killed everyone except you." He pawed at Matthias's coat. "You are God's anointed."

"I am a foolish businessman with a relic."

"You have been given the Truth."

"I have been given my undoing and yours."

"God is not through with you, brother. Noah understood."

"And he is dead, too, as is your wife. All for what? A book?"

A calmness came over Jeremiah. His voice softened. "A Bible."

"Too many have died for those pages, brother. Let the Rot consume it. Come, I will take you to the river. We'll find a doctor."

"Oh, I'm going to cross the river all right, but not the Delaware."

Matthias cradled Jeremiah's face in his hands. "Stay with me brother. We'll get help"

"No, Matthias, I cross the Jordan. I can see it now. Beth awaits."

"Now it is you who talks nonsense."

"It is you who denies what he sees. Please brother, let me lie by her side one more time. Ease my way." The sergeant staggered to his feet.

Matthias felt the soldier's trembling body press against him as he slid Jeremiah's arm around his neck. There was nothing more to do except take him to Beth.

Jeremiah whimpered at the sight.

Matthias shuddered at the sound, so pained, so full of loss.

Laying down next to her, Jeremiah pulled Beth close. With a heaving sigh, he kissed her and breathed no more.

Matthias let out a scream that shattered the silence. He raised his fists heavenward. "How can You do this? These people believe in You, and You smite them like insects underfoot. How dare You toy with us." He fell to his knees, pounding the earth. "No more of this. No more. I am not your plaything. The Bible stays locked in its crypt forever. No one else dies because of it. I swear it. Do You hear me?" The pounding stopped and sobs took over. "No, of course not. You don't hear me. You've never heard me."

A hiss emanated from above. Matthias tracked the sound to a lone buzzard circling above the trees. He looked down at the bodies of Luke, Beth, and Jeremiah. No matter how close the Order might be, he would not let them be defiled. Urgency replaced anger, and he set to work burying them.

More buzzards orbited overhead. Matthias laid the last stone upon his friends and choked back his sorrow. Perhaps now they could rest in peace. Perhaps now they were free from all the predators of this world—especially those with two-legs. He made his way to Nathan's body and spat on his face. "Burn in Hell."

Matthias turned his attention to Stanmore. He kicked the Inquisitor in the ribs. "Awake, for your time is at hand."

Gideon groaned and lifted his head. "No, your time is at hand. I offer you one chance to tell me where the Bible is."

"Or what? You'll stick a knife in my gut, too?"

"My troops are coming."

Matthias kicked him again. "Don't lie to me, Gideon. I'm in advertising. I lie to people every day. I've been lying to them every Sunday since I joined the Bank." He lifted Stanmore by the chin and dropped him. "Your troops aren't anywhere around here, and your sentries are fodder for the buzzards. You positioned your troops to drive us to this spot, you and Nathan."

Gideon looked around.

"Yes, I figured it out."

Stanmore groped at his collar. "Soldiers of the Order, help me."

"Save your breath." Matthias held out the shattered pieces of Gideon's lapel transceiver. "They can't hear you, not that you had it turned on while you tortured Jeremiah. Tell me, was Nathan an agent of yours?"

Gideon's shouts silenced.

"I bet that the Synod planted him to discover who was smuggling refugees to the Hindu Lands. He did the laundry back at camp. He must have seen my wallet and discovered who I was. I can just imagine your smug face when he got word to you that I was among the group. Did he leave a message back at the cemetery?"

"We should have killed you out on the rocks," said Gideon.

"You tried to kill everybody else, but you couldn't take the risk that I told somebody where the Bible was. You needed me alive to know. That's why you waited for a nice secluded spot like this to capture me. You couldn't even trust your own troops. Rumors would start, questions asked. Things would get out of hand."

"Get it over with."

"God, you're arrogant."

An animal called out from the forest in a repeated yip.

"What was that?" said Gideon.

It was the first time Matthias saw the Inquisitor's veneer slip into fear. "They are dogs with great appetites. They are never satisfied." He popped the clip out of his pistol, counted the bullets and slid it back in. "You'll have to forgive my quoting Isaiah. That is, if that quote actually exists, but it seems appropriate. That was a coyote. They are vicious things with a lust for blood. You've spilled enough of it to attract every one of them for miles."

"You would leave me to wild beasts?"

"I saw what you did to Jeremiah, what you and yours did in the slums. You are the beast."

"He was not with us. He was against us. I did my duty before the Almighty."

Matthias shrugged. "I don't care about your duty. I don't care about your personal calling, or your God. The things I read in the old Bible didn't speak to your authority, Gideon. That's what the Synod is so damned afraid of. But, to be honest, I just don't care anymore." He lowered himself to his haunches. "I am an Elder. I've already made a vow to myself, and you will be my witness. No one gets the book. It is my secret. Period." He tossed the gun to Gideon.

"What's this for?"

"It is a test of faith. There are three rounds left in there. You can shoot me now, and my secret dies right here. If you do that, you might not have enough ammunition to scare off the coyotes. If you have faith, two bullets will be sufficient."

Gideon grasped the pistol and rolled up on his side. "I thought you said there were three rounds in the weapon."

Matthias shouldered his pack and walked into the woods. "There are. If the first two shots don't do the trick, save the third for yourself. It's suicide, but I'm sure your God will understand."

The yipping grew louder. Snarls emanated from the forest.

"Time for me to go" Matthias headed north.

A bullet whizzed past his ear and slammed into a tree.

Gideon struggled to hold the pistol steady.

Spreading his arms, Matthias said, "Pray to your God for a steady hand and ease my way, brother."

The Inquisitor squinted over the gunsight. Flame spat from the muzzle.

It barely made a fly's buzz. Matthias resumed his journey into the woods.

Canine feet padded through the leaves around him. More snarls joined together until a hellish chorus formed.

A shot rang out.

Matthias stopped. "That was for you, Jeremiah. All is well, my brother. All is well."

Chapter 42: Verses 1-11

Cold bit through his blanket. Matthias shook. His teeth chattered.

Gray clouds met a gray forest in endless monotony. Dullness infiltrated his mind, each thought graying into the next. The death of Samuel and the others drained his spirit. Each recollection of the boy's face, or the way the sergeant and Beth held hands made him that much more reluctant to take another step.

But he went on.

When night fell, Matthias ate what provisions he had gathered from the other's packs. He slept in his coat, wrapped in his blanket, and coiled within his sleeping bag. For a time, he warmed.

By morning, the cold breached his defenses. The frosty air stole his breath. Matthias opened the tent flap. Blinding light dazzled his eyes. The sun shone from a blue sky onto a world transformed. Snow covered every surface. Gone were the gray leaves. Gone were the rocks. A brilliant white robe draped every blessed thing. He gasped and shut the flap. Spots danced before his eyes. His mind struggled to comprehend the sight.

It was unreal, the stuff of legend—yet there it was. Matthias slid his hand outside and grabbed a handful. It was fluffy and cold.

It compressed into slush and melted. He took his water bottle and let the drips fall into it.

Wind raked the tent. Snow sifted its way through the flap. Every last ounce of warmth fled. It was time to venture out or freeze in place. That in itself was a curious thought. How many times had he expected Death to take him?

Not now.

Someone needed to remember Samuel. Someone needed to remember the love of Jeremiah and Beth, Thaddeus and Theresa. Someone needed to remember the plight of Luke, of Timothy and Mary and the girls. Someone needed to recount their betrayal by Nathan. Above all, someone needed to remember the barbarity of Gideon Stanmore, Inquisitor General of the Order of St. George.

Matthias dwelled on each face. "I will remember you all." Determination burned in his soul. He took his finger and penned his name in the snow. "So saith Matthias Kent."

Chapter 43: Verses 1-15

He trudged in the direction of the rising sun, the wind lashing him with snow.

By nightfall, every inch of him was cold and his body heavy with exhaustion. Matthias teetered and fell. Matthias lay, snow drifting around him. Ice clung to his eyebrows. He no longer felt cold, only sleepy. In his waking thoughts, he laughed to himself. How funny it was to be freezing to death in a land that hadn't seen snow for seven generations.

A voice whispered to him on the wind. "It is ordained."

Delirium swept over Matthias. The voice sounded so real, yet so far away.

"You are the anointed."

He struggled to sit up. "Anointed by whom? God? There is no God." The wind slammed into him again, and he pulled his blanket around himself as tightly as he could. Numbness overtook him. His thoughts wavered.

The snow glowed red hot and turned to a lake of fire. Rourke emerged from a lick of flame. Along with him came Vanderhaggen. Each brandished a pitchfork and a sneer. Matthias tried to run, but his feet wouldn't move. Black boots tromped into view. Gideon stood over him, snorting with laughter, and raising his own pitchfork to drive it home.

The voice chastised him. "If there is no God, how can there be Hell?"

Gideon's face drew close. "Welcome, heretic."

Matthias blanched at the Inquisitor's sulphurous breath. He looked up at him and saw his black uniform turn pale. Two legs transformed into four. Hell turned ice cold, and a horse appeared amidst the blowing snow. Its snout prodded him and snorted.

"Behold a pale horse," croaked Matthias. He peeled the blanket away and saw a black rider atop its mount. "And its rider shall be Death."

The voice spoke again, this time less than a whisper. "Not Death, Matthias. Bilal."

Darkness poured over Matthias. He felt himself falling through an abyss until he landed on a cold, white cloud. As he plummeted, he repeated the word aloud.

"Bilal."

Revelation

Chapter 44: Verses 1-79

To Matthias, it was completely wrong. There was neither the glowing light of Heaven in the distance, nor a sea of fire engulfing the damned. Hell smelled like a barnyard animal, and the Angel of Death was a bearded black man straight out of *1001 Arabian Nights*.

And then there was darkness.

His eyes shuttered open to a blazing fire. He had arrived at the shores of Hades. To his confusion, the flames bore an agreeable warmth. Incense scented the air instead of brimstone. Hell might be bearable after all.

A black woman, with deep brown eyes and full cheeks, stirred a cookpot that hung over the flames. She tugged at a cowling surrounding her face and sang. It was a pleasant melody, soothing, comforting, almost like the songs of Theresa. She took some chunks of wood and tossed them onto the embers.

Shock rippled through Matthias. She just immolated a small fortune. He was in Hell after all. "My God."

The woman's eyes bulged. She dropped her spoon and ran out of the room.

Matthias attempted to get up. "Wait." The room spun. He lay back down and passed out.

Dreams came in spasms. In one, a black woman mended clothes. The next, she spooned him tea. In another, she smeared salve over his hands.

The Angel of Death would appear, hover near his face, and shake his head. More than once, Matthias heard him say, "Jihad al-Nafs."

Other times, the woman and the Angel knelt on rugs, bowing and chanting in some ethereal language.

Maybe I'm in Purgatory. Theresa and Thaddeus were right after all.

When next he awoke, a black man stared back at him. This man was different than the Angel of Death and more menacing. Three scars furrowed the right side of his face. He wore threadbare military fatigues and a skull cap. A rifle lay across his knees. Matthias understood the implied violence. That in itself was an interesting thought. The denizens of Hell didn't require guns. He was on Earth. He was alive.

The room was plain, with a concrete floor and a large fireplace. Sheet metal clad the walls on three sides. Each section bore phrases of some unintelligible, flowing script. A row of windows formed the last wall. Gray daylight lit the room.

The same woman of his delirium entered through a thick steel door. The warrior jumped to his feet.

"Sit down, Khalal. Keep your eye on him," she commanded.

"Yes, Shaykha," he barked.

Matthias sensed authority. The warrior deferred to her quite readily. "Am I a prisoner here?"

This time she wasn't alarmed. "I see you are doing better."

"How long have I been asleep?"

"Off and on for more than a week."

"Where am I?"

"My husband will answer your questions." She gestured to Khalal. "Go and get the Imam."

The word jarred Matthias in spite of his delirium. Imams were

Islamic leaders. That meant he was in the hands of Muslims. It would only be a matter of time until they took his life in some grisly public fashion. He had seen the broadcasts, heard the shrieks of the dying. It would have been so much better to perish peacefully in the snow.

Matthias hurled off the covers and dashed for an exit. His feet burned as he ran. He yanked the latch and the door opened. The Angel of Death stood before him, eyebrows raised.

"Oh my God," said Matthias. "Oh my God." His feet hurt. Dizziness overcame him. His knees softened.

The Angel laughed and came toward him.

And then there was darkness.

Matthias found consciousness again.

The man with the scars tipped his head and said, "Sheik Girard, the stranger is awake."

"Good, good." The Angel of Death sat down next to Matthias. "I am Umar Girard, Sheik of Manhattan Tribe and Imam of New York."

"Matthias Kent." He tried to sit up. "Sheik?"

"Leader."

"You are Muslim?"

"Most thankfully so."

Matthias squirmed but couldn't move. He was bound. Panic jagged through him. Umar pulled out a knife and pinned him down. Matthias waited for the sound of his neck being sawed and a rush of agony. His hands came free. "I don't understand."

"You have been fighting a great jihad of the soul—a Jihad al-Nafs. Never have we seen such distress. We bound you for safety's sake."

"You're not going to cut my head off?"

"It's been a hundred years, and the Synod is still showing those old mufsidun execution webcasts, aren't they? That is not who we are. We honor Allah who is great. The Almighty denies Paradise to any man who mistreats prisoners. Your government keeps you in fear."

Rubbing his wrists, Matthias said, "So, I am a prisoner."

Umar shook his head. "No, you are ahl al-aman."

"All what?"

"You are our guest. That is, until the ahl al-hudna come to claim you." Umar chuckled. "I'm sorry. You do not know our words. I mean, our allies to the north. We have sent a messenger to them."

Feeling the smile raise on his cheeks, Matthias said, "I am in the Hindu Lands?"

"You are in the Nation of Islam. What you call 'The Hindu Lands' are north of us. We are a proud member of the Federation of Free States."

Matthias extended his hand. To his unpleasant surprise, he saw just how waxy and dotted with Rot his hands had become.

Umar didn't shake hands. "Your flesh is unclean. Beyond the Rot, there is something more causing the swelling. It is like your hands have been scalded. The old women in the tribe say you are bitten by the frost. They say it is not bad and will pass in a short time."

Matthias regarded each finger. They itched.

The sheik rose. "You have it on your feet as well, though, to a lesser extent. You are lucky to be alive." He pointed to the scarred warrior. "Khalal will assist you if you need anything." His attention returned to Matthias. "Where are the others?"

The question jarred Matthias. He hadn't thought of Samuel and the others since he was out in the woods. The memories surged through him. He fought back his grief. "They are with God."

The sheik studied him. He seemed satisfied with the answer although saddened by it. "It is God's will. We will meet again after Maghrib. Until then, rest."

Matthias couldn't rest with the faces of the dead staring back at him. Instead, he forced himself to dwell on his new hosts and their humble surroundings. It gave him focus, and his mind cleared.

The sheik's wife came in. "My husband tells me you will be dining with us."

"Yes," said Matthias.

"How are your hands?"

"Unclean."

She shrugged. "So I have noticed. There is much Rot on you.

Pardon my rudeness, but when was the last time you bathed?"

"Days."

She turned to the guard. "Khalal, draw him a bath."

"Yes, Shaykha." Khalal nodded and hustled off.

"Your name is Shaykha?"

She chuckled briefly then returned to seriousness. "No, I am *the* Shaykha. The name my father gave me is 'Zarin.'"

"I don't understand."

"The Synod has a president, yes?"

Matthias nodded.

"Then think of me as the First Lady. Sheik—President. Shaykha—First Lady. We have these titles until our ruling council appoints another sheik. Then, I will be 'Zarin' again."

Matthias took another look around. "So, I'm a guest of the President?"

She chuckled. "Here, a man who finds another man in need is honor bound to help him. You are here because it is the warmest room in our house."

The story of the Samaritan sprang into Matthias's mind. "I am in your debt."

Khalal marched over to the Shaykha. "The bath is ready."

The bath was as warm as his welcome. The soap was as harsh as the looks he got from Khalal who locked the door once Matthias entered the bathroom.

Regardless of his host's insistence that he wasn't a prisoner, Matthias felt exactly that way. They didn't trust him. And why not, all they had was an unclean refugee. He scrubbed all the harder. The dirt came off. The Rot remained.

From what he heard, Matthias tried to gauge Umar, Khalal and Zarin. Other than their formal regard for him, there was little to analyze. Dress them differently and they might be a part of the Synod. That in itself gave Matthias concern. They were the power here. He would have to be wary.

Chapter 45: Verses 1-109

Khalal ushered Matthias into the dining room.

It was not what he expected. The room was plain, save more of the script painted on the walls. It was beautiful writing and he wished he could read it. In the middle of the space stood a long steel table and chairs. It wasn't at all like Synod's State Dining Room with its rare oak table and gold leaf opulence.

Umar stood near the window with another man. "Mr. Kent, please come in. This is Yusuf DeSilva, Imam of the Barrens Tribe. It is he who spread the news that your group might be coming through. Without him, you would still be out there."

Matthias approached the pair, noting the way Yusuf studied Umar during the introduction. There was more going on. "Then, I owe you a debt as well." He bowed. "If it is permitted, please call me, Matthias."

Both men smiled and returned the bow.

Umar laughed. "Pardon my levity, gentlemen, but have you ever seen such a sight?"

From the window, Matthias looked at the scene on the street. Children were wadding up balls of snow and throwing them at each other.

Umar laughed some more. "It is a miracle."

"Indeed," said Yusuf.

Matthias found it bittersweet. Samuel would have enjoyed such a thing.

The children halted their frolic and moved to the sides of the street. They seemed neither as amazed nor as dumbfounded as Matthias. His mouth hung open and muttered, "That's a horse."

"Indeed," replied Umar.

"Then I wasn't hallucinating out in the snow." Matthias remembered the animal's breath and the look in the rider's eyes. The same look in Umar's eyes. "You were the one who found me."

Umar smiled. "You see, Yusuf, his mind grows sharper by the day."

Yusuf studied Matthias. "Is it true your people ate horses?"

Matthias sensed disgust. "That was a long time ago, but they did. Wouldn't you, if there was nothing left to eat?"

Both men shook their heads no.

"But that happened long before I was born. How is it that you still have them?"

Umar said, "They belonged to the police and were abandoned when people left the city. Our forefathers found them and nurtured them. They considered it a gift from Allah."

Another shock rippled through Matthias. His eyes swept from horizon to horizon. If this was Manhattan, where was the city? It was empty save one tower. "Sheik Umar, I remember old photographs of the city. There were many large buildings."

Umar's head dipped slightly. "When the wars started, people fled for fear of attack. Without people, the city ceased being a city. Many skyscrapers were dismantled and their steel used to make all manner of weapons. Others were taken apart and their parts used to repair wooden homes consumed by the Rot. You are in such a building."

"And that one?"

"It is the tallest building still standing in this world, the Empire State Building. No one could bear dismantling it. We keep a light lit at its peak to remind everyone of America's greatness."

Zarin cleared her throat. "Is anyone hungry?" She placed a

large tray of meats and vegetables on the table.

Matthias wanted to run to the table and begin. Instead, he waited.

"Gentlemen?" said Umar. He gestured to Matthias to take a chair to the leader's right with Yusuf on the left.

"I am honored, Sheik Girard," said Matthias. He gave Yusuf a glance, watching for jealousy or envy. There was none.

Mimicking Yusuf, Matthias sat after Umar took his seat. Zarin passed out plates and utensils. They were plain things, adorned only with scratches. She pulled a cloth off a basket of flat bread and handed it to her husband. He took a few slices and passed it to Matthias. There was a pleasant air of informality to it all, one that reminded Matthias of the pleasures of an evening meal with his parents. "It smells wonderful," he said and passed the basket.

Yusuf took the basket and said, "How is it you made it through the blockade?"

That was news to Matthias. "I wasn't aware of any blockade."

"Yusuf," protested Umar. "Our guest hasn't eaten yet. Your questions can wait."

Matthias liked questions. It told him what his hosts didn't know. "Sheik Girard, I don't mind."

Umar nodded though the wrinkles in his forehead didn't smooth.

"We weren't stopped by any blockades."

Yusuf seemed incredulous. "Were there no checkpoints, no searches? Surely your identification was questioned."

"We were on foot."

"Ah," said Yusuf. "How long did it take?"

Matthias's mind froze. The count eluded him. "I can't be sure. I was sick a great part of the way." He searched for a starting point. "Have you heard of the recent riots in Philadelphia?"

Umar dunked a piece of bread into one of the sauces on the tray. "Yes. There was much movement of their forces then. A hunt for a heretic was the cause."

"If you can believe that," said Yusuf.

"It is to be believed, gentlemen." Matthias curved his bread into a scoop and filled it with some kind of paste. "I am the alleged heretic."

Yusuf stopped chewing.

"I suspected as much," said Umar. "Word of your exploits preceded you."

Yusuf's silence unsettled him. His gaze was cold, like Jeremiah's when he moved into combat. Heresy in this community might garner the same punishment as the Synod had in mind. Matthias decided to keep with a forthright account of things, especially since the sheik seemed so well advised.

"I am Matthias Kent, former Elder of the Bank of Job, and so-called heretic. My heresy was an unauthorized journey to the old capitol, Washington. There, I learned of secret business dealings between the Synod and those companies that have the Synod's ear. When I brought this to the Inquisitor General's attention, I was arrested."

Umar's face softened. "I see."

Yusuf seemed unconvinced. "And how did you make your escape?"

Matthias mulled the question. The sheik clearly didn't know. How could he begin to tell him of the sacrifices the others made? "There were many people who helped me find safe passage."

Umar raised a hand. "We know of Captain Finney and his good works."

"May he rest in peace," said Matthias.

"Inna lillahi wa inna ilayhi rajiun," replied Umar.

Yusuf's bowed his head. "Alayhis salam. The Captain sent many people to us. We were very distressed to hear of his death at the hand of the Order of St. George. It is they who run the blockade. No trading is allowed. There are many soldiers along the border. Our people are fearful."

The disclosure was yet another surprise in a long string of surprises. These were honest men of leadership. There seemed to be no agendas hidden in their body language, no breaks in eye contact. There weren't even any questions about the Bible. Matthias chided himself for feeling suspicious. "Your people have a right to worry. The Order had every intent on stopping us. At one point, they used an aircraft to attack us when we were in the open."

Yusuf gasped.

Matthias said, "I share that with you not to alarm you, only to inform you of the depths the Order went to track us down. That pursuit is over."

Yusuf took another slice of bread. "How can you be sure?"

"My comrades are dead, as are my pursuers. That's why Sheik Girard found only me."

"Allah truly smiled upon you," said Umar.

Matthias didn't agree but played the role of the respectful guest. "Yes, I'm sure He did." He wanted to change the subject and spoke to Yusuf. "Now what will you do now that you have no refugees to smuggle across the border?"

Yusuf looked distressed, as if some dark secret had been revealed.

Umar laughed. "You are a quick study of character, Matthias Kent. Our Minister of Refugee Relief keeps a very low profile. What else have you drawn from your observations?"

"Your people are content and feel secure except when it comes to enemy troop movements. This speaks to ample food and probably a modest security force. You have ears in the States, but those are limited or have been eliminated. Culturally, your reverence to God matches that of ours though there is a lack of religious trademarks that I find curious."

Yusuf's distress turned to astonishment. He stood and drew a dagger from his belt. "You are a spy."

Umar grabbed Yusuf's arm. "Put that away."

Regarding the knife, Matthias found his own reaction puzzling. Before, fear would have consumed him. The most he could feel now was a slight up-tick in his heart rate. "I can assure you that I am not a spy. I am not a heretic. I speak the truth and seek sanctuary from those who tried to kill me for it."

Yusuf raised the knife. "Those are just words."

Something keyed a thought within Matthias. He looked past Yusuf at the script on the walls. He missed the importance before, but now understood their significance. "As are those words on the walls."

Yusuf yanked his arm free and swung the blade at Matthias. "You dare blaspheme the word of Allah?"

Umar regained his grip. He pinched Yusuf's wrist until the blade clattered to the floor.

Matthias picked it up.

Yusuf's face shifted to panic.

"I am no spy," said Matthias. He handed the knife to Yusuf, hilt first.

Umar released his grip. "I am sorry, Mr. Kent."

"Sheik Girard, it is I who apologize. I meant no insult to your God or His words. I am who I say I am, nothing more."

Yusuf reluctantly sheathed the knife. "Allah is the God of all, even the misguided." He straightened his tunic and sat down.

"I am not misguided."

"Ahamdulillah," said Umar. "My wife would be most upset if we ignored her meal. Gentlemen, please." He grasped another piece of bread and swirled it in the food. "What was it that you did as an Elder, Matthias?"

The shift to the informal use of his name told Matthias that the questioning was over. The sheik sought to diffuse the tension with small talk. "Advertising."

Umar laughed anew, dropping his food on his plate and holding his sides. "What fools we are, Yusuf. He is far worse than a spy, he is an advertising man."

It took Yusuf a moment until he got the joke, but his face was humorless. In fact, it grew quite red. "My apologies."

"Accepted, but I don't understand," replied Matthias.

"You're going to need a new vocation, traveler," said Yusuf.

"Oh?"

"There is no need of advertising where you're going."

Umar resumed eating. "The Free States are tradesmen, farmers, and artisans. There is little in the way of life that you may be used to."

"I see. Is that where those panels came from?"

"No, they were crafted locally."

Yusuf said, "Sheik Girard is too modest. The calligraphy was done by his hand."

"My talent is a gift from Allah. I serve His word."

Matthias felt his fingers tingle. The words on the panels called to him even though he couldn't understand any of the script.

Whatever hunger he had vanished. "May I take a closer look?"

Sheik Girard smiled and said, "Of course."

Matthias walked over to one of the panels and inspected the script. There was a flow to the characters—confident, expressive, and decisive all in the same stroke. To his surprise, he could find no brush marks. "How were these painted?"

"They are not painted," replied Umar. "They are written."

A sense of awe poured over Matthias. "Written?"

Yusuf spoke between bites. "The sheik developed the etching solution and the pen by which he does his impressive work. Inventor, teacher, poet, warrior and Imam. It is no wonder we voted him Sheik."

"Excuse him again, Matthias. The Imam of the Barrens is far too generous with his praise."

A second informal use of his name surprised Matthias. "It's beautiful."

Yusuf bowed to the sheik. "Allah has blessed him with many talents."

Umar walked over to the panels and stood next to Matthias. "Our Quran was kept on plastic pages once the Rot destroyed everything made of paper. Those books were handed down for generations, but have faded. We began this project to preserve what was given to the Prophet and to honor Allah. Were it not for His words, our people would have perished long ago."

"Are your people instructed how to read and write?"

"Most can read, but, like the Christian States, most cannot write. There is little paper that withstands the Rot. We cannot afford it so we have come up with another way."

"It's the same way where I come from. Only Elders and members of the Synod are permitted to handle paper and write upon it." Matthias thought back to the Sacrament of Pen and Paper at his installation as Elder. How good it felt to caress the page, how wonderful it was to draw the pen across it. His mind drifted further back to the lessons of his mother. He imagined her hand on top of his, guiding the pen. It was like magic seeing the characters appear.

"Is there something wrong, Matthias?"

"My apologies, Sheik Girard. I was taught to write by my

mother. She passed away recently."

The imam's face beamed. "Mine passed to Allah many years ago. Her skill was twice mine."

"As was mine."

Umar grasped him by the shoulder, his enthusiasm growing by the second. "I hope that the entourage from the north will take their time getting here. It would be wonderful to see you try your hand. Perhaps tomorrow?"

"Tomorrow, it is."

Chapter 46: Verses 1-57

Mid-morning light poured through a bank of windows into the only unkempt room of the sheik's residence.

At Umar's insistence, Matthias stood amidst haphazard stacks of aluminum and steel sheeting, all on the verge of toppling over. Plaster rectangles leaned against the walls. It smelled of dust and ink and hard work. He took an instantaneous liking to the place.

Matthias focused on a four-by-eight foot sheet of metal standing against a support near the window. Red-orange letters of the same script filled part of the space while most of it remained unadorned. The grace of each stroke was the same as those he had seen upstairs the previous night. It was more of Umar's craftsmanship, and this one underway.

A table stood next to the work-in-progress. On it were arrayed jars containing a liquid of the same color as the letters. Next to the jars were a series of slender pipes.

Matthias picked one up. It was a simple thing, hollow down the barrel and one end cut at forty-five degrees to make a point.

"Pardon my lateness. Have you been waiting long?" said Umar, walking across the room.

"No sir. What is 'bilal'?"

"Who."

"Who is 'Bilal'?"

"Bilal ibn al-Harith was a slave back in the Prophet's time. His master whipped him so that he would renounce the true God. He did not. A companion of Muhammad eventually bought his freedom. We use names such as those to make it hard on Synod spies. It is much the same as the way your handlers used the Psalms." Umar assessed his work, a frown creasing his face. "I really must concentrate more."

Matthias could find no obvious flaws in the work. "It looks fine."

The sheik took the pen from Matthias. He pointed to the characters on the metal. "This method of calligraphy is called Ruq'ah. See the straight lines and compact text."

"Easy to read."

Umar smiled and nodded. "Are you sure you are not a spy?"

"Your readers must be bilingual as well. I saw street signs yesterday in English."

"We read the Quran in the language of the Prophet, but we all speak our old language. At times, they blend together."

Matthias moved closer to the writing. "What does this say?"

"It is a favorite quote of mine and one that I will take great care in transcribing." Umar opened a drawer on the table and pulled out a book wrapped in plastic. His face turned somber, reverent. "This is the Holy Quran that I spoke of last night. It is the best preserved. May God be praised." He opened it to a bookmark. "It says, 'The ink of the scholar and the blood of a martyr are of equal value in heaven."

"That's very profound." Matthias approached, more than a little awestruck. The Synod hunted him relentlessly for his Bible, yet here was a man who tucked his religion's holiest work into a drawer of a dusty workshop. He wanted to laugh and cry at the same time.

Matthias struggled to keep his emotions in check. He forced himself to look at the characters on the page, detach himself from his past. It was easier to be a critic. He studied the Quran's text and Umar's script. "Your characters are more expressive."

"Yes. There is a fine line between transcribing the Word and embellishing it."

How right the Imam was. He expected the next question to be about his Bible.

"I must let God guide my hand."

The reaction surprised Matthias. Again, an opportunity to be questioned about the Bible presented itself, and again, the sheik moved right by it. He studied Umar and found the man reading the Muslim holy book with even more reverence. His work was genuine. "God already has."

"You flatter me. Do you not do the same where you come from?"

Matthias felt embarrassed. "My job was to convince people to seek forgiveness for their sins."

"A noble career to be sure."

"At twenty-five percent interest for their transgressions. And we help them find all manner of transgressions, Umar. Redemption is the demand. Sins are the supply."

"Yusuf was right, you Christians are misguided."

"No, it's just good business. Absolutely perfect capitalism as conferred by Jesus himself in the temple greeting the moneychangers." Matthias walked back over to the easel. "Instead of steel plates, we display the words of the Bible on our computer network. Everyone gets the same interpretation." Laughter roiled in the back of his brain. Everyone had the same interpretation, except him.

"I see," said Umar, his brow wrinkling. "We are two different nations to be sure." The sheik bent over and picked up a shard of plaster. "But you and I have something in common." He unscrewed the cap on a bottle of ink and dipped a pen in. Holding his finger over the hole at the top of the pen, he withdrew it and wiped off the barrel. "So long as your finger stops the air, the ink remains inside."

Matthias nodded.

Umar brought the pen to the plaster's surface and moved it with purpose and speed. Arabic script appeared in its wake. He dipped the pen into the ink again. "You must move as quickly as the ink runs. Your turn."

Matthias mimicked Umar. The pen felt awkward in his hand,

its position seemed unnatural between his thumb and forefinger and resting on his palm. "What shall I write?"

"Anything. Your name. Your family name. Whatever you wish."

The pen touched the plaster and Matthias took his thumb from the end. The ink ran out into a blob before he got three letters onto the plaster. "Oh my. My apologies."

"Nonsense. Try again."

Matthias repeated the procedure, this time getting through all of the characters of his first name before the pen ran dry.

"Much better," said Umar, his face lighting up. It takes what few students we have many, many months to get as far."

"It's still quite bad."

Umar took the plaster and dropped it onto the floor. It shattered into bits. "God forgives our mistakes in much the same way so long as we do His will. Please, take the pen and plaster to the window and write down what you see. You are learning. We will overlook your mistakes. I will work on the Quran."

An hour passed as Matthias penned whatever came to mind. Frustration followed frustration until he forced himself to relax. He moved his arm along the surface, ink flowing out. It felt almost as good as signing the Minutes.

"Ah, you have hit your stride. Very good," said Umar.

"The pen took some getting used to."

"But look how you did. I am impressed. Your hand became confident, passionate." Grabbing a clean piece of plaster, the sheik took Matthias's pen and jotted a few characters.

"What does it say?" said Matthias.

"God is great. Please, you do the same."

Matthias hesitated. God wasn't great. He let true believers like Jeremiah and Beth die at the hands of miserable bastards like Stanmore. His hand slowed, and English appeared under the Ruq'ah.

The sheik looked disappointed. "Hmmm, this script doesn't carry the passion of your other practices."

Zarin appeared at the door. "May I interrupt the wise and powerful sheik during his artistic pursuits?"

Umar pulled in a sigh. "Yes, my dearest."

"I'm afraid you must stop. Our messenger has returned from the north. A party has come to claim Mr. Kent."

The sheik's disappointment deepened. "That is unfortunate." He turned to Matthias. "Our time together was much too short, but I consider it a gift from God. It was good to find a kindred soul." He blew air through the pipe and wiped it off. "For you." Umar handed Matthias the pen and a jar of ink.

The gift overwhelmed Matthias. "Sheik Girard, I am speechless and a fool. I have nothing to give to you."

Umar's picked up the shard of plaster that both men wrote upon. His smile broadened. "You already have shared your gift with me, my friend, and I thank you."

Chapter 47: Verses 1-135

Matthias followed Sheik Girard into the dining room.

The entourage stood at the far end of room. Despite their heavy clothes, their bodies were lean and eyes fat with curiosity.

It was his first look into the Hindu Lands. A beardless black man stood closest to the table. His forehead carried many wrinkles, and his hands-folded stance gave Matthias the feeling that he was the person in charge. Two white men flanked the leader, their cheeks taut and arms well muscled. Bodyguards.

Behind them stood a woman with dark hair. She was younger than he, attractive, with brown eyes and high cheekbones.

She studied Matthias.

When he met her gaze, a blush reddened her fair skin.

Sheik Girard rounded the table and shook the leader's hand. "Aaron, good to see you. Did you have a good trip?"

The older man smiled. "Good to see you, your Excellency, as always. Our pardon for arriving so late. The snow was challenging."

"Please, everyone, unburden yourselves and sit." Umar gestured to the table. "My guests, this is Matthias Kent of Philadelphia."

"Aaron Ennis of Poughkeepsie."

"Keith Calaman."

"Darren Fink."

"Julia Constantine."

"Greetings to all," said Matthias, taking a seat at the far end of the table. Julia sat next to him.

Zarin came into the room carrying a tray. Porcelain cups and a pot rattled with her movements. "Tea?"

"You are most kind, Shaykha Girard," replied Aaron.

As she poured, Julia said, "You did a fine job on his hands."

Zarin smiled and placed steaming cups in front of her guests. "That salve you gave us a while back did the trick."

Matthias noted the ease of the exchange. These people knew each other on a social, if not personal level. He felt a tugging at his hand.

Julia inspected each digit as though he were a medical school cadaver. "Mild frostbite. You're lucky. We have some bad cases back home with all this cold weather." She looked into his eyes with the same regard. "The Rot's come and gone in you, too. Bad fever?"

Matthias said, "Yes. Are you a doctor?"

Aaron said, "Julia is a medical aide." He took a sip of tea and addressed the sheik. "How have your people taken the cold spate?"

Umar said, "Like yours, we've had our problems. We've gone through a lot of coal. Scouts have been sent into the forests for wood to burn. That's how I found him." He pointed to Matthias. "God's will."

Matthias doubted that freezing the entire northeast just to compel one man to get firewood was a part of the Almighty's grand plan for the universe. "Our host belittles the simple fact that he rescued me. As Sheik Girard said, I am Matthias Kent, Elder of the Bank of Job and former citizen of the United Christian States. I ask for asylum in the Federation of Free States." He flashed a smile at Julia. "That is, if I passed this young lady's examination."

Julia blushed again.

Aaron chuckled. "I don't think we've ever had quite so formal a statement as that."

Umar agreed with a nod.

Aaron's face shifted into a humorless mask. "Is he genuine, your Excellency?"

The question rankled Matthias. The meeting wasn't simply an exchange, it was a judgment.

The sheik rested his hands on the table. "This man is no tool of the Synod. During his recovery, he cried out many times. His illness, and his story, seems genuine. I believe he is who he says he is."

Matthias stared at Umar. Was the hospitality extended to him part of a vetting process? "So, am I to be believed, or will you cast me into the wilderness?"

Julia's eyes widened, and she watched him closely.

Matthias noted the flaring of her nostrils, the taking in of a breath. He knew the reaction well enough. There were always women attracted to power and defiance. Things were no different in the Hindu Lands.

Umar said, "You can hardly blame us, Matthias. The Synod makes frequent attempts at infiltration."

Matthias felt disappointment grow. "Is that what the writing was about—a test?"

The sheik crossed his arms. "You presume too much, Mr. Kent."

Matthias read the body language and instantly regretted his statement.

Aaron stood up, breaking the silence. "Um, Your Excellency, perhaps we should be on our way. We thank you for your audience with us."

Sheik Girard stood and bowed to his guests. "May God grant you a swift and safe journey, my friends." He shook hands with everyone until he came to Matthias.

Matthias extended his hand, watching Umar's face. "My apologies, Sheik Girard."

The Sheik clasped his hands over Matthias's. "Keep practicing, Mr. Kent."

When they reached the sidewalk, Aaron took the lead and the bodyguards formed up the rear. The air felt warmer now, not like the last few days in the woods. Puddles formed in the streets. The children playing yesterday were gone. Dampness made him shiver.

"Are you cold, Mr. Kent?" said Julia.

"A little. May I ask where we are going?"

"The train station and then to Poughkeepsie."

The picture from one of his books leapt into his mind. Images of a sleek, comfortable liner fueled his recollection. Maybe there would be food and wine and heat.

When they arrived at the station, he peered through the fencing for a glimpse at his grand ride. A series of boxcars enrobed in graffiti hindered his view.

Aaron opened the gate and led the entourage to one of the cars. He tugged the door open and it screeched along its runners. "All aboard."

The two bodyguards stood next to the door and interlocked their fingers with each other. Aaron stepped into their grip and hopped into the car. Julia followed.

"You're next, Mr. Kent," said Aaron.

Matthias followed the others. The inside was far drabber than the outside. Its walls were painted a shade of brown somewhere between rust and feces. A stack of folding chairs lay in a corner. Julia and the guards set to work unfolding them.

Aaron swatted Matthias on the back. "It's not First Class, but it is inconspicuous. Please take a seat. We're leaving soon."

Julia lit a match and held it up to a lantern.

One of guards pulled the door shut and darkness consumed them.

It was a meager light, like the candle Samuel lit that awful night in the culvert. He remembered the toy animals, the sound of the rain.

The train lurched forward. Matthias felt the progression of movement and the sway of the boxcar. Another journey to another unknown place. The pleasant dream that was home was even further away.

Aaron plopped onto a chair. "You've got that look."

"Look?" said Matthias.

"I've brought hundreds of people into Poughkeepsie. Most everyone gets that look when the door closes."

"That trapped feeling?"

"No. Homesick." Aaron warmed his hands over the lantern. "Julia looked that way when she first arrived. Wouldn't stop crying."

Julia didn't like the teasing. "It was ten years ago. I was sixteen. My parents bought our passage a week before school was supposed to start. I left all of my friends."

Matthias watched the way her eyes conveyed a lingering resentment. "Do you miss the life you had?"

"Yes. My dad was an executive at a factory. We had servants, cooks."

"What happened?" said Matthias.

"Office politics, daddy called it. He backed the wrong candidate for a Synod position. After that, the government cancelled all contracts with his company. My father was blamed."

"And all of you were to be cast out."

"Yes."

He clasped her hands inside his. "Your parents made the right decision to come here. I've been in the slums. I almost died."

Aaron said, "You did."

"I what?" said Matthias.

Aaron rocked back on his chair, shadows filling the creases in his forehead. His face shone like a bronze bust in the lantern's glow. "The Synod says you're dead."

Matthias ran his hands along his torso and up to his chest. "I always imagined that angels would lift me to heaven." He regarded the boxcar. "It would seem as though I'm going in the other direction."

"Our sources in Philadelphia confirmed your death several times. We were very surprised when the sheik's messenger showed up."

"Several times, eh. Did your sources say anything else?" Matthias was fishing, seeking to know if they found the Bible.

"No."

Aaron twitched. There was something more, something wrong. Matthias played a hunch. "You haven't heard from your sources lately, have you?"

"No."

Matthias sensed Aaron's reluctance to continue. "You seem to put a lot of stock in the Imam's judgment. I am who I say I am."

Aaron nodded. "Yes. Yes, indeed. His people are quite thorough at ferreting out Synod spies. You were pretty outspoken back there."

"Yes, I was foolish—" He crossed his arms over his chest. "—but dead men can afford to be impetuous. Can you tell me when you heard the news of my demise? If it's not a state secret."

"About four weeks ago."

Matthias mulled it over. "And nothing since?"

Julia cut in. "No wonder they thought you were a spy."

The glint in her eye told Matthias volumes. She liked the intrigue. "Spies don't speak their mind. The best ones simply watch and listen."

She bit her lip. The discussion became a tête-à-tête. "You've met one?"

The image of Nathan's face painted itself into Matthias's mind. The gunshot echoed. Water ran out of a canteen. Nathan fell. "Yes, once."

Aaron said, "Word from pretty much anywhere inside the Christian States is hard to come by. We're hoping that changes now that the blockade of the border has been lifted."

That news buoyed Matthias's spirits. One way or another, the Order was giving up. Let the Synod proclaim him dead. "Things are returning to normal, then."

"Yes, it seems like it."

"Good," said Matthias. "I'm sure you have many questions for me."

"We do," replied Aaron, "But they can wait until tomorrow."

"When I go before your inquisition?"

"Hardly. You're a free man now. No forced persuasion. No dictates of the state upon your will. Answer what questions you feel like answering. All we ask is your honesty."

"As simple as that?"

Aaron slid down in his chair. Smoothness replaced the wrinkles on his forehead. "Yes, Mr. Kent, it is. You'll see."

Discussions fell away into small talk.

Matthias recounted life in Philadelphia to a rapt audience. No one mentioned a Bible. No one demanded that he pay penance. Even the bodyguards relaxed.

All the while, Matthias could feel the full weight of Julia's gaze and the way she seemed enthralled by his tales of life in the city.

The stories continued until the screech of brakes drowned out his voice. The train lurched to a stop. The screech became louder. The brakes grabbed. Julia tipped over onto Matthias.

He caught her by her shoulders. "Are you okay?"

Julia pulled herself up with his help. She brushed her hair back behind her ears and sat down. "I'm okay."

One of the guards dowsed the lantern. The other opened the boxcar door.

Aaron stood in the doorway. "Home sweet home. Welcome to Poughkeepsie, Matthias."

The train station, what Matthias saw of it, lurked in the cast of a single street lamp more than a hundred yards away. "No marching bands for the defecting Elder?"

Shaking his head, Aaron said, "No. We don't like to draw attention."

"Afraid of those spies, eh?"

"Not really. Poughkeepsie is kind of a frontier town, so to speak. People come and go. That's why we introduce folks like you here. Come on."

They rode in a rattletrap truck to a low brick building. It had an old façade, probably dating back to prewar days, but maintained well enough.

On the inside, clean floors and walls shone in the flutter of a single tube of fluorescent light. Voices rose and fell on tides of conversation behind the doors lining the hallway. It smelled of food—baked, fried, boiled and spiced.

Matthias's appetite rose.

Aaron led the way to the end of the hall. He unlocked a door on the right. "Mr. Kent, you're in here. The bed is in the back.

Keith will be in the front."

"So, I have a minder."

"Can't have you wandering off."

Matthias didn't like the idea of a babysitter Where was he to go in this land?

Julia pushed past into the room on the other side of the hall. "See you, Matthias." She lingered at the door, giving him another look.

It was a small apartment, cleaner than the hallway, with meager lighting and fresh bedding. Matthias flopped down onto the bed. The mattress was soft. Coarse white sheets carried a hint of bleach.

He lay there for a while until the steel entrance door echoed with a knock. Matthias heard the guard walk over and open it. A man and woman spoke. It was Julia.

"I brought some food for our guest. Go ahead and get something for yourself."

The guard walked out of the room and closed the door.

Matthias came out of the bedroom. "My thanks."

She slid a plate of dried fruit, nuts and a hunk of bread onto the table. "Sorry, but this is all we had in the pantry."

Matthias pulled out a chair and laughed. "I would have sold my soul for this a couple of weeks ago."

Julia sat down close to him. "We're you really an Elder? My father was one."

"Yes," he said. She smelled of peaches and coffee. "What does your father do now in the Hindu Lands?"

"He rests in the peace of God. Both of my parents died soon after we arrived. I was left all alone."

"I'm sorry."

"Don't be," said Julia, putting her hand on his. "And don't worry about a thing. I'll take care of you."

At first, Matthias felt reassured by her comfort but grew more uneasy the longer her hand remained on his. He pulled his hand to his side and said, "My thanks. Now, if you don't mind, I'm going to turn in."

"Of course." She forced a smile. "Sleep well."

Chapter 48: Verses 1-76

A rap on the door awakened Matthias.

"Mr. Kent, time to get up," said Keith.

It took Matthias a few seconds to orient himself in the darkness. He had a fitful sleep, laced with nightmares of coyotes and buzzards, anguished faces and black boots.

A single bare bulb lit the bathroom. He turned on the water and showered. It was lukewarm at best, but Matthias considered it a blessing.

When he came out, another set of clothes lay nearby. How many times had he changed vestments in the last couple of weeks? How many times had he taken on a new personality? Elder. Beggar. Sojourner. Muslim. What character would he assume now?

Matthias donned the clothes. They were indistinct things, a brown tunic, pants with too much room at the waist, shoes just a little too big. A thick fibrous coat covered it all. He folded the garments from Manhattan neatly and tucked them under his arm.

When he came out of the bedroom, he found the same four people sitting at the table chatting among themselves.

Julia broke away from the conversation, a dried peach slice in her hand. "Good morning, Matthias."

Matthias found her quick attention disconcerting. "Good morning."

Aaron reached for a plate of dried fruits and nuts only to have it intercepted by Julia.

She offered it to Matthias. "Breakfast?

Aaron glanced at Julia then spoke to Matthias. "Yes, better eat up. We have a meeting with the Mayor on the half hour."

The air was crisp and cold. Ice filled shallow dips in the asphalt. The sound of a distant pounding like the beat of a drum caught Matthias's ear.

Nearby buildings stood no more than four stories high, most were brick though there were steel structures interspersed on every block. Like Philadelphia, some were freshly painted while others stood faded and weathered.

What few inhabitants there were hustled about, intent on some chore or mission of their own. Some of their eyes were milky with Rot. Most were not. They paid the entourage little regard.

The clothes of the passersby were somewhat ill fitting and in varying condition. They were as nondescript as his own, and it puzzled him. After all, how could he could discern rank or class when everyone looked the same.

Another difference struck him. There were no outstretched palms, no pleading voices, no sign of Samuel and his mother. "Don't you have beggars?" said Matthias.

Aaron shook his head. "No. Panhandling isn't allowed. Everybody works."

"One hundred percent employment? That's astounding."

"Well, that's what we strive for. An empty stomach is a strong motivator. No work, no eat. And it applies to you."

They walked until they reached a steel building with dark windows.

Aaron halted at the corner. "This is as far as I go, Mr. Kent. Double doors straight ahead. Give them your name at the desk."

The inside of the building was a study in monotony. Beige walls, beige floors, and a dingy beige ceiling all lit by the listless glow of fluorescent lights.

Rather than being appalled by the lack of décor, Matthias was too busy languishing in the warmth of the room. Not since Palmerton did he feel as warm.

"May I help you?" said a woman seated behind a metal desk.

"Matthias Kent."

The woman lifted a placard and wiped a rag across its surface where Matthias's name lay. His name disappeared. Satisfied, she said, "Down the hall to your right. Look for door marked 'Mayor.'"

Matthias walked down the broad hallway, anxious and wondering why the mayor required a special audience. He bristled at the obedient sheep he became in the hands of his guardians. For a moment, he considered walking back out into the street.

Matthias halted in front of a series of murals depicting moments of Poughkeepsie history—Indians, trains, and quaint aircraft with propellers. Sailboats graced a river running under a great bridge.

"It's hard to imagine this city ever looked that way," said a stout man about Matthias's age and height. He held one arm around his waist while the other stroked his short red beard. "You must be Elder Kent." The man produced a muscled hand. "I'm Charles Higgins, but everybody calls me 'Mayor Charlie.' Come on in." The use of his former title surprised Matthias. It was the second time in twenty-four hours that someone mentioned his previous life, and it stirred apprehension in his chest.

As he entered the office, Matthias forced himself to buckle down and dismiss his reactions as weakness. There were a hundred opportunities for his hosts to give him to the Order. None ever materialized. Besides, this man knew rank. It was time to behave like an Elder. *Time to slough off the heretic's clothes and become white as snow.*

The mayor's office was a large open space with a metal desk, a table and a few chairs. A woman poured steaming tea into a mug on the mayor's desk.

She set the teapot down and approached Matthias. He guessed she was a few years younger than he, her light golden brown hair parted to one side and not an ounce of cosmetics camouflaging what few imperfections she had. The wives of the Elders would have a field day deriding her for such a thing. Still, she was pretty, and he held his gaze on her.

The woman extended her hand.

Matthias slipped off his coat and handed it to her. It was good to have servants again. "Thank you."

She frowned and hurled the coat onto a chair.

The mayor stepped inside. "This is Carolyn Decker."

Why the man took the time to introduce a servant was beyond Matthias's understanding, but he chalked it up to being a stranger in a strange land. "Carolyn."

Her frown deepened and he wondered if this Mayor Charlie maintained enough discipline among his staff.

Charlie motioned to Carolyn. "If you could leave us for a bit."

"Fine." She snapped the mug from the mayor's desk and slammed the door on her way out.

"Elder Kent." The mayor gestured toward the chairs. "Ordinarily I don't meet with refugees but you're a special case. Actually, you and your Bible have presented us with quite a dilemma."

The casual delivery shocked Matthias. He was speechless.

"Oh, don't worry. We can talk plainly here. Only myself and a few people back in Boston know that you even possess it. Not that it matters now."

"What's that supposed to mean?"

Mayor Charlie rounded his desk. "The Synod has completely Stalinized you."

"Stalinized? I'm not familiar with the term."

"It means that the Synod purged you from their digital records. Everyone in your immediate circle of family, friends and business associates have been sent through the Synod's brainwashing program.

"They call it Reformation." The sweep of it was staggering and sobering at the same time. "I no longer exist."

Charlie plopped down in his chair and mimicked Matthias's pose. "A lot of people no longer exist. A lot of people died getting you here."

Matthias felt the weight of guilt. "All over a book."

"Enough of them believed in that book."

"They fight over words. The Synod says one thing, and you say another. It's been that way for centuries. Catholics and Protestants, Muslim and Christian, Hindu and Jew, all fighting and dying over what? Words?"

Mayor Charlie remained unfazed by Matthias's outburst. "Those people died to spread the Truth and expose the Synod's corruption. Like I said, none of that matters now."

"The Federation will do nothing?"

"There is nothing we can do. Even if my government could obtain the Bible, it would be useless. The Synod would dismiss it as propaganda. You have to remember, we're a secular country."

Things weren't as Matthias assumed. "I don't understand. I thought the people that smuggled me out of the States worked for your government."

"Hardly. We've provided support to them over the years, but they were always on their own. They are the Old Believers, the ones that always knew what the Synod was doing. They're probably all dead now. And the one man that held the truth in his hands technically no longer exists. That means the Bible you found doesn't exist. That's why there's a dilemma in handling you."

Matthias's anger fell into a jag of fear. "You're sending me back?"

"No, but I've talked to my superiors in Boston. We're not sending you on. The Synod would assume our complicity if any of its spies spotted you in the capitol. Things were touchy enough when their troops were just over the border. The last thing we need is an international incident."

"That doesn't answer the question."

"We see a lot of cross-border trade. Your appearance here would be construed as normal. Think of yourself as my guest."

"Guest? I've been nothing more than a prisoner all along."

Charlie's face turned red. "I say what I mean. All we ask is that you stay here for a few months before moving on. Just don't draw attention to yourself. Other than that, you're a free man."

"Freedom is relative."

"Not here. Freedom is for all."

Matthias walked over to the desk. "That's what the Synod said to us all the time."

Unruffled, Charlie rose and stared him down. "Saying and doing are two different things. That's something you'll learn here, which reminds me. You're going to need to find something to do while you're in town. We're a market economy. No big corporations, no boards of directors and no Elders." He moved away from the desk and opened the door. "The Common Council has appointed the City Administrator to expedite things so that you can blend in that much more quickly."

Matthias looked down at his clothes, thinking back to his earlier thoughts. He understood his new mantle. A commoner in a sea of commoners. While it didn't sit well, he would be alive. His past and the infernal Bible would be behind him. So be it. At least they were assigning a man of suitable rank to make his transition easier. "When do I get to meet him?"

"You already have," said Mayor Charlie. He stuck his head outside the door. "Carolyn, he's all yours."

Chapter 49: Verses 1-104

Carolyn pointed to Matthias's coat. "Better pick that up. You'll be needing it."

He bent down and grabbed it. "I beg your pardon? Where is the administrator?"

Carolyn's face flushed. She stomped over to Mayor Charlie. "I knew this was a terrible idea."

The mayor said, "Mr. Kent, meet our City Administrator."

Confusion washed over Matthias. "Is there a shortage of qualified men?"

Throwing up her hands, Carolyn spun around and headed for the door. "I'm out of here. You deal with him."

"Hold on," said Charlie. "Mr. Kent, things will be very different for you here. We don't discriminate because of gender."

His confusion ceased. The realization smacked him in the head like a stone from David's sling. He was in a den of liberals. "Oh my God. Women in charge?" Matthias looked for a wedding ring and found nothing there. "Don't you have a man to keep you?"

Carolyn bristled. "You find him a job, Charlie. I have a city to run."

Another realization followed the first. As much as it chafed,

Matthias understood that this *woman* held sway over him. It would be like an Israelite slave insulting his Egyptian taskmaster. The result would not be good. "I'm sorry, Mrs.—um—Ms. Decker. Forgive me. Where I come from, women fulfill God's ordained roles—wives, mothers, servants."

Her face turned a deeper red. "And prostitutes, which explains why the council screwed me with you. Look, Mr. Kent, I know about your laws and customs. You can take every preconceived notion you brought with you and shove it up your ass."

"Carolyn," said the mayor.

"Don't 'Carolyn' me, Charlie. I have enough problems to deal with without some Bible thumping chauvinist from the Alleluia States questioning my credentials."

Matthias had no idea why he would thump on his Bible. It might damage the cover. He let the remark go and stuck to the issue at hand. "I'm not questioning your credentials. Please, let's get this over with, and you won't have to deal with me again."

She looked at him for a few seconds before the redness left her face. "Fine." Pulling a chalkboard from the mayor's desk, Carolyn scanned it and ran her finger to a line of script. "Get that coat on. I have just the job for you."

"Sewage Inspector?" said Matthias. His remark lifted a smile from her drawn lips.

"No, we filled that one with a qualified candidate this morning. Perhaps you can be *her* assistant."

"I see."

Carolyn huffed and waved him along. "Come on, Mr. Kent. Let's put you to work."

They left the building, Carolyn setting a pace that would have made the sergeant breathe heavily. Matthias's heart beat twice as fast as the drumbeat he heard again in the distance.

Carolyn looked back over her shoulder at him. "Part of our trip will be to introduce you to some folks who need workers. If somebody likes you, you're hired."

"As simple as that?" he said between breaths.

"Yes. Another part of our trip is to get you into transitory housing. You get the first month for free. After that, it's up to you to arrange for things. Rentals are posted on a board at City Hall. Questions?"

Matthias said, "What's that sound?"

"What sound?"

"I hear machinery banging on something." He swiveled his head around, locked onto the pounding and pointed to the west.

Carolyn nodded. "Oh, I hear that so much that I forget about it. It's the WVG."

"The what?"

"The Women's Volunteer Group—W-V-G. We call Poughkeepsie the 'Queen City of the Hudson,' and these women are its official heartbeat. Since the Second Civil War, they've kept sentries on top of the bridge. Day and night, they beat their drum to remind everyone of the hearts lost defending this place during the war. Women fought alongside men back then."

Matthias was dumbfounded.

"Don't injure that male brain of yours. It's true. My grandmother told me the stories, and I believe every one. The Christian States tried to take the bridge several times, and the WVG drove them back. Grandma said it was like the 300 Spartans the way they held their ground. The sound of their drums told the city to hang on. It gave everyone hope. Reinforcements arrived. The enemy retreated. To this day, they are the heartbeat of the city."

Matthias tried to imagine armed housewives holding off the Order. It just didn't fit. His history lessons told him the Order allowed the Federation to keep one bridge standing as a token of brotherhood between the nations. Carolyn's face eased with the recounting of her story. For all intent and purpose, she believed every word. The competing accounts were just like the differences between the Synod's Bible and his.

Carolyn waved him on. "That's your history lesson for the day. Interim housing isn't far from here. Let's take care of the room first."

Matthias took in the surroundings. Smoke bellowed out of chimneys. Citizens walked to and fro. There were no limousines, no buses.

Carolyn rounded the corner and he followed. They came upon

a series of brick four-story buildings. People stood around the façade, listless and gawking. He sensed a familiarity with them, something kindred. They looked as he felt—refugees. Thrust into a foreign land with no point of reference.

The structure looked the same as every other building on the block save its number, 1712, stenciled in flaking white paint near its door.

Carolyn led him in and spoke to an elderly man behind the desk. "What's available, Gordon?"

The man peeked out over his smudged half-moon glasses. "Carolyn? My God, they let you out of City Hall? Did you finally get fired?"

Carolyn bent over the counter and gave Gordon a big hug. "No such luck. The Council asked me to be tour guide for this gentleman. What rooms are available?"

Gordon squinted at a placard on the wall where brass keys hung. "How about 202? Only one flight to climb."

"Private bath?"

"Nope."

"This one is shy. What else do you have?"

Matthias moved out of the way as a woman hauled a bucket full of water past him.

Carolyn wrapped her fingernails on the counter. "That is, a private bath with running water?"

"407." He handed the key to her.

"Thanks." Carolyn passed the key on to Matthias. "Come on."

"We're not going to take a look?" said Matthias.

"You'll have all month to look at it."

They hustled down the street.

She looked back at him again as he tried to keep up. "You don't know a trade by any chance? Electrician? Steelwork? Plumbing? God knows we really need plumbers. Any of those?"

"Are you always in such a hurry?"

"Are you always so slow?"

"I did advertising."

She stopped and looked intently at her clipboard. "I don't

know if the markets need any hawkers, but we can give it a try."

"Hawkers?"

"Salesmen. You know, 'Apples. Apples. Get your apples here.'"

"What else do you have?"

Carolyn's glared at him. "This isn't multiple choice. How about a job in a sheet metal factory? It pays well."

Matthias chafed at the questions. He was something she dragged along until she could be rid of him. "Um, no. I grew up on a farm. Anything like that?"

"You're not allowed out of the city." It was Carolyn's turn to be annoyed. "Look, you have to remember that you're starting over. Get used to it. We place people right away so they can adjust that much more quickly. I realize you were an Elder with a car and lots of food." Her finger poked him in the chest with every syllable. "That life is over." She swung her hand toward the bridge. "You can always go back."

Matthias followed her gesture. "No. No, I can't." He felt defeated. "What else is there?"

Carolyn tossed him the clipboard. "See for yourself." She glanced at her wristwatch and looked flustered. "Shit, I have to go. Damn that Solomon."

Carolyn surprised Matthias. She just blew over fifty credits in penance, not that it mattered.

She planted her hands on her hips. "Are you coming?"

They walked along an alley named Front Street. To the right ran the Riverwall, dank and gray and throbbing with the WVG's unceasing heartbeat. It was much louder here, though the height of the wall prevented Matthias from spotting any of the heathen Amazons that pounded out the note. Did they paint their faces like Indians? Shave their legs? Wear undergarments?

To the left lay crumbling brick walls topped with sheets of aluminum. The Rot drew black spider webs along the deteriorating mortar.

"My, isn't this prime real estate," said Matthias. Some of buildings sloughed paint like molting snakes. Others were little more than tentatively arranged stacks of rubble. For a moment, he remembered his library back home with its haphazard towers about to topple.

He blinked away the sadness of never seeing it again, never touching his beloved pages. Indeed, that life was over.

"Are you okay?" said Carolyn, her grouchiness tempered by concern.

"I'm fine."

Carolyn pounded on a corrugated steel door. The building was a wholly ugly thing comprised of cinderblocks. Walls extended for fifty yards to the left and right. Shards of glass protruded out its roof like some primordial monster.

"Sol?" she said. "Solomon Dvorack? I know you're in there. Wake up. Sol."

Matthias heard the sound of bottles clinking and rolling along the floor. Footsteps slapped on concrete.

A rotund old man with wild white hair stuck his head out. He looked like a surly St. Nicolas without a beard. "Leave me alone, I'm busy." He pulled the door closed.

Catching the door, Carolyn yelled after him. "Where's my order? We have to have it ready to go by Friday."

Solomon shouted from the inside, "Then come back in three days."

Matthias caught a faint whiff of urine and some other foul smells that made his nose wrinkle.

Carolyn marched inside. "When will the reams be ready? We have a trade agreement. You better not put us behind quota again."

Matthias followed her in. He stumbled over a bottle. When he righted himself, he caught sight of what the pair was bickering about. He gasped.

Paper.

Sheets and sheets of it hung from racks near a coal stove. He reached out to touch it.

"No you don't," said Solomon, whacking Matthias's hand with a metal rod like a schoolteacher to an unruly student.

"Ow."

"Let him alone," said Carolyn.

"You make paper?" said Matthias.

Carolyn pursued Solomon around the room. "Don't you run away from me. You are going to have this ready, aren't you?" She kicked a bottle. "Damn it, Sol. You promised me no more drinking."

Solomon's shoulders drooped like the sheets of paper surrounding him. "Sorry. Occupational hazard."

"Like Hell." She kicked another bottle across the floor and gave Solomon the same disapproving glare that Matthias received earlier.

Carolyn cupped the old man's chin in her hand. "Come on, Solomon. We need this. No paper, no copper pipes. No pipes, no water. The city is depending on you. I'm depending on you."

While Solomon was occupied, Matthias ran his hand along the surface of a rough-edged sheet of paper. It was as thick as the Minutes at the Bank and looked remarkably like the paper they used in the sacrament. A tingling spread from his hand, up his arm, and along his spine. It wasn't *like* the paper at the Bank. It *was* the paper from the bank. "Carolyn, Solomon's got a deadline, right?"

"Indeed he does."

"I see that you're trading with the Synod. Paper for manufactured goods."

Carolyn whispered a reluctant, "Yes."

He knew the look. The lack of trust. The suspicion. Matthias said, "I need a job."

She caught the gist of it.

So did Solomon. "Oh no. I don't need an apprentice. Trade secrets! Trade secrets!"

Carolyn planted her hands on her hips, elbows out, and a face set as firmly as Lot's wife. "Here's the deal, Solomon. Hire Mr. Kent or you're out of business."

"You can't threaten me. I have an exclusive contract. Best product. Super-dooper. Longest lasting. A-1."

She was unmoved, unfazed in the storm of the man's protests. Something stirred inside Matthias. It was an odd feeling, a calmness and a fluttering all at the same time.

Her gaze met his. "Are you sure this isn't too menial, Mr. Kent?"

"No. Not one bit," replied Matthias.

Chapter 50: Verses 1-88

It took more than fifteen minutes of back and forth between Carolyn and Solomon until Matthias declared a winner. Of course, it was Carolyn. He knew she would win fourteen minutes ago. But, Solomon proved to be as cantankerous as he was round and wouldn't back down until he expended every breath.

Carolyn took Matthias's hand like a referee declaring a fight champion. "Matthias Kent, meet Solomon Dvorack—your new boss."

"Until Friday," huffed Solomon. "After that, he's your problem."

As Solomon ushered Carolyn out the door, Matthias couldn't resist the temptation. He touched another sheet of paper lying on a fine mesh screen.

Solomon shooed him away. "Don't touch."

"When do I get to make paper?"

"When hell freezes over and that damned near happened a couple of weeks ago. Completely messed things up." Solomon kicked some of the bottles around. "Pick these up and put them in here. And don't break any or you're fired." The old man motioned to a large barrel and headed out the back door.

Finding the bottles presented no problem. Matthias inspected a few. They varied in color and shape, but the vinyl sleeve on each one was the same—Cranberry Wine - Saugamunk Winery - 2148.

"One year old. A fine vintage." He thought it funny to have such a prodigious amount of the stuff, though it helped explain Solomon's girth. Not that many people Matthias encountered were anywhere as large, nor did they look as though they could afford anything more than common distilled.

He took a sniff. The smell confirmed his earlier encounter. The contents were beyond stale, but a hint of something tart lingered in the bottle.

Solomon came back in and tossed him a full bottle of wine bearing the same label. "Drink up."

"It's not even mid-morning yet."

"Drink up, or go get Carolyn and find another job."

"You're paying me to drink?"

"Consider it part of the job description."

Disbelief rattled around Matthias's head. He could feel the smile lift on his face and raised the bottle. "To the best job ever."

The stopper came off with a firm tug. He sniffed the contents, took a swig and swished it in his mouth.

Solomon whacked a table with his rod. "I said drink it. This isn't some soiree, outcast."

Matthias swallowed. It was thin stuff, young. No body. No depth and pretty much no alcohol. But the tartness stayed on his palette. It was unlike anything he had tasted before.

"More," said Solomon in a voice that reminded Matthias of the sergeant ordering him around. "And don't stop. Four bottles a day, every day. Trust me, the novelty will wear off. Bathroom's over there."

The restroom door sported a circle with an arrow gouged into the metal—the 'Man' symbol. Written in erratic scrawl underneath was "Women outside!!!!"

"Finish up. Soon time for the collier to show. Shovel's over there."

Matthias had no idea what a *collier* was but the shovel clearly defined manual labor. He couldn't imagine what a shovel had to do with papermaking. "When do I get to make paper?"

Solomon's face wrinkled up as if it were the stupidest question he was ever asked. "Never. Trade secret. Now drink."

Skirting the coal stove, Matthias headed toward the shovel. A huge kettle simmered on top of the stove. Inside it was a stinking mixture of brownish paste and fibers churning in the brew. Some wood chips lay on the floor. He picked one up and sniffed it. "Yellow Box Eucalyptus."

Solomon's head snapped around. "What do you know about trees?"

"We planted this kind at my parent's farm to dry up the wetlands."

"You were a farm boy?"

"I was until our crops failed." Matthias held the chip close to his nose and closed his eyes. Eucalyptus trees swayed in the breeze near the Kent monument and the graves of his parents.

Solomon's scowl slipped into a questioning look. "Oh yeah? How long ago?"

"Twenty years or so. Ended up going to college and growing money for a bank instead. I went into advertising."

"Oh, that'll take you far here."

Matthias ignored the remark and grabbed the shovel off of the hook on the wall. *Hate not hard work.*

Paper surrounded him. For the first time in his life, he stood in a place where he wanted to work, even if he did nothing more than be the janitor.

Solomon stroked his chin. He looked pensive, distant. "Twenty years, eh? That's funny."

"Why is that?" said Matthias.

The scowl returned as if a switch had been thrown. "None of your God damned business." Solomon shambled over to a thick metal plate and lifted it up. A trap door appeared in the concrete floor. The rungs of a ladder met at the opening. "Down you go, advertising man. See the coal chute?"

Matthias stuck his head into the hole. "Yes."

"Then go down next to it and wait. I can hear the truck now. When they dump their load, your job is to move it into the carts."

A hearty slap pushed Matthias toward the ladder.

Solomon chuckled. "Can't wait to tell the coalcrackers I've got an advertising man in my basement shoveling coal. The Synod must be going to hell in a handbasket."

The coal dust made it dirtier than the slums, but Matthias set to work. Over the scratch of the shovel, Solomon's laugh got louder. The men upstairs clinked bottles and let the empties thump to the floor.

When he finished, Matthias stuck his head out of the trapdoor. "That was fun."

Solomon stirred the kettle. "Outside."

"Am I fired already?"

"No, you're dirtier than hell and I can't have you within sneezing distance of my product. Wash basin is back at the end of the building. Beat the dust out of your clothes and scrub up."

Outside, a pipe round enough to fit a man gushed water over a great iron wheel. The wheel turned slowly and drove an array of gears. Belts ran off the axles, sinew to the bones of the hulking machines connected to it.

The basin turned out to be a cement block hollowed out to hold water. He took off his outer garments and smacked them against the wall. The coal hopelessly darkened them the way Rot darkened his skin. He hoped his hands would fare better than his clothes.

The water was ice cold and the chunk of soap harsh against his skin. It did the trick.

Solomon burst into the room and halted at a nondescript piece of equipment. "I don't pay you to take baths. Get over here."

Matthias donned his coat and hustled over.

Solomon grunted and threw some levers. With the water wheel's help, the contraption screeched to life. He pointed to a cart. "Bring that over here." The old man threw another lever and two-foot logs fell out of an overhead hopper. The machine shuddered and banged.

Matthias couldn't believe his eyes. There was an Elder's salary worth of wood being torn to shreds. "My God."

"Oh, shut your yap. It's full of Rot and it'd be goo a month from now anyway."

"But…"

"Get that cart over here now and don't miss a drop of oil from the mash." Solomon motioned to a door at the end of the machine. He tugged on the handle and a mass of shredded wood oozed in. "There you go, farm boy. You just saw paper being made. Time for lunch."

Matthias squeezed into the bathroom. It was a small space with a funnel for urine and a bucket for feces. While it was a primitive arrangement, a heavy dose of disinfectant reassured him that it was clean. Fresh soap sat on a sink with a single tap.

After he relieved himself, Matthias returned to the table.

Solomon plopped a white potato the size of two fists onto a plate. "Eat it, skin and all."

The plate slid in front of Matthias. "My thanks." It was huge.

"What's the matter? Not good enough for an Elder?" The old man placed a bottle of wine next to the plate.

"Quite the contrary. I haven't seen a white potato in months let alone one as large as this."

Solomon sat down on the other side of the table. Before him were two potatoes bigger than the first. "Grow them myself, I do. Best in this part of the country. You're not saying grace?"

"No." Matthias took a pull from the bottle, his gaze studying the paper hanging overhead. "I've seen your work before. I used it when I was an Elder at the Bank."

Solomon spit out a mouthful of wine. "An Elder? You performed the Sacrament of Pen and Paper?"

"Once." Matthias looked at his hand, imagining the fork as a pen and swirling it in the air. "I'm pretty sure it was your paper. Feels like it. Smells like it."

The overstressed buttons of Solomon's shirt bounced on ripples of laughter. "Smells like it, eh? They still use it for their precious Minutes?"

"Yes, they do." A wave of irony washed over Matthias. He now understood the meaning of the sacrament and its importance. It had little to do with symbolism. It was about the bank's proceedings as statement of fact. Computer data could be manipulated. The government's Bible was proof of that. Paper could not, not easily, or without great cost. Besides, every sheet of paper in the country was accounted for and stored in the government's vaults. It was the only thing of substance left in their rotting world.

That, he mused, was the issue with the paper Bible. Every word in it accused them of their treachery. Each bit of ink was like the dots of Rot on his skin, threatening to destroy its host. No wonder they wanted it so. They wanted to destroy the Bible before it destroyed them.

And here he stood, under the very pages the Synod treasured so very much. Bile formed in the back of his throat, the taste of vengeance denied. Perhaps the instrument of his revenge was right before him. *I am rescued from my illnesses and given favor. Now, if I only had the wisdom.*

For a moment, Matthias dwelled on the way the Almighty led him to this juncture. Just as quickly, he dismissed it. There was no God, just as there was no Matthias Kent in the United Christian States. And, if there was no Matthias Kent, there was no Bible.

Solomon jabbed him with his rod. "Here."

Matthias came out of his thoughts and took a jar of black fluid from the old man. "Something else to drink?"

"You don't drink it. You write with it. It's ink." Solomon rummaged through a drawer and cursed until he found his quarry, a large fountain pen. He tossed it to Matthias. "Has your hand forgotten the sacrament?"

"No," said Matthias.

"Then show me how an Elder writes." Solomon produced a strip of paper and laid it on the table.

Matthias dunked the pen and tugged on the lever to draw the fluid inside. He leaned over the table. His fingers tingled when they touched the surface. How wonderfully freeing it was to write without worry of arrest.

Matthias relaxed, looked at the old man and wrote *Solomon Dvorack*. It wasn't his best, he thought.

"I'll be damned," said Solomon. "Fine work indeed. How did a youngster like you acquire skill like this?"

"My mother taught me."

"A serious violation of the law."

Matthias laughed. "Just one more sin on my road to heresy."

He regretted the use of the word the moment he spoke it.

"You are a heretic?"

"That was my charge and the reason I fled."

Solomon nodded. "Then we have something in common, Matthias Kent." He stood and rapped the floor twice like the Bank's sergeant of arms. "But that will wait for another time. Finish up. God knows I have to get this order out, or Carolyn will have my balls for breakfast."

Chapter 51: Verses 1-59

Matthias spent the remainder of the day under the lash of old man's baritone. All the while, he tried to maintain the attitude of the prodigal son, ever so willing to do the most abject chores.

By day's end, both men were spent.

Solomon led Matthias to the door. "You have a strong back for an Elder."

The words were both insinuation and compliment. Matthias realized that the tasks heaped upon him were a test. "What time, tomorrow?"

"Ready for more, eh?"

"You showed me nothing of the craft except how to clean up after it."

"You've seen everything there is to see. Be here when the town clock strikes seven, no sooner. Where are you staying?"

"1712 Lincoln."

The address produced a nod from the old man. "Do you know the way?"

"Yes."

Solomon reached down and produced a pail of black rocks. "Your wages for the day and probably your first honest pay."

"Coal?"

"There's no penance cards here. Rot ate all the paper money long ago. And our coins were melted into bullets. Shot at your ancestors, no doubt. Everything is true-blue Yankee here. We barter for day-to-day things. Half that bucket will get you dinner, and the other will buy you breakfast. The street vendors will tell you different. They can smell a refugee a mile off. Bargain well and eat well."

Matthias set off, four of his footsteps to each drumbeat. He marched in time like a soldier of the Order. His shoes made the clomp of Gideon's boots. It brought on a consuming chill. He stopped, the picture of Gideon cowering behind the sergeant fresh in his mind. "May you rot in Hell."

Darkness filled the streets, and the cold drove most people indoors. Matthias found his apartment block. A bare bulb strained to cast its glow over the number. Vendors crowded the entrance.

"Chestnuts, walnuts, and peanuts."

They were nuts all right, worm ridden and malformed.

"Porridge, get your porridge."

A gray paste.

"Steak. I have steak tonight. Best beef for only a bucket."

Matthias inhaled the aroma from the open brazier. It wasn't steak. He moved on.

The pickings got worse as he moved further from the door. A young man and woman eyed him hopefully and shivered next to each other. "What do you have?"

The woman pointed to her pots. "Bean soup. Sweet potato bread. Peas. And apples stewed with cinnamon."

Matthias gave her food a sniff, expecting revulsion. To his amazement, it smelled good. "How much?"

"Half a pail, same as the others."

"The other vendors wanted a full pail for food far inferior to yours. Why are you out here?"

The woman cast her eyes toward the others and spit at the ground. "My husband isn't as big and strong as they." She tugged a blanket tightly around her head and shoulders.

"The free market can be like that. What's for breakfast?"

"Whatever doesn't sell tonight."

"And honest, too. Very well." Matthias handed her the bucket of coal.

"It's only half."

Matthias held out the pail. It was time to take on this new life and find people he could rely on. "Take it all. Save me a fair portion come morning. Until then, be warm. Do we have a bargain?" Even in the twilight, Matthias saw the woman's face brighten.

Gordon, the man Carolyn spoke to earlier at the apartment house, sat in rapt attention over a set of dominos on the table before him. A woman about Gordon's age sat across from him, drumming her fingers on the table.

The man gave out a disapproving grunt when Matthias came close. He spoke without taking his gaze off of the game. "Sheets are already on your bed. Just remember, you only get one clean set a week."

"My thanks," said Matthias, pleased but puzzled by the comment. There was something more in the man's voice, the lack of eye contact. He dismissed it, thinking that the game's interruption was responsible for Gordon's gruffness.

He trudged his way up four flights of steps. The stairwell carried the odor of perspiration, of grease and oil. Among the smells, he detected the slightest hint of what he could swear was peaches. But the scent faded when the aroma of cinnamon and apples overwhelmed his nostrils. It set his mouth to watering. At least the people of the Federation ate better than their kin in the States.

The lock gave way easily though the door stuck. Matthias gave it a shove and entered. One fluorescent tube lit the small room with a greenish pall. A table and two chairs occupied one side. Seated in one of the chairs was a dark haired woman—Julia.

"I thought you'd never get here," she said.

It took Matthias a moment to get over the surprise. "How did you know where I was?" He caught sight of her broad smile and intense gaze.

"I have my ways." Julia looked at the food containers in his hand and said, "You won't need that slop. I brought something for us. Have a seat."

Matthias complied. "Do all of your patients get this level of care?"

"No." Julia rose, found a bowl and spoon and set the table. The intensity in her eyes never dimmed. "Does it please you, Elder Kent?"

Unease returned borne on the memory of the women at Pharaoh's. "No one has to please me, Julia. Now that I'm here, I must make do on my own."

She brushed off his comment as easily as she brushed her hair back over her shoulder. "Have they found you work yet?"

"Yes. I am the custodian of one Solomon Dvorack, a maker of paper by the river."

Julia ladled a vegetable stew into his dish and stopped half way. Her face soured. "Solomon, eh?"

The edginess of her reply piqued his curiosity. "Does that bother you?"

She looked into the distance. "He has a hand in everything, businesses, farms, vineyards, and peoples' lives. I guess you can be that way when you have that much money. Which residence does he have you cleaning?"

"It's not a residence. It's his paper shop."

She looked dazed. "No one works in his shop but him."

"I guess I'm special."

She nodded. "I would agree with that." Julia placed the bowl before him. "Here you go."

"None for you?" he said.

"I already ate." Reaching into another container, Julia pulled out some dried peaches and ate one. She passed another to Matthias. "Dessert."

The fragrance reached Matthias's nostrils, and he recognized it as the scent in the stairwell. "My thanks. Really, you shouldn't have gone to the trouble."

Julia took out another peach slice. "It's no trouble. No trouble at all. So, tell me about making paper for the great Solomon Dvorack."

Matthias regarded her expression, a veil of pleasantry hung over the same latent anger he noticed before in the train. Now, though, it seemed more intense. He let go of the thought and chided himself for analyzing her reactions. She brought him food and conversation. He was being a bad host. "Well, I can add 'shoveling coal' to my resume…"

Chapter 52: Verses 1-100

In the morning darkness, Matthias counted the chime of the town bell—six. He had been awake since 4:00 AM when anxiousness to begin his day roused him.

He imagined himself learning the alchemy of papermaking. Making sheets one by one with Solomon—if the man who caused Julia's face to wrinkle would share his secrets.

Julia's reaction lingered in his mind, and it nagged at him. She remained an enigma right up until the time she left last evening.

Matthias rolled over in bed. A trace of peaches hung in the air. He inhaled the scent, trying to replay their conversations through his mind. He lingered on the intensity of her eyes and the way they wouldn't connect to his for more than an instant. He tried to read her emotion, but couldn't bring it into focus.

He took in another breath and smelled only the bleach in the sheets. The aroma of peaches vanished, and along with it, his concentration. He kicked the covers off. Figuring out Julia could wait. There was work to do. He could feel a smile lift on his cheeks. There was paper to make.

The morning air held more warmth than the previous night.

The sky wore its traditional mantle, clouds the color of slate. True to their word, the young couple manned their humble stall at the end of the vendors' pecking order.

The woman smiled the instant she spotted Matthias. "Good morning, sir," she said, holding out a small pot.

Matthias took it from her and handed back the containers from last night's meal. "My thanks. What culinary masterpiece do you have in store for me today?"

She looked at him as if he spoke a foreign language.

"What's for breakfast?"

"We cooked the soup down into porridge."

He took a sniff. Like last night, it smelled fine, and it was a generous portion to boot. "Very good then. And what will be on the menu for tonight?"

She laughed. "Whatever we don't sell this morning."

He arrived at Dvorack's shop before the bell tolled 7:00. Smoke chuffed out of the chimney and the stink of urine seemed stronger than the day before. It made him wonder just how much of that wine Solomon drank.

Before he knocked, Matthias remembered the old man's instructions. "Be here when the town clock strikes seven, no sooner."

His better angels pulled his fist back from the door. Dvorack had a preciseness about him and an urge to control. While arriving early might be considered conscientious in some circles, Matthias reconsidered and waited.

The bell began its peal. On the seventh chime, he knocked. The door swung open as if Solomon was on the other side the whole time. The old man smiled a facetious smile, seemingly deprived of some earthly pleasure.

Matthias smiled back. "Good morning to you, Sol. Am I on time?" He already knew the answer.

"Indeed." Solomon walked over to the table. Two bottles of cranberry wine stood atop it. He slid one toward Matthias. "What'd you have for breakfast?"

"Porridge."

"Then wash it down."

Matthias looked at the label and then at Solomon. He formulated a question designed to test Julia's comment about the old man's wealth. "Why do you drink this so soon after you've bottled it? You do own the vineyard, don't you?"

"I see it didn't take you long to find out about me. Only one day. For a refugee, that's very, very good. Did Carolyn spout off?"

"It was Julia. Julia Constantine."

"Julia. Oh."

Matthias noted the abruptness of the old man's tone. Julia was a subject best left for another time. "If it's any consolation, I would have figured it out at some point. You're not hurting for food. You run through this wine like common distilled, and you make the only paper I know that doesn't rot. You should be living on an estate."

Solomon took a pull from the bottle. "I have plenty of land, but this is where I spend my time. It's the one thing I still enjoy doing. You know, I studied your face when you saw the pages drying. It was like watching the sun rise on a cloudless sky. I said to myself, 'This one knows the value of what he sees. He understands.'"

"Will you show me how to make paper?"

"Hell, no. Why do you think I have so many holdings?" Solomon fished through the drawer and pull out the pen again. "Give me another demonstration of your handwriting." The old man's eyes twinkled.

Matthias knew that Solomon had something more in mind than handwriting, but agreed anyway. "As you wish." Matthias found the bottle of ink, filled the pen, and set his hand to write an "S."

Solomon grabbed his hand. "No. Not my name this time. Yours."

Matthias felt unsure but did as commanded.

The old man took the slip of paper, blew on the ink and laid it next to the page with his own name. "A fine hand, indeed. How often did this mother of yours make you practice?"

"Most every day until my teens."

"Very good." Solomon tucked pages into a glass jar and screwed the lid on. He looked up at it, nodding. "Very good indeed, but enough of that for now. Today, we press and trim. To the wash basin with you. Not a speck of dirt on your hands or you're fired, understand?"

Matthias carried each page to Solomon, who scanned them for defects and stacked them on a thick aluminum sheet. One by one, the pages disappeared from their clips on the clothesline until none remained.

Solomon took another sheet of metal and covered the top. "Give me a hand."

Matthias carried one side while the old man carried the other.

They walked to a machine that resembled a French guillotine and set their load onto a broad metal plate underneath the blade.

"Keep back," said Solomon, taking the sheet metal away. The old man mumbled and fretted as he slid the paper one way and then another.

For Matthias, it was like watching a diamond cutter appraise the value of a stone by the way it would be divided.

Solomon brought his hands to a great lever, stepped on a pedal and pulled. Slivers of paper fell away. A perfect edge remained.

"That is alchemy," declared Matthias.

"That is geometry, Matthias. Clear this away." Solomon pushed the trimmings back toward him. "Don't miss a single sliver."

Matthias caught them and placed them into a nearby cart.

Solomon rotated the paper and brought the blade down again and again. Soon, four neat stacks of paper emerged from the cutter. The old man lifted them from the platen and set them aside on some plastic wrap. "You wouldn't suspect it, but one ream of paper gets two loads of copper pipe. Two loads! That's enough to run water to half a city block."

"Do you run the trades as well?"

Solomon laughed. "No, not that I haven't tried. They run themselves. Have for centuries. Damn unions. I barter with them for skilled labor on my properties."

"Places like 1712 Lincoln?"

"My, you do learn fast."

"And the city provides you with unskilled labor."

Solomon finished wrapping the ream and reached for a drink.

He hoisted the bottle. "Right again."

Matthias walked over to him. "So, which am I? Skilled or unskilled?"

Solomon glanced at the jar containing the handwritten names and then back at Matthias. "Neither."

After lunch, Matthias headed to the bathroom.

When he emerged, he spotted the old man pulling two wide doors closed, locking them, and depositing the key under his tunic. Next to him was a large caldron set on top of a wheeled cart.

It was a room Solomon never approached, at least when Matthias was near. The words to Sirach came to mind. *Do no secret thing in front of a stranger, for you don't know what he is thinking.* Matthias pretended not to have seen the action.

Solomon pushed the caldron along. "Get more coal on. I need it warm in here."

Matthias descended into the basement, did as commanded and returned to the main floor.

Solomon was hard at work, his outer vestment off, and perspiration running down his cheeks. His hands were clad in long vinyl, gloves and he dipped a ladle into the milky broth of the kettle. "You wanted to know how paper is made. Pay attention."

Matthias drew close but the smell from the caldron drove him back.

"Like the wine, you'll get used to this too." Solomon dumped the contents of the ladle across a metal screen. Fluid ran through the fine mesh and into a barrel. A paste remained.

"Is that it?"

Solomon nodded. "Yes, every stinking ounce of it. Hand me that blade."

Matthias found a long, flat piece of metal and handed it over.

"Now watch." Solomon drew the blade across the top of the screen frame. The soupy mix flattened out ahead of it. When he finished, the whole screen was covered in a white mat. "Here. Put it on that rack and hand me another screen."

The instructions were simple enough and Matthias did so quickly. As he worked, he studied Solomon's movements, the way he slid the blade so smoothly, so evenly. It didn't look difficult, yet

Matthias imagined that such precision took years of practice.

They worked through the afternoon and into the evening until the caldron emptied. By then, the town bell sounded 6:00.

"Your wages," said Solomon, offering a pail of coal. "Same time tomorrow."

Matthias headed home.

Julia met him inside his apartment. "You look exhausted."

Startled, Matthias said, "You're here again?"

"I thought I'd make sure you're getting well fed."

He held up a pail of food from the vendor on the street. ""I've been fending for myself."

She frowned. "I told you I'd take care of you." Julia pointed to the table. Steam lifted from two bowls of stew. "I've taken care of dinner. Now go wash up, Elder Kent, before it gets cold."

Matthias went into the bathroom. A sense of apprehension came over him while he turned his hands over in the water. He thought of Julia's tone when he produced the food he bought and the slight admonishment it carried. It was as if his meal was some kind of rebuke to her. While it seemed like an insult to her kindness, he couldn't help but dwell on the control she assumed. The more he thought about it, more the more uncomfortable he felt.

Julia called out, "It's getting cold."

"Be right there," said Matthias. He dried his hands and sat down at the table.

"How was your day?"

He fought the growing discomfort with small talk. "Tiring, but good. I hope the next job will be as interesting."

Julia propped herself up on her elbow. "I was very surprised that you were working in his shop in the first place."

"I'm only there through Friday. Then I will be at Carolyn Decker's mercy."

Julia pulled her hand back. "You don't need her help. I can help find you work."

Her sharp tone made Matthias wary. She sounded jealous. "Perhaps there are other papermakers."

She raised an eyebrow. "That's what makes your working for Dvorack so special."

"Why is that?"

"There aren't any. Others have tried and failed miserably. The old man is the only one who succeeded. Some say an angel bestowed success on him. I think he traded his soul to the Devil for a secret formula."

Matthias sat back in his chair. "I didn't think anyone in the Federation believed in angels or devils."

"We're not atheists here."

The statement surprised Matthias. He realized he hadn't seen a single advertisement for church, a posting of required service times, or even a portrait of Christ smiling back at him. "I guess I have a lot to learn."

"And I'll be happy to teach you when I get back."

"You'll be away?"

"Yes. The clinic will be traveling around the local farms for the next couple of days. So you can eat that gruel from the street vendors."

Matthias chuckled. "I think I can manage."

Chapter 53: Verses 1-128

"That's it," said Solomon, tapping his rod on the floor. "Almost a day early. Not bad, Mr. Kent. Not bad."

Matthias washed the last of the screens off and set them into their respective racks. There was no more wood to pulp, pulp to screen, or pages to cut. His employment reached its end. "Can I count on your reference for my next employer?"

Solomon pulled out a key from under his tunic and unlocked the door to the room he spent so much time concealing. "Come here." The old man pointed inside.

It was a large windowless space packed with the remnants of trimmed paper. Matthias ran his hand through the trimmings. "So, this is where it goes."

"And where it stays. Useless to everyone, yet paper nonetheless."

"It can't be reused?"

"I've experimented with it. Unfortunately, recycling it makes it vulnerable to the Rot. I figure it will only last fifty or sixty years."

Viewing the great trove, Matthias understood. It was like his library at home, priceless and worthless all at the same time. "Why show me this?"

The old man laughed. "Christmas is coming."

"This is your gift to me?"

The laughter stopped. "Hardly. What you see is my dilemma. In the past, I simply burned it all but have always hoped to find an alternative."

"What service do you want me to provide?"

"Handwriting."

The reason for the pen and ink demonstrations became clear. The connection to a room full of confetti wasn't. "To what end?"

Solomon shifted his gaze back to the room. "As I said, Christmas is coming. I propose to reclaim this paper and have a fine calligrapher inscribe words upon it."

There was avoidance in the old man's eyes. "A fine sentiment that harks back to the golden age of the nation. But you didn't answer my question."

"What was that?"

"To what end?"

Closing the door, Solomon's cheeks reddened. He took in a great breath and let it out. "To increase my wealth, of course." The old man shuffled back to the table and pulled down the jar containing the slips of paper Matthias wrote on earlier in the week. He held the jar up. "I used to have this friend who knew about the customs of the old America. He told me how, back in the old days, a mere slip of paper was all it took to declare that somebody was born, married or dead. Along came the Rot and every shred of that past turned to dust in half a generation. For more than a hundred years, the people here wrote their legacies with chalk." Solomon unscrewed the cap and held up the slip of paper with his name. "So, how much do you think this is worth?"

Matthias shook his head. "More than any of your townspeople can afford. And, if you're thinking about selling it to the Christian States, forget it. The Synod holds all the paper. Besides, they have much more pressing needs right now."

"As an advertising man, I assume you spent time in economics classes?"

"Of course, it was part of the discipline. Sin and redemption equals supply and demand."

"Very good. How about marketing?"

"I was the director of advertising and development." The old man's prompting became more and more vexing. Matthias couldn't read his intent other than the vaguest notion that involved his handwriting on infinitely tiny shards of paper. Then it hit him. "You want to create a market using the reclaimed paper."

Solomon's face glowed. "God truly does answer prayer. Do you know how long I've hoped to bring paper back to the masses?"

"With the added plus that you will enrich yourself at the same time."

"Considerably. You see, if we produce a lesser quality paper and sell it at just the right price, it will put the pages within the grasp of many people."

Matthias's mind raced along a dozen different avenues. He understood the old man's intent. "And, my handwriting will put their words on those pages. Ingenious."

"Just like the old days."

More and more thoughts gushed into the flow of ideas circulating through Matthias's brain. One stayed in the forefront— he would be paid to write. "My payment for this service would be?"

Solomon looked at the floor. "Triple your daily wage."

Matthias laughed long and hard. "No."

"Five times?"

"I am to be a partner in this venture."

"Go to Carolyn and find another job."

Matthias headed toward the door. "My thanks for the experience. Good luck to you." He grasped the latch.

"Ten times."

The rapid ascension of pay told Matthias just how much value Dvorack saw in the venture, yet it was nothing without his hand setting ink to paper. "Partner, plus one page in ten for me to do with as I please."

"One in fifty."

He yanked the door open and walked outside, four steps to each beat of the drum.

By the third beat, Solomon appeared at the door. "Twenty."

Matthias halted. "You know, I did very well in economics. Just keep in mind that the corporations of the Synod are having a bad time and will for some time. They won't be buying nearly the paper they have in the past."

"You are the spawn of Azrael. Ten it is."

His own heartbeat beat louder than the drum. Matthias walked back to the shop. He slid his sleeves up to shake Dvorack's hand. When he did, he glimpsed at his forearm. The flecks of Rot had faded to gray. They were somehow diminished.

Solomon's face wore a shade of red blended by equal parts exasperation and anger. "You are my partner in the handwriting part of my business, no more."

"And no less," said Matthias, tightening his handshake.

Carolyn Decker stepped into the doorway. Two stout men accompanied her. "You sent word that the order is ready?"

"Greetings," said Matthias.

Carolyn let a smile flicker momentarily and brushed one side of her hair back. "Hello, Mr. Kent. I take it that your temporary job is over?"

"Yes."

Her eyes rolled. "Then you will be needing another job?"

Matthias looked at Solomon and back at Carolyn. "No. Sol here has offered me a partnership. I begin immediately."

Carolyn blinked several times as if her mind couldn't process what she heard. "Solomon, is this true?"

The old man stepped further back into the shop, yelling, "Yes, and I blame you completely."

It took a little less than ten minutes for the men Carolyn brought to load days of work onto a hand cart.

Matthias noted the process, from the way the men counted each package, to the way Solomon arranged each ream so that nothing would be damaged on its way to the Synod. Only the transfer of Penance Cards drew the same level of scrutiny.

"I have to say, Mr. Kent, that I didn't expect this outcome," said Carolyn.

"That we would have the order on time?"

"That you would still be employed."

"I'm full of surprises, Ms. Decker. Was there a wager on me?"

Carolyn frowned.

"You lost, I see. What do you owe the Mayor?"

The frown deepened. "How did you… dinner."

"Tell him to order the most expensive meal in town. Oh, and please send him my congratulations."

"I will."

"And Ms. Decker?"

"Yes."

"You'll do far better by betting on me, not against."

She nodded, her head tipped slightly. "Mr. Kent?"

"Yes?"

"Call me Carolyn."

He liked the way her name sounded, the way her lips flared as she spoke it even if it wasn't on the approved list of names. "Matthias. Please call me Matthias."

Solomon burst in. "Now that you two are on a first name basis, I'd like to remind you, Carolyn, I have a business to run. The same goes for you, Matthias."

Carolyn set her hands on her hips. "Not all of my official business is concluded, Sol. Your partner is still on my list of responsibilities." She turned to Matthias. "I take it that your housing is okay?"

Matthias nodded.

"You found adequate food?"

"Indeed."

"You're getting along with your neighbors?"

"Those that I've seen."

"Good. Very good. How about religious services? We have several that are similar to what you're used to, but it'll probably be quite a change from your prior environment."

Her statement caught Matthias off guard. The closest he came to a church service in month and a half since his escape was the sergeant's prayers. It was as if his religion died with Samuel out in the mountains. He felt almost relieved to have left it behind—just like the Bible.

Carolyn awaited a reply.

"Where do you go?"

"St. Peter's. It's a kind of Free Methodist."

"Then let's start there."

Carolyn suppressed a giggle. "I'm not sure it'll be what you want."

"Have you gone there long?"

"Since I was fourteen."

"Are you an upstanding member of your congregation?"

"I'd like to think so."

Matthias couldn't understand the evasiveness, but he remained undeterred. "What time?"

She hesitated for a full second. "I'll come by the apartment house at 7:30 AM. Service is at 8:00. How about if I show you some of the other services afterward? Deal?"

"Deal."

Chuckling drew Matthias's attention to Solomon. "What's so funny?"

The old man took a long swig from a bottle of cranberry wine and wiped his lips with his sleeve. "Nothing," said Solomon. "Nothing at all."

After Carolyn left, Solomon taught Matthias how to pulp the trimmings. When they soaked long enough, the old man showed him the idiosyncrasies of coaxing the mixture into a fine sheet of paper.

Matthias pursued the craft with fervor. Little by little, he created pages of decent enough quality to be approved by the old man. The satisfaction tasted sweeter than any wine he had ever sampled.

Evening fell though the men hardly noticed, such was the intensity of their labors.

At last, Solomon lowered himself onto a chair, wrapped a loose coat around himself, and let out a great sigh.

The old man's face and hair resembled the statue of Rodin's Balzac. It was as if Matthias were back at the bank, reviewing the works of the master sculptor in the corporation's sizeable collection.

Uncle Cornelius drifted into the memory, his eyes glowering and lips permanently set in a serpent's smile. The coldness of the Vice Elder's stare made him shiver.

"Are you okay, Matthias?" said Solomon.

"I caught a chill."

"Time to stop work for the day. I have a feeling there will be paper upon paper upon paper to make in the coming days."

"It's my first time."

Solomon stretched. "Better than sex, eh?"

Matthias ran his hand along the screens. "Well, not that good. It's just that this has a magic all its own. I can't believe I'm doing this."

"Then you should thank God for your good fortune."

The chill left Matthias. Samuel didn't freeze to death thanking God for his good fortune. Jeremiah didn't praise the Almighty for the good fortune of being disemboweled. "God and luck are two different things."

The old man shifted forward in his chair, half of his face lit by a dim bulb. "Those words would have been enough to have you sent through Reformation back in the States. You have fallen far, heretic. Don't you see His hand at work?"

Matthias held up his hands, looking for the silhouette of a cross in his palms. They were as empty as his heart. He turned them toward Solomon. "All I see are the hands of men, and it is by those hands that good and evil are wrought—not some god."

"By His hand you make a new life. That is a gift."

"It was my mother's gift."

Solomon raised an eyebrow. "And did she believe?"

Grief stabbed Matthias's heart. This was not a discussion he wanted to have. "Religion and politics are what ruins partnerships, Sol."

"I meant no offense."

"No offense taken. See you Monday."

Once Matthias retired, it didn't take long for fatigue and a full belly to lull him to sleep. But he could find no rest in his dreams.

Gideon Stanmore held a held a knife against Matthias's throat, and he wriggled in the Inquisitor's grasp.

The citizens of Poughkeepsie stood around them and gasped. Their eyes were wide with fear. The air smelled of blood and dried peaches.

At his feet, Samuel, Jeremiah, and everyone from the trek northward lay dead. A great snake slid across the carnage. It wrapped itself around Matthias's legs and slithered upward. The serpent had his uncle's face. Its tongue slipped in and out, tasting fear and relishing it.

Uncle Cornelius hissed out a single question, "Where is the Bible?"

Matthias leapt from his nightmare. His nightshirt clung to his sweaty skin. He got out of bed and flicked a switch for the room light. The glow assured him that he was alone and whole, but the nightmare played out in his conscious mind. Frozen in it were Uncle Cornelius and his question.

"Where is the Bible?"

Chapter 54: Verses 1-133

On Sunday morning, Matthias brushed his vestments out as best as he could. They still carried the smell of coal dust and the odor of pulp despite a washing in the sink the night before. It was a far cry from the finery his mother used to set out for him as a child.

Carolyn showed up a few minutes after the 7:30 peal. "Good morning, Matthias. Ready?"

Matthias thought of Solomon Dvorack's displeasure at such tardiness and dismissed it at the same time. It was Sunday morning. Precision could wait for Monday when he would begin writing.

He considered that today was the first step in his rebirth. Being seen with the city administrator would signify his importance. Matthias tugged his cloak. These crude garments would have to go.

He looked her over. She was decidedly underdressed in a simple frock and coat. It looked no better than the vestments she wore when she carried out her official duties. "All set. Can you tell me about your church?"

Carolyn led him down the steps and out of the building. "Well, we have about a hundred parishioners."

The number struck Matthias hard. How much influence could

be gained from a church so infinitesimal? "Does the mayor go there, too?"

"Mayor Charlie is Jewish. Synagogue services are Friday nights."

"He doesn't look Chinese."

Carolyn rolled her eyes. "That's a stereotype. Not all Jews are Chinese. As a matter of fact, I was taught that the United States used to have a lot of Jews."

"Chinese propaganda." Matthias crossed his arms.

Carolyn halted and brought her hands to her hips. "Maybe this was a bad idea. Look, why don't I just take you back to your place. I'll get somebody from Refugee Services to take you to some of the services."

As far as Matthias was concerned, having some tour guide wouldn't open the right doors or shake the right hands. "I'm sorry. Bad start. I was a part of a congregation many times that size. This is very foreign to me."

"You're the part that's foreign." The town bell chimed on the quarter hour. Carolyn shook her head. "I don't want to be late. Coming or going?"

"Coming."

She took her hands off of her hips and started walking again. "Okay, I'm going to give you the condensed version of the religion lecture they give all the new refugees."

Matthias hurried to keep up with her.

"Nobody holds a gun to your head to attend any particular service at any particular time. You can stay home on Sunday mornings and sleep if you want. We're extremely sinful by Synod standards. We prefer to think of it as being liberal. I said it. Get used to it. We keep an old fashioned view of the constitution—separation of church and state."

"How do you manage?"

"Shhh. I'm the teacher. You're the student. Listen up."

"God. Liberals."

"Shhh. After the Second Civil War, we were like you, rebuilding and learning to survive. Our founders saw the turmoil a hundred years of religious war caused. They decided that they would follow the pre-war constitution. No state religion. No state language."

"You probably burned the Ten Commandments on the capitol steps," said Matthias. The comment caused another stop. To him, she looked as angry as Naomi, and it imbued a bit of fear. "I'm sorry, go on."

"Actually, we left the commandments right were they were. Enough of the townspeople viewed them as a darned good set of laws to follow. Nobody complained. Well, almost nobody. We voted. The commandments stayed in the Town Hall."

"Then there's sense in your country after all."

"It's your country now. If you want to find a Christian service, we have every flavor." Carolyn counted on her fingers. "Amish, Baptist, Calvinist, Catholic, Evangelical, Lutheran, Mennonite, Methodist, Orthodox, and Pentecostal. Those are the main ones."

The first denomination stuck with Matthias. "Did you say 'Amish'?"

"Wonderful people. If it weren't for them, we'd all starve."

"Are they as ruthless as the histories say?"

Carolyn's face turned blank. "What did the Synod teach you? No. Never mind. I don't want to know. Look, you're going to have to open your mind up a bit or you're not going to adjust."

"Are there Muslims?"

She let out an exasperated sigh and sped along the sidewalk. "Of course. Hinduism and Shinto, too. It's how we got our nickname—the Hindu Lands."

A pair of men walked close to Matthias with hair like Jesus and robed in brown. They bore a resemblance to the attendants at the bank—except for the three-foot long scabbards protruding from their belts. "Who are they?"

"Jedee. A cult from England before the Holy Wars. Way left of Buddhists if you ask me. Something about a force in nature that ties everything together."

"Your government lets them carry swords?"

"As a matter of fact, yes. They settle minor disputes among the citizens and keep the courts clear for more serious problems. That, and they're absolute whizzes with what few electronics we have."

Matthias imagined himself in a robe, brandishing a sword like a Crusader and imposing righteous judgments on the townsfolk. "Where are their services?"

"They're celibate."

"Never mind."

"I figured as much. Gordon told me that Julia is spending evenings with you."

Matthias caught the insinuation edged in her voice. "She brings me food and conversation, nothing more."

"Then you might want to tell her that."

"What does that mean?"

Carolyn stopped. "From what I've heard, you're all she talks about."

At first, Matthias thought Carolyn simply relayed gossip, but he saw the concern on her face. "That sounds like a warning."

"In a way, it is. I know how women are treated in the Christian States, and you might want to be careful. She's fragile. About a year ago, her fiancé broke their engagement and married somebody else. It took a long time for her to heal. In a lot of respects, she's still healing."

The disclosure only added to Matthias's unease. "I see. I'll be careful." His attention shifted to the sound of drums. They were much louder than the Heartbeat of the City and coming from a different location.

"Her fiancé worked for one of Solomon's ventures. So did the woman that he left Julia for. She still blames Solomon for letting it happen, so you're treading on a nerve, understand?"

"Understood."

Carolyn stopped at a single-story building. "We're here. Come on in." When she opened the door, the drumming tripled in volume.

Matthias recoiled from the impact of each beat.

Carolyn laughed. "Welcome to the St. Peter's Women's Free Methodist Church."

"For the love of God."

"Exactly."

It was as though the blood drained from Matthias's body. He stood in the doorway, watching women beat on drums and dance around the hall. Other than him, not a single man was present.

A woman with gray hair tied neatly in a bun and wearing a black jacket with a cleric's collar approached. "Good to see you, Carolyn. This must be Mr. Kent. Hi, I'm Pastor Donna. Blessings."

He extended a hand. "Nice to meet you."

"I'm sure you feel uncomfortable right now, but we are a friendly church. Please come in and get settled. We've just started."

The church was a spare structure built in much the same way as every other building in Poughkeepsie, a mix of concrete and cinderblocks. A large cross wrapped with a plastic flame hung behind the altar. There were no pews, benches or chairs, only cushions arranged in a semi-circle around the altar.

Matthias was dumbfounded. He couldn't decide whether he was in a church or had blundered into a pagan Rite of Spring.

Carolyn directed him to a cushion. "We see ourselves as the daughters of Mary, Martha, Elizabeth and all the prophetesses of the Bible."

A rush ran up Matthias's spine. "Do you have Bibles here?"

"Bits and pieces. Like everybody else's, ours are fading away."

"How do you know that what you follow is true?"

"You mean 'true' as compared to what you're used to, right?"

He nodded.

"Our foremothers adopted the oral traditions of Methodism before the Rot got all the paper. We kept the Bible in our hearts and passed it along."

The thought of remembering entire books of the Bible seemed daunting to Matthias at first. Then he remembered his own drilling by the school teachers and their relentless exams. "Why the drums?"

"Another bit of lore from our foremothers. The legend goes that God gave the drum to women but that men stole it from them. For those women, it was like losing a piece of their heart. Then a few brave souls took the drums back and kept the beat going ever since."

"Hence the Heartbeat of the City."

Carolyn's face lit up. "Yes. Many of these women's husbands never get that connection."

To Matthias, the idea that some of these ladies had spouses just added to a growing pile of surprises. "Their husbands allow this behavior?"

Whatever endearment he won by his initial observation disappeared. Carolyn shook her head. "Religious freedom extends to everyone, married or not. This is who we are."

The drumming halted. Pastor Donna cleared her throat.

Carolyn shook her head from side to side. "Women have the same rights as men here. Look, I can tell you're uncomfortable. Go home. We can try someplace else next week."

He couldn't believe this was happening. How was he going to meet the town's religious elite? First he was in an estrogen den of a church, and now he was arguing theology with a *woman*. "And, for the record, women's rights are defined in the Bible, or does your interpretation conveniently leave that out?"

"You're an Elder. Don't you remember the Book of Luke? Aren't you people supposed to know this stuff inside out?"

Matthias scoured his memories. "The apostle Paul and the prophet Ruth are quite clear on the topic. What does the Book of Luke have to do with this?"

"Luke Chapter 11. Right after the Good Samaritan. The whole story about Mary, the sister of Martha, and how Jesus approved of her listening at his feet instead of being in the kitchen. We're all Mary's in there."

Then it hit him. The words weren't in Synod's Bible. "Look, I'm sorry."

Carolyn pursed her lips. "That's the third time you said you were sorry. There are a lot of women inside those doors who have heard that phrase again and again. Their boyfriends left them pregnant. I'm sorry. Their fathers abused them. I'm sorry. Their husbands beat them. Sorry. Sorry. Sorry. They all say just how sorry they are and do it all over again. Our church gives them a home and a sisterhood. Christ gives them hope. Don't presume your beliefs on them."

During the exchange, Matthias thought of Beth and how she

tended to her broken sister. How Johanna clung to that doll. Too bad she couldn't have made it this far. The recollection left him humbled. Carolyn believed. He did not. It was wrong for him to use her. Old habits died hard. "I'm sorry."

Her fury seemed to wane for a moment, and, in that moment, Matthias felt a tug in his heart. He opened the door. "I have much to learn... ...and unlearn. I'm being unfair. You're missing your service."

She stood in the doorway. "Apology accepted."

Matthias left the drumming behind and walked the streets of town. Occasionally, a hymn or a prayer lifted from a nondescript church. He wondered about those inside. At first, he felt as though he committed some grave sin by not going in, but the feeling passed.

At one particular sanctuary he brought his hand to the latch and found himself dwelling on a lifetime spent in church. How many hours had he spent studying the religious dictates of the Synod? How many souls did he bring to God during the Sunday Ecunet broadcast?

Yet, for all of his education, all of his prior work, Matthias couldn't bring himself to go in. There simply was no reason. All he would be doing is lying to the parishioners about his beliefs and hoping no one would guess his motives. He laughed. "How can you have a new beginning if the old ways never die?" Matthias stepped back, turned, and walked away.

He sat on the edge of a monument, a great granite block that bore the names of those sons of Poughkeepsie that lost their lives in the first Civil War. On another side were the names of those sons and daughters who perished in the Second Civil War—believers in freedom every one, or so the proud inscription proclaimed.

He felt around his cloak to a certain pocket. Inside that pocket was the pen Umar gave him. For a moment, he thought of scratching the names of Jeremiah, and Samuel, and everyone who deserved to have a life here. No one would erect monuments to them. No one would know they ever existed. His hand tightened on the pen.

"I've been looking for you," said Carolyn.

Her voice startled Matthias and he let the pen fall back into his pocket. "I'm sorry?"

She raised a hand. "You can stop with the sorry's. I'm being a bad host."

"I'm the one who asked to go to your church."

"And I wanted to make sure you got what you asked for."

He chuckled. "I got what I deserved."

"Well, it's my turn to apologize. I should have insisted that we go to somewhere a bit more familiar to you. Would you like some tea?"

They sat in a small teashop. It was warm, its walls painted in an Asian style of idyllic mountains with streams and cranes flying over them. Carolyn and he got the last table.

Matthias steeped a tea ball in his cup of hot water. It turned the water red-brown. Cinnamon wafted up to his nostrils and he inhaled the agreeable scent.

She did the same. "So, what does Matthias Kent believe in?"

"I believe in God, the Father Almighty, Maker of Heaven and Earth." He quit dunking his tea ball. "No. No, I don't."

Surprise filled her face. "You don't believe in God?"

He searched himself, surprised at his honesty. "No."

"That's pretty astounding considering your rank. Is that why they branded you a heretic?"

Her phrase told Matthias that Mayor Charlie didn't share the secret of the Bible with her. He groped for the right word, the right phase to divert further questions. "I came across some corruption. It was widespread and included not just officers of the bank, but representatives of the Synod as well. They were going to kill me."

"How horrible."

"It wasn't half as horrible as the things I saw carried out in the name of God. It gives me nightmares still. When I was on the run, I prayed as fervently as I ever had. My prayers went unanswered. God did not smite the evildoers. Many innocent people died."

"And here you are, having tea."

"Thanks to Umar Girard and his horse. Perhaps I should be

learning the Quran."

"Same God, different religion."

"Which is the root of the problem. Umar and his people worship one way, you worship another. I passed a dozen churches this morning, and they all worship just differently enough to hang some sign on their front door proclaiming that they know God better than the church across the street. It's a brand-awareness nightmare." He took a sip of tea. "Back home, I did everything the ministers said, tithed, prayed, fasted and prospered. Now look at me."

Carolyn rocked back in her chair. "You did everything your *religion* said. What did God say?"

"Nothing. That's my point."

She ran her finger around the lip of the teacup. "There's a story I remember Pastor Donna telling us about a woman, a Catholic woman. Her name was Mother Theresa. She once said that she heard God's voice and then it stopped. Yet, she did His will all her life."

Matthias felt a low rumble of anger. "Funny, I knew a Catholic woman named Theresa. She thought she was doing God's will right up until the second the Synod killed her."

Carolyn remained unruffled. "I'm not arguing with you, Matthias. It's just that I don't agree. That's the beauty of the Federation. Nobody has the right to tell you what to believe. We have plenty of atheists here."

"I'm not sure I believe in atheists."

She snorted her tea. "You got me there. You know, my father had a name for people like you."

"The Damned?"

She laughed again, her eyes sparkling. "No. He called them 'sojourners.'"

Matthias recalled the word. "A traveler."

"He said there were always people whose faith could never settle in one place. They always had doubt."

Bringing his hand to his chin, Matthias thought the term over. "Yes, it fits. I guess I'm a sojourner then. I like the sound of it. It sounds poetic."

The town bell chimed twice.

Carolyn jumped up. "I'm sorry, but I have to go. It's my turn to cook dinner today at the church."

Matthias enjoyed the conversation and wished she wouldn't go. "Can I see you again?"

She halted, a smile lifting the corners of her lips. "Sure. I'd like that. You know where to find me, okay?"

"Okay."

Carolyn threaded her way around the tables. "And sojourner, remember this, bidden or unbidden, God is there."

Matthias laughed and called back to her. "The same philosopher said that knowing nothing was the happiest life."

Chapter 55: Verses 1-49

If he were to carry the title of sojourner, Matthias decided he might as well earn it by touring the city.

During his travels, he found markets at different points, each one catering to a different niche.

At one, all manner of nuts, seeds and spices sat in metal drums. At another, vendors hawked vehicular parts, not that there were any vehicles around. Each market was crowded with people. Nowhere was the specter of starvation or the presence of microsonic cannon to ensure order.

His observations were secondary compared to his recollection of the afternoon with Carolyn. He felt a lightness, an inner happiness. A conversation such as theirs would have warranted a trip to the nearest Reformation Center if he were back in Philadelphia. Here though, they spoke with an unbridled openness that he savored.

By evening, he found himself back at his apartment house. It was time for rest, time to prepare for tomorrow. He reached inside his pocket to the pen Umar gave him. His thumb and forefinger pressed against it and his heart beat faster. Paper and pen—no more sacraments. Words unleashed for those that could pay the price.

"Dinner for one—or two?"

The question brought Matthias out of his thoughts. He looked over at the woman from the food stall. "I beg your pardon?"

She gave him a wry look. "Your lady is already up there."

Matthias's heartbeat doubled. *Carolyn?* He thought more of it. *Julia.* "Did she have dark hair?"

"Dark as night. Dinner for one or two?"

"One."

"Oh."

Matthias noted the reaction. The street had eyes all its own, and he received a demonstration of its effectiveness. "What is your name?"

She answered slowly, a bit uncertain and suspicious. "Greta. My husband is Nicodemus."

"Well Greta, wife of Nicodemus, I appreciate your looking out for me. Your last name?"

"Hamill."

"Is that one 'L' or two?"

She looked at him without a clue.

"Don't know, eh? Then it shall be two."

"Why does that matter?"

Matthias nodded. "I am in debt to your vigilance. Tomorrow, you will see just how much." He gave her his best, most charming smile.

The suspicion changed to a schoolgirl's giggle. "One dinner it is."

"What's that for?" said Julia, her finger pointing at the food container in Matthias's hand.

"You're back, I see." His voice trailed off as she came into view. Gone was her medical tunic, replaced by a tight dress with a plunging neckline. She looked awkward, like a young girl wearing formal clothes for the first time. He placed his dinner on the table. "Are you going somewhere?"

The rosy blush of her cheeks faded. "What am I doing wrong? Aren't I as pleasing as the women back home?"

"You're fine in that regard. God knows there are no

complaints."

"Then command me as if we were in Philadelphia. Shall I prepare dinner?"

An alarm bell clanged in Matthias's mind, almost louder than the city gate's alarm on the day he escaped. "Command you?"

"Husbands speak, and their wives listen. I know my duty."

He looked on, confused at her matter-of-fact delivery. "Husbands? Wives?"

"I'm perfect for you. I may be a doctor some day. We'll have rank. We'll meet the right people. I know the power you held. People here respect power. You will be powerful again." She held out her hand.

Matthias looked at her. His thoughts churned with the promise of wealth and position and the respect it conveyed. He would be powerful again. All he had to do was to take her hand.

At what price?

It sounded like his own voice, but it wasn't. It was the voice from the wilderness, the voice of his delirium, and it was clear and quiet and strong.

Your soul?

In his mind, Matthias argued back. *Only the Devil takes souls.*

Yes, and how can there be a Devil if there is no God?

The words rushed through him like water through a sieve. The voice flowed away.

Julia held out her hand, her face expectant.

Matthias caught a hint of anger in her eyes. Julia wasn't asking him to make a choice. She demanded his surrender. He held his lips closed, feeling them tremble one on top of the other. It felt as though all the air left the room, like he was back in the body bag and surrounded by the dead.

Her fingers beckoned. He looked down at Julia's hand. "How can there be new beginnings if the old ways never die?"

"What?"

Matthias tried to steer a course between Julia's anger and being honest with her—and himself. "You're a wonderful person, and I realize what you're offering. But Elder Kent is gone. I am just Matthias, janitor of Solomon Dvorack."

Her expectant smile changed to a sneer as if she donned a mask. "A wonderful person? Look at me. What's wrong with me?"

"Nothing. You're lovely. You've been more than kind to me."

"Am I not worthy of your love?"

"Love?" He blurted the word out just as Carolyn's warning came to mind, its impact shattering Julia.

Her eyes rounded into a white rage. Snarls leapt from her mouth. She ran to the door. "Rot in hell, Matthias. Rot in hell."

He called out, "Julia, I'm sorry. Wait. Please." But she was gone.

Chapter 56: Verses 1-92

In the morning, Matthias hoped that a hard morning's work would blunt the echo of Julia's voice. The sound of her anger lingered in his ears and the hurt on her face accused him with every recollection. He dwelled on his actions, wondering what he did to entice or provoke her. Whatever it was, it escaped him. Matthias let out a quiet sigh.

As the beat of the drum grew louder, Matthias rounded the corner along the Riverwall. He counted off the cadence, four steps to one beat. On the third step, he halted.

Each and every person wore black. They resembled a line of mourners at a funeral. Black trousers for the men. Black frocks for the women. The children that accompanied them looked every bit a miniature version of the adults. They formed a queue that stretched along the pale Riverwall and ran like a black line against a page.

Matthias cleared his throat and resumed his walk. He tried not to stare at the beards, the bonnets, and the wide brimmed hats. The look in their eyes confused him. They were happy.

He knocked on the door before the bell chimed seven.

Solomon's voice bellowed from the shop. "Please good sirs

and madams, wait. We are not ready."

"It's me, Sol. Matthias."

The sound of keys and a lock freeing off accompanied the old man's voice. "Get in here."

A wild-eyed Solomon confronted Matthias. "We are besieged by Amish."

He felt his blood drain. Every recollection of the night before flew away in fear. "Those people outside?"

"A hundred at least."

Matthias remembered the Battle of Haverford and the stand their fierce ranks made. "Oh my God. What can we do?"

Solomon yanked a jar of ink off the shelf and stacked as many sheets of paper as he could grab. "Invite them in."

"Are you insane?"

The old man danced around a stool. "I am crazy with joy. This could not be a better start."

"You've been drinking already, haven't you?"

Solomon stopped his dance. "My God, Matthias. You're scared shitless, aren't you? Come on, there's business to do."

"They're going to kill us and drink our blood, you old fool."

The joy in Dvorack's face changed to puzzlement. He studied Matthias for a moment and finally let out a great "Oh." He reached for more paper. "Good heavens, you don't know."

Of that, Matthias agreed. "What?"

"The Battle of Haverford. Complete bullshit. No Amish man alive would take up arms. Completely against their doctrine. It's all Synod bullshit."

The story Nathan told of his wife uncovering proof the Amish were peaceful surfaced in his mind. He felt stupid. "The histories lied."

"Don't look so put out. We can chat about history lessons later, but now we need to get to work. They're away from their farms, and they won't wait." Solomon tugged him out of the shop and led him to a small office. He placed the paper and ink on a desk. "This is where you'll work. I'll put the words they want on a chalkboard. You transcribe them to paper. When you're done, simply slide it under the door."

"But why can't I work out here?"

"Trade secrets. Trust me, one of those Amish folks out there sees how this gets done and you and I will be out of a job. They're hard workers and savvy businessmen. Now, close the door."

Matthias did as instructed. He listened to the sound of voices, the rise and fall of greetings, trickles of laughter, and the shuffle of feet.

A chalkboard slid under the door. It read, "Be not conformed to this world, but be transformed by the renewing of your mind that ye may prove what is that good and acceptable and perfect will of God."

Matthias set to work. It was harder than he thought. The paper held no guidelines, no margins. The pen's movement felt uncertain in his hand.

He found a flat aluminum bar and set it against the page. It became his guide. The words flowed onto the paper. He blew the ink dry and recognized the words. "Romans 12."

"All set?" said Solomon.

Matthias stacked the page on top of the chalkboard and slid it back out. He listened for cheers. He heard nothing except crying.

The demand for his work proved relentless. By late morning, he crafted dozens of biblical verses, birth certificates, and marriage vows. Both the paper supply and Matthias were exhausted.

Solomon opened the door, grinning. "We had to turn people away."

Matthias looked out. The shop looked like a treasure trove from a fable. Stacked high were jellies, pots of honey, and canned produce of all kinds, the like of which he had never seen at his own farm "My God."

"I knew we'd be a success."

He flexed his hand. "I'm glad we ran out of paper."

Solomon uncorked two bottles. "To Matthias Kent, Master Calligrapher."

"To the man with the sorest hand in Poughkeepsie. What was the crying about?"

"Crying?"

"The first thing I wrote was from Romans 12. 'Be not conformed of this world.'"

Solomon arranged the goods on a worktable, found a seat and a bottle of wine. He looked off into the distance with muted satisfaction. "Think of it as an Amish manifesto. They say it a lot during their services and inscribe it in their wares. But today, Matthias, today was the first time in more than a hundred years that they've seen it on paper like the Bibles of old. That's why they put that scripture first before all of their other needs. I cried, too." The old man's eyes filled with tears.

"Then it was a good way to begin. How did so many of them know about us?"

"I mentioned it in church."

"You're Amish? You don't wear a uniform like them."

Solomon took another pull and gave Matthias a sly glance. "I'm Lutheran these days, but I got my start with the Mennonites when I came here. They've handled refugees for the Federation for as long as anyone can remember. Anyway, I ran into an old Mennonite buddy of mine and told him what we're up to."

"I'm not getting the connection."

"The only outsiders the Amish deal with are the Mennonites. The rest of us are kind of off limits. Not me though. I kept my ties with the Mennonites, kept their refugee efforts supplied with goods and people when nobody else could. I guess that makes me okay in the Amish book."

Matthias caught the inference. "You have contacts with the Mennonites and they have contacts with the Amish. I get it. Networking. That's smart business."

The old man shook his head. "It's not about business. Sure, I've done pretty well. I'm blessed. But it's not about business with the Amish or the Mennonites. It's about a debt I owe them. They took me in when I was like you."

"You were cast out? Why?"

"I have a gift for discernment as they used to say back in Atlanta. My talents got me an appointment as Assistant Head Botanist in the Department of Agriculture. During my research, I saw how the Rot was becoming more resistant to our fungicides and made the mistake of predicting a famine unless steps were taken."

Matthias thought back twenty years and remembered the

starving masses scouring his family's fields for the most miserable scraps. He remembered the shrieks of the dying when the troops scythed them down. He remembered the soldier of the Order say, "All is well." Turning to Solomon, he said, "You saw it coming?"

"Unfortunately."

"And what happened?"

"I should have prayed for wisdom instead of discernment. I posted my findings on the Ecunet. At first, it was well received. Then I realized my folly."

"Which was?"

"I used the 'E' word. I said the Rot was evolving around our countermeasures. Can't use that word. A censor picked it up before I could retract it. The next thing I know, I'm branded a heretic and tossed outside the city gates. Was out there for months until I wandered into a SalVal. Lost forty pounds. Yeah, it's hard to believe when you look at me now. They took care of me and got me out of the country. Next thing you know, I'm working for a Mennonite cranberry farmer and his Amish buddies. They know the old ways, those Amish. I learned a lot." Solomon lifted his bottle. "To the Amish and the Mennonites."

They spent the rest of the day pulping and screening as much of the trimmings as they could.

Matthias pushed a rack full of wet paper close to the stove. A thought struck him. "Why is it that the Amish wanted paper so much? You said they left their farms to come and get it. Back on our farm, you never left things alone until all the chores were done."

Solomon smoothed some pulp onto a screen. "It's not about paper, Matthias. Any one of those Amishmen can make paper, though it would only last a couple of months at best." The old man winked. "It's about books and paper. It's about Haverford. The last stand of the printed word."

"Printed word? What do you mean? What happened at Haverford."

Dvorack shook his head. "I'll give you the Amish version. That's the one I believe."

Matthias said, "You don't trust the government here?"
"Oh, I trust the Federation enough, but governments commission histories the way they want them to read. The Amish don't couch their past with heroic tales. It would be a sin, and they take sinning very seriously. Most righteous people on the planet if you ask me."

"And Haverford?"

"To understand Haverford, you have to understand the Rot. A hundred years ago, biologists were busy trying to save people from *Pythium cronos*, not plants, or animals, or wood or paper. They didn't see how much it permeated everything until it was too late. By then, its spores were everywhere. Anything made of plant material was consumed at an unbelievable rate. That's why wood is treasured so much and why paper is almost impossible to come by."

Matthias touched the damp surface of a page. "Not for you."

"Trade secret, my friend. Trade secret." Solomon drank the rest of the bottle of wine. "Haverford College held the largest collection of books and paper records for a religious group called the Quakers in a climate controlled vault. When the college's board saw that groups like the Amish and Mennonites would lose their recorded heritage to the Rot, they offered them space. The Amish took them up on it. Things were fine for twenty-five years until the Synod came to power and began enforcing the Conversion Statutes."

"So that we could be of one religious accord."

"That accord was what started the Second Civil War—one religion, one language. Not everybody agreed."

Matthias thought back to history class. "It was started by liberals burning down a church."

"Like I said, governments decide how their histories read." Solomon uncorked another bottle. "While the liberals fought the conservatives about which church we'd all attend, the Amish marched on Haverford to get their records back. When the Synod found out, they sent a force to the college to prevent them. The Amish barricaded the doors to the library and sat down in front of it. They wouldn't fight the soldiers, but they weren't going to give up either."

"That's not right. The Amish fought them tooth and nail. It was a bloody struggle."

"Who's telling this story?"

"Go on," said Matthias.

"The histories tell you how the battle occurred, but not why and that's the most important part. You see, a Federation general named James Decker saw how the Synod forces concentrated around the college. He also realized that most of the farmers who had any success against the Rot were sitting at Haverford and not farming. Those Amish didn't use the government-prescribed chemicals. They were breeding better crops. So, the general brings his forces to Haverford to slug it out with the Synod and get his hands on the only people who are growing decent food. Decker's forces broke through to the besieged Amish."

"And they brought their records with them?"

Solomon turned somber. "No. The library was destroyed during the fighting. For the Amish, it was like the burning of the Library of Alexandria. Rot got everything the fire didn't. The Amish lost it all—birth certificates, marriage papers, and death notices. Not to mention a sizeable collection of Bibles. And then the Synod brought in their reserves. Decker's forces had to retreat all the way to the Delaware River."

The mention of Bibles slammed into Matthias with the impact of a missile. He felt as though he were John, the son of Zebedee, receiving the book of Revelation. His mind raced. Pins and needles pricked his neck. A cold clarity came to him, withering in its scope. The Battle of Haverford wasn't about heretical rebels—it was about Bibles, hundreds of them bearing witness to the Synod's treachery.

"What's the matter?" said Solomon.

Matthias didn't know how to answer. His mind fixed on a simple line of thought. If the Synod killed thousands over the Bible, they would not give up on one person. "I don't feel well."

"You worked hard, today. We both did. Go home and rest. I'll finish up. Your wages are on my desk."

After he finished his wine, Matthias collected five pails of coal, three jars of preserves and fifteen sheets of paper. He held the pages in his hand, surveying the texture and the near whiteness of its surface. How innocent it looked until ink formed words. How dangerous those words could be.

And how delightful. He chuckled and recalled his pledge to Greta Hamill. Matthias took a pen in hand and scripted out an upper case "H."

Greta sat next to Nicodemus, each of them slicing vegetables and dropping them into a broth.

"Good evening," said Matthias. "No. No, don't get up. I just came by to place my order for dinner and to give you this." He held out the page.

Greta's eyes opened wide and her hand trembled as her fingers embraced the gift. "My God, paper. Nick! Nick! It's paper. Can you believe it? What does it say?"

"'The Dining Establishment of Nicodemus and Greta Hamill.' My thanks for your good food, honest service, and vigilance." Matthias regarded their gasps and awestruck faces with glee. Blessed be the cheerful giver, he thought, leaving them behind and walking up the stairs to his room.

Chapter 57: Verses 1-89

Despite the explanations about the Amish, Matthias still regarded them with misgiving every morning when he rounded the corner and walked along the Riverwall.

The line grew longer by week's end. Other townspeople blended into the queue. Fashions changed from black hats, to hooded vestments, to hair and hairless alike. Every face reflected the same expectation—Solomon's paper and the words that he, Matthias Kent, wrote on its surface.

Their vestments were kempt and bodies on the heavy side of lean. It told him that they were well off. None of their hands pawed for a handout. None of their cheeks sank into their skulls from want.

Inside his office, though, he never saw the wealth, never shook their hands, or looked into their eyes. He laughed at the irony. All of the *right* people were coming to see him though he never met a single one. That probably wasn't what Julia had in mind.

It was late Saturday afternoon. Solomon looked like his biblical namesake, sitting among the treasures crowding the shop and working his way through a fifth bottle of wine. "An amazing week, eh partner?"

Matthias piled his own treasures on the desk. "To say the least. You know your market."

"It was easy. It's Christmas. Business will slacken after the holidays. We'll be happy to fill Synod orders by the end of January." Solomon pointed to Matthias's wages. "What are you going to do with all that?"

"I don't know. It sits in my apartment."

Solomon's face reddened. "You mean Julia hasn't gotten into it yet?"

Matthias looked at the floor. "She doesn't come by any more."

"That's not a bad thing. Didn't much like her. Hasn't Carolyn shown you the trustworthy banks in this town of hers?"

"Banks? I thought you said we bartered here."

"For day to day things, but wealth can get stolen." Solomon took a chalkboard and wrote down an address. "Go here with your booty. They will set up an account with you and trade your goods fairly. You will be extended a line of credit against the value less ten percent. Use the credit to get yourself some decent housing. God knows you can afford that now. Keep the smaller, less valuable items around to trade at your leisure."

Matthias chuckled. "The Bank of Job charged twenty-five percent. This is a bargain. I shall look them up."

"Good then. Oh, next Saturday, we will work a half-day. After that, your presence will be required for a special task."

"And that is?"

"I host a Christmas feast for everyone who works for my businesses and their families at my home here in town. It's a Dvorack tradition. Come by at 3:00 PM and eat and drink until you pass out." Solomon patted his belly. "Another Dvorack tradition is to give my employees off on Christmas Eve. You'll have three days to recover from the party."

"My thanks." The time off and the invitation brought a quiet joy to Matthias. Up until that point, he hadn't considered the holidays one bit. The joy rapidly slipped into melancholy. It would be the first year without his mother decorating the house, the first year without Naomi's roast chicken, the first year where the roof over his head was not his own. The distraction of work had been a blessing.

"Matthias?" said Solomon, his face a solemn mask of concern. "You're free to spend Christmas with us. Okay?"

"Sure."

"Oh, don't be so half-hearted about it. My first Christmas in Poughkeepsie was hell. I wept like a little child on Christmas morning. But I got over it and, well, you see the fruits of my labor. Now, get out of here and get that City Administrator to find you some proper housing."

"Did I hear my name taken in vain?" Carolyn peeked from around the entrance.

Solomon rose. "My orders are up to date, Ms. Decker. Darken someone else's door."

"I'm not here to see you, Sol. We're here to see Matthias."

"We?"

The door swung open. A dozen large men in flowing robes entered the room. Matthias recognized one. It was Khalal, bodyguard to Imam Girard.

Carolyn bowed. "May I present his Excellency, Sheik Girard, and his entourage."

Matthias bowed.

Umar Girard came in, smiling and extending a hand. "Mr. Kent, how good it is to see you again. Your enterprise has created quite a stir, and I had hoped to speak to you about it. Paper for the masses. There is hope for us yet."

Taking the sheik's hand, Matthias said, "I had no idea it would bring this much attention. I owe it all to you for saving me and nursing me back to health."

Umar's eyes danced around the room surveying the enterprise. "I merely followed where the hand of God led."

"What brings you to Poughkeepsie, more refugees?"

The answer came after a moment's hesitation. "Official business to attend to before your holidays. You Christians are impossible to deal with until after New Year's."

Matthias read a certain evasiveness in Umar's answer. He let it go and kept the conversation to pleasantries. "As Yusuf said, we are misguided with our feasting, boozing, and singing about a baby born in surroundings more humble than this place." He reached into his pocket and pulled out the pen Umar gave him. "I haven't used it yet, I'm afraid. Solomon has me using fountain pens."

"That is a pity. I had hoped to see some examples of your work."

"And so you shall, your Excellency." Matthias hurried back to his desk, uncapped the ink and dipped the pen into it. He returned a few minutes later with a sheet of paper. "For you, Umar."

The Imam held it up and read it aloud. "May Allah be with you all the days of your life, and beyond."

Matthias held out an aluminum tube. "And this is from one calligrapher to another. Please, open it."

Umar popped the cap off of one end of the tube and out slid ten sheets of paper. He ran his hands over the pages, his voice quieting. "God is great. My thanks."

Carolyn cleared her throat. "Your Excellency, I'm afraid we have to be moving along if we're going to catch the evening train."

"You have done well, Mr. Kent, and in such a short time. Surely God watches out for you."

"As He does you, your Excellency." Matthias forced a smile to his lips. Good business sense, not Providence, drove his success. "A safe journey to you and your men."

The guards slipped back out into the street. Sheik Girard regarded Matthias for a moment, then followed his men.

Carolyn stood at the door, her face beaming. "You're full of surprises, aren't you?"

Matthias couldn't help but smile. "Of that you can be sure. Will you be around City Hall any more today?"

"For a little while."

"May I call upon you to point me in the right direction for some housing?"

"Sure. You know where to find me."

Matthias stood before a wall full of chalkboards. Vital statistics of every room, apartment and home available crowded the slates. Which were good and which ones weren't? He had no idea.

Carolyn, on the other hand, stood with her arms crossed and studied the boards. "How much are we talking here?"

Matthias glanced down a sheet of plastic script the bank gave him. "I have eight thousand, more or less."

"You earned all that in your second week here?"

"Is that good?"

"You're not passing through any needles."

It took Matthias a second to get the joke. "I get it, the rich man and the needle. Laying more of Luke's Gospel on me, eh?"

"You can afford quite a bit." Carolyn pulled down four chalkboards and handed them to him. "These are all good homes. Decent plumbing and in a nicer section of town."

"What is this obsession with plumbing?"

She shook her head. "You grew up with flush toilets, didn't you?"

"Why, yes."

"I had an outhouse until two years ago."

"Indoor plumbing would be fine."

Carolyn said, "You certainly impressed the Imam."

Matthias laughed. "That wasn't the case when I was his guest. I was rude. My gift was the least I could do."

"It was the first thing he wanted to do after our meetings."

"He came to see what all the fuss was about."

"He asked for you, not Solomon and not paper."

"I see," said Matthias, though he really didn't. Why would Umar go out of his way?

Carolyn read one of the boards, her mood shifting and her words tinged in ice. "What happened with Julia? Were you rude with her, too?"

Matthias could feel himself bristle. "Ah, I wondered how long it would take for gossip to get around. What's being said now?"

Carolyn's face hardened. "It's not gossip. Julia's boss came to me. He said that Julia wants reassigned to another town. When he asked why, she said you threw her out."

Matthias tried to suppress the hot rush of anger burning up his spine. "That's not what happened." He looked at Carolyn, her lips pursed and arms crossed. No matter what he said, she wouldn't trust the answer. The strange part was that he cared what she thought. "Julia wanted me to fall in love with her and get married. Considering that I'd known her for all of three evenings, I declined. She didn't like the answer. Now, you tell me, did I violate some Federation courting ritual? If that's the case, then I'm guilty as charged. Trot out the minister and marry us so that my house may be sanctified before God."

"You didn't hurt her?"

The question rankled him even more. "I did nothing of the sort." Matthias understood. Julia trumped up the reasons for her departure to evoke everyone's sympathies. "You're being used."

"I beg your pardon?"

"Julia manipulated you to take sides. And here you are quizzing me because of your connection to the Women's church. You shelter abused women. What other conclusion could you come to?"

Carolyn didn't like the answer. "You're the one doing the manipulating."

"I'm doing no such thing," he protested. "The only thing I'm guilty of is not paying enough attention to the warning you gave me about her."

Her eyes narrowed. "Why should I believe you?"

Matthias read her expression, the way the lines in her brow softened. All it took was the right phrase to convince her. He refused. Carolyn deserved the truth. "I'm trying to start over here. I don't need any more enemies. Besides, I'm not interested in her. I can't say I ever was. I'm interested in someone else."

"Who?" said Carolyn.

Matthias looked straight at her. "You." He spoke the word without forethought, without control. The word came from inside his chest, free and unhindered from motive. It felt liberating. It felt dreadful.

Carolyn fell silent, her mouth half-open. She handed the chalkboards to Matthias. "I can't do this."

Why is it that I get in the most trouble when I tell the truth, thought Matthias, as he watched her walk away.

Chapter 58: Verses 1-102

Another week passed and the work didn't let up. The line of customers, and Matthias's thoughts about what he said to Carolyn, seemed endless. By Saturday, the supply of paper exhausted itself. The thoughts did not.

He wanted to explain himself, but she was always out of the office. She didn't reply to his messages. He laughed. Telling her what he thought was the cleanest bit of truth he spoke in a long time.

A chalkboard slid under the door.

Solomon called out, "Four to go and then we're done."

Afterward, Matthias cleaned up and made his way to Solomon's house.

The Dvorack residence crowned a hill at the edge of town. The glow of lightbulbs warmed the windows. Music played from inside.

He opened the door to a mélange of cinnamon, braised meat and baked apples. Dozens of other aromas vied for his attention. A quartet of musicians played brass instruments.

"Matthias," yelled Solomon. "You're late."

"I didn't think you'd notice." The old man's breath and ruddy complexion gave testimony to a sizeable head start in liquor consumption.

Solomon yanked two tankards from a passing tray. He shoved one at Matthias. "You're behind. Get drinking."

Matthias expected more cranberry wine and found a pint of amber liquid topped with white foam. He took a pull. It tasted of yeast and held a bitter edge. It was marvelous. He took another swig. "What is this?"

"You've never tasted beer before? Brew it myself."

"Beer?"

"A mixture of grains fermented at one of my distilleries. This recipe dates back before the Civil War and we drink it only once a year." Solomon raised his tankard, shouted "To Christmas" and drained it without a pausing.

Every man and woman cheered and guzzled their drinks.

Matthias did the same. Another tankard arrived in his hand.

"To paper," declared the old man.

"To pen," said Matthias.

The raucous crowd silenced.

At first, Matthias wondered if he committed a sin against his host. Then he studied their faces. The guests looked at him with the same kind of awe of the people waiting in line outside the shop.

Solomon wrapped an arm around Matthias, his face even rosier than before. "Yes, to pen and paper."

More cheers erupted from the crowd.

A heavyset woman joined Solomon. She wore a dress of crimson velvet under a double chin. "Is this the man?"

Solomon wrapped his other arm around her waist and kissed her neck. "Rida Dvorack, Matthias Kent."

She gave Matthias a sly smile. "So, Solomon, this is the man who flirts with your precious trade secrets."

Laughter rose from the audience.

She moved away from her husband and pulled Matthias to her chest. "Do you prefer paper to these?"

The crowd roared.

Before Matthias could extricate himself, she planted a big

kiss on his cheek. "Everyone," she declared. "I give you Matthias Kent, our calligrapher."

The crowd lifted their tankards toward Matthias. Cheers followed.

Solomon leaned in close. "You're a hero. You've taken us from an adequate year into a banner one."

The weight of the old man's words sank into Matthias. The people in the room were toasting him. Never had he experienced such a fete at the bank or even at Pharaoh's. He lifted his tankard up to the crowd.

In the back, he spotted a golden-haired woman lifting her mug. He could swear it was Carolyn. She gave him the briefest of smiles and melted into the crowd.

Solomon kept his grip on Matthias's shoulder. "There are many people to meet. Come."

For a maddening hour, Matthias shook what seemed like hundreds of hands. He met their gleaming eyes and flattered the increasingly tipsy guests.

He glimpsed Carolyn again and again. About the time she would look his way, another guest would fall into the line of sight. When they left, she was gone.

Relief finally came by way of a knock on the door. The mayor and his wife arrived and caused a happy stir. Solomon hurriedly excused himself, grabbed two tankards and became the ebullient master of ceremonies to his newest guests.

Matthias took advantage of his host's departure and maneuvered through the crowded rooms in search of Carolyn. With each new venue, he found himself glad-handing a wider and wider array of people from factory directors to farmhands. To him, there seemed to be little division by class or income. Only the most minor variation of vestment held any clue of rank. He thought of his own humble clothes. There hadn't been any time to buy something he considered more appropriate. Had he done so, he would have looked garish and a show off.

Matthias paused, alone in a room full of people, and let out a quiet laugh. He was one of the audience, not a privileged Elder expecting deference. It felt good. It felt as satisfying as the beer in his tankard.

Then he spied Carolyn.

She stood there, hesitant to come closer.

Matthias wondered what he could say or do to get her to speak to him again. He took a step toward her.

"There you are," declared Rida. "You must meet the Gillette's. They're dying to lay their hands on a page. You'll love Antonio, he comes up with the most obscene limericks."

In the space of three sentences, Carolyn vanished. Rida took him in tow to a great parlor. There, Matthias grinned through a dozen short poems involving sailors and barn animals, which seemed to be an art form all its own in Poughkeepsie.

He lost sight of Carolyn completely. Between forced chuckles and swigs of beer, he scanned the horizon of the room for her. There was no sign. Matthias resolved to drown her absence with another tankard and set off for more. He stepped into a dining hall and bumped into a woman. "Sorry," he said without looking.

"My mistake," said Carolyn. She looked up at him, her face shying away.

Somewhere between the fear and the elation of the moment, he found a calmness to himself he never knew he had. "Look, it's okay if you don't want to talk to me," said Matthias. "I mean, you don't know me. All you know is that I was an Elder and used to having my way. But, I told you the truth."

"I know." Carolyn shook her head. "We spoke with Julia. Went over her story. Things didn't add up. She lied, but we're going to honor her transfer just the same. She has problems. Maybe she just needs a fresh start."

Matthias realized that Carolyn was apologizing, and she didn't seem to be all that comfortable about it. The thought of doing such a thing made him wonder if he would be as willing if the tables were turned. He found himself looking into her eyes. "Thank you for telling me. I appreciate it."

Her face brightened. "You do?"

Rida appeared in the doorway, pressing between the pair. Her head tilted upward. She giggled, gave Matthias a peck on the cheek, and pointed. "Gothcha. Mistletoe. Your turn, Carolyn."

Hesitancy returned to her eyes. She gave him a smile and

walked away.

Matthias turned to Rida. "Am I that ugly, Mrs. Dvorack?"

Rida pinched him on the cheek. "Heaven's no, Mr. Kent. You're a gem."

Matthias gave up searching for Carolyn and distracted himself by making the rounds of the Dvorack kingdom. It held a considerable breadth. He fretted over being able to remember the details come morning when the fog of drink left his head.

By 11:00 PM, he had his fill of beer, food, and rhyming innuendo. Matthias left the party behind and headed out into the night.

His breath fogged the air and he laughed at it. A few months ago, such a temperature would send him to his heated limousine where Alexander waited to take him home. No such vehicles awaited anyone of the Dvorack clan.

Matthias took a step and halted. Before him was a panorama of the city. Lamps dotted the streets and stars dotted the sky—a rare clear night. The quartet played out a spirited tune, and its echo drifted like smoke into the streets. He sat down on the bottom step and tugged his vestments around him.

It was too bad that Samuel couldn't be here to feast on the delicacies in the dining room, too bad that Luke couldn't hear the quartet. And it was too bad that he couldn't lift a tankard to Jeremiah and Beth for getting him to this place—this blessed place.

Mother, father, if you could only be in such a place.

The sound of footsteps roused him from his thoughts.

"Had enough of the party?" said Carolyn.

Surprise rippled through him. "Anymore and I wouldn't be able to find my way home."

She sat down next to him. "Me too. Look, I hope you didn't take the mistletoe thing the wrong way."

"No, it's okay. I would imagine that I'm the last person you want to kiss."

"That's not necessarily true." Carolyn reached into her pocket, pulled out a sprig of mistletoe, and spun it between her fingers. "I just don't know if I can trust…"

"An Elder?"

"There's more to it that that."

"I see." Matthias watched fog of his breath curl skyward. "You know, I just figured out why Julia was so upset. I should have seen it much earlier. She wanted an Elder. I am no longer one. I'm a papermaker, a deed that wouldn't have occurred without your help. For that, I am very, very thankful. So tell me, can you trust a papermaker?"

She stopped spinning the mistletoe and raised it over his head. "I hope so."

Her eyes glowed with the reflection of the lights of the house, and he kissed her. It was as if he were weightless, hot and cold all at the same time. The kiss hung between them, a moment and an eternity. Matthias raised his head and swallowed hard. He never had a kiss like that before, never wanted to breathe her essence out of his chest.

A silence froze between them until he spoke. "May I walk you home?"

"Sure."

She threaded her arm through his and leaned in close to thwart the cold. They spoke about the party, about her job, and how he was doing in the city. He recited one of the limericks and got her to laugh.

They walked quickly to keep warm and soon arrived at her house.

"Thanks," said Carolyn.

"Can I see you again? Tea or something?" said Matthias.

"It's a date."

He liked the sound of that and turned to leave. "Until tomorrow then."

"Matthias, you forgot something."

"What's that?"

She held up the mistletoe again.

He obliged.

Another voice joined the pair. "So, this is why you wanted me to leave."

Matthias pulled away.

Julia stood at the edge of the cone of light at the front door. "I saw you two outside the party. Is she why you don't love me? Am I that unworthy?"

Carolyn stepped next to Matthias. "It's not what you're thinking, Julia."

"No wonder you granted my transfer. I should have known you'd steal him."

Matthias didn't like the tone. It smacked of delusion and hysterics. "She didn't steal me, Julia. You and I weren't meant to be."

"I've prayed for somebody like you, and God delivered you to me. Then this Jezebel steals you."

Taking her by the shoulders, Matthias said, "I am my own man. Not yours. Please, you're a fine person. Think this through."

Julia slapped him across the face. "I turn my back to thee Satan. Rot in Hell." She ran into the darkness.

Matthias drew close to Carolyn. "Are you all right?"

"Yes." She shivered. "Julia needs some help. I'll make some calls in the morning and see what we can do."

"I'm sorry this happened."

"No more sorry's." Carolyn took the mistletoe and pressed it into Matthias's hand.

He looked at it. "A souvenir?"

She smiled. "No. It's for next time."

Chapter 59: Verses 1-75

Matthias brought a vat of honey from his home to the tea shop for them to share.

Carolyn was happy to see it, but declined. "I'm in City Government. It wouldn't be appropriate."

"You can't accept gifts? You've got to be kidding." Matthias couldn't fathom the ethics. Gifts to Synod politicians were standard fare—*blessed be the tithe that binds* as the old joke went.

"I'm afraid not." She eyed the honey.

Matthias picked up the vat and took it to the counter. He got the attention of the owner, an Asian woman, and said, "This is for everyone. Merry Christmas."

The owner looked like she would topple over.

He returned to the table. "It's common property now. Better go get some before the word gets out."

A line had already formed. Carolyn got up, waited her turn and drizzled some into her tea. When she returned, she said, "That's two month's rent."

"It's one jar of honey. How is it?"

"Wonderful."

"Then it's worth the price."

Word spread in the tearoom, and Matthias became an instant celebrity. More than once, a "Merry Christmas" interrupted their conversation.

Matthias took it in stride, nodded and gave a "Merry Christmas" in return. At first, he found the intrusions irritating, but got into the spirit of things. He thought of Solomon and his great banquet the night before. How many faces glowed with an overabundance of food and drink? It must have cost a fortune and the man didn't care.

Afternoon tea stretched into the dinner hour, and the dinner hour stretched into evening twilight. Matthias hardly noticed.

He spent the time listening to her talk about her family and the women of her church. She spoke without guile and agenda, and he ate up every word.

Carolyn took a sip of tea and drew a breath. "I've been talking all day. I'm sorry."

"There's that word again."

She ran her finger around the cup, her earlier ease fading just a bit. "May I ask you something personal?"

Matthias figured it would be about Julia, a topic so far mercifully avoided. He nodded. "Go ahead."

"The Mayor told us about you. He said the Synod branded you a heretic, but he didn't tell us why."

The question caught him with off guard. The answer jutted into his mind—a book wrapped in cellophane and clutched by a skeleton. Another burst of memory was him reciting a vow in front of Gideon Stanmore—he would tell no one of the Bible. "When it was discovered that I didn't believe in God the government wanted to put me through Reformation."

"Brainwashing."

"Yes. Electrodes are placed on the scalp." He extended his fingertips and pressed them against her hair. It was soft, silky. He wanted to run his fingers through it. "The synapses of your brain associated with religious experience are mapped by a computer, and then a program is launched to stimulate those areas based on biblical doctrine. Good responses are given pleasure. Those that come through it find love for Jesus at a level they never knew possible." He pulled his hands back.

Carolyn looked horrified. "And those that don't?"

Matthias thought of the attendants outside the bank, simpletons happy to do the most menial things for food and attention like family pets. Or others like Blind Johnny, condemned to play the humble servant to the board of Elders. His thoughts came back to Carolyn's question. "They are given simple tasks—those that live through the process, that is."

"We knew you tortured your own people."

"It's considered an extension of the suffering of Jesus at the hands of the Jews. In doing so, He acquired New Life as told by the Bible. Just a simple application of science to provide the disbelieving with a chance for Heaven."

"You remove their free will."

"The Synod enables it."

Carolyn drew back, her face a shade paler than a moment ago. "Do you believe in this process?"

"Good God, no. I've seen its results. It's horrendous."

"And they were going to do that to you?"

Matthias laughed. "Probably, but they would've run me through Inquisition to pry my mind open and get at all my secrets first. You see, the Reformation connects certain types of behavior to the pleasure centers of the brain. The Inquisition finds your pain centers. That is what every citizen fears most in the Christian States."

She drew back even farther. "How do you know so much about all of this?"

"Don't worry. I'm a professional observer, not a torturer. Fifteen years in Marketing and Advertising. Thousands of hours of focus groups, product development and psychological examinations. I made a life out of studying human nature and how to sell to it. We knew what people feared, what they believed and, most of all, what they coveted. I saw to it that they could have everything they wanted if they just made the minimum monthly penance. Damn, I was good at my job. Hundreds of souls saved every week without the damn Reformation. Nothing could stop me." Matthias cradled his cheeks in his hands. "Not even myself."

Carolyn caressed his hands and leaned closer. "What happened?"

"I went too far. I discovered things upsetting to the Synod. When I brought it to the attention of the authorities, they threatened me. They branded me a heretic. So, I ran. And here I am."

"Thank God for your safe passage."

Her response surprised him. Most people would want to know the secrets behind his flight. All she was concerned with was his safety as granted by the Almighty. Yet the Almighty had little to do with his arrival here in Poughkeepsie. "You should thank Jeremiah, and Noah and Samuel and a host of others who lie buried along the way. If God was listening to prayer, they would be here with me now. They deserve this place a lot more than I do."

Carolyn folded her hands on the table. "Who were they?"

Voicing the recollection came hard to Matthias. His throat seized with emotion. "They are whom I owe my life to and who I have pledged never to forget. You see, I met Samuel on my way to Philadelphia one day…"

Matthias recounted the story well into the night and ended it as the shopkeeper blew out the last of the candles.

"…And here I am, wordwright to the city's richest man and seated with the loveliest woman in town. A happily-ever-after if ever I heard one."

Carolyn laughed. "Who might that be?"

He took the mistletoe out of his pocket and held it over his head.

They kissed.

The shopkeeper brought him the remaining honey.

He extended a hand. "Please, keep it and enjoy."

"Merry Christmas," said the shopkeeper.

"And to you."

Carolyn led him to the door. "You're not spending Christmas alone are you?"

He followed her outside. "Solomon invited me over. I think it's just to give his wife a different ass to pinch."

"You can always come to my church."

"I don't own a drum."

"I'm being serious. Pastor Donna's been asking about you."

"Trying to save my soul, eh? She doesn't have a Reformation processor, does she?"

"No, she employs waterboarding with Holy Water."

"Ah, the old way. It's a wonder the Synod hasn't returned to the traditional methods."

Carolyn tugged on his sleeve. "Please come. We make a Christmas meal for all the women in our charge. You can help if you'd like."

"I'm a miserable chef."

"Well, you can tell them the story of your escape. They'd love to hear it. Just think, by sharing it, many more will know of your friends and their sacrifice."

Matthias nodded. Her idea was sound and touching all at the same time. "I'll think it over."

There was no sign of Julia near Carolyn's house, much to their relief.

Matthias bid his goodbyes and strolled the city, four steps to the beat. Around him, smoke drifted up out of chimneys.

The scent of roast chicken brought back the recollection of Naomi presenting him with a long knife and fork to pare the steaming bird of a past Christmas feast. He passed the plate to his mother who slid a portion of the dark meat onto her plate. His favorite was the white, just like his father.

Matthias brought his hand to his face and found tears. "Damn that Solomon. He was right. I'm crying like a little girl."

Wiping the tears away, Matthias continued on into the small neighborhood of his new residence. He glimpsed a familiar rectangular shape pressed flat against the front window of one of the homes. It was paper. He recognized his handwriting though it looked foreign hanging there on display. The words were vaguely familiar. So many requests passed by him that they all blurred together.

"In memory of Tom Walton. May he rest in peace."

He ran his hand over the pane, wanting to touch the words he wrote. Someone inside wanted to keep a memory forever, put it out for the world to see like the books of old.

He spoke to his reflection. "In memory of Samuel, and Noah, and Jeremiah and Naomi." He pulled his hand back, and it curled into the grip he used to write. Each muscle looked primed to bring ink to paper. The tenseness of his hand swept up along his spine and an idea took hold of him so fiercely that felt his brain would burst from his skull.

"And so it will be," Matthias declared, running toward his house.

Chapter 60: Verses 1-59

A fever, burning with purpose, engulfed Matthias.

On the table before him lay the implements of his craft—pen, ink, paper. He cursed the dim bulb hanging from the parlor ceiling and pushed a table under it. A moment later, he slid a chair over, sat, and ran his hand along the page's surface. He remembered the metamorphosis of a ball of pulp into a flat page. Its transformation was amazing.

Making it had been the easy part. Now it lay before him, a white void. How hard it was to fill. He sought the words with which to begin, weighed the phrasing with a higher regard than even the Sacrament of Pen and Paper at the bank. The words hovered just out of reach, his mind as blank as the page. Instead of fighting, he relaxed. A face appeared in the emptiness.

Samuel.

Matthias found the words. "Samuel was a beggar child with the darkest eyes."

The story poured out of him faster than he could write it. The room echoed with the sound of the pen's scratch. Each word took on an economy of space. Pages filled with tiny script. One after the other, they flowed in an outpouring of ink and tears.

Night turned into twilight and twilight to dawn. On he wrote with the zeal of a prophet until he could no longer keep his eyes open, and dreams fell upon him.

He was a boy again. His mother sat next to him, her eyes trained on the way Matthias formed his script. It had the look of black thread, embroidery with ink. She nodded. "It is fine work, Matthias. Fine work. A gift from God."

"Do you think so, mother?"

"It's not a question of what I think. It's the product of what I see."

"What does that mean?"

"I don't have to think about God's touch. I know it. Back to work. Keep writing, my son. Keep writing."

Matthias awoke smelling ink and paper. The ink smacked of soot and the paper of a dry tartness. He lifted his head and pain shot from his back. His body ached from sleeping on the hard chair and lying on his hands. He needed to move around. He needed to eat.

Steel colored clouds filled the sky. Rain lurked within them. Matthias headed over to the Hamill's stand. To his amazement, there was a line. It never occurred before.

Greta yelled to him, "Matthias! Matthias! Come here." She ladled a large volume of stew into a crock and handed it to him.

He patted his clothes for an item to trade. His grogginess made him forget to bring something along. "I have to run back to the house. I don't have…"

She shoved the stew at him, well ahead of the others. "You will do nothing of the kind. Look at this line."

The Hamills were doing business the likes of which he had never seen before. "Do you have beef today?"

Greta let out a grunt. "That will be the day."

"Why are you so busy?"

She tapped on two panes of glass bound with ribbon and sandwiching a solitary sheet of paper. On it was the message he wrote. "The day after you gave that to us, our business picked up. Nick had to run to the market three times already just to keep up, and you're the reason for our success. Now, if you'll excuse me, I must get back to work. Merry Christmas."

Matthias dwelled on Greta's words. "Back to work." It was an echo from his dream. The fever returned and he sped off toward home.

He gobbled the stew down and ran his finger around the sides of the crock to lick up every ounce. His hunger surprised him. As he thought it over, he realized that the Hamills weren't serving breakfast. They served lunch. He had slept right through the morning.

After his meal, Matthias pushed his sleeves up and drew the pen. A drop of ink no bigger than a period fell onto the clean page. His eyes focused on the dot and then to the dots on his hands. The flecks of Rot embedded in his skin were a shade darker today. He fretted over the mold's resiliency. It would never leave him. They would die together.

Pulling his sleeves back down, Matthias concentrated on the scratch of the pen. The Rot mattered little. The words mattered all.

A knock at the door broke his rhythm. Matthias shuffled over to the entrance and peered out into the evening air.

Carolyn smiled back at him. "Where have you been all day?"

"Working."

"That Solomon is a slave driver."

"No, no. He gave me the day off. I'm working on something on my own." The sight of her roused him out of his trance. He wanted her to come in, but the pages were unfinished.

She tried to nudge the door open. "Like what?"

There was a gift he wanted to share with her, but not here—not now. "What time is dinner tomorrow?"

"You're not going to the Dvorack's?"

He rubbed his lower back. "I'm planning on dinner with you at your church. What time?"

"Noon. Listen, I'm going to my parent's house tonight. Would you like to come along?"

The paper twitched in the breeze. Its curled edges beckoned to Matthias. "I'd like to, but I'm not finished." He pushed the door wide open and hugged her. "I'm working on a big surprise for Christmas."

Her lips curled into an uncertain smile and a gentle laugh.

"More surprises, eh? Okay. I'll hold you to that. See you at noon."

Matthias wrote until his hand ached. To his disappointment, only a half portion of his memoir found its way to ink. Back in Philadelphia, a skilled typist could no doubt perform the task in hours and post it on the Ecunet for all to see. He wondered how the writers of olden times penned huge volumes of text and marveled at the effort it must have taken.

He dwelled on the piles stacked high in the library at home. In it were endless tomes of knowledge and stories of a past before the wars and the Rot. Atop them sat a Bible.

The history of the Bible unfolded before him, from the oral traditions to when the verses were printed on everything from animal skin to sheets of metal—an achievement not unlike Umar's great labor. Sixty-eight books handwritten until the time of Gutenberg. *Or was it sixty-six?*

Matthias mused at the difference. His own thirty-two pages exhausted him. It was longer than Second John, but not enough for a Gospel. Yet there was more to write. Someday there might be enough for a gospel, a true story of his own. He laughed and held up his pages. "The gospel of Matthias Kent."

He slid into bed as the town bell chimed midnight—Christmas. In the near-darkness, Matthias saw the stack of pages.

The irony of it all gripped him so hard that he could barely breathe. Thousands of unrelated experiences, events, and personalities led him to precisely this moment, and it humbled him. He realized the gift he'd been given and said, "Thank you."

In the morning, Matthias lay in bed looking out at the table where his unfinished gospel lay. The fever burned lower now. A compulsion to resume his work tugged at him. Other thoughts kept him in bed.

How peculiar it was not to be at the Nation's Church, sleep deprived and stressed beyond measure to control every aspect of the Christmas service. The silence of his bedroom replaced the cacophony of the control center. In that silence, he felt detached, slowly drifting away from the noise, from the chaos. There were no ads to display on the screens, no product placements for the ministerial staff to bring to the attention of a yearning audience.

Now, there was only quiet, only the words in his mind aching to be carried to paper via the ink of his pen. He shook off the numbness and clung to his purpose like a drowning man holding on to a piece of flotsam.

"Rise Lazarus," said Matthias, kicking the covers off.

He set off into the late morning gloom. The rain held off, but dampness filled the air with the constant threat of a downpour.

His gospel lay coiled inside an aluminum tube, riding inside a plastic sack full of odds and ends he brought with him. He shrugged off the chill and made his way through the streets of Poughkeepsie. Occasionally, the melody of carols or the murmur of prayer lifted from the churches he passed along the way.

How unlike the Nation's Church they were, he thought. These sanctuaries were barely big enough to hold a hundred, not tens of thousands. *How could a wide audience be reached? How could thousands be saved? How did they pay penance? Why is it that I don't care to be in any one of them?*

The tube with the pages bumped against Matthias's hip. The questions circulating in his mind about the business of churches faded. Pen and paper were his life now, and they weren't limited to the sacraments of Elders.

Today he would prove it.

Chapter 61: Verses 1-98

Matthias arrived at the church just the town bell chimed 11:30 AM. He listened for drums inside, but heard only the ubiquitous beat of the Heartbeat of the City.

The door came open with a slight push. No one noticed his entry.

The sanctuary milled with chaos. Children ran about. Mothers chased after them, begging them to behave.

Matthias chuckled at them and fretted a little. Would they hold still when he recited his gift?

Some low voices caught his attention. About a dozen men, all large enough to challenge Jeremiah in height and girth, brought tables into the room and arranged them in rows. They called out to the children.

A little girl scurried toward one of the men and wrapped her arms around his legs. The man scooped her up, lifted her up on his shoulders, and resumed his chore as if she weren't there.

Pastor Donna said, "So, you did come after all."

"I promised Carolyn I'd be here. Have you seen her?" said Matthias.

"She's in the kitchen with the cooks. I believe she'll be up soon."

He reached into his bag. "I've brought some preserves—apple, raspberry, pear and peach. I thought the congregation would like some."

Pastor Donna looked stupefied. "You bless us greatly."

Matthias read her face. "Is it too extravagant? I don't want to take away from the meal. It's just that I thought I should bring something special for Christmas."

Before she could answer, a herd of children surrounded them and the jars.

Matthias said. "It's too late to give it back now. Enjoy."

The children clamored around the preacher the whole way to the tables.

Carolyn stepped into the opposite side of the sanctuary and rounded the obstacle course of children. She came up to him and said, "Are you trying to be our Santa Claus?"

"No. I'm trying to be like Solomon. He has no problem sharing his wealth."

"That's not like an Elder."

"I'm not an Elder. I'm a calligrapher."

Carolyn eyed the tots. "Were the jellies the surprise you promised me?"

Matthias could feel a smile welling up inside. "No, but allow me to address the group after dinner. I have something else to share."

"Penance cards for everyone?"

"You couldn't afford the interest rate. Now, what may I do to help?"

"You're submitting to the will of a woman?"

"There is hope for me yet."

Matthias got to work hauling plates and flatware while Carolyn arranged them on the tabletop. The aroma of baking filled the room—yeasty breads, sweet potatoes. Children played. The men who brought the tables chased them from the preserves with mock grouchiness.

"Who are those men?" said Matthias.

"Soldiers on leave," replied Carolyn. "It's an old tradition to have them spend time with us. You see, many men died over the course of the religious wars. The Women's Church originally formed as a haven for their widows and orphans. To this day, our army sends a few troopers to help us during the holidays."

Matthias studied the soldiers the seamless way they worked with the women of the congregation. "Is that how the WVG got started?"

Startled, Carolyn said, "Why, yes. How did you know?"

"I've seen this type of cooperation in the Order of St. George. Everybody has their orders and trusts one another to carry them out."

"I hope we aren't that militaristic."

Matthias felt as though he blundered by making the remark. "I'm sorry, I didn't mean it that way. I meant that they work well together."

She looked distant. "We had to work together or the Christian States were going to overrun us. A group of war widows realized the danger and formed the first WVG Brigade. They swore to fill the ranks created when their husbands died. So, one of the generals sent soldiers to train them."

Matthias thought back to the bit of civil war history that Solomon bestowed on him and realized that he missed an obvious connection. "Did your great-grandfather begin that tradition?"

Carolyn's looked at him. "My great-great grandfather. How do you know about him?"

"Solomon. He never mentioned it. Funny, I just figured it out. Is that why you're here, tradition?"

"I'm here because I want to be here. When I'm around my sisters, I feel stronger."

Pastor Donna stood up on the altar. "Would everyone please take a seat? Our feast is ready."

After saying grace, a grand parade of delicacies wound its way around the diners. Matthias took a small portion and passed it on. For dessert, they shared small chunks of bread and the preserves he brought. Slathering on some jelly, he took a bite. Peaches. The recollection of Julia's scent sliced through him.

Pastor Donna stood again. "Our thanks to the men of the 193rd for their wonderful contribution to our Christmas dinner. May God protect you."

Applause rose up from the crowd.

She nodded to Matthias. "I'm sure many of you have taken notice of our special guest, the calligrapher, Matthias Kent."

Tingling danced up and down his spine. The title of Elder never carried as much joy.

Pastor Donna continued. "Mr. Kent provided our jams and jellies today."

The children's yells drowned out the applause of the adults.

"Carolyn informs me that Mr. Kent has something else in store for us on this special day."

Matthias grabbed his metal tube and walked to the front of the room. "My thanks, Pastor Donna. None of you know me. All you need to know was that I was a privileged and arrogant fool in my days in the Christian States. I've grown a lot in a very short amount of time."

He addressed the soldiers. "Carolyn spoke of your long-standing tradition of aid here. I come with a tradition that I hope will be one-tenth as worthy."

Turning back to the group, Matthias said, "I'm sure you mothers have told your children stories." He uncapped one end of the tube and shook out his pages.

A collective gasp sucked the air out of the room.

"There was a time when stories resided on paper and were as common as rain. I come today to begin that tradition anew."

The children stilled.

"This story is as true as any Gospel. I should know. I lived it. But it's not my story. It's the story of Samuel and Jeremiah and the man they saved."

Matthias read through the first few pages, and the room fell silent. None of the children carried on the way they did earlier. The quiet unnerved him, and he stopped. His eyes fell on a mother cradling two small children. Her face was marked by tears.

Pastor Donna clasped her hands.

Carolyn wiped tears of her own.

As if a dam burst, the children rushed him, their eyes thirsty to see his script and their hands anxious to touch the paper.

Matthias guided their fingers.

Carolyn walked over to him. "Why did you stop?"

"I didn't want to put everyone to sleep."

She laughed. "Only you would worry about crowd reaction."

"What were my numbers?"

She laughed louder. "High. I think you had a one-hundred percent approval rating."

"My life is complete." As soon as he spoke the sentence, it keyed a feeling that Matthias didn't quite know how to deal with. His life wasn't complete. He looked up into Carolyn's eyes. The words blurted out, awkward, stupid. "What are you doing later, after all this is over?"

"Going home and putting up my feet."

It was his turn to laugh. "Do you want to come over to my place?"

"No."

Her answer deflated him. Of course she wouldn't come. He was being far too bold, far too juvenile.

Carolyn stepped in amongst the children, rested her hand on his shoulder and whispered, "Let's go to mine."

They made love into the morning hours.

Afterward, Matthias lay on her bed and stroked her hair. She slept on his chest, her breathing a gentle rhythm of sighs. Never before had he experienced such a feeling of contentment.

He drew in the fragrance of her hair, a mélange of aromas from a day spent preparing the feast. The scent made him feel safe, made him feel at home, made him feel loved.

The thought took him aback. His hand stopped.

"What's wrong?" she said.

"I thought you were asleep."

Carolyn lifted her head. "I was until you tensed up." The sleepiness in her face fell away to a pained blush. "Do you want to go?"

"No." He brought her lips to his. "I'm quite happy being here with you. The happiest I've been—ever."

The words restored a smile to her face. "Me too."

A glow grew in her eyes, a depthless reflection of himself in her. There was no agenda in them, no possessiveness. Her reaction was something he had never seen or sensed in another woman. Matthias fought the urge to analyze and surrendered to the feeling of completeness that warmed his heart long after the flurry of passion. Was this how Jeremiah felt about Beth?

Yes.

Matthias stepped into the kitchen, still toweling himself off from the shower. "Hot water is a true blessing."

Carolyn sat at the table in the kitchen. She pushed a mug of tea toward him along with a plate of scones. "There's not much in the cupboard, I'm afraid. Best soak the scones first."

He sat down. Worry crept into his gut. He was all too familiar with the awkward distance the morning after. Passion was an emotion of the night that withered in the light of day. "Are you okay?"

She nibbled on one of the cakes. "I feel fine."

"I didn't mean it that way. I mean, about us, ummm…"

"Making love?"

"Yes," he replied.

Carolyn looked away. "You don't have to stay, Matthias. I understand."

The real meaning in her words reflected in the slight paleness of her cheeks, the lack of eye contact. Fear. No amount of her casual dismissal could conceal it. The same hesitancy she displayed at Solomon's party. An old wound festered somewhere inside her. Matthias wanted to erase it, heal it. "It's not a question of wanting to go. I want to stay here, but Solomon expects me. When can I see you again?"

The glow returned to Carolyn's eyes. "What are you doing later?"

Matthias took her into his arms. "Seeing you."

Chapter 62: Verses 1-109

Matthias stood at the door of the paper factory, counting down the bell chimes. When the seventh occurred, he knocked on the door. To his surprise, an eighth chime rang.

"You're late," bellowed Solomon.

Matthias said, "My apologies."

The old man darted from door to door, checking locks. His face was redder than a bishop's cape. "Save it for someone who cares. Were you in here over the holidays?"

"Didn't come near the place. Why?"

"Stuff has been moved around."

"Stuff? Is anything missing?" Panic gripped Matthias. The theft of their wares would set them back for weeks, months.

"No. That's what bothers me."

He settled down, puzzled over Solomon's actions. "Are you sure someone was here?"

The old man slammed his fist down on the table. "Yes."

"Then what are you worried about if nothing has been taken?"

"Trade secrets."

"Are your locks intact?"

"The door has been pried open."

"Is any of the stock missing?"

Solomon pointed to some broken glass on the floor underneath a shelf. "No. None of it's missing. Just one of the jars."

"All this fuss over a jar?"

"It was the one with our names in it."

Matthias studied the shelf and the dust ring where the jar containing the two slips of paper once stood. "It makes no sense."

Someone banged on the door. Solomon opened it.

Two cloaked and bearded men came in. Matthias recognized the style of the robes. They were Jedee.

The older of the two said, "Matthias Kent?"

"Yes."

"Would you please accompany us to the Mayor's office?"

"Do I have a choice?"

"The Mayor was quite emphatic. You're to come over right away."

Matthias sat in a waiting area. Murmurs and shouts emanated from the Mayor's office. The receptionist gave him little regard. She had tense shoulders and performed her duties in silent distress.

He walked over to her. "I am under arrest?"

Mayor Charlie appeared at the door. "You're here at my request. Right now, you're Number Two on my priority list today. Making it to Number One would be a really bad idea. So sit still and try not to draw attention to yourself." He slammed the door.

Matthias pushed past the obvious body language and dwelled on the mayor's choice of words. A hot rush surged up his spine as he remembered the mayor's warning him not to draw attention the day he arrived in the city. His story, his gospel, had gone too far.

The discussion in the office died down. The door swung open. Out came Sheik Girard.

Matthias rose. "Your Excellency."

Umar rushed past him. "You were from the States. Talk some sense into that fool."

More people came from the room, including Carolyn. Their faces carried the same grave concerns.

"What's going on?" said Matthias.

Mayor Charlie intervened. "Not a word, any of you. Kent, my office."

Matthias approached Carolyn and clasped her hand. "It'll be okay. Let me calm him down, and we'll all go for cranberry wine afterward."

Her lips remained straight and worry lines creased her forehead. "I wish it were that simple."

He left her behind and entered the mayor's office. "So, here I am."

The mayor faced the window and the street below. He brought his fingers to his chin. "I thought we said that Bible of yours doesn't exist any more."

Matthias's earlier instinct rang true. "I put a story to paper. The first in a hundred years."

The mayor leapt to his feet. "That story you read is the talk of the town. Everyone's heard about it. You can't tell them the whole thing."

There would be no giving ground. He leaned toward the mayor. "This story is the truth, the truth of those whose lives should be remembered."

"You're missing the point. First of all, there are still people in the Christian States who are friendly to us. Your history may get them killed. And more importantly, there's plenty of Christians running around this town. Once your story gets to the part about the Bible, they'll forget all about the people you wrote it for. They'll want blood for atonement. They will go to war. It'll be like the damned Crusades all over again, and I can't afford that right now."

Matthias wanted to counter the mayor's argument, but he caught sight of the man's stance, the way he bit his lip and his eyes casting about. He misread the way everyone looked coming out of the meeting. His gut tightened. "What's going on? This is the second time in a week that I saw Umar here."

"Sheik Girard said his scouts are reporting a lot of military activity on the roads leading to the Jersey frontier. Lots of troops, including the Order of Saint George. He's so worried that he wants us to mobilize the militia. Now, of and by itself, military deployments aren't a big deal. The Order runs exercises near the border all the time."

"Surely some refugee or trader has seen them."

Mayor Charlie raised a hand. "That's one reason the sheik is concerned. You were the last refugee they've seen cross the border."

"No others?"

"None. Trade has continued. It's a bit off from previous years, but it is the holidays."

Matthias thought back to Ecunet announcements regarding *exercises* near the Federation border. They were always rattling their sabers. But this was the first time it occurred in wintertime. "What will you do?"

The mayor walked over to the window and drew in a breath. "What we always do—send our troops to watch their troops. It's a time-honored tradition. Everybody puffs up for the cameras and then goes back home. Mission accomplished. Why they couldn't have waited for spring is beyond me."

"I'm sure God ordered them into the field. He always does, or so the Ecunet used to tell us," said Matthias. "So, did God order you to have me brought here, your Honor?"

"No. Your orders are different. You are to be moved to the capitol."

The Mayor's disclosure struck Matthias with a hammer's blow. "What?" He thought of Carolyn. "I don't want to go. I'm doing well here. Look, if it's about my story, I'll hide it just as I hid the Bible. No one will know."

The mayor slumped back into his chair. "It's not that simple. I can't countermand a direct order from the central government."

Through his rage, Matthias fathomed the logic. The Federation had to be worried about the Synod's intentions. They needed leverage. They needed his secret. "Your government wants my Bible for themselves. They weren't interested before. What's changed?"

"You already know why. So do I."

The hammer fell on him a second time. His mind raced. The

Synod wanted the Bible. More wars. More death. They would not get it. No one would. "I refuse to give them a bargaining chip. To hell with orders."

Charlie shrugged. "Orders. All I'm getting from Boston is orders, and that's what worries me most. Umar wants me to back up his troops. Carolyn doesn't want me to. Orders—orders—orders. She thinks everybody is overreacting. Says the Order is a bunch of limp dicks from the city that can't fight their way out of a plastic sack."

Matthias laughed. "They are hard men, even if their dicks are flaccid." He mulled over their motives. Nothing made sense—unless they were getting desperate. "Things are quite difficult for the Synod these days. When I left, famine was on the horizon, the Rot was getting worse and the poor were rioting. They're looking to blame somebody else for their misfortunes."

"And a certain heretic."

"They *stillinized* me."

"Stalinized."

"Whatever. I'm gone in their eyes. Millions of prospective cannibals have a higher priority. It just doesn't make sense. Fielding a force of any account will drain supplies of food and fuel. The Synod can scarcely afford it."

Mayor Charlie sat down. "We can speculate all day, but that doesn't change the orders I've been given."

The room closed around Matthias. How much he hated governments and their insipid actions. They were all posture and rhetoric while humanity flowed down the storm drain like rain. Yet all bureaucracies were consistent. "Did they give you a date of compliance?"

Charlie looked into the distance, then nodded. "The first business day of the New Year, January 2nd."

"Until then, your Honor, I will take my leave."

Solomon Dvorack paced the shop floor. "So that's it? You're just going to pull up stakes and leave me here all by myself?"

Matthias sat on a stool, downing a bottle of cranberry wine and watching the old man trundle about. "You sound like a jilted lover, and I've had enough of them to last me a lifetime."

"Why shouldn't I? You're screwing me pretty good."

"Look, how far is it to Boston? A day? Two? We can still do business. You pulp. I'll write. Just send me the chalkboards and I will do the rest."

"But what about middlemen? What happens if things get lost?"

"Sol. We'll work it out. We have a good partnership. I like what I'm doing." Matthias extended his hand. "I thought you didn't like having me here."

"I don't, but I like having you somewhere else even less. You might give away trade secrets."

Matthias snorted his wine through his nose. "As if you ever told me any." His nostrils burned with a tartness that made him sneeze.

Solomon said, "God bless you."

"If He did, I'd be staying in town." The smell lingered in his nasal passages and teased a memory to the surface. There was another time he encountered the same scent. He let his mind wander. A picture of ink on a page came to the surface. "I'll be damned. You conniving Philistine."

"What's the matter now?"

He felt as though he would burst. "Your trade secret. It's the wine." Solomon became so silent Matthias heard his eyes blink. "No wonder you have me pissing this stuff into a bucket ten times a day. And that smell! I still haven't gotten used to it."

The round man seemed to deflate once he plopped onto a stool. "Now you know. You don't need me anymore."

"We're partners. Your secret is mine. It goes no farther than between the two of us. Agreed?" Matthias pulled out a sheet of paper meant for the Synod. "You have no idea how pleased I am to know that a little bit of me is in every page we send back to the Synod. How did you ever find this out?"

The old man's spirit filled back up. "Working for the Mennonites when I was first exiled. I used to clear eucalyptus from the fields. Back then, nobody drank common distilled. We drank cranberry wine. There was this spot in the woods we'd all use for a bathroom. Funniest damned thing. All the stumps around there were chewed away by the Rot except for the one we all peed against. So, I did some investigating and found an acid in the cranberries that fights the Rot. Combine some bleach and some concentrated male urine and you have a wood pulp that didn't degrade. Knowing that made the paper possible and here I am."

Matthias pushed back his sleeve and looked at the dots on his skin. "That's why the Rot came back. I haven't been in the shop drinking this stuff all day long."

"Indeed."

"And to think of what the Synod pays." Matthias laughed and then quieted. "Thanks for everything. I promise to stop by before I go to Boston and wish you and Rida a happy New Year. Once I'm settled in, we'll resume our good business. Agreed, my friend?"

"Agreed."

Carolyn sat on the bed, her knees tucked against her chest. "When do you go?"

Matthias stood at the foot of the bed. "Next Wednesday. The mayor provided a stay of execution."

She let out a deep and labored sigh. "You know it's all going to blow over, and you'll be stuck in Boston."

"Apparently, I don't have any choice in the matter. I'm not going to flee again. I want to stay." His words seemed to sting her. Matthias sat down next to her. "What's wrong?"

Carolyn plunged her head onto his shoulder. Tears flowed. "I want you to stay, too."

"We have until Wednesday. How do they celebrate the New Year in this town?"

"Most everyone comes to the square while bands play. When the bell chimes twelve, they count down, cheer, get drunk, and stumble off to bed."

"They? What about you?"

"I'm Carolyn Decker, great-great-great granddaughter to the great-great-great general. I get to man the Heartbeat of the City beginning at midnight, banging on the drum each and every New Year's. It's only for an hour. We can meet afterward and do a pub crawl."

"A pub crawl? Sounds awful."

"You go from bar to bar and drink."

"Another job I am eminently qualified for."

She swallowed hard, and tears renewed their paths down her cheeks.

He brushed the drops away and pulled her tight. That way, she couldn't see his tears.

Chapter 63: Verses 1-58

Matthias spent his remaining days locked in a race with the chime of the town bell. The scratch of his pen kept cadence with the Heartbeat of the City.

Pages filled.

The bell rang.

Another minute, another hour, another day went by.

The nights were spent with Carolyn. The bell peal became a knell, and he hated every passing second more than November rain.

His pen marched on until the past caught up with the present. There were no more words to write, only a vast open white space. The pen hovered over the page, its emptiness disquieting him. What new chapters would he write? Who would be in them? What new things would he write about?

Matthias thought of Carolyn, and the uncertainty faded. He tucked his pen into his coat pocket, coiled the pages of his gospel together, and slipped them into an aluminum cylinder.

Tomorrow, he would write about becoming an expert pub crawler.

Matthias and Carolyn agreed to meet at the tea shop before they began their revels.

He arrived early, and found the shop mostly empty. Customers spoke in hushed tones, their eyes wary, fearful. Matthias noted the same look in the faces of dozens and dozens of the townsfolk. Even the December sky seemed to take part in the gloom, casting the town into darkness much earlier than other days.

The proprietor brightened when she saw him. He ordered a pot of tea and settled into a cozy table near a coal stove.

Carolyn came in just ahead of the tea. "Been waiting long?"

"No." Matthias regarded her, the reserve in her movements, and the way her face reflected the sullenness around them. "What's the matter with everyone? Did they close the pubs?"

"Never." She laughed for a few seconds until the laughter fell away into unease. "It's my fault, you know."

"Fault? What are you talking about?"

"I told Charlie all about your gospel. I thought he'd think it was as wonderful as everybody else did."

Bitterness and sorrow mixed together in her voice like the nutmeg and cinnamon he stirred into his tea. She was blaming herself for the problem he created. "Somebody would've told him eventually, Carolyn. The funny part is that I agree with him— mostly."

"You do?"

"Yes." Matthias watched the tea swirl, his thoughts swirling with it. "There's more in my gospel than the story of my escape. It's a history that carries far greater implications than a tale told to children and their mothers."

"What else is in there?"

He could feel her looking inside him, feel her honest yearning to know the truth. "Heresy."

"Very funny."

Matthias wove his fingers around hers. "Have you ever wondered what would happen if heresy was actually the truth?"

"Like Martin Luther?"

"In a way." He looked straight into her eyes. "I need your oath, your oath before God Himself, that you won't repeat this."

She laughed again. "Secret oaths?" Carolyn pulled her hands

away and placed her hand on her heart. "I swear not to repeat this to any living soul."

"Very dramatic. I'm serious." Matthias lowered his voice to a whisper. "I have a Bible."

She whispered back, at the verge of more laughter. "So do I. Parts of one, anyway."

"No, I have a Bible made of paper—a pre-war Bible. I came across it during an expedition and hid it away."

Carolyn pulled back, incredulous. "That can't be. The Rot ate all the old paper long ago."

Matthias put finger to his lips to hush her. "Not all of it."

Her mouth slacked.

"It's why I was cast out."

"That doesn't make sense. The Synod would have embraced such a find. They're always trumpeting what their scholars dig up."

"There aren't any scholars. The Synod is lying. They've censored the Bible, changed the meaning of verses, eliminated entire passages, and added their own. I've seen it with my own eyes. I've marketed to millions based on what they've changed."

"Why would they change the Word of God when their whole nation is based upon it?"

"Power. Their own private version of the Bible reinforces their authority. They've done so since they enacted the Surveillance Laws, allowed torture, and forced a single religion on everyone. Everything in one happy, merry accord per God's Holy Word —a Word under Synod control. An old Bible exposes their corruption."

Carolyn's face flushed with outrage. "This is wrong. You've got to tell people."

"Yes, it's wrong. Horrifically wrong. But, you gave me your oath."

"You can't hold me to that. How can you be silent? How can you be a party to the Synod's lies? This is incredible. We have to tell Charlie."

"Charlie already knows."

Carolyn recoiled back into her chair. "Are you saying our own government knows about it and is doing nothing?"

"They know, and they can't do anything about it. Look, if the Synod feels threatened, they'll attack. They're massing on the Jersey border right now just to prove that point. The Federation might be able to hold them off, or it might not. Thousands will die either way."

"But, if the Synod denies the truth, they deny the very God they worship."

"They *are* the God they worship."

"You know the truth. You have the power to set things right."

Matthias felt her quiet passion stir his soul. She was right. He felt it, knew it, but the lifeless faces of Jeremiah and Samuel surged forward in his mind. "The only power I have is to get people killed. That's a part of my story you haven't heard."

"What are you saying?"

"Everyone who helped me get out of Philadelphia is dead. Everyone. I'm responsible. Me. I'm not going to get anyone else killed."

She leaned toward him. "It's odd you said that. There's a story in my family about my great-great grandfather saying something like that the night before he left to fight at Haverford."

"Which he lost."

"Oh, he knew he'd probably lose the battle, Matthias, but he saved a nation. The Federation would have starved without the Amish farmers—just like what's happening in the Christian States now."

Matthias looked back at her. "This isn't about Haverford. It's about a book."

Carolyn rose and put on her coat. "It's about people who are starving for the truth."

Matthias stood up. "Wait. Where are you going?"

She walked to the entrance. "I'm doing what my great-great grandmother did that night."

"Your great-great grandmother?"

"Yes. She told the general to do what's right and then left him alone to make up his mind. Isn't it funny how history repeats itself?" said Carolyn as she closed the door behind her.

Chapter 64: Verses 1-144

Matthias threaded his way through the crowds in the Town Square. The sounds of laughter and merry making soured his mood all the more. He should be hand-in-hand with Carolyn, enjoying what time remained. Instead, he stood near enough to the town clock to see each minute fall away.

Her words echoed in his mind.

You have the power to set things right.

He wished he said nothing about the Bible. Passions rose far too easily. The Mayor was right. *Or was he?* And that Bible. That damned Bible. The bane and curse of his life. If it weren't for that, he'd be in Philadelphia watching a brightly lit cross and dollar sign descend from a tower near the capitol. Wine would flow, and they would eat until they burst. Not tonight.

The bell chimed a quarter to midnight.

The crowd became more boisterous with anticipation, and it drowned out the Heartbeat of the City. Matthias looked off at the immense bridge pier where he imagined Carolyn climbing to the top, taking her position next to the great drum and awaiting the signal to strike the beat.

Above the din, he could hear her words again and again.

Do what's right.

The minute hand of the clock moved forward, a knife slicing through the time he had left. The last day in the city would soon be at hand. Like his entire journey, he would be leaving another person behind. How much he wanted to say he was sorry and somehow have her with him in Boston. How much he wanted to spend year after year with her.

The minute hand announced the last sixty seconds of December 31st, 2159. Cheers went up. Voices counted down. The New Year was upon Matthias. He turned and headed for home.

While the bell chimed, he made his way through the mass. Each clang punctuated a face in his heart—Alexander, Benjamin, Naomi, Thaddeus, Theresa, Luke, Beth, Jeremiah, Samuel, his father, his mother, Carolyn.

Then as one, the crowd silenced. They turned to face the bridge and listen for the first drumbeat of the New Year. Matthias stopped and listened, too. It would be his way of listening to her heartbeat one more time.

And then he saw Julia.

She walked up to him as casually as could be, her face a gentle smile and eyes burning with fury. She placed her hands on his cheeks and kissed him.

He tasted peaches.

She said, "Happy New Year," and disappeared into the crowd.

The cheery detachment of her action brought a churn to Matthias's gut. He strained to hear the drumbeat. Nothing. He ran toward the bridge.

Murmurs circulated through the crowd.

A bright flash near the Riverwall tore the night asunder and loud volley of thunder followed it. The crowd cheered at the pyrotechnics.

The drum was silent. Matthias ran all the harder.

Another flash followed and another. More thunder echoed in the streets. The crowd grew uneasy. Matthias read their faces. Something was wrong.

A rat-a-tat pierced the night. A chill made his back arch. He knew the noise—machine-gun fire. A woman screamed. The crowd moaned. More bursts.

A man ran to the edge of the square. "We're under attack. Get to shelter." He disappeared in a puff of smoke.

Everyone poured out of the square like water from a broken levee.

Matthias tried one more time to hear the Heartbeat. Nothing. "Damn it. God damn it to Hell," he yelled. He tried to get his bearings. People slammed into him from all directions. Explosions rocked the streets. The gunfire grew closer. His gut told him to run. His heart told him to get to the bridge. Matthias fought the urge to flee and pounded a wall with his fist, "No."

Bricks and bits of concrete peppered the streets. He fought his way upstream amidst a tide of fleeing mob. Bullets clattered off the walls. There was no rhyme or reason for it all. It was a chaos worse than his escape from Philadelphia.

Matthias heard familiar shouts behind him. It sounded like Jeremiah issuing commands.

A large man pointed to and fro. Soldiers around him scurried into place. "We will hold this position until relieved. Do you understand?"

The soldiers responded with a weak, "Yes sir."

"In front of you is the enemy. Behind you are your families. Who would you rather see dead tomorrow morning?"

Another explosion rent the pavement in front of Matthias. There would be no further passage. He approached the commander. "What can I do?"

"Go to your home, citizen. You will just get in the way here."

"I can shoot as straight as any of your men. I will not dishonor you."

The commander looked Matthias over. "Very well." He handed Matthias his rifle and drew out his sidearm. "Have it your way. Make every round count."

Matthias popped the clip out of the rifle. Thirty shots. He hoped that he would not need thirty-one.

The squad hunkered down behind some debris.

It didn't take long for the first rocket to slam into a nearby wall. Two men cartwheeled into the air.

Matthias could feel the man next to him tense and get ready

to run.

The commander steadied his men. "Hold your ground. If you move, they will see you and kill you before you take two steps."

In the distance, Matthias could make out the black hulking armor of one of the enemy. A chill fell over him. It was the Order of St. George.

Another explosion rocked a nearby building. Debris showered the squad.

Matthias hunkered down.

The commander quieted his voice. "Everyone, lay still. They are well armored. Wait until you can see their faces plainly and aim for their nose. Don't waste a single shot. Give no quarter for they will kill you where you lay."

The Order's troopers shuffled from doorway to doorway, firing as they went. Matthias studied their tactic. There seemed to be no point to it all. No one opposed them. Then the answer came. They were using their weapons to cover their movements. No one would confront them as long as they were shooting.

Bullets skipped off the pavement. The commander grunted and slumped to the ground.

Matthias prodded the man and saw the fatal wound in his forehead.

The soldiers around him panicked.

"You heard the man," said Matthias. "We are all that stands between them and the city. Hold your ground. How many do you see?"

"Seven," said one.

"Eight," said another.

Matthias zeroed in on the eighth man in the oncoming squad. "I have the last man in my sights. When he reloads, I will fire." He motioned to the men next to him. "You two take the seventh and sixth men. And you two kill the fifth and fourth. Work your way to the front of the squad."

The troopers undulated from door to door. Bullets slapped into the debris the squad hid behind.

Matthias rested his rifle on a chunk of concrete and brought his weapon to bear on the last man. Glossy black boots flickered in the firelight, and he imagined the face of Gideon Stanmore on every trooper's face. He lined up the rifle's bead on the trooper's nose. The safety clicked off as the eighth man's weapon sputtered to a halt.

Matthias took a breath, let it out half way, and squeezed the trigger. The rifle bucked in his grip. More shots rang out. More troopers fell. The street took on an ethereal silence.

"Is everyone okay?" said Matthias.

The four men around him replied with a "Yes."

The man next to him patted him on the shoulder. "We did it."

Matthias watched the street for any other signs of troopers on the move. There were none, and that bothered him. He listened to the sound of fighting in the adjacent streets. Rockets and machine gunfire were plentiful, but there was something missing. "This is all wrong. There's no trucks. No armored support." Matthias looked toward the bridge. "God damn it. They've been pushing us away from the gate. Get up," he said to the others. "We're moving forward."

"Forward?" said the man closest to him.

"What's your name, soldier?" said Matthias.

"Bowerman, Private First Class."

"Well Bowerman, we need to get to the bridge. It's the only place they can bring their vehicles across."

"We're supposed to hold this street."

"If they get an armored car with a microsonic cannon into the city, we'll be sending your remains home in a jelly jar. Do you understand me?"

Bowerman looked stricken. "Who are you?"

"Matthias Kent."

"Are you an officer?"

Matthias looked at him. "I'm a calligrapher. Do you have a problem with that?"

The young soldier looked more than confused.

"Good," said Matthias. "Gather weapons and ammunition. To the bridge."

The amount and volume of gunfire rose and fell like some mad, percussive symphony. More than once, Matthias's squad found themselves behind the troopers of the Order and surprised them with a volley of fire. Each exchange gained them another street, another block, another neighborhood.

The closer they got to the Riverwall, the more intense the shooting became. A rocket split the ground near them, and they dove into a nearby building.

Matthias tripped over something and fell. In the dimness, a soldier of the Order lay on his back, eyes open. The room stank of urine and blood. A knife blade pressed against Matthias's neck.

The voice was calm. "Go to God."

"I am of the city," said Matthias.

A hooded man pulled his knife back. "My apologies. We thought we were fighting alone down here. Are you militia?"

Matthias replied, "Yes."

"I am Steven of the Jedee. We hold this block."

"I'm Matthias Kent, and we move on the bridge. Care to join us?"

They crept from building to building, closer and closer to the city gate.

Matthias clambered to the top of a building and surveyed the bridge. Fire lit half the span with a dull orange. In that glow he saw it, a tracked vehicle with a microsonic array mounted on top. An icy wash of fear froze him in place. They were too late.

Troop trucks lined the far shore, each of them waiting to take their turn on the span. There would be no stopping them now. His fear turned to dread.

And then he heard it, loud and fast—the Heartbeat of the City.

His own heart beat in time with it. He turned to the mish-mosh of soldiers behind him. "Let's show these Philistines what a group of David's can do. Who is with me?"

The dozen or so men with him yelled, charged down the steps, and headed straight to the bridge. In the same moment, more yells bellowed from the surrounding streets. Soldiers of the Order retreated to the city gate like angry black ants defending a nest.

Explosions and flames burst around them. Men on both sides died. One by one, the ranks of the Order thinned.

The militia advanced.

It began as a rumbling throb. In front of Matthias, a burst of cannon fire shredded the militiamen. More concussion blasts swept the streets until anyone in its path had been hurtled aside.

The Heartbeat of the City stopped.

While he hid behind a wall, Matthias fretted over the silence. *Was that Carolyn? Is she all right? Have those bastards killed her?* He knew there could be but one way to find out. The bridge had to be cleared.

Matthias tried to figure out a way to get to the cannon. Any head-on charge would be suicide. Dead soldiers couldn't defend the city.

Footsteps approached. Matthias saw dozens of women making their way to his position, each one armed with a rifle.

Leading them was a familiar face, Pastor Donna. "What in the name of God are you doing here, Matthias?"

"I could ask you the same thing," he said. Matthias pointed to the bridge. "We're going to regroup and figure out a way to ambush that thing when it gets to this side."

Pastor Donna surveyed the scene and shook her head no. "If it gets across, the Order will control the bridge and all will be lost. We have to stop it now."

Matthias considered her strategy. "So, suicide or Boston. What a choice."

Before he could reply, plumes of flame shot up on the far shore. Vehicles burned. Flaming men leapt into the river like embers flung from a crackling fire. Another cheer rose from the remaining militia.

"What's going on?" said Matthias.

Pastor Donna kept a hard face and shed a tear at the same time. "Reinforcements, I think. We are truly blessed. Now, we must do our part."

"What's the plan?"

"Carolyn said you didn't take orders from women."

"I have a problem with authority in general. Now, what's the plan?"

She gestured to the Brigade. "We will charge the tank. Under the bridge is a catwalk. Get some men down there and get behind the vehicle. Plug up its exhaust with these." She handed him the biggest sweet potatoes he had ever seen.

Matthias didn't understand. "What will that do?"

"It runs on biodiesel. No exhaust, no combustion."

"I get it. No combustion, no power. But Pastor, charging that thing is suicide."

"I know."

The pulse of the cannon winnowed anyone who tried to halt its progress. Matthias and Pastor Donna's soldiers crawled from body to body.

Across the river, more explosions and screams echoed off the river.

Matthias waved his men forward.

When they got to the city gate, Pastor Donna took Matthias by the shoulders. "Greater love hath no one, Matthias."

Her soldiers rose and let out a war cry. Rifle fire ricocheted off the tank. Matthias felt the throbbing hum and closed his eyes. A great tearing sound emanated ahead of him. Bodies flew.

Rage burned his fear away. "Now!"

They darted through the gate and dove off to both sides of the bridge bulwark. Two of the Jedee led the way, hurtling onto the span and extending their hands.

The cannon thrummed again and again.

Matthias took hold and made it to the catwalk. Machine gun fire spattered all around them. A soldier fell into the river. Matthias maneuvered along the metal grating until he heard the chortle of the tank above him. The potatoes looked absurd in his hands. "What a way to die."

He climbed to the bridge deck on one side while Steven did the same on the other. Bowerman and the remaining soldiers cut down the troopers huddled behind the tank.

The surprise only lasted a second when the Order returned fire. Matthias rolled behind the tank and found the exhaust, a large pipe belching heat and smoke. He shoved the potato, in and it wedged tight.

Steven arrived a second later and did the same. As he did, a bullet caught him in the chest and threw him against the tank. Bowerman's gun found the shooter and silenced him, but more troopers fired back. Matthias and his troops were pinned.

The vehicle choked and coughed.

Matthias saw the last of the Pastor Donna's troops charge the bridge ahead of him. The ground throbbed with the weapon's pulse. Explosions rocked the bridge.

With a great wheeze, the tank's engine stalled out.

Soldiers of the militia poured onto the bridge.

More gunfire rang out behind Matthias. Their situation went from bad to worse—they were now in a crossfire, and bullets had no conscience. He dove to the ground.

The troopers of the Order died one by one, their grimaced faces frozen in agony by the flash of light bursting from their weapons. Bullets ricocheted on metal in an insane percussion. All around Matthias, an orchestra of death played out, rising to a crescendo and falling away to a moaning chorus of the wounded accompanied by the hiss of burning tires. The gunfire yielded to a disquieting silence.

A voice called out from behind a vehicle. "Drop your weapons and surrender."

Matthias looked at his contingent, determination hard as stone set on every face. The Order would not have them or the town. He yelled back to the voice. "Rot in Hell. You will not take the city."

"You're from the city?"

The reply was unexpected. "I am Matthias Kent, and we defend Poughkeepsie."

Chuckles rose from behind a transport followed by the cheers of men giddy with victory.

The voice called out again over the ruckus. "Matthias Kent? Since when does a calligrapher become a soldier?"

Matthias recognized the voice and a wave of relief poured over him. "I would ask you the same thing, Sheik Girard." He rose and rushed toward the sheik.

They met in the middle of the bridge and embraced.

Umar held Matthias by the shoulders. "It is good to see you."

"You have no idea."

The sheik opened his robe, reached into his chest pocket and unfolded a sheet of paper adorned in Arabic script. "This is the paper you gave me."

Matthias read the page and recognized the script. "God is great."

"Indeed He is. We wore His seal upon our hearts, and we are victorious."

Mayor Charlie rounded the vehicle and approached the pair. "My thanks, your Excellency, but how did you know the Order would come here?

"I told you we were tracking their movements. We were quite surprised when they attacked."

"As we were." The two men shook hands, but the mayor's face remained grave.

Matthias picked up on the distress. "Is another attack on the way?"

"No. It looks like we stopped them." Mayor Charlie wouldn't raise his eyes.

"But?"

"It's Carolyn."

Matthias could feel the yawning pit of grief open up, ready to consume him. "And?"

"We have one of the Order cornered, and he has Carolyn as a hostage. He wants to talk to you."

Chapter 65: Verses 1-63

Mayor Charlie led Matthias and Umar to a warehouse a few yards from the city gate. Its walls were pockmarked by bullets and a gaping hole. "He's in there."

In the shadows, the man stood behind Carolyn. He held a gleaming blade to her neck with his gloved hand. The glove had only three fingers.

A woman dangled from a ceiling beam by a length of cord.

Julia.

The man spoke. "Our scouts found her walking across the frontier a few days ago with a slip of paper bearing your signature. She gave it up quite willingly. All she wanted to do was betray you with a kiss. I didn't even have to offer her thirty pieces of silver. Poetic justice, don't you think, Elder Kent?"

Matthias looked into the shadows for glossy boots. "Cliché if you ask me, Gideon."

"True enough."

Matthias eyed the lack of fingers on the Inquisitor's hand. "I see the coyotes were less than kind to you."

Stanmore moved into the light. The right side of his face looked like it had been stitched together by clumsy seamstresses.

"I killed them all."

"And now you've come to kill me. Let her go, and you may have your way."

Gideon sneered. "If it were only that simple. My mission remains unchanged."

The words knotted Matthias's stomach. Smoke lingered in his nostrils. The wounded lie moaning around them. "You did this because of me?"

"We want the Bible."

"No, you don't. You fear it."

Gideon pushed Carolyn into the light and raised his blade under her chin. "Julia told me about your relationship with this pagan drummer. Perhaps there is something you fear as well."

"You hide behind her like the Synod hides behind their religion."

"And you deny the rightful authority of God's will."

Matthias tried to calm himself. "Gideon, no one knows where it is except me."

"Liar."

The Inquisitor's face was too confident. There were cards yet to be played. He was buying time. Matthias yelled back to Charlie and Umar. "Tell your soldiers to prepare for another assault."

Umar protested. "We've broken their backs. Their bodies are floating to the sea."

Matthias called back to Umar, "He's hiding something. Do as I say. Do it now."

The Inquisitor said, "It won't matter."

"You've lost the element of surprise. We hold both shores. No one is coming to rescue you."

Gideon yanked Carolyn's hair, exposing an expanse of neck. "Then there will no rescue for her, either."

Carolyn displayed equal parts of rage, sorrow, and love. She tensed her body, getting ready to pull her head down on the blade. She would deny Gideon his hostage.

"No!" Matthias screamed as loud as he could.

Gideon jerked her head back even farther.

The flickering silhouette of a cross fell upon her face. The look in her eyes changed. She looked at him with regret. She looked at him with determination.

Matthias fixed the moment in his mind. After all this time he understood.

Sacrifice.

Images erupted in his thoughts—his father's death, Noah Finney, Pastor Donna, Jeremiah in the forest, Samuel, his mother. The pages of his Bible flung open to the Old Testament scene of Abraham about to sacrifice Isaac, the New Testament's Christ at Gethsemane. Sacrifice upon sacrifice burned into his psyche. *No greater love.*

Another sacrifice was needed and it would not be Carolyn.

"Gideon. You seek me and my secret. Let her go. I will go willingly. Withdraw your forces. When I am satisfied that you mean no threat to the Federation, I will tell you where the Bible is."

A sneer creased the scars on Gideon's face. "You can't be serious."

Matthias let his rifle fall to the floor. "Is this serious enough for you?"

Gideon lowered the knife.

Carolyn ran over to Matthias. "No. Don't. We can stop him. We can stop them. Matthias. Matthias."

He wiped the tears from her eyes. "I've seen what I must do. God has plans for me."

Shock rippled through her. "You believe?"

"I understand. Now get out of here before this Philistine changes his mind."

"But…"

"Just know that I love you. Now go, please."

She hesitated for a moment, her eyes bright, and her face sullen.

"Carolyn. Please. This is what I must do."

"I love you," she said, and left the room.

Umar came in as soon as Carolyn was out of the line of fire. "I see you're making progress with the negotiations."

The Mayor spoke to Gideon. "I am willing to discuss your surrender, trooper."

Matthias shook his head. "It is I who surrendered. I ask that no more blood be shed on my account. The Inquisitor and I have come to terms. I will return to the Christian States under his guard."

Umar drew a long knife out of a scabbard. "I will eviscerate this infidel before his body is cold."

Gideon tensed.

Matthias raised a hand. "Umar, put it away. I've given my word. Besides, they will come again and again until they have me. Are you and the Mayor prepared to wage civil war all over again?"

Neither Umar nor Mayor Charlie said a word.

Turning to Gideon, Matthias said, "Take your blade and cut my finger."

"What?"

"Please." Matthias felt the knife slide across his index finger and a burning pain a moment later. Blood seeped out. He reached into his pocket, pulled out the pen that Umar gave him, and drew in the blood as ink. "Do you still have that sheet of paper you showed me on the bridge?"

"I do." Umar unfolded it and handed it to Matthias.

He took it, pressed it against the wall, and wrote upon the page. "This time, I mean it."

The sheik's hands trembled as he read the words. "God is great."

Mayor Charlie blocked the door. "I can't let you do this."

"History is full of stories of people like me doing things like this. All that will be left of me are stories—true stories. Do you understand?"

The Mayor's eyes gleamed. "Yes. And we will read it every year until you return."

Matthias nodded. "My thanks." He turned to Gideon. "All is well. Let us return to the city. I'm sure my Uncle can hardly wait."

Chapter 66: Verses 1-121

At daybreak, Matthias and Gideon marched across the bridge. Matthias halted, looking back at Carolyn in the distance. The weight of their parting made him want to run to her, embrace her, stay with her. But staying would be their end.

A part of him cursed God for allowing their separation. Another part of him thanked God for her life.

His steps were heavy and laden with regret until the bang of a drum resounded from on top of the bridge pier. Another beat followed, and another. His heart seemed to beat with it. Matthias walked in cadence with the drum as if Carolyn were next to him. She would always be with him.

It took a while to find a unit of the Order. Before long, Matthias found himself in an armored transport flanked by two troopers. Fleeting glimpses out the window showed him groups of regular army amidst the familiar glossy black of the Order. No one seemed to be striking camp and heading for home. Matthias's gut tightened once again. Stanmore didn't honor his agreement. He knew there was a chance Inquisitor wouldn't, but he also knew that every hour, every minute bought time for the defenders of

Poughkeepsie.

Hours later, the troopers threw him into a cell. A voice from an overhead speaker ordered him to remove his clothes. He complied. Overhead sprayers coated him with an oozing gel. It reminded him of the bunker at home. *If home still exists.*

Once the gel evaporated, the two men escorted Matthias to another room containing what looked like a medical examination table. They strapped him down and left.

He laughed and then quieted, surprised by his reaction. The mere mention of Inquisition to any of the fine citizens of Philadelphia would evoke outright fear. And here he was, laughing at it.

The room seemed to grow colder. A whiff of urine teased at his nose. Images danced at the edge of his vision. Sweat beaded on his forehead. Matthias closed his eyes and opened them.

Gideon came in and said, "Something the matter, Elder Kent?"

Matthias composed himself and, at the same time, realized what happened. They were employing electronic trickery to unsettle him. "I'm fine. You didn't think that scent projectors and low frequency emitters were going to have me shaking in my shoes." Matthias glanced down along his unclothed body. How funny it was not to have any more vestments to change into. "That was, if I had any shoes. Truth be told, Gideon, we used stuff like that in Marketing. I'm curious though. Did you supply the urine? I remember you smelling that way out in the woods."

The Inquisitor brought his elbow down on Matthias's chest. "I prefer old fashioned methods, blasphemer."

Another voice joined in. "There, there, Gideon. You don't want to leave any marks that would be construed as torture."

Matthias struggled to free himself from the restraints. "Uncle Cornelius. I was wondering when you'd be stopping by."

Rourke walked over and stood next to Gideon. "Greetings, nephew. It's so good to see you." A sneer lifted his thin lips. "I see the Rot has taken hold of you. Now your body is as unclean as your soul."

"My soul is fine, Uncle. I've never raped anyone. I've never tortured anyone to death."

"Nor have I, nephew." Rourke turned to Gideon. "That's his job. Inquisitor, are we ready to convene?"

Gideon touched a switch under the examination table. A microphone descended from the ceiling. "I, Gideon Stanmore, Inquisitor Principal, hereby open this secret tribunal of the heretic, Matthias Kent. Do you, Chief Elder Rourke of the Bank of Job hereby accept your solemn and righteous duty as witness for the Synod as they act in God's will?"

"I do," hissed Rourke.

Matthias let out a huff. "You know, I never really listened to how many times the Synod comes first in prayer. That's some really good brand awareness."

Gideon ignored him. "Matthias Kent is given up for Inquisition until such time that he surrenders information vital to national security."

"You mean, information to make your lies secure."

"These proceedings, having been duly recognized on this, the first day of January, in the year of our Lord 2160 are hereby convened. Stanmore, Gideon, serial number 225410298435." Gideon pressed another button and the microphone retracted. His scars bunched up around a wide grin. "Let us begin. In order to see the love of God, you must understand His pain."

A machine, like an immense spider from a nightmare, descended from the ceiling. Robotic arms dangled from the device. One of the arms passed over him, its sensor array glowing, seeking. It slithered toward his forehead. He closed his eyes. The sound of suction held his eyelids open. A bright light poured in. Matthias fought its grip, but the restraints held fast.

Above him, another arm descended bearing a black ring. He could feel it compress around his head.

An amplifier echoed the Inquisitor's voice. "Your crown of thorns, blasphemer-mer."

To Matthias, it was as if someone shouted inside his skull, and he recoiled in pain. Lightning seared his brain. It felt as if every hair in his scalp were drilling through his skull. Bile rose in his throat, and he gagged.

"Welcome to what Hell feels like, heretic-tic."

Matthias fought against the pain. "Is this what you did to Blind Johnny, Uncle?"

Gideon pressed a button.

More lightning flashed in Matthias's mind. Each bolt skipped from point to point, leaving agony in its wake.

The echo ceased, and the microphone appeared.

Gideon perched over him. "Where is the Bible?"

Matthias spit at him. "Rot in Hell."

Gideon smiled. "You really have a heretical spirit. So be it."

The device returned to its torments.

Rourke stood by, reveling in his victim's screams.

Matthias didn't know which was worse, the absolute pain the machine incurred or the raw hopelessness grinding away at his psyche.

The pain stopped.

Gideon drew near again. "No spittle this time?"

The Inquisitor's words lingered in his ears a bit longer, carrying a turbulent mix of distress and anguish.

"Where is the Bible, blasphemer?"

Matthias fought back against a tide of agony. "Have your troops returned to their bases?"

Gideon sputtered.

Matthias didn't need an answer. "I have bargained in good faith with you, a bargain witnessed by God Himself. Whom do you serve, Inquisitor?"

Rourke pushed him aside. "He serves us." Cornelius punched a button on the control panel.

Matthias bucked and convulsed on the table. All of the lightning in his brain surged into one blinding fireball.

And then there was darkness.

He floated in a black void, every inch of him writhing. A warmth surrounded him and the pain left his body. The warmth coalesced into a soothing yellow-orange light. Matthias felt drawn to it. He neared the glow and it spoke to him.

"Well done, good and faithful servant."

Joy filled Matthias's heart. He rushed to join the light.

"You saved the Word of the Almighty."

He basked in warmth, felt it surround him like Carolyn's love.

"But the Word must be freed. Where is the Bible?"

The voice was sickly sweet, seductive. Seductive like the girls of Pharaohs' and demanding like Julia. Confusion engulfed him. He wanted to answer. He wanted to remain silent. The question rang in his ears.

"Where is the Bible?"

Matthias ran from the light and fought his way back to the darkness. Cold air chilled his loins. The fire in his brain simmered. Matthias opened his eyes. The torture room came into view.

Rourke stared down on him with disappointment. "It didn't work, Gideon."

The Inquisitor appeared, his face clearly puzzled. He looked at his watch. "I don't understand. He should have confessed by now. Most everyone confesses when they get a taste of the Reformation."

Matthias managed to breathe out a whisper. "The old Bible said that you cannot serve both God and money. Whom do you serve?"

"Get thee away from me Satan," shouted Gideon.

"I am no Satan. I am no demon. I am a man, and I know whom I serve."

"You are a dead man," yelled Rourke.

Matthias faced his uncle. "I died the moment you raped my mother."

Gideon's eyes flickered. He checked his instruments. "Elder Rourke, he isn't lying. What is he saying?"

Cornelius's hand slapped the panel. "You moron. The recorder is active. Strike that from the record. It is the rant of a heretic. Do you understand?"

Matthias mustered enough strength to repeat himself. "Whom do you serve?"

His uncle punched the controls again. Lightning flared. Matthias flailed against the restraints. Drool spilled from his mouth and dribbled along his chin. Darkness overwhelmed the light. Numbness engulfed the pain.

At the edge of consciousness, Matthias heard the Inquisitor

and his uncle arguing.

"Elder Rourke, one more outburst like that, and I will have you removed."

"Rot in Hell, you poor excuse for an Inquisitor. Back in my day, we would have our answers by now."

"Back in your day, he would be deaf or blind or dead. Is that what you want? Is that what you want?"

Rourke slammed his fist down. "I want the Bible."

"You will have it soon enough. Now, either sit back and witness, or I will contact my superiors. Do you understand?"

As the two men argued, Matthias closed his eyes. A cacophony of torment drowned out their words. Pain returned.

And then there was darkness.

In his dream, Matthias stood at the edge of a black void. He could feel it beckon, feel its absolute hunger to consume him. All it took was one step. He inched closer.

Stay with me.

Matthias stopped. Was it his father's voice? Jeremiah's?

Stay with me.

He heard it again, a soft and quiet tone. It stilled his pain and erased the hopelessness. He opened his eyes and felt someone's presence in the room. A rush of air filled his lungs. "Whom do you serve?"

"I serve the Lord my God—God."

Matthias heard the answer he wanted. "The Bible is in my parent's chapel. Touch your fingers to the hand of God in the mosaic and you will find it."

"And what would a blind man do with a Bible—Bible?"

The question puzzled Matthias, and he turned toward the voice. The hooded figure of Blind Johnny stood over him, holding a sponge. A chasm opened in Matthias's spirit. He imagined Gideon ordering his troops forward into Poughkeepsie. No mercy would be shown. Carolyn and Umar and everybody else would die. What was agony turned to anguish. "Where is the Inquisitor? My Uncle?"

"They have taken their leave until the morning—morning."

"What time is it?"

"Near midnight—midnight."

Matthias tried to reason it out. Would it have been enough time for Umar and the mayor to reinforce the city? He pleaded to Blind Johnny. "You must get word to the people of Poughkeepsie. I can't hold out any more. The Synod will attack as soon as they've gotten what they wanted."

A smile came to the blind man's face. "The Inquisitor has ordered a general troop recall—recall. You uncle is most vexed—vexed."

Tears streamed down Matthias's face.

Blind Johnny ran his hand along Matthias's cheek. He sponged the tears away. "I would cry for you brother, but they have stolen my tears—tears."

"It is in your darkness that I have seen the light, my old friend. Is this what they did you?"

"Yes, though their methods have improved. You will keep your eyes." He brought his fingers to his empty eye sockets. "It is an old pain, and it hurts so much more hearing you endure it—it."

"I can endure it no longer, John."

The blind man's mouth opened. "So long has it been since I've heard my name—name."

"They cannot take that from you or me."

"They will try, my son—son. When they do, you must remember the most important words of your life—life."

"And that would be?"

"I am."

Matthias listened for the blind man's echo, but it was the words that reverberated inside his soul. "I am."

Blind Johnny bent over and kissed Matthias on the forehead. "Behold the Lord's anointed—anointed."

Tears ran anew down Matthias's face. "I am a whoremonger and a fool, my friend. God does not anoint such sinners."

"Yes, He does—does. The Bible is full of such men and women—women. That's what's in the Bible you found. Go with God, my son—son. Go with God—God."

Blind Johnny shuffled out of the room.

Isolation weighed upon Matthias. He yearned for the taste of tea with honey and found only the gall of loneliness. If only he could hear the chime of the town bell, the thrum of the Heartbeat of the City. Silence filled his ears and he trailed off into a hopeless sleep.

"I have fulfilled my part of the bargain," said Gideon.

Matthias awoke. The room smelled vile. His skin looked pale. The spider-like machine hugged the ceiling, its arms folded.

Gideon spoke to him again. "I have fulfilled my part of the bargain. I expect you to fulfill yours. All of my troops have returned to their bases as of dawn."

The words wouldn't leave his mouth. Matthias didn't trust the Inquisitor. "Whom do you serve?" He could sense the question pricking at the Inquisitor's very being. "Whom do you serve?"

Gideon seethed. "I serve God and the Synod."

"He is controlling you, Gideon. He is a demon," said Rourke.

Matthias spoke to Gideon. "I serve Yahweh. That's why the Bible came to me. That's why I read its pages. That's why I got away. I have seen the Synod's lies. I have seen the truth. You will see it too. Read it. Read it for yourself. The book lies in my parent's chapel. Touch the hand of God as I did and you'll see."

Rourke cheered. "We have it. Let's go!"

Gideon began pressing buttons on the control panel. "But his Reformation."

Cornelius pushed him aside and shut the machine down. "Cast him out. Let him live with his sins and his failure. Come."

Gideon hovered between the table and the door, staring at Matthias.

"Now!" bellowed Rourke.

Chapter 67: Verses 1-22

Soldiers dressed Matthias and drove him to the West Gate. There, they tossed him out of a truck and onto the pavement.

Every nerve in his body still burned from the Inquisition, but a soothing rain fell down upon him. He raised his hands and let it wash the stink of fear from him. Matthias recalled how much he hated the rain. It felt good to hate it, and he embraced every ounce of it that fell upon him.

He got to his feet and walked away from Philadelphia. He was like the rain, a Rot-filled drop among a million other drops, each one flowing together in the alleys and gutters of the slum.

The vehicles of the wealthy whooshed by, watery plumes trailing behind them.

A black limousine hissed to a stop on the wet pavement. Matthias faced it and saw the window lowering. He extended his hand for a penance card. A flash leapt from the cavern within.

A bullet struck Matthias, and he fell to the pavement.

Beggars ran away.

A man in business vestments stormed over to him. He wore muddy, black, wingtips.

"Where is it?" screamed Cornelius.

A book thumped onto Matthias's chest. It burst open, scattering pages all around him. He didn't understand.

His uncle screamed again. "Where is the Bible?"

Another set of footsteps joined Cornelius. Matthias recognized the limp, saw the rain bead on the glossy boots.

Gideon ran his hand over Matthias's chest. It came away crimson. He turned to Rourke. "What have you done?"

Rourke grew more and more livid. "He lied to us. Where is the Bible?"

Matthias still didn't understand. He fought the burning in his chest and grabbed a sheet of paper. On it was a child's scribble, the name 'Matthias Kent' written ad infinitum. On the other side were the bright colors of crayons. They were pages from the coloring books of his library.

"Where is the Bible?" howled Rourke.

The burning in Matthias's chest subsided and a moment of clarity came to him.

Blind Johnny.

With that thought, a gentleness, a peace, washed over him with the rain. He saw Carolyn standing on top of the bridge pier, heard his heart beating in time with her cadence. Each beat grew fainter and fainter.

Matthias looked up at Gideon. "Whom do you serve?"

Gideon's eyes welled with tears.

"Then serve Him well, my brother." Matthias clutched the drawings to his chest, let his last breath rise heavenward, and smiled.

And God smiled back.

Breinigsville, PA USA
25 June 2010
240581BV00001B/6/P